KILLER PURSUIT

An Allison McNeil Thriller

Jeff Gunhus

Seven Guns Press

Printed in the United States of America

Cover design by Extended Imagery
Edited by Mandy Schoen

Library of Congress Cataloging-in-Publication Data
Gunhus, Jeff
The Torment of Rachel Ames / Jeff Gunhus

ALSO BY JEFF GUNHUS

ADULT FICTION

Night Chill
Night Terror
Killer Within
Killer Pursuit
The Torment of Rachel Ames: a novella

YA FICTION

Jack Templar Monster Hunter
Jack Templar and the Monster Hunter Academy
Jack Templar and the Lord of the Vampires
Jack Templar and the Lord of the Werewolves
Jack Templar and the Lord of the Demons

ACKNOWLEDGEMENTS

Every journey begins with a single step. The journey of writing a novel begins with the important task of surrounding oneself with great people who support, nourish and nurture the process. First and foremost, I rely on the good counsel and unconditional love of my wife, Nicole. Without you, nothing around here works. Thank you. Thank you. Thank you.

Heaps of gratitude also goes to my five kids who are so good about letting Dad write his crazy books in the mornings and trying out plots on them during long drives. All five of you continue to amaze me as you grow into full-fledged human beings. Our house is always loud and it's the music of my life. I love every minute of it.

Thank you to my parents for a childhood filled with books, travel, adventure and encouragement. And to my older brother, Eric, who consistently amazes me with his creativity.

We're told to never judge a book by its cover, but in this case I'm all right if people do so. Carl Graves of Extended

Imagery did an incredible job capturing the tone I wanted to express with this cover. I couldn't be happier with it.

Mandy Shoen once again edited the book. Your developmental edits made substantive improvements while keeping my voice and intention intact. Thank you.

Thank you to my assistant, Kate Tilton, who makes my life easier and gives me more time to write.

A special thank you to FBI Assistant Director in Charge Diego Rodriguez and the men and women of the New York FBI Field Office. The incredible access granted through the International Thriller Writer's Association answered all my questions and improved this book immeasurably. More than that, thank all of you for your tireless and dedicated service in defense of our country.

Thank you Steve Berry for your full-day Masterclass on writing thrillers. You may not realize it, but your fingerprints are all over this manuscript due to the lessons you taught that day.

Finally, thank you to my readers. I've been writing in some capacity since I was a kid, but I didn't put my fiction out into the world until I wrote *Jack Templar Monster Hunter* for my reluctant reader son in 2012. The response to those books and then to my books written for adults has been unexpected, overwhelming and humbling. I don't mind admitting that sometimes your reviews and letters cause me to choke up. Your support means more to me than you can ever know.

As always, thank you for the decision to trust me with your most valuable commodity—your time. I worked hard on this book because I take our bargain seriously. You give me your time (and a little money) and in exchange I deliver a good story. I did my level best to deliver on my side of the deal. I hope you find your trust was well placed.

With my sincerest gratitude,

Jeff Gunhus
Annapolis, Maryland

For Nicole

...because they're always for you

CHAPTER 1

Allison McNeil tensed when she spotted the first shadow dart through the mist and take cover behind a tree. In the early-morning light it took her a while to pick out all six members of the Hostage Rescue Team approaching the cabin, but within a minute she could clearly see the tactical team converging on their target.

The small building stood on a rise, up from the swampy, flood-prone land around it. Wood-slated walls tilted precariously inward, twisting the windows into deformed rectangles. Moss and dead leaves covered the roof. The place smelled and looked like decay, well on its way to inevitable reclamation by the weeds and vines choking the cabin to a miserable death.

And, if Allison was right, the place deserved what it got. Hell, if she was right, she had half a mind to take a match to the place after everything was done.

She hunkered down behind a fallen tree, her head barely clearing the top to see the building and the team closing in. A trickle of sweat started at the base of her neck and went the length of her spine. She adjusted the Kevlar vest, under her light windbreaker emblazoned with large yellow letters. FBI. It felt ridiculous to wear the windbreaker when it was in the '80s before daybreak with the Louisiana humidity hovering at about a thousand percent, but if it meant that the hotheads with assault rifles could more easily identify her as a friendly, then she was happy to have it.

Garret Morrison shifted his weight next to her, stretching out a leg and rubbing his knee. She gave him a sideways look.

"You all right?" she whispered.

He scowled at her. They both knew she didn't give a damn about him. The comment was intended as a dig at the fifty-three-year-old Garret who prided himself on being in better shape than the agents beneath him. Even though he ran the Behavioral Analysis Unit, home of the FBI's fabled profilers who spent more time in the heads of the criminals they chased than in the field, he required an aggressive physical program for his people. Everything about Morrison is a throwback to the old male-dominated Bureau. A slicked-back head of hair with just the right amount of grey to lend him gravitas without making him look old, a square jaw out of a mountaineering magazine, cold steel-blue eyes that seemed to look through people instead of at them. Unless they were trained on an attractive female, in which case his eyes gave their full attention to the area below the chin and above the waistline.

"Worry about yourself," Garret grumbled. He turned to Doug Browning, a junior agent who followed Garret around like a little puppy. "Jesus, Doug. Not so close."

Allison turned back to the cabin and raised her binoculars, not bothering to hide the smile on her lips. Garret was a legend in the Bureau for his work hunting America's worst criminals, but Allison's own legend had grown since her work on the Arnie Milhouse case a year earlier. While that case had given her credibility, she knew she was just as likely to be referred to as the woman who'd broken Garret Morrison's nose when he'd made one too many unwanted advances while she was a trainee. And, while she wanted to be known for her work, she didn't mind that piece of fame following her around.

"Alpha team in position," said a voice through the small speaker in her ear. She noticed Garret put a finger to the side of his head and nod. He looked over at her.

"You better be right about this," he whispered.

Allison shook her head. For all his brilliance—and, regardless of how she felt personally about him, she recognized that he *was* brilliant—Garret's transparency could border on the inane. What he was really saying was that if the lunatic Allison's research had tracked to this location wasn't holed up in this backwoods cabin, if the FBI's Hostage Rescue Team had been activated and deployed for no reason, then the blame would drop on her like a bag of bricks. If Sam Kraw was in there, Allison knew it would be Garret standing in front of the cameras taking credit for the HRT mission and the capture of America's most wanted fugitive.

She pushed the thought away. As long as they caught the bastard and ended his multi-year killing spree in the Southeast, she didn't give a damn who got the credit.

Allison moved her binoculars. The tactical team was in place around the cabin, peering through scopes with infrared capabilities. If there was someone hiding in the shadows of a window or doorway, they wouldn't be hiding for long.

On some signal unseen by Allison, the men began a steady, crouched advance to the building. She realized she was holding her breath so she blew out her air slowly between pinched lips.

"Relax, McNeil," Garret muttered. "You're making me nervous."

The two members of the tactical squad approaching from the front reached the deck that wrapped around the front of the building. As they strode across it, the old wood floorboards groaned. The men froze. The seconds stretched out. Allison became suddenly aware of the hum of insects in the air around her. The dampness of her own skin. The sound of a bird calling in the distance. All of her senses were wired tight. An entire year of her life was wrapped up in the next few seconds. And if she'd got it wrong, Garret would have the ammo he'd been looking for to get her out of his unit once and for all. But she wasn't worried about herself. What really bothered her was the chance that she had it right, that this was Kraw's hideout, but that somehow they'd spooked him and he'd already slipped away. If that had happened, he'd be hundreds of miles away by tomorrow, scouting for his next victim as he traveled.

Movement in the cabin. Just a flutter. Like a bird trapped in a cage. Only her intuition told her it was more than a bird. It had been an arm. A human arm. Sam Kraw.

Based on the lack of movement from the tactical team, she realized no one else had seen it.

"I've got movement," she whispered into her mic. "Window to the right of the front door. An arm."

"I didn't see anything," Garret whispered.

Allison ignored him. The men around the cabin responded immediately, reorienting to the front door. Guns pointed at the window.

One of the men produced a miniram, a high impact, brute force breaching tool. Coordinating with his partner, he crouched next to the door while the other man readied a flash-bang grenade.

There was a pause, as if someone had pressed a button on a TV remote. Everyone was in place. The air seemed to still as if the world knew something was about to happen. Allison had her binoculars trained on the window where she'd seen the movement. If Kraw was inside, then the nightmare was almost over. She'd know in a few seconds whether that was the case or not.

But in that second, she saw the movement again.

Only this time, she knew something was wrong.

It was a man's arm, she saw it clearly this time. But it was too stiff. The color was off. And, attached at the shoulder, she saw a coil of wire.

A mannequin arm on a spring.

Meant to make them think someone was inside.

It was a trap.

CHAPTER 2

Allison shouted into her mic. "No, wait!"

As the words came out, one man threw the flash-bang grenade through the window and the other reared back with the ram.

The grenade went off inside, lighting up all the windows on the lower floor, the percussive force loud even from where Allison watched. The other man swung the ram forward with enough force to smash through the decrepit door.

But the second it hit the old wood...

BOOM

A bomb detonated inside the cabin. All four walls blew out, pulverized by the blast, sending a deadly wave of splintered wood and fire roaring outward.

On reflex, Allison ducked behind the log. Even so, she felt the heat and the pressure from the explosion pour over her. Debris slammed against the log. Bits of shrapnel zinged by her head.

She looked up and saw Garret prone on the ground. She reached out for him, thinking he was hit. He flinched at her touch and glanced up at her. Something had torn a nasty gash through his left cheek, but it wasn't serious. Behind him, his assistant Doug held his shoulder, moaning. As Garret saw to him, Allison stood and surveyed the carnage.

The building had disintegrated from the force of the blast. Burning debris littered the field. Sharp boards stuck into the soil like arrows. With the smoke hanging in the air she couldn't see what had happened to the tactical team.

But she heard them. Screaming. Groaning in pain.

The smoke shifted and she saw them, laid out on the ground twenty or thirty feet from the house.

Their black tactical gear smoking.

The screamers writhing on the ground.

Others lying there. Not moving. Bodies twisted into unnatural positions.

"Agents down. Agents down," she cried out, climbing over the log. As she ran toward the nearest man, she realized she hadn't toggled her mic. "Agents down," she yelled. "Need all available medical teams."

"Roger that," came the voice in her ear, maddeningly calm and professional. "Two minutes out."

Allison slid to her knees as she reached the first man lying face down. She rolled him over and he screamed. When he did, Allison nearly vomited. One side of the man's face was gone, no more than a smoking, red smear. Smoke rose from his vest. Allison tore at the buckles and straps, peeling off the layers. The man's flak jacket was embedded with chunks of hot metal. Several had made it to the man's skin and were burning him. Her first thought was that they were nails from the cabin. But she noticed a variety of metal shards: bolts, wingnuts, screws. The bomb had been packed with them, designed to cause the most damage possible to soft flesh.

"You're gonna be OK," she lied to the man. Even if he survived, he'd never again be the person he was when he left home that morning. *Left home to come on an operation put together based on her intel,* she reminded herself. "Medical team is coming up from the staging area," she managed to say. "Hang in there."

The man didn't respond. He gritted his teeth and screamed with his jaw clenched shut. Allison moved to the next man, but Garret was already there. He looked up at her and shook his head. Dead.

Garret ran to the next man, but Allison hesitated. Something pulled at the back of her consciousness. She couldn't shake the feeling that she was missing something important.

Then it came to her. After months of living in Samuel Kraw's head she felt like she knew him as well as he knew himself. Better, actually, because she had the clinical detachment to understand why he was as fucked up as he was. There was one thing she knew about him more than anything else.

Sam Kraw would never pass up a chance to watch someone die.

Allison jerked back at the thought. She scanned the tree line all around the cabin, struggling to see through the dense smoke from the burning wreckage of the building.

Movement. In the trees to the north. A person moving.

No, that was the backup team rushing up from the secondary staging area. To confirm this, a dozen other people appeared behind the first, running in her direction.

Allison turned in place. Looking into every shadow. She knew Samuel Kraw. She *knew* the son of a bitch. "Where are you," she said, turning in a circle. "I know you're here."

"Allison," Garret called out. "I need you."

She turned and saw him giving CPR to one of the tactical agents. She was just about to run to help him when her eye caught on something to her left. She scanned the area, her eyes

8

coming to a stop at the base of a large sycamore tree. There, in the tree's shadow, was a hulking figure, hands up to his face with a pair of binoculars.

A chill passed through her.

She knew the man's silhouette from hours of studying photos of him.

She knew him from the nightmares she'd had for the last six months she'd worked the case.

Samuel Kraw, in the flesh.

Allison pulled her Glock from her side, raising it in a two-handed stance.

"FBI," Allison shouted. "Let me see your hands."

Kraw turned the binoculars her direction. Her skin crawled as she imagined the killer looking her over.

Kraw's mouth turned up in a smile and he raised a finger off the binoculars, as if waving hello. Then he spun to his right around the tree.

Allison fired two quick shots and chunks of wood splintered from where Kraw's head had been only seconds before. She knew instantly that she'd been too slow.

"Garret!" she bellowed as she sprinted forward.

"I saw him," he shouted. "I'm behind you. Go. Go."

She didn't need to be told, she just wanted to know whether she was on her own or not.

Head down, she charged toward the spot where she'd seen Kraw run into the woods. The bulletproof jacket felt like a suit of armor, hampering her movement. Still, she took some comfort from wearing it, knowing Kraw could be crouched in the bushes behind the tree, ready to pepper her with gunfire the second she turned the corner on the path. Of course, anything outside her torso and she was still a goner. But the adrenaline roaring through her veins pushed all that aside. She was so close to the son of a bitch, she didn't care about anything except taking him down, no matter the cost.

There were two trails behind the tree, branching out in different directions, each walled in by heavy brush. Kraw had to be on one of the paths, there was no way to go into the overgrowth without it being obvious. She had to choose.

Garret ran up behind her. She didn't stop to ask, but just pointed down the path to the right and said, "You check that way."

She sprinted to the left. It quickly narrowed so that it was only shoulder width, the thorny brambles on each side of her ripping through the lightweight FBI windbreaker.

She ran hard, one arm in front of her to push back the branches. But fifty yards into the chase, the path narrowed so much that it basically disappeared, no more than an animal trail through a heavy thicket.

She stopped, trying to listen for Kraw's footsteps over the sound of her own heavy breathing. Nothing.

She spun around, her gun in front of her. She couldn't see more than a few yards in any direction.

Adrenaline had brought her to that spot but now, once she stopped running, her instincts were telling her she'd made a terrible mistake.

She was being watched. Or at least, every part of her told her that she was.

Whether it was paranoia or instinct, she couldn't stop a rising panic from building in her chest.

A twig cracked behind her and she spun around, pointing her gun wildly back and forth at the bushes. Her breathing sped up, panting now, but she didn't care. She'd made so much noise that he would already know where she was.

The forest closed in on her. Pushing in around her. Kraw could be standing only feet from her in any direction. Staring at her. Silently waiting for his chance to attack. She wouldn't know before it was too late.

The shouts and screams of dying men carried through the forest, but they sounded far away now. Her brain screamed at her to run toward the sound. To get help. To seek safety.

Suddenly, birds flew up into the air twenty or thirty yards ahead of her, startled by something.

Kraw.

Allison bolted forward, her gun trained on the path ahead of her. Soon, she saw that the trail opened up to a meadow. She slowed, resuming her two-handed grip on her gun. A muffled grunt came from the meadow and she dropped to a knee, hopefully giving Kraw a smaller target if he was waiting there with a gun.

Another grunt came.

Sounded like Garret.

Allison crab-crawled forward, staying close to the brush. It wouldn't stop a bullet but at least she could keep out of sight for as long as possible.

She turned the final corner and had to stifle a cry.

Kraw stood in the middle of the clearing, holding Garret in a chokehold in front of him, a gun to his head.

"Oh shit," Allison said.

Garret struggled but Kraw was a massive man and controlled him easily. There was a new cut over Garret's eye and he looked a little disoriented. Kraw had gotten the drop on him and clubbed him in the head.

"Drop your weapon, Kraw," Allison shouted.

Kraw looked totally calm. Even now, under what had to be enormous stress, he looked like he was just taking a hike through the woods with some friends. That wasn't a good sign.

"Why don't you drop yours?" Kraw said. "Then I'll walk outta here nice and easy like."

"You know that's not happening," Allison said. "And I know you're not going to just walk away, not when you have someone's life in your hands."

Kraw smiled. "You've been studying up on me. I'm flattered. You being such a pretty thing and all." He licked his lips. "Bet you was twice as cute when you was a little girl. Woulda liked to have met you then."

Allison readjusted her grip and took aim. Garret looked horrified.

"N...no...w...w...wait," Garret managed. "McNeil. Just wait, OK?"

"'Cus if I'd met you back then, Agent McNeil, I coulda made some use of you," Kraw said.

"Stand down, McNeil! That's an order," Garret shouted.

Allison barely heard the words over the blood pounding in her head.

"When you were eleven or twelve, you probably had men looking at you, didn't you?" Kraw said. He smiled. "Ohhh yes, I can tell I'm right. Some of them try to touch you? I bet they did. And I bet you liked it too, didn't you?"

Hate burned inside her.

"You don't have to be ashamed to admit that. It's natural," Kraw said. "All my little girls liked it. I didn't hurt them. They all wanted me to—"

Allison fired.

The bullet tore through Garret's shin and bent him forward with such force that Kraw's upper body was left exposed.

Her second bullet buried itself between Kraw's eyes. The back of his head blew out in a puff of red mist. He let go of Garret and fell backward. His hulking body jerked a few times. Then stopped. Dead.

Allison stood in place, her gun still trained on the body lying prone on the ground. After a few long seconds, she realized she wasn't breathing. She drew in a sharp inhalation, the emotion of the moment turning it into a ragged, half-sob. The gun in her hand began to tremble and then shake, the adrenaline overwhelming her system.

Garret was on the ground, grabbing his leg, screaming something at her, but her ears rang from the gunshots and he sounded far away. It was probably for the best. She knew he was going to be pissed, but she also knew she'd saved his life. Whether he was going to see it that way remained to be seen.

CHAPTER 3

Catherine Fews's clients liked their sex rougher and dirtier than they could get through more respectable avenues. For most of her high-powered DC clientele, a simple blowjob was dirtier than their pearled, blue-haired wives living back with the constituency had given them in a few decades, so she seldom had to get too creative.

This man was different though. Young, strong and hung, she found herself looking forward to his visits. He didn't talk much, but what he lacked in conversation he made up for in other ways. But she meant to warn him about the bruises she received last time they were together. Marks on her skin weren't exactly good for business. The upper crust, after all, liked their meat unblemished.

But he never gave her a chance to bring it up.

The second she opened the door to her Georgetown apartment, he pushed his way inside, grabbing her arm painfully and forcing her to the side. He kicked the door shut behind him then pushed her face-first up against it.

She tried to turn around to encourage him, but he grabbed her hair and pushed her back into the door.

Clever boy, she thought. *You know where the camera is.*

She felt him hike up her skirt and his strong fingers were between her legs. But she was ready for him. Sure it was rough but it was a hundred times better than the wrinkly Viagra soldiers she usually had to cajole into action. She moaned and arched her back as he pushed into her.

Catherine owed this particular client a favor. His entrance into her life a year earlier had changed everything for her. His proposition had sounded ridiculous at first, so outlandish that she'd thought it was some kind of role-play to help him get off. But twenty grand in cash convinced her it was the real deal. Even then, she refused. It wasn't like she was turning tricks at a truck stop out on the highway. Her clientele included some of the most powerful men in DC. She knew that was exactly what made her so valuable.

But the man was charismatic and a smooth talker. Eventually, he won her over and she made the deal. For the first time she had a plan for her life that didn't include moaning encouragement to old men as they did their clumsy work on top of her. She had a lucrative exit strategy that would both get her out of hooking and set her up in style. Not only her, but her sister too. And that one thing made it all worth it.

But she'd learned in her short but eventful life that men could not be trusted. Men with money least of all. That was why the day after he installed the camera, she installed the second one in the other wall. Call it an insurance policy. Besides, even though she took the man's money and the new clients he sent her way, Catherine only worked for herself.

It seemed like such a simple thing, secret sex tapes of mid-level politicians and bureaucrats, but it had gotten out of hand. The stakes were suddenly too big when one of her clients climbed onto the national stage. Sure, most of her visitors had some level of name recognition, even if only among CSPAN and

Politico-junkies. But this was different. He was everywhere. In the papers. On the news. Catherine went from being shocked, to being nervous and then scared. Really scared. Having someone with a little power on video was one thing, but this was dangerous and she knew it.

The man paid her more, a lot more. He spoke soft words to her, convincing her there was nothing to worry about. It worked at first. He convinced her that it wouldn't be a problem. When asked what he intended to do with the videos, he didn't give specifics, just assured her that leaking them to the press or to TMZ wasn't part of the plan. They were too valuable for that.

Catherine understood the implication. She didn't like to think of the word blackmail. It seemed too much like a word someone could go to prison for. She preferred the term the man used when he explained his purpose.

Leverage.

Releasing the videos wasn't necessary, he explained. Their existence was all he needed. Just their existence gave him power.

But no matter his assurances, her intuition told her she was in over her head. In time she reached the conclusion that she needed out, no matter the cost. The man would find out that he'd taught her too well. But by then it would be too late for him to do anything about it. She had leverage of her own.

She had enough money saved up, so even if the FBI wouldn't pay anything for the information she sent them, she'd be OK. She would cut a deal and get the hell away from the East Coast and the rat's nest of politicians and lobbyists. She thought LA might be a good fit for her. She had the face and the figure to be in movies. And she didn't lack the ambition or street smarts.

In the meantime, it was clear that tonight's visit was a social call. She didn't mind giving the man a send-off. The plan had almost worked. In fact, the only problem was that it had worked too well. He'd treated her fairly, paid her well, and she was about to totally screw him over. Catherine figured that after she cut her deal with the FBI, the man would be sitting in a prison cell while she was basking in the California sun. She appreciated everything he'd tried to do for her. She didn't mind paying for the service he had provided her, especially since it wasn't going to work out the way he hoped.

But then she didn't fully understand what full payment entailed.

<><><>

The man forced Catherine's head against the door as he continued to work his fingers deep inside of her. She moaned, shifting her hips against him.

"Did you cancel the rest of your night like I told you?" he asked.

"Yes," she gasped as he plunged deeper into her.

"Have you ever told anyone about me?" he asked.

He waited for any sign of tension in the woman's body, a telltale sign that she was about to lie to him. There was nothing.

"No, of course not." She ground her hips harder against him. "Did you come here to talk?"

The man reached into his coat and took out a ski mask. He flattened his body against hers until they were both pressed against the door, her arms pinned down by his elbows, his head next to hers, breathing into her ear.

"No. Not really."

He pulled the mask over his head. She glanced back and saw it.

"That's new," she said playfully. "I like it. What do you say we—"

He pushed against her harder, making sure she didn't turn around.

"Hey, you're hurting me. Get off."

The man ignored her struggling beneath him. He leaned into her ear and said, "All right. I think I'm ready now. How about you? Are you ready?"

He felt her body tighten beneath him and he marveled at the level of intuition in the human psyche. The sexual excitement that had oozed from the woman a few seconds earlier was gone, replaced by a fundamental sense of the danger he represented.

A shudder passed through her body and he thought for a second that the tangible expression of pure fear might make him climax.

To fight the sensation, he tore the knife from the sheath strapped to his belt and plunged the blade into the woman's throat.

Blood sprayed across the door in an arc as he yanked her head backward and away from him.

Catherine's legs kicked violently as frothy red drool poured down the front of her chest.

Her arms flailed wildly as if grabbing hold of something would somehow fix the gash opened in her flesh.

The man held the gushing wound away from him to keep the blood off his clothes. Although necessary, he found it unfortunate that he couldn't see the woman's face. It was, after all, his favorite part of the kill.

With a handful of hair and the other hand holding her left arm, he dragged her to the full-length mirror on the wall opposite the foot of the bed. There he held back her head and watched the mirror in fascination as Catherine Fews stared in bewilderment at her own violent death.

The man held on, watching, waiting patiently for the money shot.

Ah, here it comes.

A convulsion rippled through the woman's body. Every muscle tensed at once, as if making one last bid to escape what fate obviously had been decided for it.

CHAPTER 4

arshall "Libby" Ashworth had not been nervous for a meeting in years. Although just turned fifty, he had seen too damn much to bother with nerves. Heads of state, U.S. presidents, celebrities, all had been part of his everyday routine for the last two decades and the novelty had long worn off. Just like anyone else, famous people used the john, got stupid when they drank too much, smelled bad when they sweat and were generally more flawed than John Q Public could ever guess.

As a staffer, he'd watched George W. Bush waddle through security briefings asking questions that proved one child had been left behind and he was sitting in the White House. Libby Ashworth was there when that sycophant Clinton said goodnight to the donors who'd ponied up the cash to spend the night in the Lincoln bedroom. He'd cried as the first African-American President was sworn in, only to see him fumble through a presidency high on promise and miserably low on results. And it wasn't just the executive branch. He'd seen Senate leaders hold up funding for needy families for no other reason than because a bill's author had bad-talked someone during a poker game. And he'd seen Supreme Court Justices so drunk they couldn't walk straight, talking trash about the sacred court on which they sat.

He'd seen enough of Washington to know better than to hold the people who worked there in enough regard to ever be nervous to meet them.

Except the meeting today was different.

This meeting had him very nervous.

And that scared him.

<><><>

The old man sat on the top step of the Lincoln Memorial. The Memorial was his favorite monument on the National Mall. There was something soothing about Lincoln's expression and the way he serenely looked out over the city from his small hill, as if he might actually be able to shame the men and women there into better behavior.

Over forty years of living and working in the center of the American Empire had worn down some of the old man's hope but not all of it. He still thought he could make a difference, but time was working against him. The latest distraction had to be done away with so that his other work could continue. The man believed he had chosen the right man in Libby Ashworth but one thing he knew for sure was that nothing in this town was certain.

He let his eyes soak in the National Mall. The reflection pool stretched out toward the Washington Monument, the tall obelisk that seemed to point to the place of honor that would forever belong to the first President. The man always felt it a shame that Washington had become a caricature, a logo more than a man. From the very beginning, Washington had been above them all. Above the pettiness. Above the fray. But the old man was a decent historian and had studied Washington the man for years. He had been as imperfect as any of them, full of vanity and contradictions, but he had been nearly perfect at the times when it counted most of all. And, in the end, that was what really mattered in a person's life. At least that was what the old man kept telling himself.

Farther down the Mall, its distant image already wavering in the heat, sat the building where even the concept of perfection was a distant thought. The dome of the U.S. Capitol building dominated the skyline, ironically crowned by a sculpture of a Native American woman, as if as a purposeful statement of the town's cynicism. *Sure we wiped out your civilization and stuck you on reservations to starve you and abuse you, but we put a statue of your people on our Capitol, so suck it up.*

The man shook his head, knowing that such thoughts only showcased his own developing cynicism. He felt tired though, more tired than ever. He just wanted to finish what he started, then he would let himself rest. But first the work had to be done.

"Excuse me, do you—"

A middle-aged man dressed in full tourist mode with bright blue shorts and grey pitted out t-shirt approached him from the right. Halfway through his question two muscular men stepped between the man and their boss, politely asking the man to move on. The old man watched the tourist crane his neck around the bodyguards to see if he could identify the person being protected, then go back to his family to excitedly tell them what happened. He imagined that the tourist would tell the story over and over when he returned home to Moline, Iowa or Orlando, Florida, or wherever he was from, and when people asked who the person was on the steps, he would just shake his head and say he had no idea.

And that was exactly how the man liked it.

"Hello, Clarence," Libby Ashworth said, trying to exude confidence he didn't feel. He carefully wiped the granite before sitting on the step. "Nice office you have here," he said with a nod toward the Mall. "Can't beat the view."

"Hello, Marshall. Thank you for meeting me on such short notice."

No one called him Marshall in this town. It was Libby, had been since prep school and the old man knew it. The same as he knew that the prestigious Ashworth name was from his mother's second marriage. The same as he knew probably every flaw and misstep in Libby's life. The purposeful error irritated him, but he left it alone. "Well, you sounded a little upset over the phone. When the Director of the FBI calls me a little worried and wants to meet on the steps of the Lincoln Memorial, I figure it's a good idea to take the meeting."

Clarence Mason smiled. "Soon the ex-Director, if your friends have their way. I hear Hernandez is the flavor of the month."

Libby nearly flinched. He knew Mason to be direct but he'd expected a little more foreplay. Not only that, but Victor Hernandez had only come up in a top-level meeting forty-eight hours earlier. The old man was showing off his sources. Libby had to admit that they were good. "Victor Hernandez is the President's multicultural young face," Libby said. "He's an empty suit."

"I know," Mason said.

"Power knows where power goes, Clarence. You taught me that. The important calls in this town will be going to you for a long time yet." He smiled but thought to himself, *Not if I can help it, you fucking dinosaur.*

Clarence Mason shrugged slightly. "I do what I can."

Libby almost laughed out loud. Clarence Mason was one of the most powerful men in DC. Not since the Hoover years had more people feared someone at the FBI so much. The old man knew where the bodies were buried, had probably buried a few himself over the years, and no one knew what his personal files contained. There were not many who cared to find out. Even before he became Director, when the President needed advice about something sensitive, it was Clarence Mason on the other end of the line. At least that was how it had been with the previous four Administrations.

"All right, Clarence. What's on your mind?"

"Your boss has some exposure that you need to know about."

Libby swallowed hard. "Recent?"

"Less than six months. Before Iowa, but not by much."

"Hard evidence?"

"Photos that place him in the home of a well-known pro. Right here in town."

Libby felt his stomach turn over. He'd dealt with issues like this before but the feeling never got better. "Is she going public?"

"Oh, I don't think so. She was murdered last week. Throat slashed and then her body was hacked to pieces. The killer was very...creative in how he left the body."

"Jesus, did you have someone..." Libby turned away, realizing that he didn't want to know the answer to the question.

"No, we were not involved," Mason said softly. "But we need to be. I thought you should know it in case it leads somewhere close to you."

Libby felt his face flush. "Don't go down that path. He's a womanizer, sure, but what you're talking about is completely different. I can't believe you would even—" He cut himself short, noticing the way Mason was coolly watching his body language. He knew he needed to get back in control of his emotions. "So why are you telling me this?"

"Call it professional courtesy."

"So it has nothing to do with my guy talking to the leaders on the Hill about you?"

"He was talking about me?" Mason said. "I had no idea."

Libby shook his head. He knew full well that half the senators had called Mason the minute they had left their offices to warn him that forces were trying to push him out of power. It had been part of their strategy all along. Who could have guessed that the old man had this ace in the hole? "All right, anything else?"

"Yes."

"Great. Don't tell me I'm going to read about this in the Post tomorrow."

"This girl made videos."

"Videos? Oh shit," Libby said. A grainy photo could be denied. Photoshop experts lined up to testify on the morning news shows how it was faked. But video? That was a different thing entirely. He really was going to throw up. "Of him?"

Mason nodded. "Your guy. And others. In this woman's apartment we found a video set up behind a mirror. The device didn't have any memory in it and the battery was out."

"Did the killer tamper with it?"

"Hard to say. But that's not the problem."

"Great."

"We found a second camera in the room. This one with a feed to the Internet."

Libby stood and ran his fingers through his hair. He had a strong urge to walk away from the old man with all his bad news, get in the car and just drive until he ran out of gas. People would talk for a while about his disappearance, wonder what happened to him, but the world would move on and people would stop asking. Then it would be someone else's shitty job to deal with this problem.

"So you're telling me that...that there's a sex video on the Internet right now? That it's been out there for six months and I'm just now hearing about it?"

"If it was being distributed you would have heard about it a lot earlier than this. As far as your boss is concerned we only recently realized he had visited this woman in a...uh...personal capacity."

Bullshit, Libby thought. *You've been sitting on this you son-of-a-bitch, waiting for when you needed it.*

"And how did you come across this piece of information?" Libby asked. "I didn't know it was legal for you guys to put public officials under surveillance."

"Never said he was. The only reason we have the photo is because the woman sent it to us to cut a deal. She wanted protection in exchange for the videos she made."

"Protection from what?"

"According to the email we received, the first camera was from someone who approached her with the idea. Paid her to set up her clientele. The second camera was her idea. She knew she was playing with fire and wanted out."

"You think the guy found out she contacted you and killed her?"

Mason shrugged. "That's one theory."

"I don't get it. Are the videos out there on the Internet or not?"

Mason smirked and Libby fought the desire to punch the son-of-a-bitch in the face.

"Our analysts say the first camera had removable memory. So those are gone. Impossible to say where. If your guy's luck keeps going strong like it has so far, then she removed the memory herself and stored it somewhere before she was killed."

"And if his luck's run out?"

"Then the guy who set this thing up has the videos. Or the guy who killed her."

"Might be the same guy."

"Might be."

"And the second video?"

Our analysts say it went out over an encrypted feed, right into the dark Internet where it's impossible to trace."

Libby had heard the term dark Internet before but didn't really understand it. He wasn't about to admit that in front of Mason. The words *impossible to trace* were all he needed to hear.

"But someone has it."

"Yes, someone has it and either they've been sitting on it or..."

"Or what?" Libby asked.

"Or your guy's been compromised and someone is using this to control him."

Libby shook his head. "No, that's not possible."

"If you say so, Marshall."

Libby spun around and pointed a finger at the old man. "You find the son-of-a-bitch. And you find him fast. Do your job, for Chrissake." He lowered his finger and took a breath. "And the name's Libby, you asshole. You know damn well I don't go by Marshall."

Mason looked at him calmly, as if they were discussing gardening tips instead of a scandal of staggering proportions. Libby turned heel and strode down the steps of the Memorial, his legs shaking from the adrenaline pumping through his bloodstream.

He knew he shouldn't let the old man get to him like that, but he couldn't help it.

They'd had their fights over the years, going back to when Libby was a young boy. But Libby hadn't lost his temper with Mason like that since he was a teenager.

But, then again, his father was always able to get a rise out of him.

Libby wondered what his shrink would have made of this father-son moment on the steps of the Lincoln Memorial. Or of the fact that Libby spent an inordinate amount of his time plotting his old man's downfall. Too bad he'd stopped going to therapy two decades earlier, because it would have been quite a session.

If there was any silver lining at all it was that the meeting had taken place at all. *Professional courtesy* his ass. Mason had called him to rattle his cage because he didn't have as much as he implied. All he had was a grainy photo they both knew could have been faked and a dead prostitute who said she had videos.

What really bothered Libby was that Mason actually believed he might know something about the girl's death. The entire meeting had been a pretext for the old man to see with his own eyes how Libby responded to the information.

No, that was just part of it. The old man knew Libby couldn't just sit on the news and wait to see what happened. Even though it was exactly what his manipulative asshole of a father wanted him to do, Libby had to tell his boss.

And it was anyone's guess how that meeting was going to go down. All he knew for certain was that Mason's spies would be on the lookout to see what reaction they got by throwing this firebomb into the enemy camp. Libby had to be careful.

A black sedan waited for him at the base of the steps in a restricted parking area reserved for police. He climbed into the backseat.

"When does the boss get back?" he asked the driver.

"Fundraiser tonight in California. A stop in Detroit on the way back."

"Did you hear me ask for his fucking schedule? When is he back to the residence?"

"Sorry, sir. Senator Summerhays will be back tomorrow at five P.M."

"Take me to the residence anyway. Make it quick," Libby snapped. He leaned back in his seat and pressed the bridge of his nose with his thumb and forefinger. Telling truth to power had never been a problem for Libby Ashworth. He just wasn't looking forward to telling the front-runner for the office of President of the United States that he was a dumb ass and had been caught with his pants around his ankles for what might be the last time in his career.

CHAPTER 5

Allison hardly noticed the dark clouds piled up to the west, marching forward with silent deliberation over the Washington DC skyline. A cold breeze kicked up dried leaves and sent them spinning among the gravestones. The trees still held half their leaves, clinging to the hope of a few more days of warmth, but even these were being ripped away whenever the wind gusted.

She wandered through the cemetery with her wool trench coat pulled tight around her, the Louisiana heat a distant memory. The wind numbed her ears and she wished she'd accepted the knit hat her dad had offered her on the way out of the car, but it wasn't bad enough to make her turn back. The car was parked some distance away even though there was an access road that led right next to the grave she was there to visit. Her dad sat in the car's passenger seat, there for company, aware enough to know she needed this time alone.

And that's why she walked through the headstones alone, carefully reading the names of strangers chiseled in stone as if she might discover among them someone she knew. She wanted the time to herself. And she wanted to put off the upcoming visit as long as she could.

The problem with anniversaries was that it forced a pause, a reckoning of what had happened in the intervening time since the last marking of time's passage. As Allison approached Richard Thornton's grave, she thought through what she'd done with her life over the last year.

Work. That was the simple answer. After Arnie Milhouse, Director Mason cleared her way to return to CID, over Garret's objections, and she dug in. Her co-workers tried in various ways to get her to talk about the night she was abducted and tortured. About how she'd managed to escape and kill her captor. But she refused. Those with high enough clearance could read the case report, but that only gave a cold, clinical rendition of the facts. The word on her was that she was a hard ass, too good to share lessons learned from the experience, but that wasn't the case. Despite passing her FBI psych evaluation with flying colors so that she could return to duty, the night haunted her. She simply wanted to leave it where it belonged. In the past, where it couldn't reach her. Only things were never that simple.

She had only to close her eyes at night to see Richard's broken body sprawled on the rocks, his eyes frozen open, staring lifelessly at the shoreline. If it wasn't Richard's face that appeared, it was Arnie's. Leering at her as he ran his hands over her body. She was strapped into the chair in his torture chamber, unable to move.

Nearly every night she woke gasping, clutching at invisible hands at her throat, unable to breathe, trying to scream for help. On the worst nights, the old nightmare of the rape returned. Only now, in some bizarre mash-up of memory, it was Arnie on top of her instead of Craig Gerty, pressing into her, licking her face with his disgusting tongue. The nightmares came so often that she didn't even consider entering a new

KILLER PURSUIT

relationship with a man. She couldn't trust herself not to wake up screaming.

But that wasn't the only reason she kept men at arm's length, even though there was no shortage of interest from them. Richard's death hit her hard even though they hadn't even been together when he died. But the reconciliation. The sense that the relationship had been rekindled. The admission of old feelings that had never left. That things were about to start new between them. These were the things that made it so hard. She knew intellectually that she had idealized the relationship that might have been instead of remembering the challenges the two of them had the first time around. But losing the second chance to do it right, especially when she was the one who walked away the first time because she was scared, was almost too much to bear.

The part of her brain where her masters in psychology held court admonished her that the attachment to Richard was a safe way to avoid new relationships and all the messiness that went with them. She hadn't ignored that idea completely and had made a few half-hearted attempts to meet new people. But every date ended early and with her feeling bad for the guy who hadn't done anything wrong except ask out the wrong girl.

The wind gusted through the graveyard, stripping the trees of more leaves. She pulled her coat collar up and shuddered. As she did, she caught sight of the gravestone in front of her and nearly stumbled.

KRAW

It was an old granite marker, worn down from decades of weather, so it had to just be a coincidence. But just the sight of the name turned her stomach. A burst of images flashed in her mind. Crime scene photos. All those little girls. Raped. Mutilated. Images that would be with her forever.

That was the last year of her life more than anything and she knew that her welling emotions as she walked through the cemetery were as much about the case ending as it was about her relationship with Richard. She felt a strange kind of grief and sense of loss accompanying the end of a case that had consumed her every day for all those dark months. But reliving Samuel Kraw's look of bewilderment the second before the round from her gun split his skull made her feel that it had been a year well spent.

She walked on and came to Richard's grave. She pulled a misshaped bullet from her pocket and rolled it between her fingers. The forensics guys had dug the bullet out from the tree behind Kraw and offered it up to her as a keepsake. She kneeled to the ground and pushed the bullet into the soil until it was deep enough to be hidden from view. She sat back on her heels and allowed herself to drift through the pleasant memories to the man buried six feet beneath her. Agnostic in her religious beliefs, she didn't know what the afterlife held, but she was pretty certain words spoken at a grave were heard only by the living. She didn't say a word but sat there for ten minutes in the cold, paying her respects, pausing to remember her love for the man whose heart she'd broken.

"You OK, sweets?" came her dad's voice behind her.

She stirred and glanced over her shoulder. Pat McNeil, a hard man who'd lived a hard life, stood shivering in the cold. Clutched in his big, heavy-knuckled hands, he held a knit cap. He held it out to her.

"You'll catch something out in this," he said. "Gotta cover your head."

Allison got to her feet, took the hat and pulled it onto her dad's head until it covered his ears.

"You're right, you do," she said. "I thought you were going to stay in the car."

His eyes darted away from hers, that look of panic that broke her heart when he realized he'd forgotten something simple he should remember. He covered it up well. Too well. It was one of the reasons his diagnosis had come so late.

"Damned if I'll stay in a warm car while my girl's out here freezing," he said.

Allison slid her arm into his and leaned against his broad shoulder. His false bluster disappeared and he put his arm around her, pulling her in tight.

"I'm sorry, sweets," he said into her ear. "Really, I am."

Buried in her father's arms, she let go of the walls built up around her and let the emotions spill out. She stood there, clinging to her father, and cried.

Even as his disease robbed him of his memory, his heart knew his little girl was hurting and still needed her father. He held her tight as she sobbed into his chest, knowing that no force on earth would make him let go of her until she was good and done.

When she finally pulled back, he wiped the tears from her cheeks and smiled. "What do you say we rent some old movies from Blockbuster? I'll make some popcorn and we'll just hang out all day and get fat?"

She smiled through the pang in her chest. The Blockbuster near their house had closed years ago and they'd talked at length on the drive up about her upcoming meeting that morning with Clarence Mason; the one where she was half-certain she was getting fired for shooting Garret in the leg. But she didn't mention any of this. She just slid her hand into his and walked him toward the car.

"Sounds good, Dad," she said. "I'd love that."

CHAPTER 6

Libby Ashworth found it interesting that a man who was only a couple of months away from being elected president could live in a normal house in Alexandria with only minimal Secret Service protection. After the election, Senator Mark Summerhays would become the most protected man in the world with an entire army dedicated to his personal safety. While some men might chafe at the idea of the trappings of the office, Libby knew Summerhays looked forward to every bit of it. The political pols may have been surprised by the senator's rise from political exile to front-runner status, but there was nothing surprising about it for Mark Summerhays. For him, it was just a matter of about goddamn time.

Four years earlier, a victory in New Hampshire had given Senator Mark Summerhays an uncommonly virulent strain of the disease that plagued the United States Senate. Presidential ambition. Since winning his first bid for congress in his Florida district over a decade ago, he had been the golden child of the Democratic Party. He'd done everything right. Served in the unglamorous but important party-building roles and made the powers-that-be appreciate his talent. Raised more money for others than he had for himself. Toed the line on votes important to the party. Spoke out against the Bush Administration before it was popular to do so. Timed the winds just right in both supporting and then distancing himself from Barack Obama. Then, when he made the decision to run for an open U.S. Senate seat, no other serious Democrat challenged him and the Republicans put up a sacrificial lamb for a candidate. The resulting landslide had prompted the national press to speculate that the handsome, well-spoken, former entrepreneur was staging a run for the White House.

He did, and did it well, until right after New Hampshire when unflattering stories about his business dealings bubbled up from the dark depths of scandal hell where he'd thought he'd paid good money to send them. Questions as to why his net worth had doubled and then tripled while serving in congress were hard to answer in a sound bite, especially because none of the answers were true.

The only thing the national press likes more than a great success story is a catastrophic fall from grace. The knives came out and in weeks the Summerhays campaign fell to pieces. Not since Howard Dean's primal scream in Iowa or Rick Perry saying "oops" after forgetting one of his own policy proposals during a national debate had someone so quickly turned from presumptive nominee to being ushered off the national stage.

But, with Libby's help, Summerhays had roared back for the next election and put himself not only in the race, but at the head of the pack as the thoughtful, intelligent choice for President, a chance to return to decent, wholesome values and get the country back on track.

Libby thought about what a sham that was as he watched the presidential front-runner pound his fists into his desk, shouting a tirade of obscenities as his face turned a deep crimson and thin lines of spittle flew onto the papers in front of him. Libby had seen the tantrums before and he waited patiently for this one to run itself out. He kept his center of balance in case Summerhays decided to throw something in his direction.

Finally, the shouting stopped and the senator placed both hands flat on the desk and stared at the spot in front of him. When he looked up, his face was composed, the anger still there behind the eyes, but the panic was stored deeper where it was disguised more cleverly.

"Seems your old man has a few tricks left in him, Libby."

"Seems that way." Libby hadn't missed the utter lack of denial in Summerhays's outburst. Normally, he would have left it at that and worked the cover-up, but this was different. This one could end the campaign in a single news cycle. "Do you remember this woman? Catherine Fews?"

Summerhays stood up from his desk and kicked his chair backward. The heavy wooded chair rocked into the small table covered with picture frames of the senator's family, knocking some of the frames over which sent others down in a domino effect until only a few were standing. Libby suppressed a grin at the metaphor.

"So you don't think he's bluffing then?"

"You tell me, Mark. Does he have it? I mean, could he have it?"

"What you mean is, did I sleep with this woman or not?"

Libby stared impassively at his boss. He'd been through this before, the stonewalling, the lies. It was what came natural to these men after doing battle long enough in the war zone called Washington DC. But he wasn't in the mood to play, so he waited.

"Fuck yes. All right. I slept with her. She was supposed to be a pro. Total discretion."

Libby rolled his eyes at the man's naiveté and thought as he often did recently that perhaps the country and the world would be better off if Mark Summerhays had faded into the sunset four years earlier instead of making his comeback. And, as his own follow up question to the witness, Libby wondered why he was still working so hard to get his man in the job.

It was the power, of course. The unbridled, absolute power of the modern Presidency. And Mark Summerhays had the goods when it came to politics. The scandal after New Hampshire had been enough to knock the campaign off-course last time around. By the time it found its feet again, the electoral map was impossible to conquer and that idiot Dick Burns swept in and grabbed the nomination. But even then, the whispering, organized by Libby, started leading up to the convention that somehow the party had gotten it wrong. The kingmakers in the smoky backrooms wanted Summerhays added to the ticket as vice-president, but Burns had said no. Ballsy, but the wrong strategy because it would have taken Summerhays off the market.

Over the next two years, Libby had successfully weaned the press off the shadowy world of Mark Summerhays's business dealings: complex corporate structures, arcane rules governing the supply of defense products to foreign governments, most friendly, others not exactly on the good neighbors list. All of this had been too complicated to gain any traction with the American public. But Libby knew that a good ol' fashioned sex scandal was a different animal altogether.

Sell weapons to America's enemies through a Byzantine network of suppliers and no one cared. Get caught with your pants down while you're getting a blowjob from a DC call girl and the whole world tuned in for twenty-four hour coverage.

"All right. Now, I'm going to ask you a question and I need to hear the truth, all right? No bullshit here. If you lie to me I can't help you out of this."

"Don't patronize me," Summerhays snapped. "If you have a question, ask it."

Libby walked over and leaned in close to his boss's ear. Even in the man's private study in the senator's home, Libby knew better than to ask his next question too loudly.

"Did you have anything to do with this woman's death?"

Summerhays took a step back, a horrified look on his face. "Of course not. How could you—"

"I want you to think now, Mark," Libby went on, still whispering. "Did you complain about this problem to anyone? Someone who might have misunderstood what you were implying?"

"I haven't talked to anyone about Catherine Fews between the night I was with her and today. It was a stupid thing. I thought that—"

Libby held up his hand. "Save it. You're not a real politician in this town unless you're screwing around on your wife."

"Yeah, but they all get away with it."

Libby suppressed a sneer at the man's self-pity. It was the same revulsion he had felt toward Clinton's private rants about the unfairness of how the press treated his extracurricular activities. How Kennedy, whom Clinton revered above all, had done much worse than anything he'd ever done while in office and the press hadn't touched him.

"Now we have to decide what we're going to do about this."

"Hey, this was your plan, remember? Shake up the establishment, rattle Mason's cage by siding with the guys who want him out. All we shook loose was this new threat he can hold over my head. Great plan, Libby. Just great."

"The plan was perfect," Libby said calmly. "We picked up endorsements from dozens of people who want to see the son of a bitch gone. If I had been informed of the complications I might face, then I could have adjusted the plan."

"You screwed up. Why can't you just *fucking* admit that?" Summerhays screamed.

"Calm down," Libby said. "This is a time for rational, collected thought. Emotions only clutter vision."

Summerhays pointed a finger at him, ready to unload a salvo of invective, but he caught himself and swallowed hard. He lowered his hand and slumped against the edge of the desk.

"You're right. I'm sorry," he said. "I'm sorry about everything."

Libby recognized this stage of his boss's manipulation technique. Anger followed by remorse, then the inevitable compliments and pleas for help. He wondered whether his father would put up with this ridiculous behavior or if he would make a stand and call the man out on his bullshit right there and then. As soon as the thought formed, he cursed himself for letting the old man get into his head. Talk about manipulation. Mason was the master at it.

"I don't know what I'd do without you, Libby. You're the sharpest hand there is, I know that much." Summerhays clasped his hands together on his lap. "This one is big, I know. I've never needed your help more than I do now. Can I count on you, Libby? Can I count on you to pull me through this one?"

"Of course you can." *And you'll let me choose the next Director of the FBI when you take office, you son of a bitch, or I'll bury you faster than a cat buries its own shit.*

"So tell me you have a plan."

Libby had spent every minute since his meeting with his father deciding on a course of action, wading through the complex political calculus of risk to come to a decision.

"Of course I have a plan," Libby said.

"Tell me," Summerhays said, leaning forward.

"It's better that you don't know."

Libby's boss stood and walked over to the floor-to-ceiling windows that looked out over the manicured back garden. Libby watched, amused at the man's transparent attempt at drama.

"Yes, I understand. Better that I don't know."

Libby nodded. "Stay loose. You have a campaign to win." He turned and left the room feeling no better than he had before the meeting but with a new sense of purpose.

He pulled a burner phone from his pocket, a pre-paid cell he'd purchased with cash. The fact that he knew the number he dialed by memory made him feel dirty. He held the phone to his ear, scanning the hallways both in front and behind.

The phone clicked and he heard breathing on the other end.

"We need to meet," he said.

"Tomorrow," a deep voice replied.

"No, tonight," Libby said.

A pause. "Tomorrow. Noon. The place I told you last time."

Click.

Libby curled his fingers around the phone and nearly threw it at the wall. He stopped himself, seeing an original Peale painting was in his line of fire. It was a rare painting of George Washington during his decisive victory at Yorktown. Libby shuddered as he thought how close he'd just come to throwing his phone through a priceless canvas of one of his heroes. One of the few truly great Americans. The first president's eyes leveled at him like a disapproving father.

He doubted Washington would have patted him on the back for the meeting he'd just set up for the following day. But Libby knew in today's world, in order to do the work of the angels, you sometimes had to get in bed with the devil.

Libby turned heel and strode down the corridor, eager to put as much distance between himself and those scathing eyes as possible. He already had one impossible-to-please father; he sure as hell didn't need another.

CHAPTER 7

Allison fidgeted in her chair in the waiting area, feeling completely out of place. She took in her surroundings. Instead of the typical government-issued grey carpeting and pressboard furniture, the room had a regal feel to it. Lush navy blue carpet. Tasteful wallpaper that picked up the accent color and gave the room a warm, rich feel. The couch on which she sat had the smoothness of a silk-blend and comfortable pillows to prop her up. The receptionist's desk, an antique Chippendale's by the look of it, guarded a double-door entrance on the opposite side of the room from the entrance where two Marines in dress uniform stood guard in the outside hallway. A look at the ancient woman serving as Clarence Mason's secretary made Allison wonder who was more fearsome in protecting the Director of the FBI, the single old woman or the two young Marines. Allison's money was on the old lady.

Shouting erupted from inside the office. It appeared not to be a very regular occurrence as the old woman looked up sharply from the computer screen toward the door. She glanced to the two Marines, but they didn't budge.

Seconds later, the doors blew open and Garret stormed out. Well, as close as he could get to storming on his crutches, sporting a thick cast on his right leg. He froze when he saw her.

"You," he stammered. "What the hell are you doing here?"

Allison stood. She hadn't seen Garret since the raid three days earlier and wasn't sure how he felt about her decision to shoot him in the leg. Apparently, he didn't feel that good about it.

"Director Mason asked to see me," Allison said. "Hey, I wanted to apologize for—"

Garret held up his hand to stop her. "Apologize? Really? Apologizing is what you do when you spill coffee on someone's notes. Or hit the wrong floor button on the elevator. You *shot* me, McNeil. On purpose."

Allison shrugged, using every bit of willpower not to let loose all the one-liners piling up inside of her, begging to get out. She reminded herself that good men had died at the raid, her raid, so playing games with Garret didn't seem appropriate.

"It was the only way I could see to--"

"She saved your life, Garret," said a voice from inside the office. "You ought to be kissing her backside instead of demanding her termination."

Garret looked horrified. He leaned in and poked a finger at Allison. "This isn't over. I'm going to finish you, no matter what the old man says."

With that, Garret limped out of the room. When Allison turned, Mason was standing next to her, watching him leave.

"That should take care of the reprimand for shooting Special Agent Morrison," he said.

"Yes sir," Allison replied, unsure as always on how to read Mason's body language. He gave her a wry smile and she relaxed.

"Hold my calls, Mrs. Watkins," he said to the receptionist. He held out a hand toward his office. "Come in. You've had an eventful few days and I want to hear all about them."

There were few places in Washington outside of the Oval Office that were more carefully designed to give a better home-field advantage. Mason's office was large, laid out in three distinct areas to give a sense of intimate spaces within the overall area. A long glossy boardroom table was to her right, surrounded by eight high-backed leather chairs, a simple vase with three red roses at the center of it. Allison pictured old Mrs. Watkins placing new flowers there each morning in anticipation of Mason's arrival. A touch of old-school class.

The other area was comprised of two couches facing one another with a low coffee table in between. A half-dozen newspapers from around the world were lined neatly down the middle so that the headlines on each were visible at a glance. There was a single leather chair at the head of the table. It was rugged and worn, out of place in the refined air of the office. *A little like Mason himself,* Allison thought.

The final area was Mason's desk, a massive, ornate structure that dominated the far end of the room. The wall behind the desk was all window, giving a view of the DC skyline from eleven stories up. Allison noted the slight distortion in the glass. Bulletproof. Hell, it was probably Stinger missile-proof. It was no secret that Mason had his share of powerful enemies. Half would be content to wreck his career. The other half wouldn't be happy until he was dead.

There was a cluster of photos on one wall. Allison walked toward it, soaking in the history. In chronological order, there was a photo with each president starting with Lyndon Johnson. The personalities of each man were on display in the photos. Carter too serious. Reagan with a smile and a twinkle in his eye. Bush the Elder standing at attention. Clinton with an arm around Mason as if they were drinking buddies. Bush the Younger smirking like he was doing a Clint Eastwood impersonation. Obama looking impatient and preoccupied. Through all the pictures, Mason looked the same. Sure, he aged, his jet-black hair turning salt-and-pepper and then totally grey and thin, crow's-feet starting around his eyes around Reagan and covered with wrinkles by the end of Bush the Younger. Yet, in each picture Mason had the same steely look, the same upright posture, the same regal bearing as if he belonged in the photo with the most powerful man in the world. The message was clear: Presidents came and went, but Clarence Mason was forever.

She felt Mason step up next to her. "There's a lot of history in those pictures," she said.

"A lot of ego on display," Mason said.

"I think you have to have a pretty healthy ego to want to sit in the Oval Office. Part of the job description, I imagine," Allison said.

Mason laughed. "I wasn't talking about them. What kind of damn fool needs a display like this in his office? An old, crusty one, I guess." He smiled and pointed to the couches. "Have a seat. Do you want some water? Coffee?"

Allison made her way over to the couch, feeling her legs tremble as she did. She was more nervous than she wanted to let on. Even though she'd met Mason before, he was still the Director, not to mention a living legend. "I suppose if I say no, I'll appear nervous. If I say yes, I'll look too eager to please."

"Which are you? Nervous or eager to please?" Mason asked.

"Neither," Allison said.

"Then what are you?"

"Thirsty," she said.

Mason barked out a short laugh and poured two cups of water. He handed one to Allison and held out his as if to propose a toast. "Back in the '60s this would have been a Scotch."

"At ten in the morning?"

Mason shrugged. "Different time." He raised his glass. "To Sam Kraw. Burning in hell where he belongs."

Allison sipped the water and it somehow tasted bitter in her mouth. Mason sat in the leather chair and studied her.

"You don't look like an agent who just cracked a major case," Mason said. "Most agents get one or two cases like Kraw in their career. You have this and Arnie Milhouse in under twelve months."

"Four men died," Allison said, her voice cracking.

"I know," Mason said. He reached to a small side table and picked up a short stack of folders. Allison could tell they were personnel files. He opened the top one. "Michael Connell, Stephen––"

"McConnell," Allison corrected. "Michael McConnell. Stephen Garcia. Dwayne Goodard. Sergio Benedict. Three of them were married. Sergio was about to be."

"None of them had children, from what I understand. A small blessing."

"Steve Garcia's wife is six months pregnant," Allison said, her voice coming out flat and lifeless. Detaching herself emotionally was the only way she could say the names of the men without breaking down.

Mason closed the folders and placed them on his lap. "Do you know how many victims' remains have been identified at Kraw's hideout?"

Allison shook her head. "Last I heard, there were nine––"

"Eighteen," Mason said. "And that's just so far. The dogs are finding graves all over the place out there. It was the middle of nowhere. Impossible to find. Except for you. You put the puzzle together and found it."

"The pieces were already there," Allison said, distracted as she digested the number she'd just heard. *Eighteen bodies. Eighteen little girls.*

"And Garret and his shop had been working with those same pieces for two years before you came along. You found Kraw. You. And the men who died were professionals. They knew the risks of the job and they still signed up for it. Think of the lives you saved, Allison. Take my word for it, sometimes that's the only way to get through all of this."

Allison nodded and took a drink of water. The bitterness lingered, but the cool water also soothed her throat. She was conscious that Mason was sizing her up and she didn't care.

"Is this why you summoned me? To tell me that those men died doing their duty so I should be OK with it?"

"No," Mason stated, taking a sip from his water with a smile. "I summoned you here to fire you."

CHAPTER 8

L ibby drove his own car past the Lincoln Memorial, round the backside and merged onto Memorial Bridge. The view as he crossed the Potomac over to Arlington National Cemetery always brought a surge of patriotism in him. For a few brief seconds, he remembered a time when he believed in words like duty, honor, sacrifice. When he believed that Washington had at least some good men willing to put the public good above politics and petty jealousies. Nothing like a few decades in the sewer filled with bureaucrats, lobbyists and politicians to eradicate that idealism completely.

Even the story of Arlington Cemetery itself was a story more fitting of today's Washington than most of the public realized. The white mansion that sits on the hill overlooking the Potomac and most of the property on which the cemetery now sits was once owned by none other than Robert E. Lee, the South's brilliant commanding general during the Civil War. After the graveyards in the area began to fill, the Union Quartermaster General Montgomery Meigs ordered new burials to take place on Lee's property. Even then, the Union general using Lee's home as a headquarters demanded the burials take place on the far west of the structure so he wouldn't be inconvenienced. On hearing this, and fearing that Lee might be able to return to his home after the war, Meigs ordered the mansion's flower garden dug up and the next internments to be immediately next to the house. Within a month, nearly three thousand bodies were buried on the grounds, making a return to the house impossible for Lee and his family. The entire property was eventually wrested from the Lee family for a meager monetary compensation and transformed into the hallowed ground it is today. Pure Washington. On the face, a place of honor and sacrifice. Underneath, the place was simply a total F U to an opponent.

Libby felt the cynicism claw away at his insides, but he didn't know how to stop it. After everything he'd seen and done, he wasn't sure if it was possible. Maybe if he could find one pure thing in DC, then some of his faith could come back. But he knew he might as well be hunting unicorns in Central Park. The only thing that mattered at the end of the day, the only thing that gave him the ability to do anything remotely good for the world, was power. Who had it? Who didn't? How to get it and keep it? These were Libby's stock and trade. And once in a rare while, power could even be used to accomplish things that helped people.

Just like Arlington, action in Washington that helped people was usually just a happy by-product of someone in power using their influence to stick it to someone else. A piece of legislation jammed down someone's throat to show dominance. Stealing funds from one district to reward one congressman and punish another. A million petty ways to play the game. Libby had learned his craft by watching his father, but now that he was in a game against him, he worried whether he was up to the task. The fact that he was having a meeting with someone like Scott Harris proved how desperate he was to get a win.

Harris was a relic of the Senator's old life. A shadowy figure that had orbited Summerhays before Libby had joined the Senator's team, years before the first White House run. Libby knew nothing about the man's personal life, hell he doubted either he or Summerhays even knew the man's real name. All he knew was that if there was a problem that needed to go away, a call to Harris would make it happen. Only the last time Libby had made that call, a problem-causing congressman ended up in intensive care after a random mugging busted his jaw, broke four ribs and punctured a lung. He'd resolved never again to use the man's services, but it turned out that never hadn't really been in the cards.

Beyond getting Harris's help, he also needed to know something before he moved forward with any of it. The only way he'd know for certain is if he looked Harris in the eyes when he asked him his question.

Libby parked his car and headed toward a rectangular gate built of red sandstone and red brick with "MCCLELLAN" carved across the top in gilt letters. He knew from his reading that the gate was commissioned by the same Montgomery Meigs who founded the cemetery, just when his boss McClellan was running for President. Below it, on one of the support pillars, Meigs had ordered a second name to be carved into the stone. His own. Libby touched the name as he walked through the gate, thinking it was two Washington staples showcased in one place: the art of sucking up to powerful men and that of unabashed self-promotion.

"You're late," said a voice behind him.

Libby stiffened and cursed himself for letting the man get the drop on him. He'd let his mind wander and hadn't been paying attention to his surroundings. He turned around and saw Harris staring back at him.

The last two years hadn't changed the man. He had a military bearing, ramrod straight posture, with lean muscle rippling with every movement. He was tan and looked younger than the late fifties where Libby pegged him. Unnatural, pale blue eyes stared into Libby's, instantly sizing him up, his lips curling into a pucker of disgust.

"I said, you're late."

Libby held up his watch. "It's four minutes after twelve."

"Which is late. But you always were sloppy," Harris said.

"And you always were a pain in the ass," Libby said. "Why the hell can't we meet at a Starbucks or something? You and your cloak and dagger bullshit."

Harris looked around the cemetery. "I like it here. This is where a lot of my friends ended up."

Libby wasn't sure if Harris was telling the truth or not. He decided it didn't matter. "We've got a problem," Libby said.

"I figured."

"Do you know what it is already?"

Harris squinted at him. "Are we playing games today? If so, I'm not in the mood."

A shiver passed through Libby. The threat of violence coiled within the man's voice was visceral, almost like there was a gun pointed at him.

"When is the last time Summerhays contacted you?" Libby asked.

Harris stared back at Libby, tight-lipped.

"I need to know," Libby said. "Did he contact you? Did he have you...take care of anything for him?"

Harris shook his head. "I'm not answering that. I'm not like you, remember? I'm not sloppy."

Libby felt his face flush with anger. "Fine, forget it then. Go back to whatever rock you were under when I called."

Libby turned and walked away. It was a game of chicken in reverse. Like walking away from the negotiating table when you were the one who most needed the deal to happen. With each step, he felt more nauseous. He didn't really have a backup plan.

"Wait," Harris called out.

It took all of his self-control not to stop. He kept walking.

"OK," Harris said. "He called me."

Libby stopped and turned. "When?"

"Last night."

Libby bit down on the inside of his lips so hard that he felt the salty taste of blood in his mouth. This was exactly the type of thing he'd promised himself he wasn't going to tolerate this time around. Whoring his way through DC was one thing, it was the man's base instinct at work, but lying right to his face and calling Harris directly showed a lack of trust that Libby knew should be a deal-breaker. He also knew he shouldn't say another word. He should just walk away from the whole thing before it got any messier. But somehow over the years, Libby knew he'd turned into a moth and the Office of the President of the United States was the brightest flame in town. He wasn't going anywhere and he knew it.

"What phone did he use?" Libby asked.

"Don't know. Don't care. Can't trace the number to me."

Yeah, but try explaining a phantom number on the official call log from a campaign phone, thought Libby. He filed that away as an issue to deal with later.

"What'd he want?"

"Not sure. I stopped him before he got going. Told him it was better for him to let other people contact me."

"And?"

"He agreed," Harris said. "But before he hung up, he told me price was no object on this one." For the first time, Harris smiled. "I can't lie, I liked the sound of that."

Libby tried to keep a poker face even though he was screaming inside. At least Summerhays hadn't revealed any details over the phone. Libby had friends over at NSA and he knew enough about the capabilities over there to know the idea of a private phone conversation was an anachronism. "How long had it been since you spoke to him before last night?"

Harris's smile disappeared and was replaced with a scowl. "Sounds like maybe you should be asking your boss these questions. Let's cut the shit. What's the job?"

"I asked you a question. How long?" Libby asked.

Harris hesitated, then said, "Not since the thing." He squinted at Libby. "Are you wearing a mic?"

"W—what? No," Libby said.

Harris waved him forward and gestured for him to raise his hands.

"I'm not wearing a fucking wire," Libby said.

"Then you won't mind me checking," Harris said, making it clear it was no longer a suggestion.

Libby was in a hurry. As much as he hated to give in to the guy, he raised his hands. Harris patted him down quickly, including a full clutch of Libby's groin. Finally, he stepped back.

"Satisfied?"

"Cell phone?" Harris asked.

"Did you feel a cell phone on me?" Libby snapped. But Harris just stared back. "Left it in the car like the other times. I'm not stupid."

Harris shrugged as if to say the last point was debatable. "Can't be too careful. Mistakes get you put in the ground. And I like the view from up here, you know what I mean?"

Libby took a deep breath. "Can we get down to business now?"

"By all means."

Libby wanted to slap the smug bastard upside the head, but he resisted the temptation. First, the man would probably lay him out before he landed the first punch. Second, Libby needed his help. "There was this call girl. High priced. We both know our friend has his appetites and he fell off the wagon. Problem is, turns out she filmed her tricks. One camera for whoever was paying her, the other--"

"Who was paying her?" Harris asked.

53

"Don't know," Libby said, although he had a pretty good idea he was related to the guy writing the checks.

"What about the second camera?"

Libby tensed. "I didn't say there was a second camera."

"Jesus, Libby. Leave the paranoia to me," Harris said. "I'm better at it. You said one camera for whoever was paying her, the other…"

Libby relaxed a little. He had said that. Maybe he was a little too on edge. "The second camera was hooked to an internet connection. We don't know where the data went or who has it."

"And that's what you want me to find out?" Harris asked.

"Yes, but when you find the person, you report it to me. You don't do anything, got it?"

"Who else is in on this?" Harris asked.

"DCPD. The FBI has some photos, but they're not great," Libby said. "But I'm sure Mason wants his hands on the videos so bad he can taste it."

"Your old man? So, this is personal," Harris said. "I don't like when it gets personal. Causes irrational thinking. Things get sloppy. And, like I said, you already have that problem."

"So you keep saying." Libby pulled out a thick envelope. "Fifteen grand now. Another fifteen when you deliver the location."

"Fifty."

"What? That's ridiculous."

"I don't know what I'm getting into on this one. It could be a foreign government. Or the Russian mob."

"Or a server at her parents' house," Libby said.

"If that was it, you wouldn't need me. No, there's something bigger going on here and we both know it." Harris licked his lips. "Fifteen now. Fifty when I deliver the location. Like the man said, price is no object on this one."

Libby made a show of thinking it over. Truth was it wasn't his money. Besides, Summerhays had millions to burn and sixty-five thousand was a bargain to make this particular problem go away.

"OK, but if you take matters into your own hands, if anyone gets hurt, then the fifty grand is forfeit."

"Deal. What was the call girl's name?"

Libby watched closely, figuring this was his best chance to determine whether Harris was lying to him. Or rather, the extent of his lies. When it came to veracity, Harris was like a politician: your best indication that he was lying was that his lips were moving. But in Libby's nightmare scenario, Summerhays had panicked weeks earlier and been stupid enough to tell Harris to "take care" of his problem. That would be one dead prostitute too many for a President to have in his past. Libby figured if that was the case and Harris was playing him, then he would be expecting to hear Catherine Fews's name.

"I need a name, place of residence, everything you have," Harris said.

Libby pulled a thumb drive from his pocket. "Here you go. Her name was Beth Kinoch."

He watched for any kind of surprise in Harris's face. He didn't expect much, the man was a professional, but at least something if he already had the real name. Nothing.

"Irish girl, huh?" Harris said without skipping a beat. "Pity, I like the Irish."

He pocketed the thumb drive and walked past Libby. "I'll be in touch."

Libby thought about telling him the real name, but decided he'd figure it out once he opened the file. He turned to walk back to his car, passing back beneath the McClellan gate, the one-time presidential candidate's name proclaimed in bold letters and Meigs's name so small and inconsequential below.

Libby knew he was playing Meigs to Summerhays's McClellan and wondered if he would, in the end, even warrant that much of a footnote in history.

<><><>

Harris patted the wad of money in his pocket as he walked. Fifteen grand had a comforting weight to it and he knew another hundred grand would feel all that much better.

Sure, he'd made the deal for fifty, but Libby hadn't even bargained. Once he had the information in his possession, the price would double and Summerhays would pay it without thinking twice.

He felt the thumb drive in his other pocket, eager to get back to his hotel room and load up the information. He hoped the job would only take a day or two, but he'd force himself to take some added precautions. There were too many variables in play, too many blind spots. It felt like there was a game of musical chairs going on and he wanted to make damn sure he was taken care of when the music stopped. If the shit hit the fan, someone had to be without a chair at the end. If he was a betting man, and he was, his money was that it was going to be Libby.

But Harris reminded himself not to underestimate the man. Somehow Libby had wedged himself into the confidence of the man most likely to be the next President of the United States. Not only that, but his father was the legendary Clarence Mason.

No, there was more to Libby than met the eye. Like the way he'd given him the wrong name as a test to see how much he really knew. It was brilliant, actually. Not good enough to catch him, but almost. Libby obviously suspected he still had a direct line to Summerhays, probably even thought that he had something to do with Catherine Fews's death.

He would have to step carefully on this one. But then again, he always did.

CHAPTER 9

"This doesn't sound like you're firing me," Allison said. "It sounds more like a job offer."

Mason folded his hands on his lap. "And is it a job offer you're interested in?"

Allison met Mason's stare. Her nerves had given way to a cold anger once Mason had explained his proposal to her. "No."

Mason didn't flinch. He simply lifted a hand, indicating that she should continue.

Allison cleared her throat. Choosing her words carefully wasn't something she did very often but she knew she was about to tread through dangerous waters. Mason was not a man who was often told no. Especially by a lowly Special Agent.

"Suzanne Greenville," she said, letting the name hang in the air, searching Mason's face for hints of recognition.

"What about her?" Mason asked.

"The call girl who was murdered while I was tracking Arnie Milhouse down."

"I know who she is," Mason said.

Allison felt chastised. Mason's memory was legendary in the Bureau; dredging up facts from cold cases decades old enabled him to make connections that no computer ever could. Of course he knew who Suzanne Greenville was. His look sent her a message: *I may look old, but I haven't missed a step. Not yet, anyway.*

"The cases are too similar," Allison said. "When you gave me permission to follow my gut about Arnie Milhouse, you were hoping he had videos from Suzanne Greenville. Also a call girl taking video of highly placed clientele."

"But he didn't," Mason said. "And we never conclusively proved he committed that murder. But none of this is what's bothering you, is it? And here I thought you were a straight shooter."

"It's too much of a coincidence."

"Unless..."

"Unless Suzanne Greenville and Catherine Fews were being coached by the same person." Allison's mind took her down a dark path as she considered the possibilities, but she pulled back from it, shaking her head. "But sex scandals are the oldest currency in Washington. Clinton got a blowjob in the Oval Office and he survived."

"But what if there had been a video of it?" Mason said. "Such a thing would go viral in a matter of seconds. A politician with a future would do anything to stop that from happening." Mason leaned forward. "But ask the question you want to ask, Allison."

"I don't know if you'll tell me the truth." Her stomach turned over as she said the words, essentially calling the Director of the FBI, her ultimate boss, a liar straight to his face. Stupid at best. Career suicide at the worst.

Mason smiled. "Ahh, that's the Allison McNeil I thought I knew."

"Did you?"

"Did I what?"

She steeled herself. She was already in over her head, so why not go all the way? "Were these two women working for you?"

"No, they were not," Mason said coolly. He may have anticipated her line of questioning but he obviously didn't like the way the accusation sounded out loud.

Allison sat back in her chair. Even if Mason had been running the women as an operation, she didn't expect him to come clean with her. The suspicion was ugly, and she hated doubting Mason, but the cases were too similar. She realized she didn't believe him.

"Did you have them killed?" she asked, her voice coming out a whisper.

"No," Mason said, his voice flat.

Silence. Allison searched his face for clues but knew Mason had been in the business of lying for more years than she'd been alive. Most people would elaborate, go through the logic argument for their innocence, try to persuade. Mason did none of that. He simply stared at her, unreadable. For someone who prided herself on being able to get into other people's heads, she felt like Mason might as well be carved from granite, an impenetrable wall of training and experience.

"If not you, then who?" Allison asked, deciding to play along.

"That's what I need to know," Mason replied.

"But you don't want a full investigation because it might lead back to you."

"It would never lead back to me," Mason said. "But to the Bureau, maybe. That's part of the solution set I've considered. Was this a blackmail operation inspired by the Suzanne Greenville case conducted by some overzealous group in our organization? Perhaps in some other part of the intelligence community? All possible. The Greenville videos were all low-level people, but it might have gotten the wrong type of people thinking about the possibilities. Frankly, I hope that proves to be the case."

"Why?"

"The people on the videos Fews claimed to have were on a different level. Congressmen. Senators. Powerful businessmen. What if it was a foreign government who set this up? Or a terrorist group seeking leverage? Let's hope it was us."

"Because the FBI can be trusted, right?" Allison said. When this had happened with Suzanne Greenville, she'd felt like the videos falling into Mason's hands actually would be for the greater good. Give him some relief from the near-constant witch-hunt by a few members of congress who had an ax to grind with the director. But if he'd gone out and set this up and a woman had died because of it, she couldn't accept that.

"Why me? DCPD can work this. And there must be dozens of agents you know better. Whose discretion you can trust more," Allison said.

"The regular investigation will continue as is. They will have no knowledge that you are also working the case. Maybe they will beat you to the punch. Nothing but dead-ends so far, so I doubt it."

"Still doesn't explain why you want me."

"You're not the only one who is adept at reading people," Mason said. "You're exactly the right person for this. Your work on the Kraw case proved your ability to put pieces of a complex puzzle together and the Milhouse case showed that you can work alone. Shooting poor Garret in the leg gives me a reason to put you on administrative leave pending a full investigation, carving out time for you to dig in. And, most importantly, you'll do it for the right reasons."

Mason grabbed a folder from the table next to him and tossed it onto the coffee table in front of Allison. It landed open. One side had an eight-by-ten photo of Catherine Fews, a bright smile, hair down over her shoulders, wearing a conservative black dress. On the other side was a shot of the crime scene.

It was a bedroom with a four-postered bed. The sheets were drenched in blood with a dismembered torso in the center. Each bedpost had a bondage rope tied to it. At the end of each rope was one of Catherine's legs or arms. Allison took a deep breath. Photos like these were her profession but she still felt an initial wave of nausea each time she saw a new crime scene. She supposed the day she stopped feeling that would be a good time to start thinking about a new line of work. As she scanned the brutality on display, she noticed something missing.

"Where's her head?" Allison asked.

Mason tapped the crime scene photo and Allison leaned forward to look more closely. There was a fireplace in the bedroom with a wide mantle across its length. In the middle of it, perched like a souvenir brought back from a vacation, eyes wide open, was a dismembered head.

Allison leaned closer. She heard the screams of the victim. She pictured the killer standing in the center of the carnage, imagining what could possibly drive someone to do something so depraved.

"He's forcing her to watch," she whispered. "Were the eyes fixed in that position? Adhesive? Stitching?"

Mason nodded. "The eyelids were pinned open. Five needles in each eye."

Allison touched her finger to the photo, slowly working her way back and forth over the image as if it were a braille document. She absorbed every detail. Placing herself in the scene. Imaging the feel of the room. Putting herself into the mind of the killer as he positioned the head perfectly so that it faced the bed. She felt the tension coiled inside of him as he turned to do his work on the rest of the body. The grip of the knife. The smell of the blood in the air.

Mason rapped a knuckle on the coffee table and Allison jerked back from the photo, blinking hard to clear her senses.

Mason studied her for a few seconds, then covered the crime scene photo with the image of Catherine Fews when she was alive. "I want to find out who has the videos and what they intend to do with them," Mason said. "But you don't care about that, do you?"

Allison shook her head. She held up the photo. "If what you're saying is true, then if I find the videos, I find the killer."

"That is the assumption. The last video transmitted from the camera to the unknown location would be of the murder itself. Do your job as I know you are capable, and I will make sure the videos are not in the wrong hands and you will get your killer."

Allison had interacted with Mason outside the normal chain of command on the Milhouse case, but she'd still walked into the meeting nervous and overwhelmed by the trappings of power surrounding her boss. But now she felt more like herself. The aura of legend she'd ascribed to Mason had lost some of its glow in this meeting. He was just a man, flawed like everyone else. And she still wasn't sure that she trusted his motives for choosing her for this assignment.

"And if I refuse?"

Mason shrugged. "Administrative leave makes sense. Garret pounded the table pretty hard today that you didn't have to shoot him in the leg. That you had other options. He wants a full investigation and hearing."

Allison was surprised at the directness of the threat. She expected him to be more nuanced in his approach, but it appeared he was ready for this discussion to be over, one way or the other. She considered administrative leave and that it would give her time to be with her dad. But it was the investigation that had her worried. Garret was a powerful force in the Bureau. Without Mason looking out for her interests, he might just have the clout to get her reassigned to a field office in Omaha or Cleveland.

Mason stood and extended his hand. "Do we have an understanding?"

She stood, feeling a slow burning anger at his manipulation of the situation to his advantage. Still, the bottom line was that she wanted to find whoever killed Catherine Fews so there really was no decision to make. She shook his hand. "I'll work with you to find this killer, but if the trail leads back to you in any way, I won't stop."

Mason nodded, keeping his face unreadable. "I'd expect nothing less." He crossed the room to his desk and retrieved a small, flat box. He handed it to Allison. "Inside is the complete file on Suzanne Greenville and Catherine Fews along with database access codes."

"Won't people see what I'm looking into if I access the database?"

"These are special codes," Mason said. "No log will be made of your access."

"I have a guy, a tech guy. I want to use him on this."

"You're talking about Jordi Pines," Mason said, frowning. "I know of his involvement with the Kraw case. The man's not much better than the criminals we chase."

"He's a big reason we got Kraw," Allison said.

"I can give you access to someone who can do anything you need," Mason said.

She didn't like the idea of someone reporting on her to Mason, not until she had a better idea what his real involvement had been. "I'd like to use Jordi. He has the clearances."

"Which are constantly up for review for violations," Mason muttered. Then he nodded, giving in a little too easily for Allison's taste. It either meant he was desperate or he didn't really think she was going to be able to find anything. Either way, there was something Mason wasn't telling her. And it made her nervous.

Mason nodded at the box in Allison's hands. "Inside the box you'll also find a phone preprogrammed with a number to reach me, not to be used for anything else, and a pre-paid credit card with all the funds you need. If you need me to run interference with the locals, use the cell phone. You tell people that you're on administrative leave pending the review of the Sam Kraw shooting. You decided to spend your time researching the call girl murders for a technical paper you're preparing."

"Instead of using the break to go to the Bahamas?" Allison asked.

"Anyone who knows you would find the research project more believable."

"Looks like you thought of everything," Allison said, poking through the box. "Did you ever consider that I might say no?"

Mason grinned. "The thought never crossed my mind."

CHAPTER 10

Scott Harris took out a Corona from the mini-fridge, cracked it open and took a long drink. He closed his eyes and imagined himself on his favorite beach in Playa Del Carmen. Powder white sand. A pleasant breeze against his tan skin warmed by the sun. Senoritas in skimpy bathing suits giving him looks as they walked by. No worries. Not a care in the world.

When he opened his eyes he let out a disappointed groan that his attempt at teleportation had failed. He was still in his short-term rental unit in Southeast DC, just a shabby motel room with a small kitchenette. The place was a dump. Poor lighting. Stains on the carpet. Dirty water coming out of the taps. It'd been a shithole to begin with and he'd just added to it. Pizza boxes and fast food wrappers littered the floor. Empty beer bottles stood in formation on the counter like they were lined up in front of a firing squad. He had the money to stay at the Four Seasons, but he was working. When he was on a job, it was all about staying places where people knew better than to ask questions. Besides, he'd stayed in worse places. Much worse.

Harris looked through the information on the thumb drive Libby had provided him. He didn't expect to find anything he didn't already know, but he hadn't gotten this far in his career by cutting corners. He dutifully went through every file, reviewed each photo, read every word of every report. When he got to the end, he went back up to the first folder and read through it all a second time.

Neither pass added anything worthwhile to what he already knew, a fact that pleased him. Although there wasn't an official seal anywhere in the files, he recognized the FBI's layout. He wondered whether Libby's father had been the one to give him the information. If so, he guessed there might be some data missing, data which might be the essential ingredient to tracking down where the second camera had sent the video images.

Harris opened the photo of one of Catherine Fews's severed legs and zoomed in on the image. The resolution degraded quickly and the picture turned blurry and dark. The photographer had botched the job. He decided a trip to the morgue to get a look at the body would be his next step.

Harris closed the file and sipped his beer. He needed to see who was on the case for the Feds. Maybe if Mason had chosen the right agent for the job, he could just hang back and see where the FBI led him.

CHAPTER 11

Allison smiled as Richard reached over and caressed her arm playfully. She knew exactly what that touch meant and she was more than open to the idea. She slid her feet backward under the sheets until they were intertwined with his. Richard's caressing fingers went from her arm, up her shoulder, through her hair. She felt his warm body press up behind her and she moaned softly, the urgency building in her. She wanted his mouth, wanted to feel his chest against her own. She rolled over and opened her eyes...

...to an empty bed.

She stared at the bedcover, an entire side without a wrinkle in it since her habit was to sleep on only one side of the bed. She reached out and placed a hand in the center of it. The spot was cold to the touch and the emptiness brought tears to her eyes. The image of Richard's broken body sprawled on sharp rocks flashed in her head. A casualty of the Arnie Milhouse case but also a casualty of her bull-headedness and her willingness to take risks. In her semi-awake state, her brain jumped to the other casualties she'd laid at her own feet, times when her choices had put men in harm's way and gotten them killed. The faces of the four men on the tactical team in Louisiana came to her, an odd mix of images, one second their official photos from their personnel files, the next their burned and mangled bodies.

Allison sat up and clawed for the bucket next to her bed, heaving into it. It wasn't the first night since Louisiana that the guilt had woken her up this way, and she doubted it would be the last.

The shrink the Bureau sent her to after Arnie Milhouse had told her it was typical of most agents to have difficulties after killing in the line of duty. Arnie wasn't her first. There was the time before when she'd saved Richard's life in the field by killing Harvey Madel. She'd made the mistake of being honest with the shrink that time, only to have the supposedly sealed conversation thrown back in her face during her first meeting with Clarence Mason. Allison did have trouble dealing with the shooting. She had trouble with the fact that she liked the feeling of power and justice it gave her. From her studies, she knew most people experienced remorse even when killing to defend themselves or to protect a loved one. She must be missing that gene because she didn't waste one second on Madel. Or Arnie Milhouse. Or Sam Kraw. Maybe it was that the human mind was only capable of bearing so much guilt and all that she felt for Richard and the four tactical guys made it impossible to feel anything for the bad guys.

It was a nice thought, one that bestowed on her the benefit of the doubt and ascribed human traits that could make her feel better about herself. But it didn't explain Madel. No one had died then. The only real conclusion was that she felt no remorse because she was happy to put the sons of bitches out of their misery when she had the chance.

She wiped her mouth and sipped some water from a glass on her bedside table, a throwback to her childhood when her father always made sure a glass was there. She wasn't sure when it started, but it was part of his ritual to bring her a glass and a goodnight kiss, something he did without fail all the way through middle school and high school. He offered to stop doing it once when she was in tenth grade, asking if it was foolish of him. She told him he could stop if he wanted to, that she didn't care. Then once he left the room, she cried like a baby, not really sure why, but unable to stop. The next night, there was a glass of water on her bedside table.

She cried one other time as well because of his small, quirky gesture. It was after she quit the United States Naval Academy. Her father hadn't said a word the entire ride home, unable to find the words to soothe a daughter who'd been raped by an instructor and then discarded by an institution they had both thought they loved. But that first night at home, as she lay in her bed clutching the covers to her chest, doing her best to hold herself together, her father knocked softly on the door. She didn't answer but he came in anyway, glass of water in hand, and set it on her bedside table and kissed her cheek. He didn't say a word as he left the room and he didn't have to. She cried herself to sleep that night not because she was alone, but because she felt loved.

The clock glared at her, the digital numbers showing it was just after three in the morning. Late enough that she should be fast asleep, too early to just pack it in and get up for the day. Even so, she knew there was no chance of falling back to sleep so she took the second option and dragged herself out of bed.

The file from the Fews case was spread out across the length of her breakfast table, which she supposed could double as a dining room table if she was ever home for dinner or had guests over. The Georgetown apartment was new in the last year, a chance to start fresh. The rent sucked, but the location couldn't be beat. Only a few blocks off Wisconsin Avenue, she was within walking distance of restaurants and bars. Not that she took advantage of it that often. At least there were great runs to be had crisscrossing Georgetown University, or through the maze of brownstone mansions belonging to diplomats and politicians, or down to the waterfront along the steady-flowing Potomac.

She waited impatiently as her Keurig gurgled its way to a perfect cup of coffee. What had once seemed a delightful extravagance was now just part of her morning routine, the thirty seconds to make a single cup sometimes feeling like an eternity. The machine finished and she took the first sip a little too quickly, burning the tip of her tongue, but still relishing the all-important first taste of morning coffee.

Turning to the table, she looked death and depravity right in the face. Hours of study had given her very few details about either Catherine Fews's life or her death. Clearly, she'd been using an alias as there was no record of a Catherine Fews until she suddenly appeared in official records four years earlier.

There were no run-ins with law enforcement, not even so much as a speeding ticket. Not until her murder case was opened, anyway. The FBI computers had been unable to find a match in their vast archives of any record showing what the woman's real name had been. It was the first mystery Allison intended to solve.

One surprising data point was that at the time of her death, Catherine Fews's net worth was over two hundred thousand dollars. Either turning tricks with the DC elite paid far more than the FBI did or someone was funding her for the videos up front. She didn't think the money came from Catherine using the videos for blackmail on her own, but she couldn't rule that out either. She figured the other team, the real investigation, had likely already chased the money to find the source and had come up empty. Allison needed a different way in.

Most of the documents Mason had given her didn't shed much light on Catherine Fews's life, just her death. Close-up photos of her severed limbs hanging from the bondage cords on each bedpost. She was no pathologist, but she knew enough to be dangerous. Using a jeweler's loop, she magnified sections of the photos, looking for details that might tell a story. Just like the other dozen times she'd looked at them, she found nothing except frustration at the photographer who had done a crappy job of memorializing the scene. She wondered if it was someone young, someone overwhelmed by the scene. Still, it was sloppy work with shadows in important areas, blurs in others. She didn't want to admit it, but her first visit in the morning needed to be the coroner's office to look at the remains herself.

Allison picked up the eight by ten of a very alive and very beautiful Catherine Fews and stared into the young woman's eyes. She tried to imagine how it was possible that a young woman with so much potential ended up as a prostitute. Allison realized that if she wanted to know how Catherine Fews had died, she needed to know more about the life she'd led.

"What happened to you?" Allison said, her voice echoing in her empty apartment. Allison sat at the table sipping her coffee, rereading the file and feeling a new determination seep into her blood, not just to stop this man from killing again, but to avenge this young woman who must have caught a hard break somewhere along the line. And catching a hard break was something Allison could relate to. So, there at her kitchen table, at three thirty in the morning, the thing that happened at some point in every case happened. It was no longer just a case. It was personal. That usually meant the killer didn't stand a chance.

CHAPTER 12

Jordi Pines squatted behind a bank of computer monitors, his eyes twitching between screens as his fingers flew over the keyboard on his lap. Allison stood quietly off to the side, letting him do his magic. They were an unlikely pair, brought together by a mutual distrust of authority and a fervor for ending the careers of serial killers. Her intuition had pointed them in the right direction on the Kraw case, but it was his unique search algorithm that had been the real breakthrough.

Grossly overweight from countless hours at his computer fueled by pizza, Cheetos and Mountain Dew, Jordi wore tacky Hawaiian shirts, decorated his room with skulls and Dungeons and Dragons memorabilia, and showcased no noticeable internal filter when he spoke. It was as if he had gone down a list of geek programmer stereotypes, dutifully ticking off each item.

He had an English accent that made the socially awkward things that came from his mouth seem somehow funny instead of creepy. But the really odd thing was that Jordi was from New

Jersey and had never even been to England. When Allison asked where his accent came from, he looked at her like she was crazy and asked what accent she was referring to. Allison knew that genius sometimes came wrapped in a little bit of crazy and Jordi Pines had the crazy side of that equation working. She never brought up his accent again.

"You right bastard," he muttered at the screen in front of him. "You think you have me? Take this, bitchness."

It'd been over ten minutes of this one-sided conversation with his computers. As near as Allison could gather, someone smarter than Jordi had protected the data he was trying to access. If there was one thing Jordi couldn't stand, it was coming across someone smarter than himself.

The speaker made a harsh, grinding noise and the monitor flashed red. Jordi grabbed a handful of popcorn from the bowl next to his computer and threw it at the screen. "Fuck off, you twat."

"How's it going?" Allison asked.

Jordi looked up in surprise and Allison realized he had forgotten she was there. Once he dove into cyberspace, the real world faded for him. He'd shared a story once of another analyst who came into their shared office to find a small fire in one corner of the room and Jordi hard at work programming, oblivious to the smoke rising around him. Since then, Jordi had been given his own lair in the basement of the Hoover building since no one really wanted to work in the same space with him. Uncle Sam wasn't sure how to best use Jordi Pines, but he knew he wanted Jordi on his side instead of out in the world available to the highest bidder.

"Any luck?" she asked.

"There's no luck involved here, love," Jordi said.

"So, you've got something?"

Jordi scrunched up his nose as if a terrible smell had entered the room. "No, not really. Come have a look."

Allison slid around behind the desk, stepping over old pizza boxes. Jordi sized her up as she did so. "Have you put on a few pounds? Your boobs look bigger for some reason."

When they'd first started working together, that was the kind of comment that had shocked her speechless. But it was just Jordi being Jordi, unfiltered and prone to say the damnedest things. It helped that Jordi was gay. Unless he'd converted overnight from his predilection for large, hairy men, she knew there was nothing sexual about the comment.

"No," she said. "New bra."

He stared at her breasts and then her hips. He didn't look convinced. "If you say so."

Allison hit him in the shoulder. "Careful, I'll drag you out of this dungeon and force you to come to the gym with me."

"And then you'd be responsible for my heart attack, wouldn't you?"

"You'd be fine. It's just a matter of time before I break you down." Allison said as she leaned in and tried to decipher the data flashing on the screens. "So, lay it on me. Are you able to figure out where she sent the videos?"

"No," Jordi said. "The first analysts were right. The way it was set up is untraceable."

"This is the part where you make fun of the other analysts for missing something obvious," Allison said, "proving that you're better than them."

"That I exist on an entirely different plane of existence than them," Jordi corrected.

"Exactly."

"Not this time," Jordi said. "Look at this." He typed a few lines and the screen flashed lines of code at them, none of which made any sense to her.

"Oh, yeah," Allison said. "I see what you mean now."

"Smart ass." Jordi pointed to the screen. "It's set up to go through the dark web."

"You mean like the Silk Road, bitcoins and all that?"

Jordi looked impressed. "Yeah, you've got it. That's more in the news nowadays. What people don't realize is that the dark web is about five hundred times larger than the world wide web everyone is used to."

Allison's mind reeled at the idea. "How is that even possible?"

"Oh, it's possible," Jordi said. "The world has a way of wanting to keep its shit secret. Wasn't long after we figured out how to share everything that we figured out how to not share anything."

"So, our call girl had to be pretty high tech then, right?" Allison said. "Or she had help."

"Not really," Jordi said. "This goes through TOR, a free software program that a ten year old could use. It's free, simple and impossible to break."

"Even for you?"

"This thing takes what you're sending and breaks it into application layers of encryption." Jordi's hands sliced the air, mimicking data packets rushing through the air. "It bounces it around a randomized sequence of over five thousand relays all over the world, with each relay only able to decrypt one part of the data and that data is only the next step in the relay circuit. By the end of it, the final relay to the destination doesn't even know where the message came from. It's...it's...you know...fucking brilliant."

Allison shook her head. "So how do you unravel it?"

"That's just it," Jordi said. "There is no unraveling it. You want to know where your videos are? They were blown up into millions of encrypted pieces, scattered across the globe on random computers, then anonymously reunited and reformed. They were everywhere, then they ended up somewhere, but even the computer that received them has no idea where it came from."

"Maybe not," Allison said. "But the person who received them knows who sent them."

"Not necessarily," Jordi said. "She could have just set up a dummy server somewhere and sent the videos to herself."

"I don't think so," Allison said.

"How do you know?" Jordi asked.

"Because you know computers, but I know people. When you're scared and you have an insurance policy, you send it to someone you trust. A best friend. A family member," Allison said. "Trouble is, the original investigation already canvassed all of Catherine Fews's friends here in DC. Just acquaintances. Nothing strong enough to warrant that kind of trust."

"So it comes down to her alias," Jordi said.

"But the other team already searched all the databases we have access to. No match for either facial recognition or prints," Allison said, reaching out and digging through the bowl of Skittles on his desk, picking out all the red ones.

"Those other guys are pukes," Jordi snorted, staring down her hand as if he might swat at it.

"You found something?" she asked, tossing the candy in her mouth.

Jordi picked up his Skittles bowl and put it on the other side of his computer, out of her reach. "No. Nothing yet," he admitted. "But I wrote this killer little program that's crawling through all these restricted access databases to see what I can turn up. It's breaking about a dozen civil liberties regulations, but if those NSA assholes are allowed to do it, why shouldn't I?"

"Jordi," Allison scolded.

"It can't come back to us," he said. "That's why it's taking some time. I'm not running the query through the regular FBI servers." He went on to describe his methodology, something about mirrored systems and truncated alias paths that sounded like another language to Allison. Finally, she held up a hand.

"OK, I get it. You're super smart," she said.

"Damn right I am." Jordi grinned.

"But tell me this," she said. "If you find her in these hidden databases, and especially if you somehow find the videos, can you keep it under wraps? Make it so no one else knows? I'm talking even if Clarence Mason calls you into his office to give up the goods?"

Jordi grinned. "You know me, love. The only thing I like more than doing you a favor is giving the system the middle finger. This is just between me and you."

Allison leaned forward and gave Jordi a kiss on the cheek. "You're the best."

"Don't I know it," Jordi said. He swiveled in his chair as she left the room. "Where are you going?"

"I'm going to do that old-timey field investigation thing. You know, interview witnesses. Inspect the victim's body. Want to come?"

Jordi laughed and gestured to the room around him. "What? And leave all this? No thank you. I'll race you to see who can find Catherine Fews's real name first."

"If I win, you come to the gym with me for a month," Allison said.

Jordi clutched his chest in a mock heart attack, then added, "And if I find her first, you're buying my pizza for a month."

"You've got a deal," Allison said. "Good luck."

Jordi turned back to his computer screens, fingers dancing across his keyboard. "Yeah, baby. Only thing better than pizza is free pizza."

Allison smiled and left Jordi hard at work. Part of her wished she could just let him find the information she needed, but she knew she couldn't count on it. The other team members, the ones Jordi derided as "pukes", were actually top forensics professionals who had scoured FBI databases looking for a match. Maybe Jordi did have some magic mojo he was going to drum up to solve what the other team couldn't, but there was no way she was going to just sit around and wait to find out.

Even so, she dreaded where the path naturally led her to next.

CHAPTER 13

The mortuary drawer slid out with a grating sound of metal on metal. In the silence of the two-story, linoleum-floored room, it was loud enough that Allison half-expected someone to fling open the door and demand what the ruckus was all about. The man helping her, a young orderly named Maurice Hunt, smiled as if to apologize for the noise. He was a mouse of a man, wiry and slope-shouldered, his too-small nose made to look ridiculous by the oversized glasses poised on its end. Allison noticed his fingernails were grown out long but kept immaculately clean. He kept his eyes carefully averted from her, as if in fear of accidentally making eye contact.

"How long have you worked here, Maurice?" Allison asked.

"Six years," he said, pushing his glasses back into place. "No, eight, I guess. Time. You know how it goes."

Allison couldn't help but wonder if the man had turned odd after working in the morgue for eight years or if he'd come into the job that way.

Maurice unzipped the body bag and Allison could have sworn she saw him draw in a deep breath, creating an unnerving impression of a chef opening an oven.

"I'll take it from here," Allison said. Her FBI badge had gotten her this far, but she was acutely aware she was somewhere she wasn't supposed to be. She hadn't cleared the visit through regular channels, trying to keep a low profile. Having Maurice the morgue ghoul hanging around asking questions wasn't part of that plan. But it didn't look like getting rid of him was going to be an option.

Maurice frowned, insulted. "I'm supposed to stay," he said. "Even if you are with the FBI. Besides, I watch all the shows. *CSI. Bones. Forensic Team Challenge.* Maybe I can help?"

Allison figured Maurice actually might know more than she did. She wasn't a pathologist, or even particularly adept at forensics. Her Masters degree in human psychology had led her to a career track in the FBI's Behavioral Analysis Unit, the shop the public knew from countless TV shows and movies about profilers. She'd gone through the Academy like everyone else in BAU, a rigorous four-month training program that taught her the basics of fieldwork and weapons handling, but most of the last seven years had been spent at a desk with only rare excursions into the field. The fact that those few times had turned into face-to-face confrontations with the men she was tracking made her by far the exception within BAU. Still, while she knew her way around a dead body, pathology wasn't her strong suit. But what she was good at was noticing things that other people missed.

"Suit yourself. Gloves?" she said.

Maurice reached into his pocket and handed her a pair of latex gloves. He pulled on a pair of his own. "The head's not attached, you know," he said eagerly.

"Yes, I know," Allison said, unable to keep an edge from her voice. Maurice caught it and took a step back to give her room. She reached into the body bag and found that there were six separate bags inside. The torso, head and four limbs. Someone had arranged them in place.

"Did you do this?" she said.

Maurice nodded. "Seemed like the nice thing to do. In case...you know...her parents came down or something."

Allison pursed her lips, recalibrating her judgment of the strange orderly. Maybe if Allison did her job right, this girl's parents would eventually be contacted and able to mourn their daughter and collect her remains. "That was nice of you. Here, will you help me with this?"

Maurice jumped forward, all smiles. He reached out as Allison handed him the bags containing the limbs, one after another. He piled them up like firewood at the end of the flat iron bed of the morgue drawer.

"Should we transfer them to an examining room?" Maurice asked. "That's where the ME does the examinations."

"No, this is fine," Allison said. "I'm not doing a full exam. I just want a closer look." She wanted to make the visit as short as possible. She figured it was inevitable that the DCPD and the FBI team investigating the case would eventually become aware of her snooping and she wasn't overly anxious to have to use the lie Mason had given her about doing research. The idea didn't make her nervous because she was some kind of Girl Scout. It was more that she was just a terrible liar.

Allison opened the largest bag first. The stench of decaying flesh rose from the bag like heat off pavement. Allison turned her head and tried to catch her breath. A great sucking noise came from above them and she realized Maurice had crossed to a wall and turned on a high-powered vent for the fumes. He walked back, holding out a nose-plug for her. Allison waved it away. He shrugged and held out two pairs of toothed forceps, one for her and one for himself. She took a pair and smiled. It was nice to have an assistant, even one as strange as Maurice.

"OK, let's see what we have here," Allison murmured. She rotated the torso to look at one of the shoulders. The wound was grey, dead flesh now, but it still told a story. It was a surgical incision, not the frantic hacking of a killer expressing anger or hate. No, this was controlled and calculated. She used the forceps to lift a flap of skin to examine the shoulder joint. This area was rougher, with gouges throughout the glenohumeral joint where the humerus met the scapula. The killer had trouble removing the arm here, suggesting he (and it was almost always a he) wasn't a doctor or a butcher as she'd seen hypothesized in the report Mason had given her.

She inspected each of the four other cuts: the three other limbs and the neck. These showed the same indications as the first cut: a smooth first incision and then problems getting through the bone and joints efficiently.

Next, she reexamined each cut, mimicking the sawing motion needed to do each one, moving around the body to try the same cut from different angles.

"Are you trying to get into the mind of the killer by acting out the crime?" Maurice asked. "That's so wicked."

Allison smiled at the use of the term *wicked* which Maurice obviously felt was cool, but that she was pretty sure was out of date by about five years. "No, I'm trying to figure out for sure if our killer was left or right handed."

"How can you tell?" Maurice asked.

"Come look at this," she said, pointing to an incision in the upper thigh. "If you were going to cut off someone's leg, how would you do it?"

"With an electric saw," Maurice said, a little too quickly, Allison thought.

"I mean, which side would you stand on? Where would you cut first?"

Maurice thought about it, then positioned himself next to the torso. "I guess I'd stand here, reach across the leg I'm not cutting, and start from the outside."

"Good, so we look to see if that matches up with the evidence. Take out the left leg."

Maurice grabbed the bag. "You think he cut off the left one first?"

"No, the right one," she replied. "See how the left one is cut higher up on the thigh, up to the pelvis?"

"Because he didn't have a second leg in his way when he was cutting that one off," Maurice said excitedly.

Allison smiled. "Exactly. Pretty sharp, Maurice."

It was an odd image seeing Maurice beaming from ear to ear because of her compliment just as he held Catherine Fews's severed leg out to her.

Allison took the leg and inspected it. "There, look." She pointed to a series of thin parallel lacerations on the top of the leg. They were at an angle, higher toward the inner thigh and lower toward the outside of the leg.

"That's from the saw when he was cutting the other leg," Maurice said excitedly. "But wait. That could be from either a left or right handed person, depending where they stood."

"Correct," Allison said. "But imagine you're standing on the right side, cutting this leg and you're right handed. First, the direction of the cut is awkward, but doable. But if you did, then once you got down to the bone, you'd probably hit the top edge of the saw against the inside of the opposite leg." She rolled over the left leg. "No indication."

"The killer was left-handed," Maurice said softly, obviously impressed. "Is that a big deal?"

"Only 10% of the population is left-handed," Allison said. "I'd say taking 90% of potential suspects out of consideration is a pretty big deal."

Maurice raised his left hand. "I guess I'm a suspect," he said. "I'm a lefty. Can you believe it? You know left-handed people are more creative and smarter than average?"

"Well, let's hope the killer is neither of those things," she said, inspecting the ankles of both legs. Then the shoulders of the amputated arms.

"What are you looking for now?" Maurice asked.

"Anything that can tell me who this was," she replied.

Maurice pointed to the paperwork tucked into the plastic holder on the side of the bag. "Catherine Fews. Says right there."

Allison was about to explain that all they really had was the girl's work name. She needed to know where she came from, how she had ended up turning high-class tricks in DC with video cameras pointed at her bed. Who she'd been before her life in DC might be the key to answering those questions. But she stopped herself, reminding herself that she was supposed to be operating on the down low.

"I know," she said instead. "I'm looking for clues about how she lived. Maybe signs she took drugs. Old bruises. Something."

"The ME would catch all that," Maurice said. "There was someone down from the FBI for this one; our doc just assisted."

Allison nodded. It was probably an exercise in futility, but she'd already turned up one fact missed in the forensic report that proved important. But that was a clue about the killer, not the girl.

"Sometimes things get missed," she said.

Maurice squinted at her, looking back and forth between the cadaver tag and Allison. "That name. It's not her real one, is it? It's like her call girl name. You're looking for some way to ID her."

Allison didn't respond at first, but she had to admit the little weirdo was actually kind of clever. She decided it wouldn't hurt to let him know. "You got it," she said. "All we have is her alias." She went to the torso and inspected the lower back, the hips, the girl's chest and then finally her pelvic area. "So I'm looking for details that can help us deduce who she was."

"I deduce that she was someone who used tanning beds. In the nude," Maurice said, his voice unable to mask an awkward emphasis on the word *nude*. Allison shot him a disapproving look but he didn't see it. "She overdid it, though. Makes her tat show."

Allison looked where he was pointing. Right at the bikini line was a small, irregularly shaped area of skin several shades lighter than the skin around it.

"A tat? You mean a tattoo?" Allison asked.

"Yeah, we see it all the time here. Really bad tattoos that got removed. They've gotten to a point now where they can get rid of most of it, but you can still find them if you know where to look."

Allison pressed the light-colored skin but saw nothing underneath it. If there had been a tattoo there, it might have been the clue she needed. But it was long gone.

"You should see some of the ones we've found," Maurice said, starting to laugh in short snorts through his small nose. "Mostly names of old boyfriends or girlfriends. *Together forever*. Oops, right? But the best are the misspellings. *I'm Awesme*, with no *o* in awesome. *Regret Nohing*, spelled n-o-h-i-n-g. Bet he regretted that, right?" Maurice was enjoying himself, laughing out loud at his own comments. "Or my favorite was *Sweet Pee*. Get it? Like his pee. Freaking hilarious."

Allison watched Maurice giggle like a high school girl, his body shuddering so hard that his oversized glasses nearly fell off the end of his nose. Suddenly, he turned serious. He pointed to the patch of light skin on the torso in front of them. "Do you want to see what her tattoo was?"

Allison nodded, a thrill of excitement in her chest. "Can you do that?"

Maurice made a show of looking around the room even though they both knew they were the only ones there. "It's kind of against the rules," he whispered. "But I won't tell if you won't."

Allison smiled. "Of course. Just between you and me."

Maurice clapped the air and then spun around and headed toward the door. "Back in a jiff," he called.

Allison watched the door shut behind the young man and wondered, not for the first time, whether he had a few screws loose. When he returned with a scalpel in one fist, she wondered if maybe it was more than just a few screws.

"What do you plan on doing with that?" Allison asked.

"This is how we solve the mystery," Maurice said.

"Slow down, hard charger," Allison said, holding her hand up. "Why don't you explain to me what's going on here before you do anything stupid."

Maurice looked taken aback by Allison's serious tone. He lost his manic grin and seemed to refocus himself. "Do you have a tattoo?" Even with his new self-control, his eyes roved over her body as if he were imagining where such a tattoo might be hidden.

Allison shook her head. "No, do you?"

Without hesitation, he pulled up his shirt on one side, exposing the pasty white skin of his ribcage. There was a tattoo seven or eight inches tall of an astronaut on the back of a bucking horse, a lasso in one hand. Maurice looked at her, obviously expecting a reaction.

"Wow," she said, trying to stifle a sudden urge to laugh. "That's something."

Maurice looked disappointed. He sang, totally off-key, *"Some people call me the space cowboy, yeah. Some call me the gangster of love."* He looked incredulous. "The Steve Miller Band?" He went back to singing. *"Some people call me Maurice."* He pursed his lips and swung his hips. *"Weeee, oooooh."*

"Oh yeah," Allison said, just wishing he would stop. "I remember that song. Cool."

Maurice lowered his shirt, not buying it. He pointed to the patch of light skin on the torso. "The way it works, see, is you get the offending tattoo, usually when you're drunk, sometimes from someone who is drunk."

"Or just a bad speller apparently," Allison said.

"That too. Then years later, once you get respectable, you decide the tattoo was a terrible mistake that needs to be erased from the history books. Only, like most mistakes, this one is permanent."

"How about less philosophy and a little more getting to the point?"

Maurice scowled, obviously a little bummed that his captive audience didn't seem that captive at all.

Allison chided herself. The way to get through to this kid was to stroke his ego, not bash it. "Sorry, go ahead."

"The point is everyone knows you can get tattoos removed, but few people know how it's really done."

"You're right. I have no idea, but I'm guessing you do." Actually Allison had a pretty good idea, but Maurice smiled at the comment.

"A tattoo is inked down into the subcutaneous level of the skin, which is why it's permanent. Tattoo removal doesn't remove the tattoo, it just uses light therapy to fade out the top layers. If I wanted to get rid of my space cowboy tat, which I don't, it would take like thirty or forty treatments to make it look gone."

Allison felt a thrill of excitement. "But the tattoo would still be there, in the subcutaneous layer." She eyed the scalpel in his hand with new interest. "Are you saying that if you cut the top layers off, we'll still see it?"

Maurice nodded. He leaned in and whispered, "We do it all the time down here."

Revulsion dulled Allison's excitement as she pictured Maurice and his vulture friends cutting chunks of flesh out of cadavers to have a good laugh. She decided to worry about that later. Right now, she needed Maurice's ill-gotten expertise.

Maurice pressed the scalpel against the cadaver, then looked up at Allison. "Are you sure? Usually we just do this on John Does and the low-income people whose families would rather we just take care of the bodies. This is an active investigation, isn't it?"

Allison hesitated. She wondered how whoever was in charge of the actual investigation would react when he discovered an off-duty FBI agent had instructed an unlicensed morgue orderly to perform an unauthorized dissection. Even though she had Mason's blessing to do whatever it took to do her job, he also wanted it done quietly. She didn't think this was what he had in mind. Not only that, but the tattoo might be nothing more than a seahorse blowing bubbles for all she knew. There was only a small chance it would give her any clue at all about the girl's true identity.

"Go ahead," she said, the words seeming to come out all on their own. "On my authority."

Maurice gave her a crooked smile, as if to say he knew she didn't have the authority...and that he really didn't care. The scalpel was pressed against soft flesh and there was no going back for him. She felt a chill as she considered the knife's edge the young man walked, his traits matching so many of those she found in the killers she hunted. She wondered if Maurice Hunt might one day be a name in a dossier on her desk in the Criminal Investigations Unit.

As she watched him sink the scalpel into the flesh with a feverish excitement, she considered that the idea wasn't too far-fetched. But for right now, she just hoped the weird little man wasn't full of shit and that she hadn't just let him cut into this poor woman's body for no good reason.

CHAPTER 14

Maurice glanced up at the FBI agent leaning over the body as he cut into it, savoring the way her breasts hung forward, her blouse coming open just a little so he could see the top of her white bra against her tan skin. A shudder passed through him. It wasn't that he didn't see beautiful women very often, Washington DC was full of them, but it wasn't that often that one spent an entire hour alone in the same room with him. She wasn't quite a ten in his book, more like a solid nine. He liked girls with a bigger chest. The bigger the better as far as he was concerned. Like the girls down at the Rhino who invested their dancing money in massive tits that looked like skin balloons tied off with a nipple. Now that was awesome.

Still, he had to admit that the agent had it going on. Killer body, amazing supermodel face and wicked smart. Usually that turned him off. Smarts usually came with all that bitchy pretension. Like those lawyers and political women who wouldn't even talk to him at the bars, even when he sent them a ten-dollar drink from the end of the bar like they did in the movies. One look at him and they immediately decided they were too good for him. Not that it ever stopped them from slurping down the drink he sent them. But this was different. She had been nice to him the whole time. He hoped the tattoo delivered what she wanted. If it did, he thought she might be willing to show him some gratitude and go out on a date with him. And if that happened, he saw no reason they wouldn't end up in bed together. Maurice silently rooted for the tattoo to be something important.

He worked his way all around the edge of the area of light-colored skin, leaving an extra two inches around it. Then he peeled back one side and sliced the slab of flesh from the torso.

"Is it that deep?" the FBI agent asked. Maurice was terrible at names and had already forgotten hers. *Something Irish,* he thought. She didn't even need a name as far as he was concerned. She was just the hot FBI agent.

"You'll see," he said.

He turned the chunk of meat sideways, using Catherine Fews's rib cage as a cutting board. It looked like a New York Strip steak, one of those thick ones from an expensive restaurant; only the meat was grey and spoiled.

"Are you ready for the big reveal?" Maurice asked. He was getting off slow-playing the whole thing, adding to the drama. He felt like a bad ass.

The agent, Allison McNeil, that was her name, damn if he didn't just remember it, nodded for him to continue.

He sliced the hunk of meat about three quarters of an inch below the skin, making a clean cross-section incision. After he got through the first two inches of extra border, he saw black ink in the flesh.

"Houston, we have a winner," Maurice said.

He sliced through the rest, exposing more black ink.

"What is it?" Allison asked.

Maurice purposefully covered the image with his hand as he cut, just because he could. He liked the feeling of this beautiful woman needing something from him.

He finished his cut and turned the result toward him and away from Allison. The image was a little blurry but clear enough to read. He threw it back on the cadaver's rib cage so that it landed facing the FBI agent.

"You might want to play the lottery today," Maurice said, "because it's your lucky day."

He watched as her face lit up. She pulled out her cell phone and snapped pictures of the tattoo.

A graduation cap, the name Harlow High and the year two thousand and six.

He was no fancy FBI agent but it seemed like a trained monkey would be able to track the girl down with that information. He was bound to get at least dinner out of the deal. And probably a blowie.

But when he looked up, Allison was packing up her things, her demeanor clearly showing she'd gotten what she wanted and now she was getting the hell out of there. He had to take his shot.

"So, I was thinking," he said. "Maybe we could get a drink sometime? Talk about the case, you know. That kind of stuff."

Allison smiled the same smile Maurice had seen from countless attractive women in his life. It was the *Go eat shit* smile that he returned through gritted teeth.

"I'm sure you're a great guy," Allison said. "But this isn't a really good time for me."

She looked like she was being nice about it, but Maurice knew she was laughing at him on the inside. He looked away, hoping she didn't see the anger flash across his face. "Sure," he said. "I get it."

He flinched as she put her hand on his forearm.

"Thanks," she said. "You really helped me out today. I appreciate it."

The words felt great. A sudden warmth spread up from his chest to his face. He realized he was probably blushing bright red. "It was nothing," he said, ready to take another shot at asking her out.

Her hand gripped his arm tighter. Her eyes narrowed and there was a flash of anger that he hadn't seen there before. "But you and your buddies can't do this anymore. You got that? It's not a game. These people deserve better than to be cut up and laughed at. You seem like a good guy. I think you know they deserve better."

Maurice hung his head, feeling the same way he did when his mom caught him whacking off in the bathroom as a grown man. Embarrassed for being caught. But more angry at the way she stood there judging him, all pissed off and self-righteous.

"You hear me, Maurice?"

He nodded, refusing to make eye contact. She let go of his arm and stepped back. "Thanks again. I couldn't have done this without you."

And, just like that, she turned and headed toward the door. No goodbye. No phone numbers exchanged. Not even the courtesy of lying about grabbing a drink with him in the future. Nothing at all.

He stole a sideways glance and watched her ass for as long as he could, until the door closed behind her.

Maurice pulled out his phone, his fingers dancing over the screen even before he was looking at it.

FBI just left. Allison McNeil. Found tat on CF. Said Harlow 2006 w grad caps. U owe me 200$.

At least her being a bitch at the end made selling her out that much easier. He'd let the guy know when Allison had first gotten there, so if she'd gone out with him, he probably would have had to eventually come clean with her. It was better this way. Less complicated. And with his two hundred bucks he could have a pretty good night at the Rhino. At least down there, the girls were always nice to him.

He picked up the slabs of flesh, layered them back on top of one another and put them back in Catherine Fews's torso. He liked the way they fit like the last pieces of a jigsaw puzzle. He didn't think he would take the FBI agent's advice about stopping his little hobby. It was just too much damn fun.

CHAPTER 15

Allison felt like she needed a shower after her experience with oddball Maurice. The trip had paid off, but she felt dirty from being in the same room with the guy. She had no doubt that the orderly and his buddies would keep up their practice of carving into the unclaimed bodies, having chuckles over their bad tattoos. She felt the violation even more than if they were cutting into the dead flesh for fun or just out of boredom. A tattoo someone paid to have erased was too personal, a mistake someone went to lengths to hide from the world. For private reasons, it was something they didn't want exposed for everyone to see. But, like most mistakes, they lingered, literally just under the surface, never really gone.

The psychiatrist the Bureau had made her see after the Arnie Milhouse case would have told her she was internalizing this tattoo thing. Making it about herself. About her past mistakes that she hoped to keep hidden from the world. The outrage she felt toward Maurice's macabre practice wasn't just for the dignity of strangers in a morgue who deserved better, but the idea that her own mistakes could be dredged up just as easily. A few layers stripped away and there she would be, exposed to the world, fodder for others to laugh at and shake their heads in condemnation.

She didn't want to raise awareness of her visit just yet, but she decided that once the case was over she'd make a return visit to Maurice and make sure the practice stopped once and for all.

Allison exited the building, the sun already high overhead. Even so, there was a chill in the air and a breeze that rustled the leaves on the trees. She pulled her jacket tight around her and pulled out the burner phone Mason had given her. She hesitated and pulled out her other phone and sent the image of the tattoo over to Jordi. She added the text: *If you find her with this, we can call it a tie. Free pizza AND the gym.*

She powered up the burner phone and searched the contact list. True to his word, there was one number stored there, the word HOME listed as the name. Allison smirked at Mason's choice of name, ostensibly as in "home base" but it also carried connotations of safety and protection. Clarence Mason was not a man who made idle choices and she figured this small word had been a conscious decision.

She dialed the phone. There was a series of clicks as if the call was rerouted several times. Finally, it rang once and then was picked up immediately.

"Any progress to report?" Mason said. The soft paternal tone from their meeting was gone, replaced by a clipped speech that told her to keep things short.

"I rechecked the body. I believe the killer was left-handed," she said.

The sounds of paper on the other end. "That's not in the original report. Are you sure?"

"Ninety percent," Allison replied. It was a joke in the BAU: ninety percent was as good as it ever got. There was always an out-of-the-box possibility that could prove any conclusion false.

What if the killer had faked being left-handed to throw investigators off the trail? What if he simply had a blister on his right hand and used the left hand for convenience? There were a thousand variations of this idea. Still, in chasing bad guys, the principle of Occam's razor was fully in force. In the face of competing hypotheses, the simplest solution is the most likely to be correct. In this case, that the killer was left-handed carried the fewest assumptions, so she was going with it.

"Anything else?" Mason asked.

"I have a lead on Fews's real identity," she said. "She had a tattoo from her high school that the coroner missed." She was about to tell Mason what the tattoo said, but something held her back. She decided to keep the information to herself.

"Sounds like we need to fire the pathologist who did this work-up," Mason grumbled.

"I'd take it easy on him," Allison said. "It was easy to miss. I'll explain later. I'm going to track down the lead to this girl's hometown. See what I can find."

Allison felt the prickle of her hair standing up on her neck, that unsettling feeling that someone was watching her. She spun around. A man in a black overcoat stood right behind her, only five or six feet away. While that would be giving her a wide berth on a busy sidewalk, on the deserted steps of the city morgue, it was practically in her face.

She whispered into the phone while she kept her eyes on the man. "I've got to go." She slid the phone back into her pocket. "Can I help you?"

The man held up his hands, an acknowledgement that he had taken her by surprise. "Sorry, I was just waiting until you were off the phone."

Allison relaxed a bit. The man's voice was deep and smooth, using perfect inflection to add reassurance to the words. She knew better than to trust it, though. Some of the most successful killers in history were known to be smooth talkers.

The man was handsome, which didn't hurt. Short, well-groomed black hair with neatly trimmed sideburns framed a rugged face with fine lines that made the man look like he'd not only seen the world, but had actually lived in it. He was clean-shaven, tan and flashed her a wide smile. She felt a nagging sense that she ought to know his name. An FBI colleague? Some long ago blind date?

"I'm afraid I overheard a little of your conversation," the man admitted. "But please know that I didn't mean to and I won't use it unless you give me permission."

Use it? she thought. *Permission?*

Then she placed the face and her stomach turned over. Mike Carrel. Reporter for the Washington Herald. Covered the FBI, especially the serial killer stories. He had a knack for getting information that wasn't ready for public consumption. Based on the number of stories featuring Garret Morrison in the Herald, there were rumors that Carrel's access was a quid pro quo for making Garret look good. Even more rumors were that an internal investigation had looked into the matter but that no disciplinary action had been taken. However, the flow of information slowed considerably for a while. But the fact that he was on the steps talking to her showed the information certainly hadn't dried up completely.

He held out his hand. "Mike Carrel. With the Herald. You're Special Agent Allison McNeil, right?"

Allison ignored his outstretched hand. "That was a private call. Anything you heard––"

"I told you, I won't use anything I heard," Mike said, pulling his hand back. "Although, technically, I could."

Allison turned and walked away. She knew there was zero upside to talking with a reporter, especially someone like Mike Carrel. She just needed to get some space between them before she said something stupid.

"However," Mike called out, "if I get the same information from other sources, I'll have to use it. I'm sure you understand."

Allison kept walking.

"So, where is Harlow, anyway?" Mike called out. "Is that Virginia or West Virginia?"

Allison stopped in her tracks, her blood suddenly throbbing at her temples. It was the feeling she got right before she threw something or cussed someone out. She turned and looked back at Mike Carrel, the smug son of a bitch grinning like a fool down at her. He must have guessed from her expression that she wanted an explanation of how the hell he knew.

He sang his answer, doing the song considerably more justice than Maurice had done. *"I'm a joker, I'm a smoker, I'm a midnight toker, I sure don't want to hurt no one. Whooo-whoooo."*

Allison fought the urge to march back into the morgue, find Maurice and pummel the little weasel for selling her out. Instead, she walked slowly back to Mike.

"What do you want?" she asked.

"Just a cup of coffee and a chat," he said.

"Off the record?"

"Deep background. No attribution," he offered.

She shook her head. "Completely off the record. You print a word and SWAT guys come and break your legs."

"And in return?" he asked.

"If we talk, then you don't print anything you learned from the goddamn space cowboy," she said.

He looked away, making a show of thinking it over. A move she knew to be complete bullshit, but telling in its own way. Hopefully he would continue to make the mistake of misjudging her.

"Tell you what," Mike said, smiling. "Why don't you try to convince me that I shouldn't run it and we'll see where it leads?"

She matched his smile. "I always thought you looked like an asshole in the photo next to your byline. I guess the photographer really captured your essence."

Mike's smile evaporated as Allison turned on her heel and marched away.

"Come on, then," she called over her shoulder. "Let's get this over with."

CHAPTER 16

Libby sat across from Summerhays in the limo even though the seat next to his boss was unoccupied. He told himself it was a more comfortable position to have a conversation, but part of him just didn't want to be any nearer to the man than he needed to be. It was a childish reaction, but Libby didn't care. Summerhays had looked him right in the eye and lied to him about contacting Scott Harris. It was an inconsequential lie, something Summerhays could have easily admitted to. That's what made the lie all the worse. Something was off. Libby was pretty sure that Harris had lied to him too.

"Right, Libby?" Summerhays asked.

Libby snapped back from his thoughts and tried to pick up the trail of the conversation. The man had been prattling on about the fundraiser he had that night with the Teacher's Union, how he wished he could tell the teachers to kiss off and stop their complaining. Libby had heard the whining before so figured he hadn't missed much.

"If you say so, sir," Libby said, not bothering to feign interest.

"What's eating you?" Summerhays asked. "You're as much fun as a hunting dog at a picnic."

Libby winced. He hated it when Summerhays tried to sound folksy. He was always mixing his metaphors and coming up with sayings that made little or no sense. He thought it connected him to the regular people. Libby thought it just made him look like a jackass.

Summerhays leaned forward. "It's not that thing we were talking about, is it?" he asked. "I thought you said you had that all under control."

"I didn't say it was under control," Libby said. "I told you that I would handle it."

Summerhays leaned back and looked out the window dramatically. It was the same look he liked to use in photo shoots. During the campaign they called it the *thoughtful statesman*. Libby knew it was a sham, just a pose. But it was better than the senator's usual pose in private, *fucking idiot*.

"Maybe we should call in some more help with this," Summerhays said. His voice was loaded with gravitas as if he were discussing a solution to the Israeli-Palestinian conflict instead of a cover-up of his screwing a hooker on video.

"What were you thinking?" Libby asked, a pit forming in his stomach as he guessed where the conversation was going.

"Maybe you should call Scott Harris," Summerhays said. "He's good at this sort of thing."

Libby searched Summerhays's face for any sign of guilt or shame for lying to him a second time. There was none. Libby chided himself for thinking that there would be. With sudden clarity, he realized it wasn't the second time the man had lied to him. It was probably the hundredth. The thousandth for all he knew. *Politician lies* wasn't exactly a news headline, but it left Libby cold.

He was supposed to be on the *inside.* That was the only reason to put up with it all. Being lied to so easily, so boldly, made him feel like a sucker. As if all the compromises he'd made to hitch a ride on the Summerhays train had been pointless. He wasn't in on the game. He was a pawn, just like everyone else.

"Did you hear me, Libby?" Summerhays said.

"Yeah, I heard you," Libby murmured.

Summerhays arched an eyebrow his direction. "You all right? You're acting...off."

Truth was, he was buying some time to work through the position he was in. It occurred to him that Harris might have already told Summerhays they'd met. Maybe this entire thing, this seemingly casual suggestion to call Harris, was a bizarre loyalty test, checking to see if Libby was still playing for the right team. He considered just admitting he'd met with Harris already, but that came with its own levels of complications. There was a good chance Summerhays was actually testing Harris, trying to see if the man had told Libby they'd spoken. As much as he disliked Harris, Libby didn't want him discredited. At least not while he was still useful. Either way, he felt jammed up. Say he hadn't spoken to Harris and Summerhays might catch him in a lie. Admit that he had and make Harris look bad. He was trapped.

Libby glanced up and Summerhays was studying him through squinted eyes. Maybe he had misjudged just how ruthless the man could be. Even though Summerhays could be an idiot, idiots didn't make it this close to running the free world by luck. He was reminded that underestimating the man could be dangerous. For the first time since confronting the senator, he thought Summerhays might actually have had Catherine Fews killed.

"I'm fine," Libby said. "Under the weather. Puked my guts out last night. Just trying to work through it. That's why I'm sitting over here away from you." It felt good to lie to him. A small victory.

Summerhays scowled, obviously not satisfied. "And Harris?"

Libby drew in a deep breath and leaned forward in his seat, lowering his voice. "Look, this thing is bound to get messier before it gets cleaned up. Even if I did call Harris, hell, even if I'd already met with him and discussed our little issue, you wouldn't want to know that information. If this thing goes south, it's not just a scandal, it's depositions, lie detector tests, prison time. You don't want to know anything I do."

Summerhays leaned back, the hard look in his eyes from just seconds before fading back into his usual vacant look. Libby realized that he didn't really know Summerhays at all. The face he'd been around for the last decade was a mask, the stern man beneath was the real guy. A shudder passed through Libby.

"But you're forgetting the most important thing, Libby," Summerhays said.

"What's that?"

"I had nothing to do with that woman's death," he said. "You know that, right?"

"Of course," Libby said. He realized for the first time that he didn't really mean it. "I know you're not capable of something like that. You're innocent in all of this."

"Good," he said, looking out the window as they entered the White House grounds for a meeting with the man Summerhays meant to replace. "Don't you forget it."

CHAPTER 17

Allison waited for her coffee-date to park his car and catch up with her. She had chosen to make him follow her across town to Tryst in Adams Morgan. As someone who studied human interaction and psychology, the manipulation was almost second nature. Mike Carrel thought he had her backed into a corner. Her choice of venue was a small thing but it put her back in charge. If they were going to battle it out for information then, like an infantry commander, she would at least choose the ground where the engagement was going to happen. Tryst was one of her favorite places. It was her turf and she guessed that the eclectic look and feel of the place was not the reporter's usual environment. She pegged him as more of a two-times-a-day Starbucks guy.

But the location was only one advantage. The other was that the ride over gave her a chance to Google the hell out of the reporter and dig up a few details that might prove helpful.

"Did you find anything good?" Mike said as he walked up.

"What do you mean?" Allison said.

"Either you were looking me up on your phone the entire way over here, or you're just about the worst driver I've ever seen."

"Which of those things gets you the most girls? The big ego or the insults?" Allison asked.

"They both work pretty well, actually," Mike said. "On the kind of girls I tend to date, anyway."

Allison smiled. Certainly he had to know a sexist comment to someone in a male-dominated world like the FBI would strike a chord. It had been purposeful and deftly played. Rather than being annoyed by it, she found herself admiring the work. She was self-aware enough to know that his looks were playing into her reaction to him. Studies showed that good-looking people were generally more trusted and, while Mike Carrel's smug expression might have made her want to knock him out, she couldn't deny that he belonged on a magazine cover. Not only that, but what she'd learned about him on the way over also cast him in a good light and dramatically changed her perception of him.

"Let's grab a seat," Allison suggested.

Mike held his hand out. "After you."

"An asshole and a gentleman," Allison murmured as she walked by him into Tryst.

The popular coffee shop was always busy. The fact that it had a full bar and some of the best mixologists in DC working behind it had something to do with keeping the place hopping into the night. During the day, the attraction was ostensibly the coffee and fresh baked goods, but the real draw was the chance to hang in a space that was so purposefully *not* a Starbucks that being a patron felt like a stand against homogeneity and the corporatizing of America. There was a hodgepodge of irregularly shaped couches, unique chairs and tables of all sizes. The walls were a deep red and pocked with built-in shelves filled with books set loose in the wild by staff and patrons to find a home in someone's hands for an afternoon. The clientele was as oddball as the furniture, everything from K Street lobbyists to young techies writing code to artistic-types writing longhand in pretentious journals. The hiss of the espresso machine spouting steam into stainless steel mugs of milk mixed with a soundtrack of alternative music piped in through speakers in the ceiling. Allison felt like she was walking into her own living room.

"Want something?" Allison asked.

Mike pulled a phone out of his pocket and read the screen. "I'll have whatever you're having," he said, distracted.

"Two Cuban coffees," she said to the young man behind the counter. She stole glances at Mike as she completed her transaction. "Everything OK?"

Mike slid the phone back into his pocket. "We all have bosses, right?" he said. "Mine just happens to be a fifty-year-old man who discovered texting about six months ago. Now he just can't stop himself. Emoticons and everything."

Allison smiled. She had the same experience except it was her dad, not her boss. And with him it was FaceTime on his new iPhone about a year earlier. He thought it was the coolest thing and had called her a few times each day from different locations in their hometown or on his day trips to trout streams around Maryland and Pennsylvania. Until his mind started its downhill slide, that was.

Now the FaceTime calls came from inside the house or from the backyard on a warm day. She nearly shared that information with Mike but checked herself. This wasn't a social meeting. The man had inserted himself into her investigation and she needed equal parts charm and coercion to keep him from ruining it by releasing the information she'd just uncovered at the morgue.

A tattoo carved out of a dead prostitute's body by an off-duty FBI agent was the kind of juicy news that the American public loves to obsess over. Her name would be trending on Twitter within an hour and the entire press corps would be trying to scoop each other by trying to decipher Catherine

Fews's real name. Not exactly the under-the-radar investigation Mason had asked her to do. She knew if it leaked out that her time left on the case would be measured in minutes instead of hours.

"Not your typical law enforcement hangout," Mike observed as a tattooed woman with bright red hair and a nose ring passed them.

"There's caffeine and alcohol," Allison said. "What's not to like?"

Mike shrugged. "Cops like conformity. Can you imagine Garret Morrison in here?"

Allison tried not to betray her shock that he'd play his hand so openly. She assumed his relationship with Garret would be something he'd hold close. She took the two Cuban coffees from the barista behind the counter and handed one to Mike. "I forgot you and Garret are buds."

"And you and Garret are not," Mike said, following her to a small table in the least busy corner in the large open room.

Allison took a seat, searching for the best way to respond. As usual, the most direct route won out. "But that's not why I shot him."

Mike laughed, nodding. They both knew that her role in shooting Garret was not part of the public report but the story had made the rounds. It was an acknowledgement that she knew Mike had sources deep in the Bureau and that it didn't faze her.

"No, but given Garret's reputation, I'm sure you found some kind of enjoyment in it," Mike said.

Allison shrugged and decided to get down to business. "How much did you pay Maurice to tip you off at the morgue?"

"Couple hundred and some killer Caps tickets right on the glass," Mike said. "Turns out, the weird little guy is a hockey fan."

"Anyone else stop by the morgue except me?"

Mike looked at her blankly, sipping his coffee, as if the question had just passed through him. After a few beats, he put the coffee back on the table and leaned forward. "What are we doing here? I have all the information I need. I have the high school name and year. That's enough for me to go dig up this girl's history and have an exclusive story that will sell a shit-ton of papers and get my boss off my back."

"You do that and it corrupts my investigation. Makes it harder for me to find the killer," Allison said.

"Not my problem," Mike said. "And from what I understand from a few calls I made on the way over here, it's not yours either. Not officially anyway." He held up his hands. "Don't worry, I was discreet. Only asked who was working the case. Your name didn't come up so I left it alone. Having information other people don't is a good thing in my profession."

Allison felt some relief but was also conscious of the man digging his claws deeper into her. Or at least he thought he was.

"I'm taking some time off," Allison said, sticking as close to the truth as possible. "Not uncommon after an agent is involved in...in something like what happened with Kraw."

"See, now that's something I'm interested in," Mike said. "What exactly happened there? How did you all find him to begin with?"

Allison got it. This was the real reason he was there. The play-by-play of the grisly deaths down in Louisiana was what he was really after. Catherine Fews was just a bargaining piece.

"I've read your work," Allison said. "It's obvious you know people in the Bureau who like to run their mouths when they shouldn't."

Mike shook his head. "Not on this one. I've pieced together a few things. Made a couple of good guesses based on the official report that make me think there's more to the story than is getting out."

"You mean Garret Morrison didn't want to tell you a story where he wasn't the hero," Allison said.

"I never said Garret was my source."

"The only people who think that's still a secret are you and Garret," Allison said. "He's just using you."

"I've had a front seat at every major serial killer investigation over the last fifteen years. You tell me who's using who. *If* Garret was my source, that is."

Not every serial killer case, Allison thought. The press after the Arnie Milhouse case had been kept to a minimum, likely again due to Garret's influence. Or, more accurately, the lack of him leaking the kind of details that made the press go crazy.

Even Charlie Rangle, the young man Allison had inadvertently gotten involved in the whole mess, had resisted every offer to tell his story to the press. When Allison asked him about it he admitted it was tempting, especially since girls went nuts over a guy on TV. But he just didn't want to talk about it. Being tortured by a madman and knowing with absolute certainty that the only escape was death had a way of changing a person. For Charlie, it put a darkness into his otherwise carefree, go-with-the-flow lifestyle. Refusing to talk about it was his way of keeping it at bay. In fact, he'd moved to California after his injuries healed just to get away from people asking him about it. Allison still checked in on him once a month or so by phone to see how he was doing, knowing from her own experience with the darkness that it could only be ignored for so long. Eventually, it fought its way out. And when it did for Charlie, she wanted to be there for him.

"Are we here to make a deal?" Mike asked. "Or did you just want an overpriced coffee?"

Allison sipped her drink, savoring the sweetness of the raw sugar that had been added to the espresso as the barista made the pull. She would have paid double the price for it. But Mike was showing the first signs of impatience. That was good. "I'm not here to make a deal with you. I'm here to explain to you why you're not going to print the information you got today."

"Let me help you out here," Mike said. "Here are three points to consider. First, I have the information about the girl's tattoo. If you don't give me a better story to write, then I'll go track down this new one."

Allison's phone vibrated in her pocket. She ignored it at first, but then she realized it was the burner Mason had given her. She pulled it out.

"Second," Mike continued, a little slower, unsure that he had her attention.

"I'm listening," Allison said.

"Second, I know you're investigating a murder case on the down-low, apparently without the knowledge of the guys who are really investigating it."

Allison read the text a second and third time, as if rereading it would somehow reorganize the letters into a different message.

"If you were an investigative journalist, you would probably find that very interesting, right?" Mike said. "Are you even listening?"

Allison stood. "I've got to go," she said.

"What?" He looked down at her phone. "What happened?"

"Maurice from the morgue..." she started.

"Our weird little friend? What about him?" Mike asked.

"He's dead."

CHAPTER 18

Harris checked his teeth in the rearview mirror, picking at the bits of salad stuck there. He hated salad but he forced himself to make that one of his meals each day. After hitting fifty, the pounds were easy to accumulate if he wasn't careful. It wasn't like the old days when he could down a plate full of bacon and eggs and waffles for breakfast, destroy a couple of burritos for lunch, then steak, fries and beers for dinner. He still ate too much fast food, but the one salad a day made him feel that he was at least putting out an effort. Still, later that night, he planned on having a porterhouse steak at the nicest place he could find. It was a cheat since the cut of meat was really two steaks in one: a New York strip on one side of the bone and a filet mignon on the other. He wasn't technically breaking his self-imposed rule. One steak per kill. Even with this rule, his cholesterol was still too high.

Harris wasn't completely sure if he should count Maurice as a kill. He had been more of a creature than a man, sniveling and weak, unworthy to be stacked up next to the other people in Harris's list of victims. He relived the exchange, trying to find some buried pleasure in it because the entire event had been less than satisfying.

One thing the little dipshit had done well enough was text him as soon as the FBI agent arrived. The arrival of the reporter to the scene at about the same time he got there showed the weasel was at least entrepreneurial. He had to hand it to the guy. But even though there was never any mention of exclusivity in the original transaction, it still pissed him off.

After the FBI agent and the reporter left, entry into the hospital was simple enough. Security was lax and the few cameras on the property wouldn't matter with his coat collar pulled up and a hat and glasses in place to obscure his face. Maurice had been surprised to see him, more than a little nervous actually. FBI agents, reporters, strangers offering money for information about who takes an interest in a dead girl. While it sounded in theory like a fanboy's wet dream, it was a lot of pressure for a weasel like Maurice to bear. The kid had already been on edge when Harris arrived, but he really got nervous once Harris cornered him alone in the morgue. The one with the cameras that didn't work so Maurice and his buddies could play their games with the bodies.

Maurice had not been very forthcoming with the information Harris wanted. Damn intuition kicking in, giving the kid some misguided idea that he ought to hold back to protect the pretty FBI agent. But Harris was very convincing and Maurice finally shared everything with him.

Less than twenty minutes after walking into the hospital, Harris walked back out through a service door, crossed the street to his car, climbed in and drove away, certain Maurice would never be able to identify him. On the way, he tossed the phone Maurice had used to text him into a dumpster. They wouldn't be able to use it to track back to him anyway, but he liked to be thorough.

While he didn't have the heady rush from the kill he usually had, there was a certain amount of pride in how he'd done it, especially since it hadn't been preplanned. Then again, inspiration was like that. It could strike at any time and, as an artist, he just had to keep an open mind so that when it did show itself, he was ready.

As he pictured the scene the police would find in the morgue, he allowed himself a smile. One thing was for sure, he damn-well deserved a steak dinner.

CHAPTER 19

Allison came to a stop in front of the young uniformed cop blocking her way.

"You don't want to go in there, ma'am," he said, holding out his hand to block her way.

Allison held up her FBI credentials, expecting him to wave her through. He didn't.

"I understand, ma'am," the cop said. "I know you *can* go in there, I just don't know that you want to."

Allison felt a surge of anger at the cop's condescension, her sexism radar pinging at full speed. But then she noticed his ashen face and the slight tremble in the hand he held out in front of her. She understood. Whatever was inside was something the young cop wished he hadn't seen. The anger drained away and she felt sorry for him.

"Thank you," she said, meaning it. "I'll be all right. Thanks for looking out though."

He hesitated a second, but then lowered his hand.

"It ain't pretty," he whispered.

Allison walked past him. "It never is."

The morgue had a few more uniformed cops, a crime scene investigator taking photos and two homicide detectives in suits talking to a professional-looking man with a hospital nametag. She was surprised how quickly people had been mobilized to the scene. Must have been a slow day.

They blocked her from the crime scene, possibly by accident, or just out of decency to shield the only door into the room from a direct sightline at the body they were all there to discuss.

But as she approached, her credentials in hand, they parted to let her pass. As she took in the scene, she realized the young cop had been right. She really didn't want to see this.

Maurice was on the floor, legs and arms splayed out in all directions. His head was covered by a plastic bag, cinched at the base by a drawstring. The plastic was transparent and showed his bulging, open eyes staring up like they were asking her a question. His tongue lolled out of his mouth through his yellowed teeth.

More disturbing was that his pants were down around his ankles so that his white, pimpled legs and butt were exposed. Allison took a couple of steps around the body, but she already had a good idea what she was going to find there.

Maurice's penis was shriveled, drooping on the cool linoleum floor, coated with a glistening layer of lube. A quick look at his right hand showed that it was covered with lube too. It was the kind of crime scene that might be used in the first day of a forensics class. An open and shut scene wrapped up in a bow.

Autoerotic asphyxiation, choking to the point of passing out during orgasm, was fairly common, especially among young, socially alienated males who primarily relied on masturbation for a sexual outlet. From what little she knew about Maurice, she felt pretty sure he wasn't going home to some nice girl after he was done carving up cadavers for fun with his morgue buddies.

No, he fit the profile. And the practice, especially when doing it solo, sometimes led to death when the person misjudged the amount of time they could choke before passing out.

What made the scene even worse was that Maurice had pulled a female cadaver from a drawer to help him out. Not Catherine Fews, but another one. Something a little fresher.

Allison stifled a gasp. Not because of the sight of lube on the dead woman's naked breasts. Not because she wondered what else Maurice had done to the rest of the body. But because across the length of the woman's chest, carved into her flesh in capital letters with a scalpel, was a single word. A word that told the world what was going through Maurice's mind as he masturbated his last time.

ALLISON.

CHAPTER 20

"You were the last to see the deceased?" the detective asked. His name was Neil Briggs. He was African American, his head shaved, wearing a thick goatee as if to prove he could grow hair. The tone of his voice told her as far as he was concerned, the investigation was already over. The questions he had were just to complete the paperwork.

"I don't know if I was the last one," Allison said. "I was with him in this room about an hour ago. I don't know what he did after that."

"I can tell you what happened after that," the second detective snickered. "This loser and Jane Doe here got it on."

The detective carried a beer belly under his cheap suit, an off-the-rack number with food stains on the lapels. He hadn't bothered to introduce himself to Allison, but she caught the name Grady on his badge. He grinned as if this crime scene was a present just for him, a hilarious story for him to tell over the next couple of months in bars across DC. If there was one thing cops loved, it was a good story that could one-up their friends.

"I mean, I don't know if he spoke to anyone after I left," Allison said, addressing Briggs who seemed professional and in control, especially compared to his partner. As soon as she said the words, she realized Maurice had spoken to someone after she left. Mike Carrel. She was about to correct herself but stopped short. She didn't want Mike dragged into this. Nor did she want her own activities with Maurice scrutinized. If it were material to the case, she'd have no choice but to share it. But she'd seen Mike immediately after she left so it wasn't like he was a suspect. She convinced herself to hold her cards close and engage in the little white lie. As she did, she could hear her father's admonition in her head: *You know what another name for a white lie is? A lie.*

"And what was the nature of your visit?" Briggs asked.

"An active FBI investigation," Allison said. "I'm sorry, I can't give you any details."

Briggs nodded as if expecting the answer. Grady was less forgiving.

"The Bureau's always into our shit," he complained. "And then they act like God's gift to law enforcement."

Allison met Grady's eyes. "You have to admit, we are pretty good."

"And you don't think we are?" Grady challenged.

Allison knew she should bite her tongue. Grady was a college fraternity guy stuck in a middle-aged man's body and allowed to carry a gun. There was no good to be had locking horns with him. In fact, it was better if these two shut this case down as a simple accidental death and moved on.

"That's not what I meant," Allison said. "Sorry."

Grady made an oversized gesture, grasping his hands together in fake appreciation. "Thank you. Thank you," he said.

"Cut it," Briggs said to his partner.

Grady looked chastised. It was clear where the power lay in their relationship. He turned back to Maurice's dead body and murmured, "We know Maurice here thought *you* were fine."

"Grady, I said enough," Briggs growled. He nodded to Allison. "Sorry."

"It's all right," she said. "I've dealt with his type before."

"My type?" Grady said, whirling around. "What's that supposed to mean?"

"Middle-aged man, joined the force to knock heads and get bad guys. Disillusioned with the job after you realized it was mostly breaking up domestic disputes and filling out paperwork. Thought about joining SWAT but that old football injury to your right knee kept you out."

"It was wrestling," Briggs said, obviously enjoying himself.

"I should have known," Allison said. "Next best thing? Making detective. You weren't quite smart enough for it, but you're a good ol' boy, so strings were pulled. You told yourself making detective would change everything. But it didn't. You started eating more. Drinking more. Probably a divorce or at least woman problems. You hate feeling your incompetence every day working next to your partner who actually earned his spot, so you make up for it with this bullshit, macho personality trying to mask your almost crippling sense of inadequacy." Allison turned to Briggs. "Did I get him right?"

"Oh no, I'm staying out of this one," Briggs said, even though he grinned like he'd just watched a magician perform a card trick.

Grady screwed his face up into a scowl and looked like he was gearing up for a great comeback. But nothing came. He noticed the uniformed cops and the photographer staring at him, flushed red and marched out of the room. "I'm not staying here for this bullshit. I'll be outside."

Allison immediately felt guilty for picking the man apart. She knew what it felt like to be plagued with an overwhelming sense of inadequacy. And, just like Grady, she erected her own walls to protect herself. Still, it didn't give him a license to be an ass wipe.

Once he left the room, she turned to Briggs. "Sorry about that."

Briggs gave a low laugh. "Hell, that was the most fun I've had all week. Did you two used to date or something? You nailed him pretty good."

"Date?" Allison said. "He's not exactly my type."

"And what's your type?" Briggs asked, his tone changing just enough for Allison to realize the point of the conversation had changed. It was a smooth transition from business-only detective to just enough of a hint that he was interested in more than her statement.

"A strong, silent guy who doesn't pick up on women at a crime scene," Allison said.

Briggs made a show of scribbling the information down on a notepad. He handed her his business card while putting a finger to his lips. After she took it, he pantomimed that he'd almost forgotten something and flexed his bicep and pointed at it. Allison laughed, admiring how he'd managed to pull the sequence off as a joke while still looking smooth and confident.

Allison held up his card. "I'll call you if I think of anything else about Maurice."

Briggs smiled and nodded, committed completely to the strong and silent shtick. He closed his notebook, gave her a wave and then walked past her to the scene photographer. Despite everything going on, Allison took a second to enjoy the sight of him walking away. The reaction surprised her, but she couldn't deny an attraction for the detective. She decided to throw him a bone.

"Briggs," she called out.

He turned.

"Are you a good detective?" she asked.

"I'd like to think so," he said.

"Did you notice Maurice there only has lube on his right hand?"

Briggs looked at the body then back at Allison with a questioning look.

"He's left-handed," she said. "Let me know if you turn up anything." She turned and left the room.

It was a thin fact, but one that had bothered her since she first looked at Maurice's body. There were a hundred reasons why Maurice would have used his opposite hand. He wanted his dominant hand available to operate the bag over his head. He carved the name in the girl's skin with that hand. Or maybe going righty was just the way ol' Maurice liked to do the deed.

But there was another consideration. That this wasn't an accidental death at all, but an elaborate staging to cover up a murder. A staging where the killer incorrectly assumed Maurice was right-handed.

If that was the case, then she was dealing with a pro. And it had to be about Catherine Fews. While Maurice's extracurricular activities at the morgue might have given more than a few people reason to put a bag over the guy's head, it was too coincidental that this had happened so soon after she left. She harbored no doubt that Maurice had given up the details about the tattoo to the killer at the first threat.

That meant the killer was a step ahead of her now, on his way to Catherine Fews's hometown.

And that wasn't all. She pictured the letters carved into the girl's flesh and an uneasy realization settled into her chest.

If someone had killed Maurice, then they knew who she was.

CHAPTER 21

Allison pushed her way through the crowd gathered in the hospital lobby. She spotted Mike mingling with the hospital staff standing in small clusters. The stratified nature of hospitals was on display, with orderlies, nurses and docs naturally segregating themselves into different groups, each whispering and pointing toward the yellow police tape stretched across the stairwell. A uniformed cop stood sentry in front of the elevator bank to keep anyone from going down to the morgue. Mike excused himself from the people he was talking to and fell in step next to her.

"You all right?" Mike asked.

"Fine," Allison said. With her solitary lifestyle, there weren't that many people outside of her dad who asked her that question. And he was asking it less and less.

They walked out the front door together into the late afternoon sun, away from the small crowd of onlookers. "The rumor mill was working overtime up here. I heard everything from he hung himself to he died of a heart attack while having his way with a cadaver. None of his coworkers seemed to think that last one was too much of a stretch, which says a lot."

"There was nothing crazy like that," Allison said, avoiding eye contact with him. "Not much to it."

"Really?" he asked.

"Yeah, accidental death. Pretty run-of-the-mill. Unfortunate, but these things happen sometimes," she said, feeling embarrassed because she knew how obvious the lie was. She just needed some space. Some time to breathe. Having a reporter in her face wasn't helping with that.

"Interesting. Because what I was about to say," he continued, his expression shadowed by anger, "was that I finally found the nurse who discovered the body. She gave me the details. All of them."

Allison felt her stomach clench. She hated the feeling of being caught. It was probably why she was such a terrible liar. But she didn't stop walking and she didn't apologize.

"I'm not your source and I don't have time to hold your hand," she said. "I have work to do."

Mike jogged a few steps ahead of her and blocked her path. She came to a stop.

"Just think this through. If you block me out, I'll have to file the story I have so far," Mike said. "Maurice's kinky death is exactly the kind of thing that sells papers and you know it."

Allison pulled her keys out of her pocket and clicked the fob. Her Audi A4 chirped back at her as if agreeing with her that it was time to go.

"You said earlier you wanted the Kraw story," she said. "I'll make that deal. Don't run any of this until the case is wrapped and you get all the gory details about what happened in Louisiana."

Mike grinned. "Nice try. No, that deal's off the table. Something big is going on here and I want in on it."

"Go ahead," she said. "Run the story. The second you do, every reporter in town will be chasing down your lead, trying to figure out who Catherine Fews really was."

"That's where you're wrong," Mike said. "The way I'm going to write it, everyone is going to be asking who Allison McNeil is. They're going to be asking why an FBI agent on administrative leave is investigating a case she wasn't assigned to. But what they're really going to want to know is what was happening between her and the weird hospital worker who carved her name into a body while he was whacking off with a bag over his head. I can have it in the online edition in the next hour. My best guess is that you're done working on this case by dinner. Or do you think it'll take that long for you to get pulled?"

Allison took a deep, steadying breath. "I told you, I'm just researching this case during my leave," she said. "There's no one to throw me off the case."

Mike smiled. "Anytime you want to play poker, you just let me know. You might be the worst liar I've ever met."

"This conversation is over," Allison said.

"I know the Bureau. I know law enforcement," Mike said. "How many years will you find plastic bags with cinch strings left on your desk? Bottles of lube sent to you in the mail? How many dirty jokes will have your name as the punch line?"

Allison knew he was right. She could roll with it, of course. Join in the jokes to defuse them. But Mike was right on both counts. Her reputation would go from profiler with an uncanny knack for being involved in big cases, to a name inserted into every off-color joke imaginable. And the second thing he'd been right about was that she'd be off this case. Mason wanted her involvement kept under wraps. If her name appeared in the Herald tonight, she'd be done. And that meant exile from BAU because of Garret. She couldn't allow that. But if Mason found out she had Mike Carrel as a ride-along for this off-the-books case, then the exact same thing would happen.

Either way, she was screwed. And that pissed her off.

The only possible out was if she broke the case and found the videos before Mason discovered her little deal.

"Let's suppose I did let you come," Allison started, struggling to push aside her anger for being boxed in.

Mike grinned. "I'm listening."

"You do as I say. You're observing, not investigating."

"OK."

"You don't tell anyone what you're doing. Not your editor. Not your assistant."

"Easy, I never tell my editor anything anyway," he said. "As for my assistant, you must not follow the news business much if you think the Herald gives me staff."

"And I get approval of any story before you file it," Allison said.

Mike shook his head. "You know I'm not going to agree to that. No self-respecting journalist would."

"You could have lied to me and just agreed," Allison said.

"But, like you, I'm a terrible liar," Mike said.

"But a pretty good blackmailer."

"Not blackmail," Mike pointed out. "I'm just proficient at listing out things as they are, especially when they're not what people want them to be."

Allison found herself nodding along with that comment. Human nature, hell, her nature, was to realign facts to fit a preconception of the world. A fact without context was just a data point. With context, it could take on a totally different meaning. Everyone walked through the world influenced by confirmation bias. Seeing the world for how it really was could be both a gift and a curse.

A pleasant evening stroll down an urban street for one person was another's terrifying walk where every shadow contained a threat. Standing there, she struggled to strip out her bias and view her decision as a series of data points. There couldn't be a worse possible scenario for keeping an investigation secret than inviting a reporter on a ride-along. But if she didn't, it was going public anyway and she'd be done. She really didn't have an option. And she hated that more than anything else.

"Get in the car," she said. "First time you get in my way, I'll shoot you in the leg and leave you on the side of the road."

Mike grinned. "Deal."

CHAPTER 22

L ibby hung up the phone and leaned back in his desk chair, rubbing his eyes. The news was good. Harris had a lead on the girl's real identity, which he could use to track down who might have the videos.

He stood and crossed his office to the well-stocked liquor cabinet he kept in the corner. An afternoon drink was a throwback to a different time, but he needed one. As he poured himself a whiskey, he considered for the hundredth time whether Mason's claim that all of the leads to Catherine Fews's connections in her DC life had been dead ends. If nothing else, his father was a master of the well-placed lie. He'd proven that when Libby was just a kid, using work as the reason he was away from home for nights on end. Turned out Mom wasn't a bad detective herself. She eventually discovered the late nights at work often ended in a suite at the Four Seasons in Georgetown with a revolving door of young girls.

The lies didn't stop there. Libby was fool enough to believe his dad's promises to be at his sports games. To take him on a trip, just the two of them. That he actually gave a damn about his son.

Not one of those things came true.

It wasn't until his mom remarried when he was thirteen that he discovered what a father was supposed to be. Roger Ashworth was an old money blue blood who adored Libby's mother, a deep love that spilled over into a relationship with Libby from the very beginning. More than that, Roger's first marriage had ended ten years earlier with his wife's death in a boating accident before they had children. Marrying a woman with a young son was an enormous positive in Roger's eyes and he took to being a father like it was the job he'd been waiting for his entire life. Being rich and in control of his time helped. The three of them traveled the world together and led the life Mason's promises had described but never delivered on.

So when Roger had visited him during Libby's senior year at Harvard to tell him about the cancer, Libby's world was shaken to its core. Stage four. Only a few months to live. Libby wanted to drop out of school but Roger wouldn't have it. He made Libby promise he would finish what he started and do something good with his life. Something significant. In a tear-filled conversation, Libby promised that he would, but asked for something in return. That he could live that life with the Ashworth last name, the name of the only father he loved. Months later, Libby held his mother's arm as she buried her husband the same week that he strode across the stage with his diploma in his hand. On it was the name Marshall Liberty Ashworth.

Libby stared at the framed diploma on his office wall as he drained his glass. The diploma was surrounded by other memorabilia of the life of a DC powerbroker. There was his Masters degree from Georgetown. Photos with presidents ranging from Bush 41 to Obama. And, near the center of it all, a photo of him and Mark Summerhays dressed in hunting gear, arms over one another like the best of friends, a row of dead pheasants lying in front of them. Libby shook his head at the photo and considered how fitting it was. The pheasants were just props. They'd run out of time on the trip to actually go hunting together so the photo had been staged to show how folksy Summerhays could be. A real man of the people. Except it was all stagecraft. A fancy, inside the Beltway term that was really just another way of saying it was all a lie.

Do something good with your life. Something significant.

Is that what he was doing? Fighting for political wins. Peeling the scabs off his opponents' wounds at every opportunity. Power for the sake of power was what the game had become. Everyone played it and sitting out wasn't an option. Sitting out meant you got run over. The worst thing about it wasn't that the battlefield in Washington had become so petty and shortsighted; it was that Libby had discovered he was really good at playing the game. Despite his adopted father's lessons about ethics and the common good, Libby had proven to be as crooked and manipulative as the politicians he held in disdain.

Libby walked to the diploma and ran his finger across the glass where his last name was written. There was a smudge on the glass there, reminding him that he often performed this personal ritual. A touchstone to a last name that meant more to him than anything in the world.

But it was a behavior burdened with guilt and insecurity, not remembrance. It always led him to wonder what Roger Ashworth would think of him now. What he would think of all the compromises he'd made to become the right hand to the man about to ascend to the Presidency if all the pollsters had it right. A man who was conniving, amoral, remorseless and power-hungry. The kind of man Roger Ashworth wouldn't deign to invite to a dinner party, let alone support for office.

He pictured his adopted father's kind eyes, actually younger at the time he adopted him than Libby was now. He remembered the way he wouldn't cast judgment or show anger no matter what Libby did. Instead, when he messed up, as all kids did, they would register profound disappointment. And that was more vicious than anything he could say or do to him.

Libby thought how those eyes would look right now if Ashworth were still alive and if he reviewed the life Libby had led. The small early signs of purpose and achievement derailed by latching himself to powerful men on the rise through the political ranks. No wife. No kids. No legacy.

No, if Ashworth were still alive, there would be no handshake or pat on the back. No warm embrace to show his pride in his adopted son. When Libby closed his own eyes, he only saw Ashworth's staring back at him.

And the sad disappointment in them nearly brought Libby to tears every time.

"You OK?" Summerhays asked.

Libby's eyes snapped open. Summerhays stood in the doorway, a folder in hand, looking at him oddly.

"Yeah, damn migraine," Libby said, rubbing his temple. "Trying to battle through it but it's kicking my ass."

Summerhays seemed to accept the explanation and looked at Libby's diploma on the wall. "Seems like a million years ago, doesn't it? Being an undergrad, I mean."

Libby nodded.

"Look, I know I've been leaning on you pretty hard," Summerhays said. "I hope you know how appreciated it is. How essential you are to what we're doing here."

Libby's stomach clenched. How many times had he watched Summerhays give this pep talk to members on the Hill? Fifty? A hundred? Every word rang false. All it meant was a big ask was coming.

"Thanks. I appreciate you saying that," Libby said, dutifully playing his part.

Summerhays grinned, pleased. "What would I do without you? We're going to run the country some day, you and me. Together."

"Then we can do something good. Something significant," Libby said.

Summerhays stumbled over his words, not characteristic for him. "Yes, yes, of course. That's the goal."

"We could start right now, you know," Libby said softly. "The President's education bill is floundering. It's a good bill, but it's not going anywhere with Johnson and Murphy threatening a filibuster. You delivered their seats to them. They owe you."

"And you think I should call in my chits with them over the education bill?" Summerhays asked, arching an eyebrow.

"It's a good bill."

"It's the *President's* bill, Lib. Not mine," Summerhays said. "Why would I want to give him a win right now?" Summerhays looked disgusted. "Jesus, use your head."

Libby rubbed his eyes and nodded. "No, you're right. Not thinking straight. This damn migraine."

Summerhays looked him over carefully. "Are you sure that's it? You've been a little, I don't know, *off* the last few days." He squinted at him. "It's not this thing you're working on for me, is it? Did you call Harris yet?"

Libby was starting to get an actual migraine, Summerhays's every word digging into him. Harris mentioned he'd already called Summerhays before he called Libby. The bastard already knew Harris was on his way to West Virginia, driving to avoid any paper trail of his whereabouts. So why this charade? Libby wasn't sure yet, but he intended to play along to find out.

"No," he said. "I'll call him and see if he's turned anything up. But even if he does, I don't think you want to know about it."

Summerhays waved his hand, dismissing the idea. "Let's just get this wrapped up. I don't care how you do it. I know we'll all feel a lot better once this is behind us."

Libby nodded. That part was at least true.

"And take better care of yourself. I need my best players on the field right now. I need to know you're on top of your game," Summerhays said, smiling even as the tone of his voice delivered the line as a threat.

"Just a cold is all," Libby said. "I'll be fine by tomorrow."

Summerhays stared at him for a few beats, stretching the moment out between them. For a moment, Libby thought he saw a flicker of sadness pass across the man's face. One second there and then gone.

"All right. Get yourself better and we'll talk later."

Libby nodded as Summerhays strode out of the office, leaving him standing alone in front of his wall of photos and diplomas, haunted by the ghost of the man who gave him his name and his love, but perhaps not the courage to live the life he hoped for his son.

CHAPTER 23

Allison threw the car in park in front of her dad's well-kept rancher and looked over at Mike in her passenger seat. She'd spent the short drive over trying to figure out a way to get out of their deal, but she'd come up empty. "You stay here," Allison said.

"Is this your place?" Mike asked, looking over the neatly kept rancher.

They were in Silver Spring, Maryland, just outside the DC limits. The neighborhood screamed suburban Americana: green lawns, trimmed bushes, basketball hoops in the driveways and the stars and stripes hanging on the front porches.

"Doesn't concern you," Allison said. "Just give me five minutes."

"Boyfriend?" Mike asked.

Allison shot him a look and he raised his hands, smiling. "Sorry, I ask a lot of questions. Occupational hazard."

Allison climbed out of the car and walked to the front door. As she approached, she saw that it was already open by a foot. Out of habit, she took a position to the side of the door, her hand instinctively coming to a rest on her gun. She didn't pull it out, realizing there was probably a simple explanation. Still, she carefully rolled around the doorjamb and entered the house scanning for any sign of trouble.

"Dad? Maria?" she called out. "Hello?"

She moved systematically through the house, making a mental note of every detail. No sign of a struggle. TV on in the living room. Half-eaten sandwich on a dinner tray.

"Dad?"

Down the hallway. Into the kitchen. Orange juice splashed all over the linoleum among shards of glass. Smears of red mixed with the juice.

"Dad, where are you?"

Allison heard the stress in her voice. This was her fault. She should never have left him alone. But she hadn't. Maria was supposed to be here. Where were they?

She ran down the hall and burst into the first bathroom. There were hand towels in the sink spotted with blood. There wasn't a lot of it, which Allison registered in her rising panic as a good thing.

The two bedrooms were the last places to look. She sprinted to his bedroom. Nothing.

Loud voices came from the front door. It took her a second to realize one was her dad. The second was Mike. They sounded like two buddies coming in from a night on the town.

"Come on in, mind the mess on the floor," her dad said.

"Sure thing, Pat. Watch your step."

Allison turned the corner and saw Mike helping her dad into the kitchen, an arm around his shoulders. Her dad only had one shoe on, the other foot was bare. He wore a sweater appropriate for the cool fall day, but had only a pair of boxer shorts below. His legs looked withered and frail. Patrick McNeil had once been a beast of a man, full of energy and life. Time and the heartbreak of burying a son and a wife had whittled him down to a ghost of what he once had been.

"Just sit me down there, Ed," her dad said. "Did something to my foot is all."

"Yes, sir," Mike said. "How about this chair right here?"

"Perfect." He looked up and saw Allison. "Alley-cat, when did you get here? Look, Ed's home."

Allison put on her best smile. "I was just waiting for you. Where'd you go?"

"I was going...I was...there was..." A flicker of doubt shadowed his face as he tried to remember. He pushed the question aside. "Doesn't matter." He turned to Mike. "Ed, why the hell don't you come around more, boy? What have you been doing with yourself?"

Mike glanced at Allison for guidance. Allison crossed to a small table near them and picked up a framed picture of a tall, lanky young man. It was a good photo of her brother, with him posed outside near a body of water, looking full of life and promise. Two things that Arnie Milhouse had cheated him out of over a decade earlier.

Allison kneeled next to her dad and placed her hand carefully on his arm. She held the photo in front of him. "This is Edgar, Dad. Remember? He's not with us anymore."

Her dad shook his head, still grinning madly. He pointed at Mike. "What are you saying? He's right here. In front of your nose."

Allison blinked a tear away. "No, Dad. This is Mike. Ed is right here," she took his hand and placed it on the photo. "Ed died a long time ago."

It tore her up to see his expression change from such joy, to confusion and into slow realization. And with that realization came the flood of emotion of a grown man discovering the son he loved was dead all over again. His lower lip trembled. His eyes filled with tears. The hand on the photo of Edgar pawed the glass as if he could get through the barrier and touch his son one last time.

When he looked up at Allison, it was the same haunted look she'd known since her brother's death. The same from the day he'd picked her up at the Naval Academy and driven her home in stone-cold silence. Like each time before, she swore the next time he was confused she would just let him keep thinking Ed was still alive. It was the easier way out, perhaps kinder, but it felt like a final surrender to the illness. She worried that if she didn't keep pulling him back, no matter how painful the experience was, that she might lose him permanently.

"Do you want me to stay?" Mike whispered. "Or..."

"Can you wait in the car please?" Allison said.

"Sure."

"And Mike. Thanks for bringing him in."

Mike nodded. He leaned down toward her dad. "Nice to meet you, sir," he said, but he received no response.

Pat hugged the photo to his chest, tears flowing freely down his cheeks as he rocked in the chair. The moment Mike left the room, she lost it. Still kneeling next to her dad, she wrapped her arms around his neck and rocked with him, trying to return some small part of the comfort he'd given her throughout her life.

"It's OK, Dad," she whispered. "It's OK."

Eventually, they both collected themselves. Allison pulled off the one shoe her dad had on and revealed two cuts from stepping on the glass. She retrieved the first-aid kit from the bathroom, sparking a memory of how many times her dad had used the same kit to patch her up. Always a skinned knee or elbow for Allison the tomboy. It wasn't the first time she'd been struck with how their caregiving roles had reversed.

She cleaned the cuts with hydrogen peroxide, then applied some Neosporin and a Band-Aid. Her dad sat through it all quietly, looking out the window into the backyard. She wondered where his thoughts took him.

On most days he was perfectly cogent and totally aware of the disease eating away at his ability to remember. This was both a blessing and a true cruelty. A blessing in that they were both acutely aware that the good days of remembering and sharing stories of the old times were finite and dwindling. And a curse for the same reason. Allison had moved in not long after the Alzheimer's diagnosis, keeping her apartment in Georgetown but staying there only a couple nights a week when she worked into the small hours of the morning. In the last six months they'd had their share of long, late-night conversations, laughing and crying as they relived the days when they had been a family of four, instead of only two.

Only in the last month had things taken a turn. The blank spots in his memory more noticeable. The inability to remember making him lash out in anger that Allison knew was just fear taking hold of a proud man.

"Hello?" came a voice at the door. It was Maria, the woman who was supposed to have been watching him when Allison couldn't be there.

"I'll be right back," she said.

She met Maria in the hallway. A retired nurse in her sixties, she was a stern, no-nonsense woman, a trait Allison thought would be a perfect fit for her dad. But not if she left him unattended.

"Where the hell were you?" Allison said, not bothering to hide the accusation in her voice. "I told you that he can't be alone."

"What happened? Is he all right?" Maria asked, her face drained of color. She looked past Allison, trying to see into the room behind her.

"Yes, because I happened to come by when I did. He was outside in his boxers, going God-knows-where. He cut his foot."

"Oh God. Is it bad?" Maria looked panicked. She made a move to walk past her into the house but Allison slid over to block her path. The nurse took a step back, her expression

JEFF GUNHUS

pinched, as if readying herself to deal with the obstacle in front of her.

"So? Where were you?"

Maria's panic was gone, replaced by cool condescension. She pulled a white pharmacy bag from her purse. "You said you were going to get his meds, but you never did. He was completely out."

Allison felt a pang of guilt. She *had* promised to bring the meds by. Heart and blood pressure. Maria was just covering for her. "Why didn't you take him with you?" Allison asked.

"He dug his heels in," Maria said. "Refused to come. You know how he is."

At least the woman wasn't incompetent, which was Allison's larger fear. The agency could send someone new but that would take time. Maria would have to do.

"I'm sorry I snapped at you," Allison said. "It just scared me."

"It's all right," she said, putting a hand on Allison's arm. "We want the same thing here."

Allison appreciated the gesture, especially since she was about to segue into asking for an enormous favor. "Listen, I have a work thing that's come up. I need to go out of town."

Maria's eyes lit up, as if she were excited by the news. But the expression quickly passed and she shook her head with disapproval. "For how long? You just got back."

"A day. Two at the most," Allison said.

Maria looked past her into the room where her dad now sat on his couch. "He misses you so much when you're gone. He needs you, you know."

Allison nodded, wondering at how guilt could feel like a physical thing, a pressure building inside of her. Maria was right. There weren't that many good days left for her dad, but she needed to do her job too. She knew the in-home care agency could provide the care, but her dad seemed most comfortable with Maria. She was the only nurse he ever asked about. "Only a day or two."

Allison had been prepared to strong-arm the woman into staying, but Maria didn't argue. Maybe she was worried the incident would be reported to the agency. Whatever the reason, Allison was happy to have someone covering for her.

Allison went to her bedroom. She kept half her wardrobe there and she threw a few pieces of clothing into a bag. By the time she was ready to leave, Maria and her dad were sitting next to one another in front of the TV, looking more like an old married couple than nurse and patient.

"I'm leaving, Dad," she said. "A work thing."

"Maria here told me about the nice-looking fella in the car," her dad said. "Have fun *working*. That's not what we used to call it."

She started to protest but decided to leave it alone. It was nice to see him smile and have a little twinkle in his eye. She leaned down and gave him a kiss.

"I love you, Dad."

"You too, Alleycat," he replied. "Don't worry, me and Nurse Ratched here have things covered."

Maria gave him an affectionate jab to his arm. "I told you not to call me that, Pat," she said.

Her dad reached out and patted her knee, chuckling.

Allison caught the exchange and wondered how she could have missed the signs. When Maria came in the door, she wasn't afraid for her job, she was afraid for her dad. And now seeing them together, Allison realized that somehow in the last few months, the relationship between the two had blurred from nurse and patient into that of mutual companionship. Maria's expression when Allison told her she was going to be gone for a day or two made more sense now. She wanted Allison to stay because she knew it was what her dad wanted, but like a teenager left alone for the weekend, Maria was excited to have the house to themselves too.

As she left the room, she glanced back and saw Maria slide closer to her dad on the couch. Allison smiled and walked out the door.

CHAPTER 24

They rode in silence for the first half hour. Allison appreciated that Mike didn't feel the need to fill the silence with small talk but was willing to just let the quiet stretch out between them. When her phone rang, it caused them both to jump. She answered the call.

"I have her name," came Jordi's voice over the phone.

"That's great," Allison said.

"Even with the tattoo, it wasn't easy," he said. "The only photo record online was her high school picture, and that wasn't a public database. I had to get into the school servers to access their archived records. And their systems were old. I mean, like going-into-a-crumbling-condemned-building old. But I Indiana Jones'ed it and got the info."

"Awesome," she said. "Can you send me over everything you've got?"

"Have I taught you nothing?" came Jordi's reply. "You want this intel to stay secret or not? Assume anything on this phone is heard by a room full of old white guys. *Hey, old white guys listening right now, fuck you! Hear me, you twats?"*

Allison held the phone away from her ear and Jordi's voice blasted from the speaker. Mike raised an eyebrow but she ignored him.

"Jordi, how many cups of coffee have you had today?"

"Not nearly enough," he replied. "I set you up with a Darknet alias and I'll send the info that way. First initial, last name for user. And the password is the thing I said to you this morning that made you mad."

Allison thought that through, realizing it wouldn't make any sense for him to give her the password on a call that he thought was monitored. *The thing I said to you this morning that made you mad.* She didn't know what that was. "You always say a lot of things that make me mad," she said.

"Try 'em all, love," Jordi said. "It'll be fun."

Click.

Allison held out her phone, wondering if she'd dropped the call. She had four bars. Jordi had just hung up on her.

"Interesting friend," Mike said.

"You have no idea," Allison replied. "But he came up with the girl's name. He's sending over the details via email."

"So the old white guys won't listen?" Mike asked.

"You have a habit of eavesdropping," Allison said. "It's not polite."

"Do you know what you call a polite reporter?" Mike waited a beat. "Unemployed."

Allison groaned but gave him a smile. She navigated around a slow-moving truck and pushed her speed up to eighty. They had a lot of road to eat up and getting around the Beltway before the afternoon traffic started could mean an hour of saved time. Besides, she couldn't help thinking they were racing against the killer going to the same destination. She knew it was a stretch, but her intuition was telling her they weren't the only ones on their way to West Virginia that night.

"How long has your dad..." Mike's voice trailed off and she heard the hesitation in it, the underlying question whether the topic was off-limits or not. When Allison didn't answer right away, he followed up quickly with, "Sorry, if you don't want--"

"No, it's fine," she said, surprising herself. Maybe it was the way he'd helped her dad into the house, or the way he'd spoken to him so easily, careful not to make her dad feel self-conscious, but she felt her guard lower just a little.

"Alzheimer's, I'm assuming," he said.

She nodded. There were other forms of dementia, but Alzheimer's was the most common, so it was a safe guess. And it suited her father. He would have been horrified to have something exotic, something people raised a fuss about. No, he preferred a run-of-the-mill degenerative neural disease. *Old-timers*, as he liked to call it.

"It's just been in the last year. Really since my mom passed away."

"Sorry, I didn't realize..."

"No, it's fine," she said. "It was a long illness. She was ready. My dad thought he was too, but he...you know..."

"You can never really be ready," Mike said.

"Married for nearly forty years," she said. "Had my brother and I late. They really lived a great life together. Endured a lot together too."

"Your brother?" Mike asked.

Allison shook her head. She had never revealed to anyone that Arnie Milhouse had been the one to kill her brother Edgar in the convenience store shooting all those years ago. It would have just complicated matters. Questions would have been raised why an agent with such a direct personal connection to the suspect was allowed near the case. Arnie had known at the very end. He'd known that she'd hunted him down like a dog. That she'd outsmarted him and, in his last breaths, that she'd out-fought him. She had meted out justice for her family and sent Arnie to his grave.

She wasn't about to share any of that with a man she'd just met, let alone a reporter.

"My brother died when he was a teenager," she said, staying with what was in the public record. "Shot at a convenience store hold-up in Baltimore."

Mike took a deep breath, obviously feeling guilty for dredging up all the memories of dead relatives.

"I had no idea. I'm really sorry to pry."

"At least you didn't ask about my dog. Just last week, it…" Allison allowed her voice to trail off.

"Why? Did it…" He stopped himself, catching her wry look. He shook his head. "C'mon, I already feel terrible and you're going to do that to me?"

She laughed, enjoying seeing the uber-confident reporter back on his heels a little. "Just trying to lighten the mood."

"You have an odd sense of humor."

"I've been told," she said, laughing. She turned off the Beltway and headed north on I-270. They still had four or five hours of driving ahead of them. At least it was starting to feel like it wasn't going to be a completely unpleasant experience.

"So it's just you and your dad then?" Mike asked.

She nodded. "At first I thought he was just disoriented after my mom died. It's not uncommon for a surviving spouse to have difficulty adjusting. Especially after being a caretaker for a long period of time. He hid it well too. If I'd paid better attention, the diagnosis could have been made six months earlier."

"Would it have made a difference? In treatment or how it progressed?"

"Maybe not," she said. "Probably not," she admitted.

"But you still feel guilty about it."

It was a statement, not a question. She didn't correct him. She did feel guilty. She felt guilty at that moment for being on the way to West Virginia instead of sitting next to her dad on their couch watching reruns of *Jeopardy!* Guilty for not picking his brain for every story about his life before the memories deteriorated away with the rest of him.

"I felt that same way with my mom," Mike said. "Also Alzheimer's. It's a slow, painful descent into the dark."

Allison snuck a look over at him and saw that he was staring out the passenger window.

"My mom called the disease her shadow," Mike continued. "She said she felt her memories in the back of her mind, lingering, as if she could stare into the shadow long enough and her eyes would adjust to the dim light and she'd be able to see them again." He touched the window with the tips of his fingers, tracing shapes there. "The real cruelty came in the moments of false hope, those rare times when a light switch goes on and chases the shadows back and everything is clear for a minute or two. But the light burns itself out quick enough. The shadows return. And then, one day, more sudden than you think, you're on the bottom and there's nothing but shadows forever. The same eyes that once lit up when you walked into a room just stare back at you with no recognition at all. And it breaks your goddamn heart." His voice cracked with emotion at the end.

Allison discreetly reached up and wiped away a tear from each of her eyes, hoping Mike didn't catch the movement. His words went right to the center of her fear of what was coming with her father. And her guilt for not being with him.

"Sorry," Mike said. "I didn't mean to go there. It wasn't that long ago and seeing your dad..."

"No, that's fine," Allison said. "I appreciate you being open like that."

An awkward silence came next, filling the car like a living thing. Allison tried to think of a direction to take the conversation, but nothing seemed quite right. His fidgeting hands showed he was struggling too.

"Radio?" Allison offered.

"Perfect," Mike chimed in, a little too loudly.

Allison turned on the radio and flipped through the stations. That started a conversation about the merits of rock versus hip-hop, which led to stories about past concerts they had both gone to. That led them to college and old stories there, then high school and hometowns and stories about how they were raised, how they grew up.

The miles and hours clicked past. In the back of her mind, Allison recognized the conversation she was having was the same one that she had on every first date she'd ever been on. The difference was that she was enjoying herself and the person sitting beside her was actually articulate and interesting.

Allison realized that if this had been a first date instead of a car ride on the way to go catch a killer, she'd have to say it was going extremely well.

CHAPTER 25

Harris pulled into the gas station just outside of Harlow, West Virginia, around ten o'clock. He rolled over the rubber hoses that snaked across the cracked concrete, causing a tire bell to sound. The place was deserted. Seemed the good people of Harlow had sense enough to get their gas and their lottery scratch cards at a more reasonable hour.

The terrain for the last two hours had turned mountainous. Even so, he made quick progress on I-70. Engineers from the 1960s and 70s hadn't been handcuffed by bureaucratic blowhards in the EPA so they'd just blown chunks out of the mountains wherever they wanted to give travelers a convenient ride. Nowadays, Harris figured, the interstate probably would have needed to be elevated so it didn't disturb the migratory patterns of the black bear, or not built at all so that some rare mushroom could be saved from extinction.

Harris looked to the dingy, cinderblock building behind the pumps for any sign of life. The left side of the place was two stories tall with a service bay for mechanical work, covered by a rollback door that looked to be more rust than metal. Faded banners hung stretched across it, one for Marlboro Reds and the other proclaiming a big sale on Bud Light. Judging by the age of the signs and the rust, it appeared the mechanical needs of the hamlet of Harlow were being served elsewhere and had been for quite a while.

The single story box attached to the side of the service bay was lit up from inside although Harris saw no movement inside. He could see that one wall was lined by a refrigerated case with beer and sodas, and that the little floor space there was inside was given over to display racks of grease, fat and sugar packaged in bright paper. And people wondered why America was getting so damn fat.

The slot where credit cards were accepted at the gas terminal had a little piece of paper taped to it: "Broke. Come inside." Harris wondered if the note referred to the gas station owner or just the slider for the credit cards. Didn't matter to him, he planned on paying with cash anyway. He had a few cards that were theoretically not traceable back to him, but he hadn't survived as long as he had without a certain amount of paranoia. As he walked to the building to find someone to pay, he heard a motor coming up the road behind him.

A pickup turned the corner, souped-up with extra suspension and big, knobby tires. Harris watched as headlights turned toward him, bouncing as the vehicle hit the potholes where the asphalt met the gas station's concrete slab. Country music blared out from the windows. The truck pulled into the pump in front of Harris's car, a dead deer sticking out the back of the bed. It was a big six-pointer, not a monster, but probably big enough to hang on someone's wall.

The truck door swung open and, out of habit more than anything else, Harris sized up the man who came out. He was in his late twenties, six foot and maybe two hundred pounds, hard to tell with the coveralls and the hunting jacket. The man's thick neck and posture marked him a jock that spent time in the gym.

Harris noticed how he paused behind his door when he first got out, using it as a shield, while his eyes darted to the tree line outside the halo of light from the station, searching for threats. Harris recognized the behavior. He looked to the back window of the pickup and saw the USMC sticker there. Ex-military. Maybe a tour or two. Enough to still make him look for something moving in the shadows that might kill him.

If he was a local, then he was exactly what Harris was looking for.

"Don't think anyone's here," Harris called. The man looked at him strangely, like he was making fun of him. "I mean in the gas station. At least, I haven't seen anyone."

"Nah, Earl's in there somewhere. Probably jacking off in the back room."

Harris noted the man wasn't wearing a hunting jacket. It was military camo with a name patch on the front pocket that read "Doyle". Harris made a mental note that he ought to have picked up on that detail earlier. Not for the first time in the past year he considered the dubious idea that he might be losing a step. He didn't like that thought at all.

Doyle spit a gob of chew at the ground and gave Harris a once over. "Where're you from?"

"Nowhere special," Harris said. "You?"

Doyle laughed. "Me too. You're looking at it. Born and raised." He spit again, looked him over again, then walked to the convenience store. Harris followed behind, limping on his right leg and wincing. It wasn't a very convincing performance but it got the job done. Doyle noticed.

"Hey, you think you could give whoever's in there this forty bucks?" Harris said, hitting his leg with his fist. "Got a bum leg here."

Doyle squinted as if trying to figure out the scam. He looked around again as if there might be a band of robbers ready to set on him if he reached out to take the money. Seeing nothing, he reached out and grabbed the bills.

"Thank you," Harris said, slumping his shoulders forward. "Appreciate it. That's pump two."

"There are only two pumps here, pal." Doyle laughed. "I got you covered." He turned and marched to the small building. "Earl!" he shouted, beating the window beside the door before he opened it and walked in. "Put your dink back in your pocket and get on out here."

Harris returned to his car, careful to keep the gas dispenser between him and the building. A plan was coming together. And having the guy working the night shift see him wasn't part of it. He considered that Doyle might force the guy to come out to gawk over the dead buck in his pickup bed. If so, it would change the plan a bit. Nothing major, but it would make things messier.

He limped over to the pickup and looked inside the cab. Just as he hoped, there was a shotgun and a box of shells on the passenger seat. He smiled as he worked his way down to the end of the bed to look at the deer. For a second, he worried that he might have forgotten which leg he'd faked the limp on, but he was pretty sure it was the right one. Losing a step. That was the constant worry.

The buck stared up at him with lifeless black eyes and his blood-covered tongue hung from the side of his mouth. The exit wound right behind the buck's foreleg was a crater of torn flesh.

He peered around the edge of the gas pump and saw Doyle talking to someone in the store, must have been Earl. There was a pudgy girl with too much makeup standing next to him. Harris smiled. Looked like Earl hadn't been jacking himself off after all, but had found someone willing to do it for him.

But then Harris frowned. *Three* people. Things were starting to get too complicated. Like many things, this one was out of his control. He just needed to wait and see who came out of the store with Doyle.

He gripped the buck's antlers and gave them a tug. They were thick and gnarled, perfect for fighting other bucks over a piece of ass, basically a buck's driving force in life. Holding the animal's antlers, smelling the unique scent of musk and blood, took Harris back to his times hunting with his dad.

His dad had warned him there were a lot of people in the world who didn't like hunting. No, more than that, some people hated it. Were absolutely repulsed by the idea. But these hamburger-eating, steak-loving assholes were pure hypocrites. According to his dad, strict vegetarians had a legitimate argument, but everyone else just needed a heavy dose of shut-the-hell-up.

Harris's dad wasn't a big religious guy, but he did like the part in the Bible about how man was meant to be lord over the earth. He'd never actually read that part in the Bible, but his old man, Harris's grandfather, had told him it was there and that was good enough for him. It was right next to the part where it said slaves were all right to have, that gaywad-ass-suckers would burn in the fires of hell and that if a woman cheats on you, it was fine and dandy with the Lord of Hosts if you beat her senseless. The Bible actually said you could throw stones at her until she was dead, but Harris's dad warned him that law enforcement was filled with non-believers, so they didn't look kindly at that sort of thing.

His dad thought the rule about man's dominion over things, the words as handed down by God Himself, extended to every living creature walking the earth. That included his wife who, because Harris's dad was not in his words a *faggot* or *butt-muncher*, was definitely of the female persuasion. As Father Tom at the local Baptist church liked to say, God had handed the keys to the kingdom to *men*, not *wo-men*. What that meant to Harris's dad was that when your wife talked back to you or didn't cook a good enough dinner, or if she screwed up in any of dozens of other ways, then it was the man's job, hell it was his duty, to set things right.

Harris's mom spent a lot of time explaining to emergency room technicians and social services how clumsy she was, how the stairs into their cellar were too steep, how she should have known better than to walk on ice without decent shoes on. Harris thought his dad only had things part right. Man was meant to lord over the Earth, including over women. Sometimes they got what was coming to them for bad behavior. What his dad hadn't figured on was that a boy's mother wasn't just another woman; she was something else entirely. She was a figure to be revered. She was something a boy, especially a boy like Harris, would do anything to protect.

"You all right there, hoss?" Doyle said, startling Harris.

The man was at the pump. Harris hadn't even noticed him coming toward him.

Jesus, get yourself together, he admonished himself. Allowing himself to daydream like that wasn't losing a step, it was damn near incompetence.

"Sorry, just thinking about the last time I went hunting with my dad," Harris said.

"You a hunter?" Doyle said, pushing the gas nozzle into his tank.

Harris checked the store. Earl and his fat little girlfriend were nowhere to be seen. Probably back to porking away in the back room, making a little mutant baby. Perfect. No one had seen his face.

"Yeah, I'm a hunter," he said. "It's been a long time since I shot a deer though. I moved on to other things."

Doyle's phone rang in his jacket pocket. He held up a hand toward Harris and excused himself as he answered it.

Harris faked his limp back to his car, put in the fuel pump and eavesdropped on snippets of the conversation.

"...got to butcher the deer tonight..."

"...nah, I'll just shack up here. Probably hunt all day tomorrow..."

"...I tol' you I was huntin' this week..."

"...whatever, Bess. Go ahead an' do what you want. I tol' you I was huntin'..."

There was a long pause and Harris sneaked a look. Doyle held the phone to his ear, his face slowly twisting in anger. Whatever Bess was saying wasn't sitting well.

"...I don't have to explain shit to you, OK...Bess? Hello? Shit."

Doyle looked at his phone, finger poised to dial, then he closed the phone case and slid it into his pocket.

Harris replaced the pump and screwed the gas cap back on.

"Sorry to bother you," he called out. "But Harlow is that way, right?" he said, pointing down the dark road.

"What do I look like, your damn tour guide?" Doyle snapped. After a beat, he held up one of his hands as if to apologize. "Sorry, man. Goddamn girls, right?"

"Can't live with them," Harris said.

"And you can't kill them," Doyle said.

Well...technically...

"You got that right," Harris said. "So, Harlow..."

"Yeah, man, another six miles," Doyle said. "You'll think you're lost, nothing but forest and darkness, and then you'll hit town. Don't blink or you'll miss it."

"Thanks."

"I'm heading that way if you want to follow me. Just give me ten minutes to fill up and hit the john."

"No, I'm good," Harris said. "Good to meet you. Congrats on the buck."

"Thanks, man. Take it easy."

Harris limped back to his car and climbed in. He watched as Doyle lit a cigarette, either oblivious to the giant NO SMOKING sign right in front of him, or just not giving a shit about it.

"Yeah, man, see you around," Harris said quietly to himself inside the car.

Harris started the engine and turned left toward Harlow. It was only six miles away but he suspected it would take him an hour or two to get there.

CHAPTER 26

Allison pulled off at a truck stop with about a hundred miles left to drive. They needed gas, but she was also eager to check the information Jordi sent her. The place was one of those big interstate jobs. Fourteen pumps, double-sided so that twenty-eight cars could fill up at a time was small compared to the other side of the complex where dozens of big rigs guzzled fuel or sat silent in parking lots while their drivers slept.

A metal canopy soared over their heads, piping in a local country station. The whole place was brightly lit and dozens of TV monitors embedded in the pumps told travelers how good the hot dogs, Slurpee's and beer was waiting inside the convenience mart that was larger than the grocery store in most small towns.

There was also an ad for a "State-of-the-art Internet Café." She sent Mike to try to find them some halfway healthy food while she went looking for it. In a Wi-Fi world, Internet terminals were fast becoming an artifact of a different time like the payphone booth or beeper. But it was exactly what Allison needed to check Jordi's info. She'd considered using her phone to access the data, but even with Jordi's encryption, once it was on her device, it was vulnerable. One thing Jordi had done well was instill in her a sense of paranoia.

The computer terminals were through the store and out the back, down the twisting halls of the truck stop complex. It was nicer than she had imagined, with gleaming linoleum floors and freshly painted walls. Signs pointed to showers, a TV room and a lounge area. There were even sleeping rooms available to rent for the truck drivers tired of stretching out in the narrow space behind their seats. A sign listed the rates and insisted that patrons strictly adhered to the one occupant per room policy. Allison grinned and wondered whether the idea to charge for bedrooms by the hour at a truck stop was the worst business idea ever or the best. She guessed it depended on how serious management took their own rule about one person per room. And how soundproof the rooms were.

She found the bank of five computer terminals, each with its own semi-private area with a cubicle half-wall on either side. None of them were in use. She tried to imagine who the customer was for the terminals nowadays. Probably limited to people who had lost their phone recently. She didn't think the Internet café would last much longer in the world, but she was glad it hadn't disappeared quite yet.

Allison logged on and was asked to slide her credit card. She heard Jordi's voice insisting that every electronic transaction was bagged and tagged by the feds, ensuring that if she used her card then her location would be known. Still a hundred miles from their destination, she wasn't too worried about that. But she did worry that somehow whatever information she looked at would somehow be visible on this computer. Short on time, it was a chance she had to take.

She swiped the card Mason had given her and logged in. She pulled up her email and found the message from Jordi with the Darknet access portal. Clicking through brought her to a blank screen with a text box in the top right corner. She placed her cursor there and rested her fingers on the keyboard.

The thing I said to you this morning that made you mad.

Allison had been thinking what the password might be since talking to Jordi. She knew generally what he was talking about but wasn't sure how his warped mind would turn it into a password.

Looking behind her first to check if she was alone, she typed in:

gainedweight

Nothing.

gettingfat

"Jordi, why are you such a bastard," she muttered to herself.

biggerboobs

Nothing.

yourboobsarebigger

The screen remained blank. With a groan, Allison typed in:

fatboobs

The screen flashed and switched to an interface of multiple boxes with messages and files.

"Asshole," whispered Allison, although she couldn't help but give a short laugh imagining how much Jordi enjoyed coming up with the password.

She made a quick study of the screen layout and clicked through to a file labeled Executive Summary. A picture of Catherine Fews filled the screen, only it was a teenage version of the girl, wearing a hoodie with her hair pulled back into a ponytail. There was no sign of the heavy makeup she wore in all the photos in her DC life. Without it, she was a natural beauty, emanating a healthy glow and a warm smile. Allison knew she must have broken hearts all over the county.

It was hard to believe this was the same girl wrapped in six separate pieces in a DC morgue. But it wasn't, not really. This was Tracy Bain, graduate of Harlow High School. Allison scrolled through the report Jordi had pieced together, clicking through the links to photos from either the school yearbook or the local county newspaper. The girl had been a two-sport varsity athlete, basketball and track. It was no accident that Catherine/Tracy was prominent in the coverage. The camera loved her. And the only thing that sold local papers better than local sports was local sports done by a drop-dead gorgeous seventeen-year-old girl.

Hard to imagine what had happened between the sweet pictures of the girl in the paper and her life as a DC call girl.

Allison clicked through the photos and documents swept up in Jordi's net. She had to back click after passing by an image too quickly. It caught her eye because there was a text box inserted on top of the photo from Jordi. He'd flagged a page from the yearbook and drawn a thick line from his note to the image of Tracy standing in a group of boys. It was a photo for the computer club. The boys surrounding her fit the geek stereotype with bad bowl haircuts and goofy smiles. Tracy stood out like a supermodel walking into an engineer's luncheon, except she also managed to fit right in too. She had her arms over the shoulders of the boys next to her and her hands held forward, fingers parted in a Vulcan salute from Star Trek.

Tracy Bain may have been homecoming queen and an athlete, but she was also a computer geek. Jordi's note made her smile. *I'm in love,* it said. Certainly, having someone like Tracy in high school computer club was probably the fantasy of computer geeks everywhere. But for Allison, it was another piece to the puzzle that fit into place. One of the things she'd been wondering was how Catherine, *Tracy,* she reminded herself, managed the fairly sophisticated technology of the encrypted video feed.

The working theory that someone had come to Tracy with the idea for the first camera but that the second camera had been her idea seemed to bear out with these new facts. She'd started out the trip to find out where that signal went and who could have set up the camera system for her. Now she considered that Tracy hadn't needed anyone's help setting it up, either in the room or on the back-end where the images were stored. Maybe she did it all herself.

If that was the case, then maybe her earlier assumption that she'd sent the videos to someone she trusted was wrong. With her technical skills, she could have sent them somewhere remote where she could access them later. To the cloud or some kind of external data storage. But she would still want the videos to come out if she went missing.

Allison clicked back to the homepage of the interface Jordi had created for them. There was a chat box there.

Jordi? she typed.

Hey love, came the reply almost instantly. *See you figured out my password.*

I just thought of the most childish thing I could.

Sound strategy. Like the data?

Allison paused. She didn't want to think of Tracy Bain as just data points. There was always a point in every case where that happened though, where the human beings disappeared, leaving behind just a mystery to be solved, an itch that needed to be scratched. She looked at the photo of Tracy in one of the boxes on the sidebar, feeling a surge of sadness for the young life cut short. She held on to that sadness, hating the feeling but hating it worse when she didn't feel it.

Great job, she typed. *Thinking maybe data on cloud, remote server. Not physical location. Possible?*

There was a longer pause. Jordi typed about as fast as an auctioneer could talk, so she assumed he was entering a long, technical explanation. She was surprised when the answer came back.

Don't think so.

More specific? she replied.

Cloud-based services don't play nice with the Darknet. All those drugs and guns sold there makes them antsy. Relooked back end to make sure I didn't miss something. Simple but elegant programming. Old school open source operating system called Zope. No one really uses it now.

OK, less specific.

Ways to fool cloud services to store something they don't want to. Whoever did this either not sophisticated enough for that...or so sophisticated that I can't catch what they did. That last option is ridiculous...of course.

Allison laughed and a truck driver walking through the corridor behind her jerked his head her direction. She turned the screen slightly away from the man. He got the message and moved on.

Of course. You're the best. Thanks.

Right, love. I'll update here if there's anything and text you if there's something new. Be careful.

Always, she typed, trying to remember the last time being careful had been a priority for her.

She clicked through the photos and files one more time. She felt like she was missing a pattern but she couldn't quite place it. She opened the file with the images of the local newspaper stories and scrolled through them, watching Tracy's high school career play out in the papers. Sports. Academic awards. Homecoming court.

Then an idea struck her. She went back through the images another time, ignoring the stories and just looking at the dates. There was nothing from what would have been Tracy's senior year.

Allison went back to the yearbook folder and clicked through. Same thing. No mention of Tracy in any club or sport that year. Her only appearance was as part of the graduating class and her senior photo. And the photo showed a different girl than the one showcased in the rest of the file. In the picture, she wore her hair pulled back tight. Her cheeks were sunken and her eyes had dark rings beneath them. It looked like perhaps she was in the middle of having the flu and had barely managed to come in for pictures that day.

But Allison didn't think it was the flu. Something had happened to Tracy Bain before her senior year of high school. And whatever it was had changed her.

Allison had been that person once. She'd been on each side of the situation, the golden kid who seemed destined to lead a charmed life, to the frail girl with the thousand-yard stare once everything tumbled down on her after the rape at the Naval Academy.

She jotted down a few notes, entered one number into her phone, then closed her connection to the site. As she stood up and stretched, she knew one thing for certain. There was no risk of Tracy Bain becoming just a data set to her. Not this time.

Every step along the way, the case felt more personal. While the murderer took her life, whatever happened to her before she left Harlow was what had set her on a path that put her in that Georgetown bedroom. Allison intended to uncover all of it.

As odd as it seemed, she felt both a bond and an obligation to Tracy Bain. Allison closed her eyes and Tracy's senior photo was there, that haunted gaze staring beyond the camera as if she wasn't there anymore.

It was too late to do anything to save the girl, but it wasn't too late to avenge her death.

CHAPTER 27

Harris staggered into the road, waving his arms at the approaching headlights. He wiped at the blood that dripped into his eye from the cut on his forehead. It stung, making his eyes water so that the truck's headlights turned into a starburst for a second. He wondered if Doyle was digging around in the glove compartment or something, because the son of a bitch didn't seem to be slowing down. Even though the limp was fake and the cut on his hairline was just a shallow self-inflicted slice with a razorblade, he wondered if he'd be able to jump out of the way in time if the redneck didn't stop. It was a quick thought, but there long enough for him to feel the irony inherent in it.

Fortunately, whatever Doyle was up to, he finally must have noticed him in the road because the tires on the truck locked up. The back tires slid out to the right a little but it wasn't bad. Soon, the truck came to a stop and then rolled over to the shoulder. The driver side window came down and Doyle stuck his head out.

"What the hell are you doing? I almost ran--"

The blood did its work and Doyle went from pissed to concerned in a split-second.

"Man, you OK?" he asked, getting out of the truck. "You're bleeding."

"Am I?" Harris asked. He wiped the cut with his palm, pressing on it to make it bleed a little more. The effect was probably overkill, but Harris liked to be thorough. He made a show of being surprised by the sight of the blood, buckling his legs slightly.

Doyle got out of the truck and reached for him. "Easy there, man. C'mon. Why don't you sit down?"

"Maybe I should," Harris mumbled. "Deer came across the road. Tried to miss it."

"Where's your car?" Doyle asked.

Harris jerked his head to the right. "Got out on the soft shoulder. Lucky there was an old farm road or something. Bounced down there. Then I found a ditch."

"Do you need an ambulance or something?"

"No, just give me a minute. I'll be OK," Harris replied. The guy was being so helpful that he almost felt guilty for what he planned to do. Almost.

"I do need a tow out of the ditch though," Harris said. "I'd appreciate the help."

Doyle looked down the dark farm road where Harris had indicated earlier. "You must be way back there."

Harris nodded. "I kept going, thinking I could find an easier place to turn around. Found a ditch instead."

Doyle gestured for Harris to climb into the cab. "What the hell? It's not like I have any plans for tonight. C'mon, let's get you pulled out."

Harris walked around to the passenger seat. "Thank you. I can pay you for your time."

Doyle was already in the cab as Harris climbed in. "Pay me? C'mon, man. What do I look like to you? I'm happy to help out. Hell, I just hope I can find the deer you hit. Two deer are better than one, you know what I'm saying?"

The truck rumbled to a start and Doyle backed up until the tire tracks from Harris's car were visible in the pickup's halogen headlights. He spun the wheel and followed the tracks down the short embankment to a leaf-covered dirt road.

"This is Leif Gustav's old farm back here," Doyle murmured. "Died about ten years ago; no one's worked it since, I don't think."

"That's right, back at the station you said you were born and raised here. You must know about pretty much everyone in town."

"Hell, you could know everyone in town yourself in a day or two," Doyle said. "Damn, man. Where is this car at?"

"Keep going," Harris said. "Just down here."

"Did your brakes stop working or something?"

"There," Harris said, pointing to the left. His car was buried nose-first in a thicket.

Doyle put the truck in park. "You can't get out of that? Doesn't look like it's in much of a ditch."

Harris shrugged. "Well, I sure couldn't get it out."

They both got out of the truck and walked around to the front.

"Keys?" Doyle asked.

"I left them in it. Figured it wasn't going anywhere."

Doyle walked up to the car and got down on his knees to look underneath. He got up, climbed in and cranked the engine. The motor revved and then the car lurched backward, coming out of the thicket so easily that Doyle nearly careened into his own truck. He opened the door and was about to climb out when something inside the car seemed to catch his eye. Harris walked back from the truck cab just in time to see Doyle reach up and pull the photo off of the sun visor where he'd left it for the man to find. There was a long pause as Doyle studied the photo. When he finally climbed out, he still had it in his hand.

"What's this about?" he demanded. "Who are you?"

"Do you know who that is?" Harris said, standing right next to the truck's headlight so that Doyle couldn't see him.

"Sure, that's Tracy Bain," Doyle said. "I thought you said you were just passing through."

"I'm afraid I wasn't being entirely honest with you," Harris said. "Tell me what you know about her."

"Fuck yourself, man," Doyle said. His body tensed, it was the same body language Harris had noticed when the man had gotten out of his car back at the gas station. Hyper-aware. Seeing danger in every shadow. The difference was this time Doyle was right. There was something in the shadows to be worried about.

Doyle walked toward Harris. "Wait, did you set this up? Is that why––"

The shotgun blast hit Doyle's midsection, picking him up off the ground and throwing him backward. The smoke from the barrel swirled in the shafts of light from the pickup's headlights. Harris lowered the shotgun and walked up to where Doyle writhed on the ground.

"You know, you really shouldn't hunt alone," Harris said. "When accidents like this happen, it's best to have a buddy with you."

Doyle cried out through gritted teeth.

"Come on, roll over," Harris said. "Let me look at it."

He pulled Doyle's arm and the man rolled onto his back with a scream. The camo jacket was shredded and drenched in blood. Harris wrinkled his nose at the foul smell.

"Nothing worse than a GI tract ripped open," Harris said. He took on a sympathetic look. "Hope you don't mind me saying this, but you smell awful inside."

Doyle curled up, clutching both hands to his abdomen. He seemed to get the pain more in control. Enough anyway to cast a look of pure hate toward Harris. "I'm going to kill you."

Harris laughed. "No, you're not." He kneeled down on the ground next to Doyle. "But I bet you know how gut shots work,

163

don't you? Long, nasty business. So, here's our plan." He held up the photo of the girl he'd only known as Catherine Fews up to this point. "You're going to tell me everything you know about Tracy Bain. I want to know who her boyfriends were. What she has for family. Where they live. All of it. You got that?"

Doyle tried to say something but it came out as a mumble. There was a lot of blood in the man's mouth and Harris worried that he might have punctured a lung or two. That would make the interrogation a short ride. Doyle kept mumbling and Harris moved closer to hear what he was saying.

"What is it?" Harris said.

"F...fu...ck...off..." Doyle said.

He lurched up and spit a mouthful of blood into Harris's face, then fell back, mewling in pain.

Harris stood, spitting and wiping the blood from his face. He pulled out a knife, sliding a finger across the blade.

"You know what?" he asked Doyle. "Part of me was kind of hoping you'd say that."

CHAPTER 28

Allison had the car running as Jason Aldean sang a sweet song to her on the radio. She thought about texting an update to Mason, but quickly put the thought aside. She wasn't convinced that he was completely innocent in the deaths of Suzanne Greenville or Tracy Bain. The circumstances around them were too much of a coincidence to be swept under the rug.

Mason had the big three dialed in: means, motive and opportunity. With essentially unlimited means through his position and with the last year to develop and execute the plan, there was no doubt it was something he could pull off. As for motive, it was clear that the videos would give him tremendous political leverage at a time in his career when he needed it most. But her nagging doubt wasn't the same thing as incriminating evidence. There were hundreds of plausible explanations how Tracy Bain had come to mimic Suzanne Greenville. But it didn't seem likely that they happened completely independently of one another. There was a connection somewhere and she couldn't discount the fact that Mason was the most obvious choice, but only if she was willing to believe he could stoop that low.

She had to remind herself to separate her idealized version of Mason-the-savior-of-the-Bureau from the more realistic Mason-the-career-bureaucratic-infighter. To survive as long as he had in Washington, there was bound to be a ruthless side to the man. Just wanting the videos showed that part of his personality, but what if that wasn't all there was to it? What if he'd been the one to recruit the girls and set them on the path that led to their deaths?

No, it was ridiculous to imagine him personally discussing such a thing directly with a woman. But he might have set the program up. Tasked someone to run it for him. Or, more likely, he'd been disappointed when the hoped-for windfall never appeared from Suzanne Greenville so he'd taken matters into his own hands and replicated the model with Tracy Bain.

But if he already had the videos, why did he need her to find them?

The answer she wanted to believe was that he cared about who killed Tracy Bain. Or that he was truly worried that the videos might be used to compromise government officials.

She was afraid the real answer was that he only had some of the videos and he wanted the rest. Not only that, but he knew that the videos were only valuable if he was the sole owner of them.

Allison opened her phone and dialed the new contact she had just put in the phone from Jordi's notes. She checked her watch. Almost eleven o'clock. Her father used to say that no good news came by phone after ten o'clock. In her career, she'd delivered enough bad news to people to know it didn't discriminate and could come at any time. The call from a lawyer to let you know a rich uncle left millions in his will came during business hours. But the late-night call held the most potential for terrible, life-changing revelations.

The tentative voice that answered the phone sounded aware of this truism.

"Hello?"

"Is this Natalie Bain?" Allison asked.

"Speaking." Allison heard country music and the sound of men laughing in the background.

"Ms. Bain, my name is Special Agent Allison McNeil. I'm calling you regarding your sister, Tracy." A long pause. "Do you have a sister named Tracy?"

"She owe money or something?" Natalie said. "I don't have anything to do with her. Haven't seen her in years."

"No, it's not like that. I'm with the FBI."

A harsh burst of laughter belched from the phone. "Yeah right, nice try," Natalie said. "Listen here. Don't call again. I want nothing to do with her and she damn well knows it."

"I'm coming up to Harlow and I'd like to talk to you. Tonight if possible. I'm about an hour and a half from town. I know it's late, but do you think--"

"I'm working tonight, lady," Natalie said. "Leave me the hell alone."

The line clicked and went dead. Allison would have thrown the phone at the windshield except that she needed both of them intact.

She spotted Mike emerging from the convenience store, a couple of hot dogs, bags of chips and two huge fountain sodas balanced in his arms.

"Everything OK?" Mike asked.

Allison ignored the question and redialed the phone. It went straight to voicemail.

"Damn it," she said, waiting for the message to end. "It's Allison again. I really need to speak with you tonight. It's urgent that I—"

The automated voice chirped at her through the phone, "Recording ended. Press one if you want—"

Allison hung up.

"Boyfriend?" Mike asked, sliding into his seat.

Allison considered telling him everything. He was going to find out once they got into town anyway. She had the feeling he wasn't going to be content to wait in the car like an obedient dog on a road trip. But she decided against it. Truth was, she'd spent the last hours trying to figure out how to welch on her deal with the reporter while retaining the most dignity and integrity possible. No simple task. So far the only plan she'd been able to concoct was to bean Mike over the head with the car's tire iron and hope for a bad case of amnesia. She didn't think that move was in the Bureau's approved handbook of how to deal with the press though. She decided to punt.

"No," she said. "It was nothing." She nodded toward the pile of junk food in his arms in a bid to change the subject. "Ever heard of fruit and vegetables?"

He looked down at the mass of junk food, apparently willing to continue to play the game where she kept all the secrets. "Oh, are you hungry too? I should have gotten you something. This is just for me."

"Is that so? You always eat two of everything?" she asked.

"Emotional eater." He shrugged. "If you want I can go see if there's some fresh fruit. Maybe some tofu and wheatgrass?"

"I'll take a dog and some chips," Allison said.

He held them toward her. "Regular or this one's filled with nacho cheese and jalapenos."

Allison laughed. "Nacho cheese and jalapenos. Go big or go home, right?"

He handed over the hot dog and little packets of mustard, ketchup and relish. "And here're napkins because I assume you're a messy eater."

"Hey, what's that all about?"

"Am I right?"

There was a reason she usually stuffed an extra shirt in her bag. "No, you're not."

He grinned. "Like I said, you're a terrible liar."

Allison accepted the clump of napkins, finding that she enjoyed the small gesture. Enjoyed someone pampering her just a little.

She put the car into gear and steered with one hand as she devoured the hot dog. She felt bad for all her negative thoughts about junk food earlier. The dog was simply goddamn delicious.

"What did you find out?" Mike asked, his tone casual. Almost too casual. "Do you have her real name?"

Allison tensed. Nothing like a direct question from a reporter to ruin a great meal.

"Yeah, I have a real name," she said.

Garth Brooks had taken over on the radio. One of his old songs about a truck driver finding his cheating wife. It was amazing that even with the music, it felt like there was an awkward silence in the car.

"So, what are the rules here?" Mike asked. "You plan on keeping me in the dark? Maybe blindfold me or something?"

Allison stared at the road, thinking it through. Truth was, she wasn't sure how to play this.

"So who was on the phone?" Mike asked.

She wiped her mouth while steering with her knee. "Just trying to get in touch with people in the girl's hometown."

"It's going to be past midnight before we get there. Shouldn't we just try in the morning?"

Allison remembered the background sounds she heard on the phone call. It was a long shot but it was worth trying. "Whoever the killer is wants the same thing we do. If he tracks down the girl's hometown the way we did, then these people could be in trouble. We're going up there tonight."

"If they're in trouble, then we should warn them, right?" Mike asked. "Or shouldn't we have taken a helicopter up? The FBI still has those, don't they?"

Allison shrugged.

"So either you're willing to put innocent people in harm's way so you stay off the radar," Mike continued, "or you don't really think they're in any real danger and you're just using that as an excuse."

"An excuse for what?" she asked, not really liking his ability to read her so easily.

"I don't know. To play super-cop. To find the bad guy doing something no one else would do." Mike finished off the last bite of his hot dog and chewed with a goofy smile. "Fine with me. Makes for a better story."

Allison scrunched up the empty food wrapper and tossed it in the backseat. She didn't know why she felt she needed to defend herself to this guy. Maybe it was because he'd tapped into the small splinter of guilt that had been working its way into her conscience since the morgue. She was withholding evidence in a murder investigation from the team tasked with the case. That wasn't going to win her any friends in the Bureau, with or without Mason's blessing. She decided to come clean, even if just to see how the justification she'd come up with in her own mind sounded out loud.

"OK, you're right. I don't think it's likely the killer could beat us up there, not even with the info from Maurice about the tattoo. If he did, he wouldn't know what he was looking for. Flashing a photo after midnight saying you're looking for a woman whose name you don't know would draw too much attention."

"Isn't that what we're going to do?"

"*We're* not doing anything," Allison said. She mulled over how much to tell him about the phone conversation. Not much. "I'm reaching out to a family member."

"Who's the family member?"

"Can we stop with the questions? Our deal was that you hold off on the story and I bring you along. You're here, aren't you?"

"Come on," Mike said. "If I wanted to screw you over I could have made a call while we were back at that gas station and got my researcher to dive into the Harlow High School archives. Not only that, but I could have filed a story on my iPad about the murder at the morgue to run in tomorrow's paper. Or even posted it right to the online edition."

Allison shot him a look. "Did you?"

"No," Mike said. "Because I promised I wouldn't."

Allison barked out a short laugh. "A promise from a reporter?" She felt bad the second the words were out. It felt like she took the last few hours of enjoyable conversation and dumped them right into the trash. If Mike was offended, he didn't show it.

"OK, let's take trust out of the equation," Mike said. "Let's go for pure, unadulterated self-interest."

"Now you have my attention," Allison said.

"You guessed it right earlier. All the way back in Tryst. Garret has been a great source for a lot of years. It's the perfect relationship. I get access to serial killer cases that no one else can get."

"And Garret gets the spotlight."

"Exactly," Mike continued. "And we both know he loves being the center of attention. But it's not going to last forever. It's clear that you're the rising star over there."

"I wouldn't say that."

"The whole Arnie Milhouse thing last year was buttoned up. Garret said he was maintaining confidentiality on it for reasons he couldn't tell me, but I think he just didn't know shit and was embarrassed to be iced out."

"That was one case. Shit!" Allison said as a glob of nacho cheese squirted from the hot dog onto her lap. Grinning, Mike passed her extra napkins.

"Garret gave me his version of Sam Kraw," Mike said.

"Yeah, I saw it in the paper," Allison said.

"So you do read me."

"I looked it up at the truck stop."

"And?"

"Decent. I mean, half the facts are wrong, but you used a lot of five-dollar words that made you sound smart."

Mike flushed red. "There were a few details taken out at the Bureau's request."

Allison nodded. It was common practice for the team to hold back a few details from the public. It made it easy to identify the sickos who called in trying to take credit for the murders. That and copycat killers who hoped replicating a murder in the headlines would get their crime scene to just blend in to a larger investigation. "Those weren't the details I was referring to," Allison said coolly.

"Then let me set the record straight. Tell me what really happened."

Allison took another bite of her hot dog and spoke through a mouthful of food. "This...is...good..."

"You're not going to talk about Kraw, are you?"

Allison smiled, pointed to her full mouth and shrugged.

"OK, let's leave Kraw for now. How about we just agree that you seem to have a knack for ending up in the middle of the most interesting cases?"

Allison nodded. It reminded her of the old Chinese curse: *May you live in interesting times.* In her world, an interesting case meant some innocent person, or usually several of them, had met untimely and gruesome deaths.

"OK, so?"

"So, I'm only relevant if I have access to stories that other people don't have," Mike said. "My relationship with you is a long-term investment. I'm not going to go around you for just this one story. I'm here to build trust between us."

"You're here because you threatened to release details of what happened at the morgue. Blackmail is a tough start if you want a trusting relationship."

"True," Mike said. "But that was just a way to get your attention so I could have some time with you and ply you with all my charm and wit."

"You're saying the threat to run the story was just to get time alone with me?"

"Yeah."

"So, if I let you out here, you wouldn't run the story at the morgue? The tattoo? My name?"

Mike made a show of looking around the lonely stretch of dark highway they were on. "You'd drop me off out here?"

"The thought has crossed my mind."

"If there's Internet out here, then the story would be in the online edition within ten minutes."

"See?"

"What do you mean, see?" Mike said, throwing his hands up in mock exasperation. "You're the one who left me on the side of some abandoned highway. What'd you expect? That I'd thank you and put the story in a bottle?"

"Then you're still holding that story over my head."

"We both have something," Mike said, turning more serious. "I have information that you don't want getting out in the mainstream press just yet. You have a front row seat to the big leagues of chasing bad guys."

"I'm not Garret. I don't want the spotlight."

"You don't have to be in the spotlight. It's up to you if you want to provide anything to me or not. All I'm saying is that if you do give something to the press, I'm just looking for a little advance notice. In my business, an hour head start might as well be an exclusive."

"Mutual self-interest," Allison said.

"Exactly. If I screw you on this one story, I'd be shooting myself in the foot."

"What makes you think I'll feed you information in the future once you don't have something hanging over my head?"

Mike shrugged. "Maybe you won't. But things have a way of working out. I'm an optimist."

Allison figured the optimism was more borderline arrogance, but she held back on making the observation. Whether she liked it or not, Mike was along for the ride. And she couldn't deny that she'd enjoyed the last few hours they'd spent together. She wasn't sure when she'd spent that kind of time with a man having a conversation. Hell, she didn't really have a girlfriend she even spoke with for that long either. Her dad and her cases absorbed all the bandwidth she had. But that was another reason for her to put up her guard. She didn't want there to be any blind spots in her judgment simply because he could carry on a decent conversation. Still, maybe there was reason for optimism.

She smiled and then chuckled softly. "Shooting yourself in the foot?" Allison said. "Pretty cliché for a writer."

"My writing gets the benefit of editing. Speaking...not so much."

Allison took a deep breath. "Her sister's in town. Works at a bar from the sounds I heard in the background. That's where we're going."

Mike nodded. "Thanks. I appreciate you trusting me."

"It might not be too valuable though. You were right earlier, hard to say how close the killer might be to Harlow. If we don't come up with something tonight, I'm calling in the information I have. Once I do that, I'm likely off the case."

CHAPTER 29

Clarence Mason stood from behind his desk in the small home office and stretched his neck left and right, moving slow and careful. At his age, even stretching felt like a risk. He knew it was all in his head, but he couldn't help but imagine that a wrong rotation could snap a dried-out ligament or crack a brittle bone. Growing old was a terrible thing. Not a day passed without some kind of indignity. Whether a sideways glance in a mirror after a shower that showed drooping, splotchy skin hanging from his boney carriage, or the sixth visit to the john at night that resulted in the barest dribble of urine, or catching a subordinate speaking more slowly or louder than normal as if he were a normal run-of-the-mill octogenarian sliding downhill back toward infancy where he would gum his food and shit his pants.

He also noticed it took a little longer each morning to get himself going. It wasn't until he pulled his tie knot snug to his collar that he began to feel like himself. Decked out in a suit from Anderson & Sheppard, a landmark tailor on London's Savile

Row, he looked not much different from the man he remembered seeing in the mirror twenty or thirty years ago. Thinner on top and more wrinkles etched into his face to be sure, but the posture and the confidence were there once the suit was on. And if he looked hard enough into his own eyes, he could imagine the twenty-five-year-old altruist staring back at him. But that young man was long gone. Clarence Mason had seen too much for that version of himself to have survived.

But on nights like this one where the hours slid by without his really noticing and the thought of sleep held no appeal, he felt age catching up with him no matter what he was wearing. He padded through his apartment to the kitchen where the decaf coffee waited for him in a steaming pot. He poured the dark roast into a cup and savored the smell before taking a sip. He read the text message a third time, gaming out the conversation he was about to have. Turns out he didn't have time to prepare as his phone rang ten minutes earlier than the time promised in the message.

"We're speaking twice in one week," Mason said. "People will start talking."

"Any news?" came Libby's voice through the receiver. His voice sounded hoarse and tired.

"There's always news, Marshall."

A heavy exhalation from the other end. Mason pictured his son in a dark hotel room somewhere on the campaign trail, perhaps working down a bottle of booze while he was at it.

"I'm not in the mood for your games," Libby said.

"You never were," Mason replied. He thought he heard the clink of ice in a glass. "Macallan?"

There was a long pause and then a soft sigh of contentment. "Johnnie Walker Blue. An old friend of yours, I think."

"One I haven't seen in many years." Mason sat down at his kitchen table. There was nothing about this call that matched his prediction. It made him nervous. "You ought to be careful. That dog can bite."

Libby's laugh came back quick and harsh. "You're giving me drinking advice?"

"In case you forgot, you called me." A pause. Mason let it play out. Another clink of ice in a tumbler. Mason hated how the sound made his jaw ache, anticipating the taste of a drink he'd wanted for over a decade.

"Is there news?"

"I don't know what to tell--"

"Did you have the girl killed?"

Mason clutched the phone tighter and felt his shoulders bunch. For a man trained to never show his emotion, even when alone in a room, it was a telling reaction. He glanced at the mirror on the far wall and felt a rising disgust for the weak, old man staring back at him.

"No, of course not," Mason said.

"*Of course not,*" Libby mocked, doing a pretty good imitation of his father. "Because you'd never do anything like that, right? You're one of the good guys."

Mason heard the slur in Libby's voice again.

"How about your Senator Summerhays?" Mason asked. "Is he one of the good guys?"

"I don't know," Libby whispered. "I hoped. But then this." Then his voice grew bitter. "You just couldn't stand it, could you?"

"Stand what?"

"Seeing me succeed. Why is it such a terrible thing for you? I don't understand it."

Mason sighed and leaned back in his chair, a palm pressed against his temple. "We're not really going to do this, are we?"

The clink of ice again. This time Mason felt the saliva rush into his mouth. He caught himself looking to the apartment's kitchen, imagining the spot where he used to keep his own bottle of Johnnie Walker Blue for the nights when his mood matched the label. He knew the spot was empty but the impulse was still there.

"No, probably not. That would take two people being honest with each other. Not sure if either of us is up to that. It's just...I don't know...I just..."

"What do you need, Marshall?"

"I just need to know who to believe in. Maybe the answer is no one. Not any more. This fucking town, right?"

Mason felt tears well in his eyes. He wondered at his own reaction. Libby's voice had cracked just a bit as he spoke, but he couldn't fathom why it would have hit him so hard. Maybe it was hearing his own cynicism thrown back at him. Or perhaps it was the deep-seated need of a father wanting his son's love and admiration. And the honest self-appraisal that he likely deserved neither.

"This fucking town," Mason agreed.

Clink. Clink.

That long pause and Mason felt his throat constrict as if he were doing the drinking instead of his son on the other end of the line.

"Help me out on this one," Libby said in a detached boozy voice. "I don't need to know if you had anything to do with the girl's death. Just Summerhays. Tell me that."

Mason rolled over the possible answers in his mind, wanting to choose his words carefully, not quite trusting himself given his unusual emotionalism. Libby filled the silence.

"Just tell me why you have this second investigation going outside the regular channels. Is there something that bad coming?"

Mason sat up straight in his chair, the sensation of ice-cold water pouring down his back. He'd caught a slight change in Libby's tone and a realization struck him with the force of an electric shock. His emotions went from shock to anger to embarrassment, and then to a perverse sense of pride in his son.

"How's the ice water, Marshall?"

A long pause, then a few clinks of ice and a slurping sound. "Refreshing," Libby said, all traces of his boozy speech pattern gone. "It's a Diet Coke actually."

"Those things will kill you."

Libby laughed but there was no joy in it.

"Pretty decent idea, playing on the emotions of an old man, calling late, apparently drunk. Going for the sympathy card," Mason said. "Impressive."

"How about rewarding the effort with some information?" Libby said, his speech alert and clipped. "This Allison McNeil. What's she after? Why is she working outside the system on this case?"

Mason cursed under his breath even as he again felt pride about the intel his son was able to collect. "Allison McNeil? The agent on the Kraw shooting? She's on administrative leave as far as I know."

"So I hear," Libby said, leaving the implication that he had his own sources into Mason's beloved Bureau to hang in the air. "But then she turned up to examine Catherine Fews's body at the morgue. After she left, the orderly who helped her turned up dead. Odd way to spend your time on administrative leave."

"Everyone needs a hobby," Mason replied. "I just hope that interfering in a federal investigation isn't a new hobby of yours, Marshall. That would be a damn shame."

"Is that a warning?" Libby asked.

"No, a threat," Mason said softly. "Goodnight, Marshall. Thank you for the interesting call. We should do it again soon."

Mason ended the call and held the phone to his chest. He considered that he'd underestimated his son and perhaps his new boss as well.

There was nothing more dangerous than underestimating one's adversaries, a lesson he'd learned the hard way over a lifetime in the rough world of DC politics. He didn't intend to allow it to happen again.

CHAPTER 30

The road twisted deep into the dark mountains, skeleton trees poking bony fingers at them, potholes in the old asphalt rattling their ride. Bored, Allison purposefully drifted off the road so that the car's right tires ran over the rumble strip beside them. The rattle shook the car and Mike jerked away. He rubbed his eyes, sat up and looked at her.

"Want me to drive for a while?" he asked.

"Do I want you to drive the last half hour of a six-hour car ride?"

"Should have asked earlier, huh?"

"If you were trying to be polite."

"Would you have let me drive?" Mike asked.

Allison thought about it. "No. Probably not."

"Then I really wish I'd offered. Could have looked good and still taken a nap. Best of all worlds. Where are we?"

"Middle-of-nowhere, West Virginia and about to go even farther off the beaten path."

"This is coal country," Mike said. "I investigated a story in a place like this a few years ago. One of Garret's cases."

"Oswald Perkins," Allison said. "Ten years ago."

"Ten years? Jesus, you're right." Mike shifted in his chair. "One sick puppy if ever there was one. I met him a few times."

Allison wasn't impressed. "I've watched the tapes of his interviews with Garret."

"No, I mean I met him a few times before Garret figured out he was the guy. Before the standoff and the fire."

This had her attention. She'd studied the case, of course. She'd studied every major serial killer case in the last forty years, but even in her world of aberrant behavior, Oswald Perkins stood out. He was special. And that meant he was doubly deranged and wicked in his killing ways.

"How did that happen?" she asked.

"Garret had the wrong guy at first, a preacher named Dan Jenks. Remember that? Brought him in for questioning but had to turn him loose. Didn't have anything specific, just suspicions from some of the locals and a few circumstantial facts that gave him opportunity on some of the missing girls." He paused, popped the lid from his drink and rolled an ice cube into his mouth.

"And Garret told you this while the investigation was still active?" Allison asked.

Mike crunched the ice with his teeth and shrugged. "Let's just say I didn't decide to drive out to Taylorsville, West Virginia all on my own."

Allison shook her head. "Jeopardizing the case."

Mike considered the comment. "Looking back, you're right. I shouldn't have gone up there. But not for the reasons you think. The case was fine. I knew enough from working with Garret not to make a mess of things. Hell, there've been a few times when I've helped him out and given him information I found on my own. But Oswald Perkins was another matter all together. Did you ever meet him?"

"No," Allison said. "There was a plan for me to interview him. He'd been in custody for years at that point. I think Garret was playing out his *Silence of the Lambs* fantasy, but his Hannibal Lecter didn't cooperate. Perkins hung himself before it happened."

"Do you buy that it was a suicide?"

Allison nodded. "I read the report. Sloppy work by the on-duty guards to give him enough time to do it, but the investigation came out clean."

Mike gave her a look showing that he didn't buy it for a second. "Even if Perkins had turned up with three shots to the chest from the guard's gun instead of dangling with his toes six inches off the floor, that coroner's report would have listed it as a suicide."

"Maybe." She didn't care for the insinuation that she was naïve, but she felt like he might also be right. After what Oswald had done, it was surprising it had taken as long as it did for something to happen to him. But that wasn't the part of the story that held her interest. "Tell me about when you met him," Allison said.

"It was at Pastor Jenks's church, Taylorsville First Methodist. I knew the good pastor wasn't there so I didn't see any harm in looking around. I just wanted to see the church for myself, you know. Get the lay of the land. The caretaker was around back so I went around to say hi."

Allison knew Oswald Perkins had been the caretaker of the Methodist church in Taylorsville. She realized her stomach was clenched tight as if she were walking with Mike up to one of the worst serial killers in recent memory.

"He was digging a hole in the back and he looked up with those blue eyes of his," Mike said, staring out the window as if he were back on the church grounds. "And they just kind of locked on me. You've seen pictures, right?"

Allison nodded. "And video."

"They don't come close to capturing it. I shit you not, when that man looked me in the eye, every hair on my body stood on end. It was primal. The animal part of my brain knew the man was not like the rest of us."

"Did you talk to him?"

"You know, I must have," Mike said. "I probably asked him about the property. Maybe about Dan Jenks. But what's crazy is that I don't really remember what we talked about. It was like he drew the energy right out of the air."

Allison thought about Sam Kraw, that last haunting look he'd given her right before she pulled the trigger and blew out the back of his skull. She remembered Arnie Milhouse and how his face had changed once the charade was over between them, especially on the catamaran as they fought to the death, the human mask stripped away so there was nothing left but the monster visible underneath. She'd seen the look Mike described and knew the power inside of it.

"And how did it make you feel?" she asked softly.

Mike looked away. She noticed him biting his lip. With a glance down, she saw one of his hands gripping the door handle and the other clutching his leg.

"I felt judged," he whispered. "Inadequate. That somehow I was less than I ought to be. Less than I could be. But that's not what bothered me." His hand opened and closed on his leg, making a fist. "It's more that I...I don't know, it was like I..."

"Wanted his approval?" Allison asked, flicking her eyes from the road to her passenger, reading all the body language.

Mike nodded. "I didn't just want his approval. Within a few minutes of talking to him, I needed it. I craved it." He let out a short bark of a laugh. "How screwed up is that? Especially given who he really was. All those horrific things he did." He looked embarrassed. "I don't know why I'm even telling you this."

"Nothing to be ashamed of," Allison said. "Serial killers are often charismatic figures, especially ones that unite their personas with religious imagery."

"Unite their personas with religious imagery?" Mike asked, the bitterness clear in his voice. "Is that what the textbooks say? 'Cause that's a pretty fucking clinical description of what that asshole did to those little girls. Did you see photos in a class? Read a report? Well, I saw the girls in person, OK? What was left of them. I saw what he did. It was too much." His voice trailed off. "Too much."

The silence hung in the car between them. Allison realized that at some point in the conversation her hand had reached out and instinctively turned off the radio. The only sound was the thump of the tires on the road and the low *whirr* of the car's heater. Allison had been in enough therapy herself to know it was best to let the moment breathe.

After a minute, Mike let go of the door handle and folded his hands across his legs. He took a deep breath and exhaled slowly. It came out in short shudders, as if he were suddenly cold. "Wow, didn't expect to go there," he said. "Sorry I got so worked up."

"Don't apologize," Allison said. "The things we see, the world we live in, it wears on you after a while. I know, trust me. Sometimes I wonder if it's worth it."

"Then why do you do it?"

Allison considered the question, mentally clicking the dial on the level of honesty she was willing to give this strange man who had been in her life for less than a day. "It used to be so I could make them stop. You know, catch the bad guys."

"Used to be?"

"I still want to stop them," Allison said. She hesitated, knowing she ought not to say the next words. But she liked this guy and he'd shared something personal with her, so it felt like a betrayal holding back the truth. "When I shot Sam Kraw, I pretended to feel bad about it, but I didn't. He deserved it. No, he deserved worse than what I gave him. I should have shot him in the gut and let him die slow. The longer I do this, the less I think about stopping them. What I really want, more than stopping them, more than putting them in jail..." She hesitated, but then decided to push through. "What I really want is to punish them."

Mike nodded and looked out the passenger window. She glanced over, trying to gauge his reaction, immediately regretting what she'd said. But it was out there now and like he'd said earlier, there was no editing feature on the spoken word. Besides, it was true. And saying it out loud felt good.

"I've been trying to make sense of what I do for years now," he said, shaking his head. His voice was distant and flat, so different from his usual tone. "I don't know why I can't stop." So quiet now that she almost couldn't hear. "It's just something inside of me. It's who I am. I don't think it's possible for me to stop, not even if I wanted to."

Allison realized that Mike's beat covering serial killer cases, especially with the special access afforded him by Garret, put him on the front lines like any of them at CID. Only they were trained to deal with it and were surrounded daily by people who knew to look for the warning signs of someone burning out. Even so, there was a revolving door at the dark, murky corner of the Bureau where the worst cases ended up. Eager crime fighters came in, ready to find and arrest the big bads of the world. Months later, many of them left, cynical and damaged, wracked with nightmares no amount of self-medication could stop. She imagined crime reporters experienced the same thing.

She'd seen it happen both ways, either a slow build of too many crime scenes over a long period that wore someone down until their nerves were paper thin, or a single scene that broke them in two. The cases with children were the hardest, of course. The juxtaposition of the innocence of a child and the depravity of a diseased mind. The Oswald Perkins case had retired a few agents from the field.

The photos of the scene Allison had studied were stark and over-exposed from the powerful external flashes set up by the crime scene photographer. It was in a cave, an off-shoot of one of the old abandoned mines that dotted the area. The five girls had been positioned in a wide circle around a fire pit in the center of the cave. The pit was just a pile of ash and charred wood by the time the picture was taken, but it wasn't hard to imagine a fire going, smoke going up a natural flue in the cave ceiling. Oswald Perkins had later described how he liked to sit next to that fire, crouched down on his knees in prayer, shuffling in a circle around the fire pit. As he did, he looked through the fire at each of his girls, arms spread wide, feet together, nailed to the rough-cut wooden crosses made from old mining timbers.

The heavy nails went through their ankles and wrists, both for historical accuracy and pragmatic reasons, as Oswald later explained. Even though the oldest of the five girls was only nine and well under eighty pounds, a nail in the palm of the hand wouldn't support the weight. Bone was needed for that job. Otherwise the nail just ripped through eventually. And it needed to last because Oswald Perkins liked to keep the girls alive for as long as possible.

The suffering was necessary for their purity, he explained later in the interviews. *I think they were thankful for it. Yes, come to think of it, I'm sure all my girls enjoyed their time with me. Why wouldn't they? I made them pure.*

Allison thought of the way Oswald had died, strips of his own clothing tied together into a hangman's noose. Nothing in his profile suggested he would commit suicide. If anything, he loved the attention he was getting. It fit perfectly into his messianic complex, a prophet brought before the Pharisees for persecution. Maybe Mike was right. Maybe it was those lines about the girls liking it that finally did it for the guards who decided to personally reinstate the death penalty in West Virginia and save the taxpayers the expense of incarcerating Oswald for the rest of his life.

186

"Maybe we think we're still doing good," Allison said. "Preventing the next victim."

"Maybe you are," Mike said, his voice trailing off as he stared out the window.

They passed a rusted sign that proclaimed that the town of Harlow was only five miles away. Mike rubbed his face with his hands and shook his arms loose. He reached out and turned the radio back on. It was two parts country music and one part static, but it filled the air with something other than their own dark thoughts. It was a clear signal. Therapy was over. Time to get back to work.

"OK, boss," he said, the over-confident bravado back in his voice. "What's the plan?"

CHAPTER 31

Some towns appear to be ghosts of their former selves. The kind of place where old, stately mansions crumble in their last stages of life, with sagging rooflines and flaking paint, segmented into apartments for working-class families. These towns usually have the vestiges of a downtown, a few blocks of plywood-covered brick storefronts, laid out in a grid with plenty of parking for non-existent shoppers. There might also be a wide public square with an oversized gazebo where the band used to play on Friday evenings, only it's fenced off as a hazard of rusty nails and splintered boards.

The town of Harlow, West Virginia had none of these things. This wasn't a town that had lost its grip on past greatness, nor was it one with greatness ahead of it, if the last hundred and fifty years were any indication. It had never been a trading post for settlers traveling westward in pursuit of a better life, nor had a railroad once made a fortuitous stop there, which was often the happenstance that turned once small, rural villages into full-blown towns. There had never been a strike of a coal vein rich enough to cause one of the large companies from Pittsburgh or Baltimore to pump investments into the town the way they had in nearby Evansburg and Falston Heights. Harlow was about as Podunk as a town could get and still have the balls to give itself a name.

Allison coasted through the tiny downtown, a collection of eight buildings, four on each side of the road. Three of them were shuttered. Two were diners with signs in the windows declaring their price war on breakfast. *Coffee 50c! Hungry Man's Breakfast $1.95.* The other stores were a general grocer, a hardware store and a feed shop. All closed.

"Finally, a town without a Starbucks," Mike said.

Allison pointed to one of the diners. In the corner of the front window was the ubiquitous green mermaid and the tagline: Proudly serving Starbucks coffee.

Mike pointed to the other diner. The owner of that establishment had the same logo and tagline, only there was a red circle and a line through it and the word "NOT" inserted between the words proudly and serving.

"The battle lines have been drawn," Allison said.

"I know where I'm going in the morning," Mike said, nodding at the diner with the negation sign over the mermaid. "That's the owner I want to meet."

She scanned the streets but didn't see any sign of life.

"So, what are we looking for?" Mike asked.

"The bar noise is all we have to go on. Usually, even a little town like this has at least one watering hole."

"The best dive bars are on the edge of town, not in the middle of them," Mike said. "I'm sure even a place like Harlow once had its share of town mothers who didn't want all the drunks and fast girls right where everyone could see them. Keep driving."

"You seem to know a lot about dive bars."

"My occupation requires it," Mike said. "Look, up there. You can kind of see a glow. Bet you a buck it's a sign that says something like Mike's Place or Billy Ray's."

Allison drove by the last few houses in town and followed the road on a curve to the right. Sure enough, there was an old lit-up sign on a rusty pole in a parking lot with a dozen cars. It was an odd building that looked like three different shacks had been smashed together and had their common walls torn down to create enough space inside so most of the town could get drunk together if they wanted to. Half of the lights in the sign were out and those remaining flickered. Even so, it was possible to make out the name of the place. Billy Ray's Saloon.

Allison looked over to a grinning Mike who held up his iPhone. "You know, they have apps for this stuff nowadays."

"Anyone ever tell you you're a smart ass?"

"All the time. Look, it's one of your fellow law enforcement officers."

Allison followed his gaze and saw a sheriff's blazer parked next to the side door. She groaned. Locals weren't always excited about the FBI poking around in their back yards. Sometimes you'd get an overeager FBI wannabe who fell over themselves to help out, but usually it was the exact opposite and they were just a pain in the ass. It was one of the few things the cop movies got right.

She parked the car. "He's probably off-duty. No reason to bother him if it's not necessary." She turned off the ignition. "Don't suppose you'll stay here and wait for me?"

Mike nodded to the bar. "A single woman looking the way you do walks into a local dive bar alone at midnight. How do you think that's going to go?"

"You're worried whether I can handle myself?" Allison asked. "That's sweet."

"I have no doubt you can handle yourself," he said. "I'm just saying that if you go in alone, you'll be fending off the sharks instead of doing what you need to do. Besides," he added, opening the door, "there's no way I'm staying in here." He climbed out.

Allison got out and met him at the back of the car. "OK, but let me talk to her. Don't forget you're the guest on this trip."

"Yes, ma'am."

As they walked to the door, Allison noticed that the sheriff's blazer was parked in the only handicap spot. Even better, a bumper sticker of a large-breasted woman with a police hat and handcuffs covered the rear fender. *I Love Badge Bunnys,* it proclaimed.

"Class act," Mike said.

With a deep breath, Allison stepped into the bar.

Billy Ray's Saloon was low-life enough to give dive bars a bad name. Poor lighting that cast long shadows. Musty air that smelled of stale beer, peanut shells and a faint whiff of urine. A dartboard. Pool table with so many stains on the felt that it looked like a work of splatter art. There were tables and booths spread throughout the place, few of them matching any of the others. While the mismatched look was popular in some trendy cafes, it didn't take much to guess that Billy Ray, if there really was someone who still owned the place with that name, had simply pieced together a collection of furniture from whatever sources he could. An old jukebox hugged the wall near the pool table, pouting in the shadows with a thick power cord wrapped into a knot and thrown on top of it. Still, country music played in the background from speakers over the bar, probably plugged into someone's phone. The ceiling height varied in elevation in the three sections, each eight feet or less, giving the space a compressed feel. Everywhere, that was, except at the bar.

The ceiling here soared to twelve feet which, after walking through the rest of the establishment, felt like a cathedral-sized space. In a way it was, and the supplicants here took their prayers seriously. Instead of rosaries and Hail Mary's, they washed away their sins through other rituals.

Shot. Beer. Shot.

Peace be with you.
Salt. Tequila. Lime.
And also with you.

A low rectangular platform at one end of the room was ostensibly for a band to play, a time when the rickety chairs could be pulled back for a dance floor and the place could roar with good times. But it didn't look like that had been Billy Ray's scene for a lot of years, maybe ever. There were a few guys in their twenties at the pool table, missing easy shots, smoking, joking and wasting their paychecks, but they were the exception to the serious drinkers at Billy Ray's.

This wasn't a place to party. It was a place where fifty-year-old men talked about high school football games where they were heroes. Where lonely women, the kind dragging a luggage train of bad decisions behind them, used too much makeup and wore revealing clothes to show they still had the goods. A little worn, a little saggy, but goods nonetheless. It was the kind of place where those hunched over on their barstools imagined lives different from the ones they'd lived and did their damned best to drown out the voices in their heads that whispered mean truths about their value to the world. The kind of place where once the bell rang and the last drink was poured, the slow game of musical chairs would begin. Who went home alone and who got laid changed from night to night, but no matter how it turned out, they'd all be back the next night to roll the dice again.

By the look of things, Allison sensed the night was winding down. The few women she spotted in the place were all pressed up near a man, or pinned between two vying for her attention. Heads turned to look at them when they entered but it wasn't the record scratching to a stop moment she feared. Mike was right about one thing. As soon as he walked in behind her, the men turned back to their drinks and their thoughts.

She spotted the sheriff in a booth to one side, sidled up to a large woman with a nest of hair with enough product in it for an entire salon. He was in uniform and the table in front of him was covered with empty beer bottles. He didn't even bother looking up when they walked in.

The layout made sightlines through the place easy enough and it was clear that the person she was looking for wasn't there. According to Jordi, Tracy's sister was twenty-five. None of the women here came close. She walked up to the bar and an old coot with gnarled hands and a bald head thumped two drink napkins on his bar.

"What'll it be?" he asked.

Allison checked out the tap and saw Bud, Bud Light and Pabst Blue Ribbon. Behind the bartender a neon sign proclaimed Budweiser to be the King of Beers. She didn't agree, but it would work for that night.

"Two Bud Lights," she said.

"Shot a' rye for a buck?"

"You bet," Mike said. "Are you Billy Ray?"

"Nup."

"What's your name, friend?" Mike asked.

"Sure as hell ain't friend," the bartender growled as he pulled the beers. "Ned's fine."

Allison noticed the glasses Ned was using weren't quite spotless. Nothing the alcohol couldn't kill.

The glasses were slid toward them and Allison took a drink. Even though she usually dismissed Bud Light as beer-flavored water, she had to admit it tasted damn good after the long ride. She asked, "Natalie here tonight?"

"Don't know any Natalies," Ned said without looking up. He busied himself pouring the two shots of rye.

She glanced at Mike and could tell from his expression that he didn't believe the old man either.

"Sure you do," Mike said. "Town like this." He turned to Allison. "What was her last name again?"

Allison's eyes burned into him. It was a cheap way to get the information out of her. She had to answer and he knew it.

"Bain," she said. "Natalie Bain."

Ned the bartender wrinkled his nose as if catching a whiff of something in the air. "Nup, don't know the name. No Bain's around here I know of."

"I talked to her earlier tonight and I thought she said she'd be here," she said. "Did she already leave?"

Ned slid the shot glasses across the bar. "Best hurry these off. Closin' soon."

Allison leaned forward. "Look, I'm not going to waste your time and pretend I'm some relative or a family friend looking for her." She opened her credentials and showed them. "My name is Allison McNeil. I'm a Special Agent with the FBI. I have reason to believe Natalie might be in danger."

Ned was good; decades of listening to blowhards on the other side of the bar had perfected his poker face. But Allison noticed an involuntary wince when she said Natalie could be in danger.

He nodded toward the sheriff. "We got our own law enforcement around here. Suggest you talk to Sheriff Frank if you think there's any trouble comin' up for this Natalie person you're talking about."

Mike stepped forward. "Looks like your sheriff has enough trouble on his hands tonight."

Ned looked over at the booth and a sneer of disgust bared his teeth before his blank expression returned. "Could be. I was married to that bitch fo' eleven year. All the places to pick up on men, she comes here."

"Women, they can be terrible creatures, man," Mike said, ignoring Allison's withering stare.

"Amen to that," Ned said. Out from below the bar, his hand came up with a shot glass of his own and he slugged it back.

"Come on," Mike continued. "You've got the FBI here at midnight looking for this girl. She's in real trouble."

"In trouble or in danger?" the bartender asked. "She said danger. Big diff'rence."

"In danger," Allison said, feeling a swell of excitement that the bartender was coming around. "Not in any kind of trouble, I swear."

Ned looked from her to Mike and waited. Mike was slow to pick up on the cue, so Allison nudged him.

"No trouble," Mike said. "She's done nothing wrong. We're purely here for her own protection."

Just then the double doors that led to the back area flew open. A young man in his late twenties backed out in a hurry, hands up in front of him. He slammed into a table and went down to the floor in a tangle of chairs. A young woman followed him out, striding toward him with purpose. She was dressed in jeans and a Billy Ray's t-shirt. Her hair was pulled back in a ponytail, revealing a beautiful face with the same high cheekbones and jawline that looked so much like her sister's that it could only be Natalie Bain.

But what was most striking about her at the moment wasn't how she looked, it was the gun she clenched with two hands in front of her as she marched toward the man on the floor.

"I'm gonna kill you this time, you son-of-a-bitch," she said. "Gonna kill you like the pig you are."

CHAPTER 32

O n impulse, Allison reached under her jacket and put her hand on her Glock. It was a reaction drilled into her by years of training but she didn't pull the gun out. Instead, she stepped in front of Mike and pushed him back, turning to the side to reduce her profile just in case bullets started to fly.

"You piece of shit, Carl," Natalie yelled. "I told you if you ever hit her again I'd shoot your nuts off. Didn't I tell you that?"

"This is between me and my wife. You need to jus' stay out of it, you crazy bitch," Carl sputtered, back-crawling through the pile of chairs behind him.

Natalie stepped closer. "Excuse me? What did you just call me?"

"You're just a crazy bitch who's gonna get hers one day," Carl said.

Allison's eyes flashed up to the back of the room where Sheriff Frank was hefting his sizeable bulk up out of his booth, leaving behind a disappointed woman who saw her chance to be that night's badge bunny slip away. He didn't seem too flustered or in too much of a hurry. In fact, looking around the bar, she realized that people were watching with interest but not shock. Just another night out at Billy Ray's Saloon where the patrons got assaulted with a gun by the waitstaff.

Natalie cocked the gun and the tone in her voice took a dangerous turn. "Threaten me again, Carl. C'mon. Let's just see how crazy I am."

"All right now, that's enough, Natalie," Sheriff Frank called out, his voice the same inflection as a parent tired of telling his kids to stop jumping on the furniture. "You've scared the piss out of him. Put the gun down."

"Did you see her, Frank?" Natalie asked, her voice trembling for the first time. "Bruises all up and down her back and arms. Used a baseball bat this time."

"She fell down some stairs," Carl said, addressing the entire bar.

Sheriff Frank stepped closer to Natalie, his hand out for the gun. "We'll deal with that shit later. You can't be pulling guns on people, even shitheads like Carl here."

"C'mon, Sheriff," Carl complained.

"Shut your hole, boy," Sheriff Frank said.

He might have been a small-time sheriff more interested in making out with Ned the bartender's ex-wife than stopping bad guys, but he was no fool. He'd picked up on the same thing Allison had. Natalie was winding up, not down. If the gun had started as a way to scare the man, it was something else now. Natalie's hands had been steady when she first walked through the door, but they shook now. The color was gone from her face. The yelling had been replaced by a flat, lifeless tone.

"Nothing's going to change, is it?" Natalie said.

"Calm down now," Sheriff Frank said, his hands up in front of him like he was walking toward a wild animal. "We'll sort this out. Get Becky in and I'll take a look."

"She fell down some *stairs*," Carl said.

"Shut the hell up, boy," Sheriff Frank muttered out of the side of his mouth. "One more word and I'm gonna shoot you myself."

Allison noticed the mood in the bar had changed. What had started as the mild interest in a fender bender had all the focus of a major train wreck about to happen. Nothing better than having a good story to tell. *Hell yeah, I was there the day Natalie Bain came raging into Billy Ray's and shot Carl's nuts clean off.* It would be a great story to have in the back pocket. Only not so good for Allison's purposes.

"Natalie," she called out.

The room turned to look at her. Everyone except for Natalie. She looked lost in her own world.

"Miss, please stay out of this," Sheriff Frank snapped.

"Natalie Bain," Allison called out louder, ignoring the sheriff and walking to the space between the woman and Carl on the ground. "We spoke on the phone earlier. I have news about your sister."

Natalie blinked hard, coming back from whatever future she'd been picturing for herself. Maybe one where she wore an orange jumpsuit for a few years with great moral authority. She stared at Allison.

"I told you, I don't want nothing to do with her," she said.

Allison took a few more steps forward, hands out to her sides.

"Can we go somewhere and talk? It's important."

Natalie shook her head and moved to the side, aiming the gun back at Carl. "Lady, I don't know who you are, but you better get out of my way. And I mean right now."

"Miss," Sheriff Frank said, raising his voice. "You better sit the hell down and let me deal with this."

Natalie laughed bitterly. "Deal with this? If you had dealt with this then Becky wouldn't be all bruised up again, would she?"

"I told you I didn't––" Carl whined.

"Shut up!" Natalie yelled.

"Natalie, calm down," Sheriff Frank said, sounding nervous for the first time.

"Not this time," Natalie said, her voice cold and laced with such finality that it seemed to suck the oxygen out of the room.

"Oh Jesus," Carl whimpered from the floor as if just realizing things were coming to a head and that he might actually get shot.

Allison watched the girl's hand grow steady as she took aim. She hated what she was about to do, but she had to break the momentum of the situation.

"Natalie," Allison said softly. "I'm sorry to tell you. But your sister's dead."

There were a few gasps around the bar. Clearly other people knew Tracy Bain. She noticed the sheriff drop his head to his chest and shake his head. But Allison mostly watched Natalie's reaction. It was impassive at first, just the cold hard stare into Carl's eyes as she contemplated the cost of gelding him right there on Billy Ray's floor. But then her eyes softened and raised just slightly so that they were staring at a point on the far wall. Tears appeared in her eyes and then welled over, tracing lines down her cheeks. Her chin quivered and her hands shook harder. Unfortunately for Carl, she didn't lower the gun even an inch.

"When?" she asked, emotion thick in her voice.

"It happened a few days ago," Allison said. "I'm sorry to tell you like this. Why don't you just hand me the gun? We'll go somewhere and I'll tell you everything."

"How?" she blurted. "How did she die? Was it an accident or something?"

"She was killed."

Murmurs among the bar crowd. This was the kind of news that would fuel bar conversations for months on end.

Sheriff Frank shot an angry look around the room and the spectators quieted down. In the silence, the country music wafted through the air, making the place feel empty and lonely. Lyrics about loss and heartache would have been appropriate, but instead some cowboy was singing about drinking and high school football, just adding to the surreal feeling of the moment.

"Come on," Allison said, stepping closer. "Hand me the gun. I don't even know this guy, but I can tell this piece of shit isn't worth going to jail for."

"But he won't stop," Natalie said, pure rage in her voice. "They never stop."

Allison turned to Carl. "Carl, are you going to stop?"

Carl nodded. Piece of shit or not, he'd clued in on the fact there was still a fifty-fifty chance he was about to get shot.

"What are you going to stop?" Allison asked.

Carl looked at her blankly.

"What did you do to your wife that you're going to stop doing?"

"I'm gonna be nice to her from now on," Carl said. Allison glared at him and he lowered his head like a scolded child. "I took a baseball bat to her. Beat her some. Didn't mean anything by it."

"Didn't mean anything by it?" Natalie demanded.

Allison put her hand up and, to her surprise, Natalie took a step back. "Have you done this before?"

Carl glanced around the room and everyone staring at him. He reluctantly nodded.

"What's that?" Allison said.

"Yes!" Carl blurted out. "OK? I hit her. But she hits me sometimes too."

"Oh, Carl," Allison said. "And we were just starting to get along." She kneeled down to his level on the floor and whispered, "I'm a psychological profiler in the FBI. I know for a fact that Natalie behind me has enough rage and grief and other conflicting emotions right now that she's prone to make an irrational judgment. In fact, I think if I stood out of the way right now, she'd shoot you right in the chest. Or probably the nuts the way she promised. Is that what you want?"

Carl shook his head.

"If I were you, I'd tell her you're going to stop. And you'd better mean it."

"I won't do it again," Carl stammered. "I promise. I swear on my mother's grave that I won't beat on her the way I've been doin'."

"OK, that's better." She turned to Sheriff Frank. "Enough of a confession for you?"

Sheriff Frank nodded and reached for his handcuffs. "C'mon, Carl. I'm taking you in. I'll read your rights in the car."

"What the hell is this?" Carl screamed. "She's the one who pulled a gun on me."

"Looks like it was a citizen's arrest to me," Sheriff Frank said. "C'mon, on your feet."

Allison took a position between Natalie and Carl as the sheriff hefted him to his feet and cuffed him. He looked at Allison. "I'm gonna put him in the car and then you and me are going to have a little chat."

Allison acknowledged him with a nod but turned her attention to Natalie, who had finally lowered the gun.

"I get it," Allison said. "I've been where you're standing. You made the right choice."

"Hey, Natalie!" Carl called from the front door, putting on a tough guy act to save some face with the bar crowd. "Like I said, you're gonna get yours one day, you crazy bitch. You think you bested me? Wait 'til I see Becky next. Jus' you wait. She's my wife. All do anything I damn well want with her. You got that? Anything I want."

"No!" Allison called out, but was too late.

Natalie raised the gun with a cry. The explosion in the enclosed space felt like it shattered the air. She fired a second time, but Allison was already on the move. She grabbed Natalie's arm in a lock, shook the gun loose, then dropped the girl to the ground, pinning her there.

She looked up at the door. Sheriff Frank and Carl were both on the ground.

Jesus, she shot them both, Allison thought.

Mike ran to the door but both men were already climbing to their feet before he got there. Neither of them had been hit. Both bullets had soared well over their heads and added some extra circulation to Billy Ray's Saloon. Allison slowly pulled Natalie upright from the floor.

"What the hell were you thinking?" she asked.

"I've been shooting since I was a kid. Wasn't even close," Natalie said. "I think I made my point, though."

The sheriff took the cuffs off Carl and walked over. He nodded his head for Natalie to hold out her hands. She did and he clicked the cuffs on her.

"After what you just heard about your sister?" he said, shaking his head. "This is the shit you're going to pull?"

"I pictured you driving Carl to his house and letting him go," she said. "And tomorrow Becky would have a black eye or another broken bone and you wouldn't do a damn thing about it. Just like I can't do a damn thing about what happened to Tracy."

Allison grabbed her by the arm. "The reason I'm here is that I think you can do something about what happened to your sister. I think you can help me find the killer."

Sheriff Frank dragged Natalie toward the door. "You two can talk down in the jail. I'm getting her out of here. Right now." He called out to Carl. "Boy, I'll be talking to you tomorrow, so don't you dare leave town. You got that?"

Allison thought about trying to stop him, but decided against it. With Carl still in the bar, it was probably for the best. Besides, if the killer was on the same trail she was, then having her in protective custody wasn't the worst thing in the world.

Mike walked up and stood next to her. "Are things always like this for you?"

Allison nodded. "Pretty much."

"Good work with her," he said. "She was teetering on the edge."

"She still took a shot at him. And at a cop."

"You heard her, those were just warning shots," Mike said. "Before that, she was thinking of doing the deed. You could see it in her eyes. She could feel the raw animal power of it and it almost dragged her in. Without you, ol' Ned would be mopping red off his floor tonight."

Allison wasn't sure what to think. Playing the events back in her head, she figured she could have played it differently at some point. Taken the weapon away more quickly was the obvious one. But, ultimately, she sensed the sheriff was the kind of guy to give her a break, especially since it seemed that he had a personal reaction on hearing about Tracy Bain's death. At least this way, she had a captive audience for questioning. As long as the sheriff played ball and gave her access.

"Come on," she said to Mike. "We're going to jail."

CHAPTER 33

I n a booth against the wall of Billy Ray's, over by the broken jukebox, Harris tipped back the last of his beer and wiped his mouth with the back of his hand. Doyle had been spot-on with his intel, even if he'd been reluctant to hand it out. Luckily, or unluckily for Doyle, Harris had a particular expertise in helping prisoners overcome their reluctance to talk. His time in beautiful vacation destinations like Syria, Afghanistan, Qatar and other "allies" of the United States intelligence apparatus had paid off. In black locations, CIA parlance for doesn't-exist, Harris had learned from some of the best in the business. And despite what the namby-pamby liberals thought, they did their jobs with more restraint than the enemy deserved. Waterboarding and stress positions were a hell of a lot better treatment than American captors could expect if they were captured. Did they get a little carried away sometimes? Sure. But it was for a greater good. And, if he was being honest, it was kind of fun.

His conversations with first Maurice back at the morgue and then Doyle in the field off the main road didn't carry any of the restrictions from those old days. That made things go a little quicker. Threatening to cut off someone's dick unless he talked was one thing, actually doing it made more of a statement.

Doyle had recognized the picture of Catherine Fews immediately. Harris could tell by the kid's reaction, but then he'd clammed up as tight as a dehydrated asshole. Still, it took all of five minutes to transform Doyle from a hard ass ex-Marine into a quivering mass willing to tell him everything he knew, not about Catherine Fews, but about Tracy Bain, once the beauty queen of Harlow, West Virginia. The old adage that there were no secrets in a small town proved true and he got more information than he expected. One piece of intel was the location of Tracy's father, Doug, a small-time drug dealer who grew his own mushrooms and had a habit of sampling his own wares a little too often. Once he'd gotten everything he could out of the guy, Harris made sure to thank Doyle properly and end things for him in a timely fashion. He wasn't without compassion in such situations. He didn't hate Doyle the way he'd hated the al-Qaeda bastards he'd dealt with back in the day. The kid was just in the wrong place at the exact time Harris needed information. Besides, the kid was a veteran, and that counted for something. He gave him a quick death, one right between the eyes.

Harris drove out to the middle of nowhere to the broken down, rusted out trailer where Doug Bain lived and found nothing, including Doug Bain. Based on the man's set-up, there was no way any kind of Internet connection was streaming data into a hard drive. Shit, the man got TV reception with a wire snaked up through a hole in the roof of his trailer attached to an old-school antenna that was tied to a tree with a rope. Still, he rifled through the place looking for anything interesting. It was a dead end, so he drove to the bar where his buddy Doyle had thought the sister, Natalie, worked some nights. Since Doyle had no idea where she lived and there was no record of an address online, Harris had resigned himself to waiting to see if she showed. The drinks were just an extra bonus.

He'd been there for an hour when the FBI walked in. Maurice had told him all about Allison McNeil and, with the help of his contacts at the FBI, he had a good read on what she was all about. Her personnel file didn't do her justice though. She was a hot piece of ass just as Maurice had insisted, but he wasn't about to let that cloud his judgment. The rumor was that she'd shot Garret Morrison in the leg to take out Sam Kraw. A woman with that kind of balls deserved his professional respect and he intended to remember that.

He also knew about the man with her although he was surprised to see him there. Maurice's low pain threshold meant it hadn't taken much to get the kid to spill every secret he had. Just like Harris, Mike Carrel had paid Maurice good money for intel on who came to check on Catherine Fews, now Tracy Bain's, body. That a reporter who specialized in serial killers would be aggressively tracking the case wasn't surprising at all. He knew Carrel had contacts in the FBI the same as he did, so he felt a grudging sense of respect for the man's thoroughness in paying off the morgue tech instead of just relying on his regular sources. Hell, he might have paid off the night staff too for all he knew. All on a hunch that paid off. But what was really impressive, so much so that it bordered on the bizarre, was that he'd somehow convinced an FBI agent to let him tag along on the investigation. Now *that* was ballsy.

Harris had remained content to watch them from his vantage point in the bar. The fact that he was there first made it nearly impossible for them to make him as a stranger. His car was parked around back so his out of state plate wouldn't raise any eyebrows. His clothes fit in with the locals and he'd adopted a slumped over, my-life-sucks posture so he wouldn't attract attention, not that the local sheriff appeared to have any Sherlock Holmes powers of observation in his DNA. Harris looked the part and simply held his position, waiting to see what would happen.

Then the whole thing with Natalie Bain went down. The events with the gun had been brilliant, better than any Broadway stage play or Hollywood blockbuster. It was exactly his kind of entertainment. A little bit of blood would have paid the whole thing off better, but nothing was perfect. He put a ten-dollar bill on the table and slid on his coat.

The girl's arrest complicated things, but it was nothing he couldn't handle. The FBI woman was a little tricky too, but she had to play by different rules than he did. In fact, he didn't have to play by any rules at all. And, in the race to get the video cache filmed and transmitted by Tracy Bain, he intended to take every advantage he could get.

Still, time wasn't on his side. He figured he had twenty-four hours, maybe less, before people started looking for Doyle. Worse than that, once word spread in Harlow that the FBI thought a killer might be making a visit to their town, it was going to be impossible to walk down a street without a dozen eyes flagging him as a stranger. He had to work fast. Fortunately, that was what he was good at. All he needed was a few minutes alone with Natalie Bain. She would tell him everything fast enough. That he knew for sure.

He walked outside and breathed in the cold, mountain air, stretching a little as a gentle reminder that rushing too fast led to mistakes. He still had to be careful. Patience was a virtue. Perhaps the only virtue he still possessed.

CHAPTER 34

Allison and Mike sat in the front room of the Harlow sheriff's office. It was in an old building that had an open area large enough for two file-covered desks, a set-up which reminded Allison of the set for the Andy Griffith show, one of her dad's favorites. She pictured Andy and Barney standing vigil over the good folks of Harlow. Only Andy and Gomer didn't have calendars on the wall with a large-breasted woman sprawled over the hood of a police cruiser or straddling a police motorcycle while dressed in a bikini and looking over her shoulder, biting her lower lip. Classy.

The holding cell was back behind a door and down a hallway. Allison had tried to go down there to talk to Natalie when they first got there, but Sheriff Frank didn't much care for that idea. He'd sent her to wait in the front room until he and his deputy, a pudgy man with a bad comb-over named Cal Swanson, got their prisoner settled in.

"You think ol' Frank is going to let us talk to her tonight?" Mike asked.

Allison nodded. "The only question is how much information I have to give him to make that happen. If I can get him to believe Tracy's killer might be on his way up here to look for the same information we're looking for, then he might be more willing to cooperate."

"But you don't really want to tell him all that, do you?"

Allison shook her head. "Kind of like I wasn't planning on telling you Natalie's last name until I was ready. What was the deal with forcing my hand?"

"What are you talking about?"

"At the bar. You asked me the girl's last name in front of the bartender. You knew it wasn't necessary. How many Natalies could work there? That was just so you could get the name. It wasn't even sly."

"Sorry," Mike said. "But sitting around watching is driving me nuts."

"You're a reporter," Allison countered. "I thought that was your deal. To observe and not make yourself part of the story."

"That's journalism class, not the real world. Could you imagine a lifetime of only watching and reporting? Of being a spectator and never playing in the game?"

Allison noticed a rough edge to his voice. She'd hit a sore spot. "Isn't that what you signed up for?"

"The writer in me agrees with you," Mike replied, shifting his weight in his chair. "But the other part of me, the part that wants to live and experience and feel, that part is never content to just watch."

"I suppose everyone feels that way on some level," Allison offered. She stood and crossed over to the door that led to the cell block, looking through the small square window in its center. The sheriff and his deputy were at the far end of the hall speaking to Natalie in her cell. "Most people want to get in on the act," she said to Mike without turning.

"You really think so?" Mike asked. "All I see when I look at the world are these fat-asses sitting on their couches watching TV. Kids with their faces buried in their electronic devices, hardly looking up when they walk down the street. Suits scurrying to their cubicles to hide and manage their fantasy football teams when their bosses aren't watching. Blue-collar guys digging holes for fifty hours a week so they can wash down painkillers with cheap beer on the weekends. They're not living. They're not experiencing. They're just passing through time and waiting out the clock."

Allison turned from the door and wandered over to Deputy Cal's desk, looking over his personal photos. Mostly pictures of a young boy spanning a lifetime from infancy to high school graduation. Allison held up a framed photo of the deputy and the teenage boy holding up a giant catfish together. "Is that so bad?" Allison asked. "Think about it. We're surrounded by death. By the worst kinds of depravity. And we do it by choice."

Mike shook his head. "Not really by choice. We can't help ourselves. It calls to us. We have to be part of it because we know the truth."

She put the photo back in its place. She didn't really care for the direction of the conversation. "Really? And what's the truth?"

"That only death can make you truly value life," Mike said. "It's why people leave funerals and change the way they act for a few days. Take better care of themselves. Reach out to family members. Take stock. But they're no different than the millions of people who go to the gym after the New Year. Within a week or two they fall back into their old patterns."

"And death becomes something they ignore," she said softly.

"Exactly. But we see death every day. We know exactly how tenuous life really is. A car veers into your lane. Done. A blood clot reaches your brain. Game over. The wrong guy picks you out from the crowd and you're his next victim. And you never know how or when it's going to happen. And trying to understand why it happens? Forget about that. All you need to know is that when your number's up all you have is what you've done up to that point. What you plan to do tomorrow means absolutely nothing."

"And here I thought you were a sunny optimist this whole time," Allison said.

Mike grinned. "I guess that's saying something if a top FBI profiler can't read me. I must be really complicated."

"Or just really screwed up," Allison said.

Mike faked a hurt look and held his hand over his heart. "Man, I see why you chase serial killers instead of doing therapy. Your bedside manner sucks."

"Granted. But while you're a master at changing the subject, it didn't work. I'm still mad that you manipulated the situation at the bar to get Natalie's last name out of me. We had a deal and I expect you to stick to it. "

"I just thought I could help."

The lock in the door leading back to the jail clanked open.

"Stop thinking that," Allison said, standing up.

Sheriff Frank and Deputy Cal strode out looking like pallbearers at a friend's funeral. The deputy dragged a tear from his eye and looked miserably at the floor. Sheriff Frank patted him on the back and sent him over to his desk before turning to Allison. "Against my advice, she wants to talk to you," he said. "Empty your pockets before you go in there."

Allison tried to disguise her annoyance with the sheriff but she dug in her jeans and pulled out her credentials, car keys and money clip and tossed them on the desk. The sheriff nodded toward her and she removed her gun from her shoulder holster and placed it on the table. "Good?"

"Fine," the sheriff said.

"My associate will stay here," Allison said, pointing to Mike.

Mike started to object but Allison glared at him and he slumped in his chair.

Allison followed Sheriff Frank through the door and into a narrow hallway. "Is your deputy OK?"

The sheriff stopped and turned to her. Standing next to one another, they blocked the entire hallway. He was an imposing man, but his expression softened as he glanced back toward the room. "The thing about small towns is everyone knows everyone, see?" He spoke in a low voice, probably so it wouldn't carry back to Natalie's cell. "Cal back there, his son was a couple years behind Tracy in school. His boy never dated her or nothing like that, but he'd had a crush on her same as pretty much every boy in Hereford County. We all watched her grow up from a little kid."

"Including you," Allison said softly.

Sheriff Frank scowled and his right eye twitched. "Yeah, me too. So, this isn't some FBI case, where you can just roll in and call the shots. This is personal for us. Got that?"

"If I did anything to make it seem like it wasn't personal for me, then I apologize," Allison said. "I'm here in the middle of the night because I think I have a chance to find Tracy's killer. I'm damn good at my job. All I'm asking is that you let me do it so I can make the son of a bitch who did this to her pay."

Sheriff Frank looked her over as if resizing her up, this time not her physical measurements, but by the type of lawman she was. She stared up at him.

"Now are we going to stand here and measure our cocks," Allison said, "or can I get to work?"

Sheriff Frank snorted and gave a nod that she assumed was one of approval. He pointed down the hall. "Down there."

She nodded. "Thank you."

As she walked away, Sheriff Frank called out, "Tracy was a good girl," he said. "Everyone knew it. Damn shame."

Allison had no response for the man. The image of the crime scene came to her, the one where all four limbs of Tracy

Bain's body were clearly visible, each hanging like meat from the bondage straps tied to a bedpost. She wondered how much the sheriff might know about what caused a girl like Tracy Bain to become a woman like Catherine Fews.

She waited until the sheriff turned, walked down the hall and let himself out. If Natalie didn't prove helpful, she had a suspicion that Sheriff Frank just might.

CHAPTER 35

Allison walked the twenty feet to the last jail cell. Natalie sat on the bed, knees pulled up to her chest, eyes red from crying. Gone was the confident woman brandishing the gun and threatening Carl the wife-beater. She looked smaller now, as if the cell had compressed her and made her less somehow. If Allison had the keys, she would have let her out just to see that fire she'd seen at Billy Ray's return.

"You OK?" Allison asked.

Natalie nodded. She rubbed her right wrist where Allison had grabbed her. It was already bruising up. "You have a strong grip."

"Guns make me nervous," Allison said, smiling. "Guns going off around me make me really nervous."

"You think he got the point?"

Allison paused and looked away. She wanted to play this straight. The girl deserved it. "No," she said. "Probably not."

A flash of anger and then acceptance. "You're probably right." She stared at her hands. "What happened?"

It didn't take her master's degree in psychology to catch the shift in the topic of conversation. The way the girl's voice cracked was heartbreaking.

"Tracy was murdered."

"How?"

"Doesn't matter," Allison said. It had the added benefit of being true.

"You're trying to protect me," Natalie said. "Do I look like someone who needs to be protected?"

"Yes, you do," Allison said without hesitation.

"Well, you're wrong about that."

Allison softened her voice. "I don't know what happened to Tracy. I don't know what happened to you," she said. "But I think you've needed protection for a while."

Natalie lifted her hands to her face and leaned forward, her shoulders giving away the crying she was trying to hide.

"The way you reacted to Carl, that was something more than anger for a friend," Allison said. "That was something far deeper. I know because I've been there."

Natalie swallowed hard, then looked up and wiped her swollen eyes. "You don't know anything about me."

"Maybe not. But I know that anger. And I know a little something about pain," Allison said. She hesitated. She was moving too fast, but she thought there was a chance to strike quickly and convert the girl over to her side. She decided to just lay it all out. "I saw pictures of your sister in high school. Something happened her senior year." She watched closely and saw that Natalie tensed at the words. "You know what I thought when I saw her picture from that last year in school?"

"What?"

"That I'd seen that same look in the mirror before. It was the person looking back at me for an entire year after I was raped."

Natalie rocked back, looking at her differently. It always happened when Allison revealed that dark part of her past.

People's body language shifted ever so slightly, showing their discomfort, sometimes their pity, other times their revulsion. But Natalie had none of those reactions. She simply looked as if she completely understood.

"I was a student at the Naval Academy. A young instructor took an interest but I refused him. He saw me at a party, followed me out with a couple of his friends. Once I was away from everyone he raped me."

"Just him?" she asked. "Not his friends?"

This gave Allison pause. No one had ever asked that question before. "Just him. But that was enough."

Again, a simple nod and that look, *I understand.*

"The Naval Academy covered it up, basically told me to move on, suggested that I was to blame somehow. Word got around and people made it hard. So, I gave up and quit. And when I went home, I looked just like your sister did in those photos."

Natalie looked away.

"What happened to her, Natalie? Maybe it wasn't exactly the same, but something happened to her."

"Our mom..." Natalie whispered so soft that it was more like a breath than a word.

"What was that?" Allison said, leaning her head against the steel bars separating them.

"Mom died," she said. "Summer before Tracy's senior year. Things sort of...you know...fell apart after that."

Allison closed her eyes, letting the twang she felt of missing her own mother rattle around inside her chest for a second. When she opened her eyes she saw the distant expression on Natalie's face and her instinct told her this wasn't the entire story.

"I'm sorry to hear that. Did they ever find who killed her?"

Natalie looked sharply at her and Allison worried she might have gone too far.

"I said she died, not that someone killed her," Natalie said. "Are we playing games here?"

"No, I'm sorry. I just thought that since your sister changed so much, that trauma can…"

"So you don't think losing your mother is trauma enough?"

"I've lost my mother too," Allison said. "I know how it is."

This admission tamped down the rising tension in Natalie's voice and body language. She slumped back against the wall of her cell but her expression remained rigid.

"Convenient," she said coldly. "I'm starting to think maybe you're just full of shit. Sheriff Frank warned me about you FBI people. That you'd say anything to try to bond with me. To get me talking."

"That's what Sheriff Frank says, huh?"

"Your mom is probably home right now baking cookies and reading romance novels. I bet you made the whole thing up just so you can…"

Her voice trailed away as Allison held up her phone, screen forward. It was a picture of Allison next to an ancient, shriveled woman lying in a hospital bed, not much more than a skeleton with thin, yellowed skin stretched over it. The woman was done up with makeup and a wig and sported a brave smile that didn't quite hide her pain. There was an IV in her arm and an oxygen tube around her neck, lowered from her nostrils just for a second for the sake of the picture. Allison's smile was filled with the sadness of someone who knows they are taking a final picture with someone they love.

"She died two days later," Allison said. "So you and Sheriff Frank can kiss my ass."

"I'm sorry," Natalie said. "I shouldn't have…"

Allison waved the comment away. "Listen to me closely. If you don't want to tell me what happened to Tracy, that's OK. But there is something I need you to tell me the truth about right now."

Natalie nodded.

"Tracy had a video camera in the room where she was murdered. That video feed went to an encrypted Internet connection and was stored on a server somewhere."

Natalie seemed confused for a second, but then looked excited. "Then you know who killed her."

"We can't track where the signal went."

The confused expression returned. "But you're the FBI."

"It's complicated. She used a simple but effective way to cover her electronic footprint. She set up a physical server somewhere, a computer where all the video is stored."

Understanding was followed quickly by an incredulous look. "Wait, you think I have this computer?"

"I was hoping so, yes."

Natalie laughed but there was no joy in it, just hopelessness. "You're really no help then, are you? I haven't seen Tracy in over four years. No, it's been five years now. Not since the day she just...you know...left me here."

Allison felt the disappointment claw its way up from her stomach and into her throat. She hadn't realized until this moment just how much stock she'd put into this strategy. In her mind she'd pictured Natalie walking her over to a nearby house and opening a back closet to reveal a computer nestled on a shelf, happily blinking away as it waited to reveal the identity of Tracy's killer. That wasn't going to happen.

"Maybe your dad?" she asked.

Natalie's laugh turned harsh and mean. "Step-dad. Our real dad took off when we were still in diapers." She closed her eyes and leaned her head back against the wall. "That's a dead-end."

"I have to try," Allison said. "Where can I find him?"

"Trailer outside of town," she said softly, her voice growing distant. "Still right where Tracy left him. Right where she left me."

Allison caught something in her voice. The pieces weren't quite together yet, but she felt that they were floating near one another, wanting to coalesce.

"You feel like she left you behind." It was a statement, not a question.

Tears back in the girl's eyes. "That's what she did, isn't it? Left me there. With *him*. She got out, but I didn't. I had to stay there. She had...sh...she had to know what would happen, right?"

"What happened, Natalie?"

"Why didn't she come back for me?"

"You can tell me if you want. It's OK."

Natalie wiped her eyes angrily and sucked in a shuddering breath. She shook her head. "Nothing happened," she said. "Nothing at all."

"Everything OK back there?" Sheriff Frank called out from the end of the hallway.

Allison didn't take her eyes off of Natalie.

"We're fine. Just a few more minutes, please," she said.

"No," Natalie called out. "I think we're done actually."

Allison reached through the bars. "I've been where you are. I can get you help."

Natalie turned away, crossing her arms and hugging herself.

Sheriff Frank walked up and shot Allison a questioning look. Allison stood and walked past him. As she did, she heard the sheriff whisper in a tender voice, "I'm gonna let you get a night's rest here, Natalie. Get you home in the morning. I called the house and told them not to expect you tonight. I think that's best. All right?"

Allison didn't hear a response and she doubted there was one. The poor girl was likely tackling demons from her past, fighting them back and forcing them down into the cages where she kept them in her daily life. She remembered those days all too well, back when the smallest thing could trigger a flash of memory so real that it took her back to that night on the grass with Craig Gerty pawing at her like an animal. If the stepfather had sexually molested her, then Allison thought there was a good chance he had molested Tracy too. Maybe that was the source of the thousand-yard stare in the pictures more than just the loss of a mother.

Regardless, it still put her no closer to finding the videos and the killer than before. If anything, this was looking like a complete dead-end. If Tracy hadn't seen her sister in five years, and there seemed zero chance she'd contacted the stepfather, then there wasn't much to go on. An old boyfriend, maybe? Or a business where she used to work? But would she come all the way up here and not visit her sister? Allison didn't think it possible.

She opened the door to the front office area ready to admit defeat and call in the information she knew about Catherine's true identity to the main investigating team. They would have the resources to shadow Natalie in case the killer showed up to question her. It wouldn't make Mason happy, but this was too big of a data point not to share. There'd be hell to pay when the team found she'd withheld the information as long as she did, but what was done was done. Ensuring Natalie's safety was the most important thing.

But when she walked into the front office, Mike was gone. Only Deputy Cal was there, Facebook open on his desktop screen.

"Where's Mike?" she asked.

"The fella you were with?" Deputy Cal said. "He left the minute you walked into the back."

"Where'd he go?"

"He asked me where Natalie lived 'cause he said there weren't no address for her online." Deputy Cal looked smug. "Guess the FBI don't know as much as they think, huh?"

Allison thought he was at least right about that. "Where does she live?"

"Not too far from here. The Smith-Shelly house. Owned by the town. It's for women and kids who need a place to stay. Natalie's been running it the last couple of years. She was pickin' on Carl Wilson about one of the women who stays up there sometimes."

"Pickin' on Carl Wilson?" Allison asked. "Is that what she was doing?"

The dark cloud on Allison's face wasn't lost on the deputy. He flushed red. "No...didn't mean it like that...c'mon now..."

"What's the address?"

"Three-twelve Prescott Street," he stammered. "Go out here, turn right about a mile, then left another mile. Big white house on the hill."

Allison turned and hit the door as the deputy called out behind her.

"That thing I said about Carl, I didn't mean it like that."

She ignored him and stepped outside. She knew exactly how he meant it and she couldn't care less. The only thing she was wondering at that particular moment was what the hell Mike Carrel thought he was up to and why. A few seconds later, she was wondering how she was going to get to her destination since the bastard had taken her car.

CHAPTER 36

Allison glanced out the window of the sheriff's Blazer as they pulled up to the Smith-Shelly House and parked behind Allison's car.

"I thought you said he was with you," Sheriff Frank said. "That he was FBI."

He hadn't been too excited to give her the ride over, but he'd relented easily enough. The news about Tracy Bain and his chat with Natalie had left the man edgy and emotionally spent. Allison figured it was a tough way to spend a night, especially when only a few hours earlier he would have bet good money that he would have been in Ned's ex-wife's bed about then, with his stomach full and his balls empty. Allison wasn't giving him the whole story and she could tell he was getting tired of it.

"No, I told you he was with me, but not that he was FBI," Allison said.

"What is he? DC police or something?"

"He's a reporter." Allison popped open the door and climbed out to get away from the bitching she knew was about to follow.

"Aw damn," Sheriff Frank said, also climbing out. "Damn, damn, damn. I hate those pricks. Always making the police out like we're the bad guys. Who knows what I might of said in front of him. Let alone Cal. He's a good man but he's got horse manure for brains sometimes, you know?"

"I should have told you earlier."

"No shit. Whatever happened to professional courtesy?"

"You mean like what you've given me?" Allison said, feeling her temper flare. "You tried to convince Natalie not to talk to me. Then you warned her that I would lie to try to get her to talk. Is that what passes for professional courtesy around here?"

Sheriff Frank squared his shoulders to her as they stood on the front yard, halfway to the front door. Allison squared off just the same, not backing down.

After an awkward silence, Sheriff Frank grinned. "You're a tough som-bitch, aren't you?"

"Can be."

A scream erupted in the house behind her.

Sheriff Frank's smile disappeared as he looked over her shoulder.

She turned. It took a second to register what she was looking at, but once it did, every internal alarm bell went off. Windows on the top floor of the old home glowed orange. Fire.

Allison broke into a sprint, hearing the sheriff making a call to the fire department behind her. The description Deputy Cal had used echoed in her head. *It's a place where women and children go.*

Women and children.

A fire alarm finally went off inside the house, ridiculously late. Allison burst through the front door and was hit with a wall of smoke. Screams came from upstairs and the back room. A large African American woman came running down the stairs clutching a baby in her arms.

"This way," Allison called to her. "Outside."

The woman ran toward her, eyes wide in panic.

"Is there anyone else upstairs?" Allison asked her.

The woman shook her head as she pushed past to the main door. "I don't know. Maybe." She didn't wait for Allison to ask a second question. Holding her baby tight, she escaped out into the night.

Allison turned to see two little boys in matching Captain America pajamas run down the stairs, eyes wide, hands to their ears to block the piercing sound of the fire alarm. Allison ran up to them.

"It's all right, come with me," she said.

The boys may not have been able to hear her above the noise, but they were more than ready to have an adult help them. They quickly followed her the rest of the way down the stairs, both of them hacking and coughing from the smoke. As she got to the door, Sheriff Frank was running in. She handed the boys off to him. "Where's your mother?" she asked, yelling over the piercing alarm.

One of the boys, the older by only a year or so it seemed, pointed upstairs.

Sheriff Frank shouted something at Allison. She couldn't understand the words but the meaning was clear. He wanted her to take the boys outside and let him go in. But she knew she was faster and more agile than the overweight cop who'd been drinking his worries away only a few hours earlier. She turned and sprinted up the stairs.

The smoke was worse on the top floor. She pulled her shirt up over her mouth and shielded her eyes as much as possible. Even keeping low to the floor, she hacked and sputtered. Her eyes burned and blurred from tears.

The landing on top of the stairs was in the center of the house. The hallway stretched in either direction with a row of doors on each side like a hotel. To the right was a wall of smoke, to the left fire was licking up through the floorboards from the level beneath. She'd seen the fire in the upstairs windows though so she knew the fire had to be in at least one of the bedrooms already.

"Anyone up here?" she shouted.

Allison ran to the left, thinking that side likely had less time before caving in. If someone was trapped, they needed help right away.

The first room was empty. So was the second. As she ran to the next, the floor gave way beneath her feet, a section of it falling into the inferno raging in the room beneath her. She jumped across and came up short, landing from the waist up on the hallway floor, her legs dangling through the hole.

The heat was incredible. In her mind's eye, her skin turned black as it burned, curling up at the edges in thick, scabrous layers. But she dragged herself up from the hole, scraping her shins on the rough edge, and patted her smoking pants with her hand. She hadn't been burned. Not yet anyway. By the looks of things, that possibility wasn't too far out of the question. She had to hurry.

She ran to the next room but could only get the door open a foot or so. Something heavy lay on the other side. She put her shoulder into it and the door slowly slid open. Smoke and heat poured out as she looked in. The far corner of the floor had been eaten away by the flames. The curtains caught fire in a sudden flare, turning that side of the room into a wall of flame.

Allison looked down and confirmed her fear.

A young woman in sweats and a t-shirt lay sprawled on the floor, her hands up to her mouth. Allison ran over to her, fell to her knees and felt for a pulse. Weak, but there.

Part of the outside wall crumbled away and the roof fell in right behind it. The new source of oxygen gave the fire a burst of energy. It swirled and spun, looking for more to consume.

Allison lifted the woman onto her back in the fireman's lift she'd learned at the Academy. Luckily the woman was small and fairly light. Allison didn't know what she would have been able to do if she'd found a two hundred and seventy-five pound woman there instead.

Coughing violently and barely able to see, she went back the way she'd come. The hole in the floor was bigger now and she had a clear view down into the living room below. There was movement there. Mike.

"Hey! Up here!" Allison shouted, but it was no use. He couldn't hear her. She wasn't sure what he would have been able to do anyway. He was hunched over, picking his way through the burning embers. In a few seconds, he was out of sight, having darted through the room.

Allison didn't have time to consider what she'd just seen. She needed to get the hell out of the building. She eyeballed the distance over the hole in the floor. She could jump over it easily on her own and then run down the stairs to safety. But there was no way to get the woman across it. Even if she tried to throw the woman over it, she was deadweight and there was no way she'd make it.

She turned back and went into the room where she'd found the woman. Putting her on the bed, she grabbed a chair and threw it through one of the two windows. She put her head through and sucked in a few quick breaths of gloriously fresh air, trying to steady herself.

She was on the side of the house now, but she had a clear view of the front yard. It was filled with people, some running, others standing and hugging whoever was closest to them as they watched the place burn.

A piercing wail filled the air and a fire truck pulled up to the curb, lighting the neighborhood in red strobing flashes. Good news for the building, but Allison knew Harlow's finest wouldn't get to her in time.

"Hey! Over here!" she screamed anyway, waving her arms. "Help!"

But her voice was lost in the crackle of the centuries-old house going up in flames.

If she was going to get the woman out of the building, she had to do it herself.

She looked down and saw that the house bumped out below her, giving her a short, slanted roof to climb onto. From there it would be another ten-foot drop to the ground. Piece of cake by herself. Infinitely harder when she was a plus one.

Taking a deep breath and pulling her shirt over her mouth, she turned and stumbled back into the room. The heavy smoke burned her eyes, making tears run down her face. She quickly gave up trying to see and just dropped to a knee, hacking and coughing as she groped her way back to the bed where she'd left the woman. She found the bed.

There was nothing on it. The woman was gone.

CHAPTER 37

Allison climbed on the bed, waving her arms madly across the sheets.

She tried to remember if she'd seen more than one bed in the room when she first came in, but she could have sworn there had only been one.

She slid off the far side of the bed, belly crawling to the floor, hitting it with a thump. Dizzy and disoriented, she nearly didn't notice that her landing was softer than it ought to have been. The woman. Allison didn't stop to wonder how she'd gotten there, she just grabbed her under the arms and dragged her to the window, hoping that she was heading the right direction.

She tried to peer through squinted eyes but was rewarded only with searing pain from the smoke. There was a low crack behind her and a sudden rush of heat. Even without her sight, she knew that part of either a wall or the roof had caved in. She didn't want to think about what was going on beneath her, but she imagined the fire raged there. If the floor caved in, it would be a short ride down to a fiery death for both of them. The thought kicked in her survival instinct. Self-preservation demanded she let go of the woman, a stranger no less, and get herself the hell out of there before it was too late. It was the only sane thing to do.

But the thought just pissed Allison off. She yelled and pulled harder at the woman, pushing away any idea of leaving her behind. It was a weakness she would not tolerate.

She hit the wall with her back and reached up behind her, expecting to feel the open space of window. Instead it was solid wall. She'd gone the wrong way. Somehow gotten turned around in the smoke.

Desperate, she reached out to her left. Nothing. Then to her right. She was about to give up on that direction too when she felt the rush of hot wind pass by her hand. The window. It had to be acting like a flue, a spot for the heat to rush to the outside.

She dragged the woman with her, crying out from the effort. The wind intensified, a barely tolerable heat, but she knew it was her salvation. They reached the window and she stuck her head out, gasping at the air once again, this time only a series of hacking coughs, but still a relief.

A loud snap came from behind her and a belch of heat and smoke erupted through the window. She didn't have much time. She dragged the woman up until her limp legs hung over the windowsill. Allison lowered her as slowly as she could down to the roof of the bump out below. With no better option, her plan was to drop the woman the rest of the way and hope she didn't roll off the edge. The ten-foot fall was better than the certain death of staying in the house, but not by much. There was a chance the woman would break her neck in the fall and still die. But at least it gave her a chance.

She finally had the woman hanging as far as she could and was about to let her go, when the floor beneath Allison gave out. She fell, but only a foot, keeping her grip on the woman who now dangled on the opposite side of the wall, a counter-balance keeping Allison from falling to her death.

She kicked her legs over the inferno below, trying to find purchase on the wall. She finally did and, using the woman for leverage, hefted herself over the windowsill.

She and the unconscious woman fell through the air in a mix of limbs. They hit the roof hard and rolled off together. Allison tried to orient herself to be able to brace for the impact, but she couldn't tell which way was up. Either way, it was going to hurt.

But the blast of pain didn't come. Instead, she landed on top of a small crowd of people who'd gathered below the window. People who'd seen her the first time she'd come out for a quick breath.

Still, stopping her and the woman's fall was no simple thing. Allison heard several grunts and a few cuss words when she rammed into them, and still felt the jarring impact of the ground when she slid through their outstretched arms. But it was manageable, no more than rolling off a park bench onto the grass. Allison leaned up on the grass, still hacking the smoke out of her lungs, but aware enough to take a mental inventory of her limbs and joints as she moved. Nothing broken. A few sore spots that would end up as nasty bruises, but nothing that was going to hang her up for too long.

"Damn, woman," said an old man dressed in a tattered bathrobe. "You jus' crazy."

"H...h...how is she?" Allison sputtered. "The woman?"

Other people hovered over her but they turned to the old man. It seemed since he'd spoken to her first that it was his job to communicate with the stranger that jumped out of burning buildings.

"She's fine, girl. Don't you worry 'bout it none," the old man said. But she saw the look in his eyes. In all of their eyes. They didn't want to upset her.

"No, no," she said, pushing herself to her knees but stopping as a punishing coughing fit wracked her body. As she looked up, the crowd parted and she saw the woman on the ground, a man alongside her conducting CPR.

She had to blink hard, thinking the smoke inhalation and the mucus that had formed in the corners of her eyes were making her see things. But no, it was Mike administering chest compressions and mouth-to-mouth. By the looks of the people around him, he might as well have been administering last rites.

Shortly, two paramedics rushed up and inserted themselves into his role, placing a breathing bag over the woman's mouth and checking for vitals. Mike turned and looked toward her. He quickly walked over and knelt next to her.

"You all right?" he asked.

She nodded, unable to take her eyes off the woman. "She had two kids. Make sure they don't come over here."

The old man looked around quickly. "I know 'em. Not here yet, so that's good. I'll go find 'em and keep them occupied." The man strode away to the front of the house.

A stretcher appeared, manned by a fireman and a paramedic. They loaded the woman up and Allison's stomach turned at the way her arm hung limp off the side. She felt a hand on her shoulder.

"Come on, we need to get away from the building," Mike said. "It could come down at any time."

Even though she felt her strength returning to her with each breath of cool, night air, she leaned heavily on Mike and allowed herself to be led away from the house.

"I did everything I could," she said once they were a bit away from the immediate heat from the fire.

"You did more than everyone else," Mike said. "Including me."

Allison froze at that, remembering seeing Mike in the room below her when the floor caved in.

"What were you doing there?" she asked. "Why did you leave the jail?"

Her tone must not have masked the accusation and suspicion she felt, because he stepped back and looked at her, incredulous.

"You think I had something to do with this fire?" he asked.

"What were you doing there?" she repeated, not liking his tone.

"I came to ask someone to go into her room and get Natalie a change of clothes, toothbrush, all of that," he said. "I figured she didn't need to spend the night in those crappy clothes she was wearing and I..." He stopped as if realizing she wasn't buying his explanation. He held his hands up. "Jesus, you're like a human lie detector. OK, I admit it. I came over to see if I could find her computer."

"Why would you do that?"

"Once you went back to talk to her, all I could think about was what you said about someone else, probably the killer, being on his way up here too." He shrugged. "I figured I had good cover to take a quick look around her room and report back to you. I didn't see the harm."

"A woman died tonight."

"I had nothing to do with that. I knocked on the front door. No one came, but I thought I saw a light on in the back. I walked around to the kitchen door and that's when I saw the fire inside. I broke the door in, tried to put it out, but..." He nodded to the inferno behind them. "Obviously it was no use."

"I saw you downstairs in the living room during the fire," Allison said. "Why weren't you able to get out faster?"

Mike looked surprised, but this look was quickly replaced with a withering resentment.

"I was making sure there was no one left in the building. The same as you," Mike said, an angry edge to his voice. "Any other questions, counselor? I mean, shit, what're you thinking?

232

That I came over here and just decided to torch a building with a bunch of sleeping women and children? That's just nuts."

Allison knew it was unfair, but instead of feeling guilty for accusing him, she felt a surge of anger. Had he really done everything he could to stop it? Why hadn't he looked up when Allison had called to him? She might have been able to lower the woman to him and she'd still be alive.

"Jesus, you do think that," Mike said, misunderstanding the expression on her face.

"No," she said. "No, I don't." She rubbed her burning eyes. "I'm sorry I jumped at you. I'm still a little out of it."

Mike's expression transformed into a look of concern. Allison thought it was almost too calculated, too measured, but he was under a lot of stress too, so she discarded the observation.

"We should get you checked out," he said.

She shook her head, wiping the ashes and soot from her eyes with the edge of her shirt like she was removing mascara at the end of a long night.

"No, I'm fine," she said. "I don't believe in coincidences. The night we're here to question Natalie about the location of the hard drive is the same night the place where she lives just happens to go up in flames? I don't think so."

"Someone else is looking for the video files."

Allison nodded. "Yeah and if this is one of their tactics, then they are just as interested in destroying the files as they are in recovering them."

"Tracy's killer?"

"I think so."

The realization hit Allison like an electric shock.

"If he's here, even if he found the video files, he's not going to trust that's the only copy. He's going to tie up all loose ends."

"Natalie," Mike said. "But she's safe at the jail."

"Locked up in a fixed location with only Deputy Dawg guarding her--"

"--and the rest of the town tied up here."

Allison ran toward her car. "You call the jail, I'll drive."

CHAPTER 38

arris liked the look of the old jailhouse. Its brick front and arched windows harkened back to a time when law enforcement was recognized as the bedrock of any community, no matter how small. As a kid, he'd loved the old western movies, the black-and-white ones with the greats like Randolph Scott, Yul Brenner and Gabby Hayes. The kind where the good guys wore actual white hats to mark them as the ones to cheer for. Even back then, Harris felt himself relating more to the other guys, the black-hatted baddies who wanted to shoot up the town, steal cattle, get into fistfights and wrestle with the corseted brunettes in the saloons. What wasn't to like?

Even so, he also liked the character of the small-town sheriff, a lone voice of law and authority, set apart from everyone else because of the tin star on his chest. He remembered towns back then, at least in the movies, always had a church, a dry goods store, a schoolhouse, a few saloons and a jail. How nice the jail was lent a certain amount of seriousness to the town. By the looks of things, the founding fathers of

Harlow, West Virginia took law seriously and invested in a nice building. It just so happened that the town never grew much past the need for the original jail.

It seemed like a shame to shoot up the place.

"Can I help you, sir?" asked the pudgy-faced deputy when Harris walked in.

Harris already knew the deputy was alone. Ten minutes earlier he'd first watched Mike Carrel leave, then the sheriff and Allison McNeil. He followed them to the other side of town and saw the FBI agent run into a house fire. He wasn't sure how the fire fit into things, but he knew a gift when he saw one. He didn't wait around to see if the FBI agent made it out. He'd rolled down the street with the lights off, made two turns and headed back to the jail. Now he stood in the front room, talking to the idiot behind the desk with his nametag pronouncing that he was Deputy Cal. An old-fashioned police radio squawked from a shelf on the wall. Fire, ambulance and police talking over one another.

"I'm here on behalf of Ms. Natalie Bain," Harris said. "I've been retained as her attorney."

Cal jerked up from his chair. He grabbed an empty Big Gulp cup and hocked a gob of chew into it.

"We're a little busy right now. Fire up at the Smith-Shelly House. You'll have to come back later."

"No, I'll see my client now," he said. "Unless you want to be the one who drags this town into a civil rights violation lawsuit."

"C'mon. Really? Frank's gonna cut her loose in the morning anyway."

"I don't intend to let my client stay overnight in a jail with God knows who bothering her."

Cal stood up and walked out from behind his desk. "There's no one else here." He brought out a set of keys from his pocket. "Just me. So I don't think--"

The world had to do without knowing what Deputy Cal thought because the brain that had formed the idea was suddenly sprayed over the back wall of the office. The big man slumped into a kneeling position, weirdly balanced so that he remained upright on his haunches, chin to chest, as if sleeping or at prayer. Blood pooled around him, spreading smoothly on the painted concrete floors. The image took Harris a little by surprise and he froze for a couple of seconds, waiting for him to fall over. Finally he walked up, smoke still spilling from his gun's silencer, put a foot to the man's chest and nudged him over. The body fell, arms splayed wide, the way it was supposed to. It made Harris feel a little better.

He grabbed the deputy's handcuffs and keys, then dragged the body a few feet so that it would be out of sight if someone happened to walk by the sidewalk outside. The blood splatter was off to the side, perhaps visible, but the average person would explain it away. Maybe an exploded soda or a plate of spaghetti thrown at the wall as a prank. The idea that it might be little bits of brain and blood clinging to the walls wouldn't even enter their mental vocabulary.

He flicked through the keys, smiling when he saw that Deputy Cal had conveniently labeled each with red nail polish. He fought the urge to pull off one of the deputy's boots and socks to see if he'd find perfectly painted red toenails. He suspected he just might and pushed down a giggle at the image of the chubby painted toes.

Jesus, where's your focus, he thought to himself.

He took a steadying breath and selected the key that said *J Door.* Seemed like a reasonable jump that J stood for jail and the keys marked with a C and a number were for the cells on the other side of the door. He slid the key in and turned. The lock clicked and the door, its hinges bent or just a little off-center in the old building, slowly opened on its own. An invitation. One he was happy to accept.

"Natalie Bain?" he called out in his official-sounding voice, the one he used when impersonating someone in law enforcement or the military. He walked down the hallway, the brick wall on his left and the cells on his right. He assumed she hadn't been able to hear the silenced gunshot through the heavy jail door. "My name's Harris. I'm with the FBI. My colleague Allison McNeil spoke to you earlier this evening."

Movement at the far end of the hall. A pair of hands pushed through the bars and there was a flash of hair as she leaned her face against the bars.

"I told her I was done talking to you people," she said. She didn't say it loud, but the sound carried well enough. Her tone gave Harris hope that she hadn't cooperated with the other two yet.

"Sorry, I didn't want to startle you is all," Harris said, checking each cell as he walked to the back. "You're here alone, huh?"

No response. He wondered if something of his intention had slipped into his voice. He didn't think so, but he was starting to realize he wasn't the best judge of those kinds of things lately.

"In any case, just got word from DC that I'm to bring you in," he said. Things were always easier when people came willingly. It wasn't necessary in this case, but it was still preferable to clubbing her on the head and dragging her out to the street. Although once she saw the mess he'd made of Deputy Cal in the front room he would probably have to subdue her anyway. "Just for questioning, you understand. Nothing more."

"There's no way I'm going to DC," Natalie said. "I told you people I don't know anything."

Harris looked through the keys, selecting C-4 and sliding it into the lock. "Just a day and back. As long as you cooperate."

Natalie looked past Harris's shoulder. "Where's Sheriff Frank? Or Cal?"

Harris opened the door, pulling the handcuffs from his pocket. "Not available right now. Hands out, Ms. Bain." He tried to look apologetic. "Just policy. You understand, right?"

"Frank! Cal! Get back here!" she called out. "I'm not going anywhere with this asshole."

"Shhh," Harris said. "I already told you, this is my operation now. They can't do anything for you."

"Sheriff! I want to--*uuggghhh.*"

The Taser hit her in the chest, the voltage crackling in the air. Harris didn't mind using the weapon, but it usually meant his persuasive skills had failed somehow so it was also an admission of failure. He watched as the girl fell to the floor, jerking from the electricity, spit drooling from her mouth. It was clear she was going to be a pain in the ass to deal with and he didn't have time for pain in the asses. All he needed was the sheriff to come back from the fire and find the murdered deputy, all while he was stuck in the cellblock with no way out. It was time to go.

He stopped the Taser and knelt down next to Natalie, who blinked hard as the world came back into focus. He snapped the cuffs on her, hands behind her back so she couldn't scratch his face.

"W—who are you?" Natalie whispered.

"Just someone who wants something you have."

"You're not with the FBI, are you?"

Harris yanked her to her feet. "What do you think?"

Natalie threw her head back and clocked Harris right on the bridge of his nose and it exploded in a sunburst of blood. She ran out of the cell, pushed against the door with her shoulder and slammed it shut.

Harris reached out at the last second and inserted his hand between the door and the jamb. The bones in his left hand crunched as the door slammed into it. He howled in pain, but the sound ended with an animal growl of anger.

He pushed the door back open and ran into the hallway in time to see Natalie already halfway to the door.

Harris tried to pull his gun but his mangled hand was too damaged and it was impossible to pull the gun from his shoulder holster using his left hand. Besides, he didn't trust himself shooting righty. If he killed the girl by accident then he'd be empty-handed.

He ran after her. In most jails, the door would need to be key-opened to go out, but this one didn't. She already had it open.

"Stop or I'll shoot you in the back," he said, bluffing.

She didn't bite. She was through the door and he was still a few steps behind.

He tore open the door just in time to see Natalie slip on the blood slick oozing from Deputy Cal's body. Handcuffed, she hit hard on her shoulder and the side of her head took a bounce off the concrete floor. She tried to scramble back to her feet, but she succeeded only in sliding around in the blood, smearing it all over herself.

Harris managed to get his gun out from his holster by hooking it with his left thumb and then transferring it to his right hand. Natalie froze, covered in Deputy Cal's blood, terror in her eyes.

Harris tasted salt in his mouth. He reached up and felt his nose. It was cockeyed to one side, clearly broken, and his hand came back covered with blood. He shook his head at Natalie.

"This was going to be so simple," he said. "Short and sweet. You give me the information I need, and I give you a painless death." He pointed to his nose and held up his mangled hand. "Plans have changed."

CHAPTER 39

Allison hung up the phone after getting the sheriff's voicemail a second time.

"Any luck at the jail?" she asked, taking a corner too fast.

"No answer," Mike said. "The sheriff?"

"Same," Allison said. "Busy with the fire. This might be nothing, but..."

"...but seems too convenient," Mike said. "And I don't believe in coincidences. That house was the most logical place for Natalie to have a computer set up or store a hard drive. It goes up in flames right when everyone is looking for it. I find that hard to believe."

Allison was thinking the same thing. Her eyes were still draining from the smoke and she smelled like a campfire, but her mind was churning. It was the old feeling, the one she inevitably got on every case, where only three or four more pieces were left to complete a five-hundred-piece puzzle, only she couldn't quite yet see where the pieces fit.

She saw she had a phone message from Mason. It was from over an hour ago. She pressed the button and held it to her ear.

"The word is out that you're working this case. You should have told me the details about the death at the morgue. I'm taking you off this. You're compromised. I want you to immediately--"

Allison pressed the delete button and slid the phone back into her pocket.

"What was that?" Mike asked.

"Just an old friend lending me his support," she said.

"Mason?"

"Nice try," she said.

Mike shrugged. "Habit."

They came to a hard brake outside the jail. The lights were on and it looked the same as when they left it.

"Maybe I was wrong," Allison said.

"Let's hope so."

They got out. Allison pulled her gun and held it low to her side. Even though things looked all right, her intuition told her another story. Over the years, she'd learned to trust what the little voice in her head told her.

Even before opening the door, she knew there was a problem. She spotted the splatter of red on the wall. Hundreds of hours of splatter analysis meant she knew exactly what it was. She waved Mike back and raised her gun.

"What is it?" Mike whispered.

She ignored him. Craning her neck left and right, she saw the puddle of blood next to the desk and one of Deputy Cal's legs sticking out. There were footprints leading from the blood, growing fainter as they neared the door. They were small, the shape of running shoes, exactly what Natalie had been wearing.

"Oh shit," Allison said.

She pushed the door open, covering the room's corners with her gun. It looked like whoever had come had taken Natalie away, but she had to be sure. And she didn't know whether someone had been left behind to clean up any loose ends. The concern in Mason's voice took on new meaning now. Whoever these people were, they likely killed Maurice, set fire to a house of sleeping women and children and killed Deputy Cal. An FBI agent unofficially investigating a case wouldn't give them any pause.

Mike came in behind her. Stepping carefully around the blood, he crossed over to Deputy Cal. He recoiled when he passed behind the desk and finally saw the deputy's head. Allison went around the other direction in the room, gun trained on the door that led to the cells. Once she reached the door, she looked back and saw the ash-white face of Deputy Cal staring right back at her, a single bullet wound right between the eyes.

Allison knew logically from the amount of blood that the deputy was dead, but seeing the entrance wound and the man's death stare made her shudder.

She chanced a quick look through the window that led to the cellblock, her mind warning her that she just might get a shotgun blast in the face for the effort. But in the one second look, she saw that the hallway wasn't filled with assassins and hit men. It was empty.

She slowly stood up and took a longer look, moving her head to try to see into the nearest cell, but she couldn't see much. But at the end of the short cellblock she did see that Natalie's cell door hung open.

Carefully, she entered the cellblock, gun raised, and made short work of checking out the cells. Nothing in the first three. In the last, she spotted drops of blood on the floor. Not good.

"You think it was whoever killed Tracy?" Mike asked, standing at the cell door.

Allison nodded, beating herself up for leaving Natalie unprotected when she suspected the killer might be following the same bread crumbs they were to the videos. But how had he managed to catch up to them? Even if he had killed Maurice, and if Maurice had told the killer about the tattoo, they'd left almost immediately and found out Catherine Fews's real name while on the road. The killer could have flown out, but it meant that he'd pieced together Catherine's identity on the way too. And without the help of the FBI's resources and Jordi...

She stopped her train of thought, not liking where it was going. Clinically, she recognized the rising sense of paranoia clutching her chest, but knowing that didn't help. What if Jordi was sharing information? Or maybe Mason had more than one off-the-books operative looking for the videos, someone without the scruples he knew Allison to have. She looked at Mike, waiting outside the cell for her. Wasn't it too convenient that he'd shown up at the morgue when he did? Could he be on Mason's payroll as an operative?

The last thought about Mike got pushback from her logic. She knew why Mike had shown up when he did. He'd bribed Maurice to let him know who showed an interest in the Catherine Fews/Tracy Bain corpse. It fit in with his job. Ironically, the stranger she'd met the day before was the one person she felt she could trust right then.

"What do we do now?" Mike asked.

Allison pulled out her phone, the one Mason had given her. It was her communication link to one of the most powerful law enforcement agencies in the world, but at that moment, it was just a tracking device telling Mason and God knew who else exactly where she was and what she was doing. She slid off the back casing and pulled out the battery. She slammed the phone on the corner of the metal bed frame and busted it in half.

"So, I guess calling in the cavalry isn't an option," Mike said.

"Actually, that's exactly what I'm doing," she said. "We need all the help we can get."

"Then why'd you break your phone?"

244

"I'm not sure the person on the end of that line can be trusted anymore." She raised her other phone. "I'll call with this."

The phone rang in her hand, surprising her. She looked at the number. Blocked call. She smirked and answered it.

"So you *were* tracking the phone," she said.

But it wasn't Mason on the line. It was a very scared, very desperate Natalie Bain.

"Help me," she cried. "Oh God, please help."

CHAPTER 40

Harris took the phone from Natalie's hand but didn't hang it up. He laid it on a rough work table, not much more than a piece of plywood balanced on two saw horses, right next to Natalie's outstretched hand. The room was filled with sharp shadows cast by two battery-powered commercial lamps, the kind with metal cages around the fluorescent bulbs. He'd brought these himself, figuring that the power to the old factory would have been long cut off.

The advance work he'd done online had paid off and the abandoned quarry just outside of town had proven to be a perfect place to hole up. It was enormous with dozens of places to hide and multiple escape routes if that turned out to be necessary. Most importantly, it was totally abandoned so there was no one around to get in his way.

He turned the phone just slightly on the table so that the microphone was right next to Natalie's fingers, then he grabbed her pinkie and snapped it sideways. The crack of the bone was drowned out by the scream that followed it. Harris picked the phone back up and held it up to Natalie so that Allison the FBI agent could hear her whimpering in pain.

"Are you still there?" he asked.

"Leave her alone," came the reply. Strong and in control. He didn't much care for that. He'd hoped the female agent would be a little more emotional.

"If we keep this local, then I will," he said. He couldn't be certain the rest of the FBI hadn't already been notified, but he was playing a hunch. "Start making calls and I take her apart, piece by piece, then dump her body where you'll never find it."

"Just like you did to her sister?"

"Special Agent McNeil, I'm disappointed. Still trying to solve your case even when you should be focused on other things." Harris grabbed Natalie's mangled hand and squeezed it, eliciting another scream.

"OK, I'm here," came the reply. "Just don't hurt her." More emotion this time. Harris relaxed a little. That was more like it.

"I need to have a chat with you and your reporter friend. In person. If you call in support, if you bring anyone with you, I kill young Natalie here. She fought back a little too much, so I'm not going to make it easy on her either."

He described where to meet him and what they should do once they got to the meeting spot, then hung up.

Natalie held her right hand to her chest, crying softly while managing to look pissed off at the same time. Her right eye was swollen shut where he'd had to clock her one for not paying attention, and three toes on her left foot weren't quite as long as they'd been before. It was amazing how the tips off a few toes was usually all it took to get even the toughest prisoners talking. And this girl was no easy mark. Usually the first toe was enough. Or just the threat of it. But she'd endured three before telling him everything.

She finally admitted to Harris that she'd lied to the FBI agent. Her sister had been in contact about a year earlier. They were in a fight for some reason Harris didn't give a shit about, but her sister said she needed her help with something. Something big. Enough to set both of them up. Maybe move together to California. Her sister said she didn't even have to do anything, just maintain a computer and a backup. She would do the rest. The only caveat was that if anyone came looking for the computer, anyone at all, she had to hide it.

Harris held up a small, flat silver rectangle, about the size of a hardcover book. It had a USB cable dangling from one edge. They'd made a quick stop at Billy Ray's Saloon to pick it up.

"So this is the backup off the laptop that burned down in the house?"

Natalie nodded.

"Why did you have it at the bar? There's no way you just carry it around with you."

"Once the FBI woman called, I went home and grabbed it," Natalie explained. "I thought they were coming to take it."

At least the girl wasn't a total idiot. She was right that they'd been coming to take it. The only thing still in dispute was whether Mike Carrel had gotten his hands on the girl's laptop before the fire started. He thought it was likely, and that he'd started the fire as a cover-up that he'd taken it. It was the play Harris would have made if the roles were reversed. He was just surprised the reporter had the *cajones* to pull it off.

Regardless, he had to close the loop one way or the other. It wouldn't work for there to be additional copies of the videos out in the world. He had to be certain. He checked his watch. Looked like he'd know in another fifteen or twenty minutes.

He opened the Mac PowerBook he'd brought. It was an air gap computer, no internal modem and it'd never been connected to the Internet via a wired connection either. He plugged in the USB and waited, humming out snippets of an old melody.

The external drive appeared in Finder and he accessed it. An encryption prompt appeared asking for a password. He looked over to his prisoner.

"I don't know it," Natalie said. "I swear to God. I've tried to get into them, but I've never been able to."

Harris turned his back to her. He had a few toys on his computer. This wasn't the first password-protected file he'd faced. He opened a decryption program, a sophisticated one thanks to his buddies over at NSA. The five-character password slowly filled in one at a time and then his computer chirped like an appliance telling him his toast was done.

He was in.

Harris opened the files. There were thumbnails of dozens of videos. He clicked on one at random. It was inside of Tracy Bain's bedroom where she lived her life as Catherine Fews. A grey-haired man walked into the frame, someone Harris recognized from congress. A representative from the great state of Kentucky, if he wasn't mistaken. Tracy walked in behind him, hands on his shoulders, then arms, taking off his coat. Harris turned the monitor toward Natalie.

"Want to watch?" he asked.

Natalie shook her head in disbelief. Whatever her sister had told her, Harris figured it hadn't included the truth about what she was actually doing with her time in DC.

"Yeah, me neither," Harris said, closing the window.

He changed the settings to enlarge the thumbnails, but still couldn't find what he was looking for.

"Is this everything?" he asked, spinning to look at Natalie.

"Yes, I swear," she said.

He turned back around and went through the thumbnails again. Halfway through, he noticed a subfolder with an odd label that looked like a random series of numbers and letters, like a computer-generated backup file. He clicked it and found a second subfile labeled VIP. He clicked it.

Bingo.

There were four separate files. The bastard Summerhays had copped to only two visits to the woman. He couldn't help lying even when there wasn't a reason to. Harris clicked on a few spots in the middle of the video and couldn't help but let out a howl of laughter. He found it fitting that the man who was front-runner to lead the free world got off on playing the submissive. Harris's favorite screenshot was of the Senator with a gag in his mouth, hands tied to the corners of the four-postered bed with Tracy Bain in full dominatrix costume. The best part was that she was doing something to the man's rear end that Harris was pretty sure the conservative voters in America's Bible Belt would have trouble stomaching.

He closed the video and then did exactly what he swore to Summerhays and his flack Libby he would never do. He made a copy for himself.

Only a sucker didn't have an insurance policy when the stakes were this high. And while Harris was many things, he wasn't a sucker.

While the computer copied the large file, Harris went back to the main folder and rolled through the thumbnails until he came to the last file. He opened it and watched the first four minutes of the video, mesmerized.

"I'll be damned," he murmured.

He could have kept watching, wanted to keep watching, but he knew his guests would be coming soon. Harris selected the video of Tracy Bain's murder and copied it to his hard drive. He didn't know if it would ever prove to be useful, but it was nice to have.

Harris picked up his gardening shears. Once he'd tried the medical version, but found the run-of-the-mill version available at Home Depot to be the most effective. He usually loved the weight of them but he was using his right hand because his left was still throbbing from being slammed in the cell door. Despite feeling awkward in his hand, the shears definitely got the job done.

"This hard drive and the laptop were the only copies?" Harris said.

"Yes, I told you that already."

She was eyeing the shears. Harris liked that.

"Anyone else know about them?"

Natalie shook her head. "I only know about the FBI woman. I told you everything I know." Her lip quivered as she stared at the shears. "Please, I didn't even know what was on there until now. And Tracy told me I was the only one she sent these to. I was the only one she could trust."

Harris clicked the shears thoughtfully, enjoying the sound of the hinge and the metal blades scraping against one another.

"I'm going to take off one more toe."

"Nooooo, pleeease," she whined. "I did everything you said. *Pleeease.*"

"I'll make you a deal," Harris said, placing his elbows on the table and leaning toward her as if they were a couple deciding which movie to go see. "I'll let you choose which toe."

Natalie kicked and bucked, screaming angrily, but the zip-ties around her ankles and wrists just dug deeper into her skin. Harris waited until she wore herself out, knowing there was no risk of her getting loose.

"You don't like that idea?" he asked. "OK, I'm a reasonable guy. You tell me about one more copy that you made and you can keep your toe."

Natalie started to cry. Low, baleful sobs of someone who understood the hopelessness of their situation.

"But there are no more copies," she cried. Harris liked this part, where the person's pride was gone completely, replaced by pure fear. "I never even looked at the files. There was a password. You saw. I didn't even know what's on them."

Harris clicked the shears and bent down to inspect his captive's feet. It was a shame because they were pretty feet, well kept, painted a fashionable red. One of the toes he'd cut off even had a little yellow flower painted on it. He thought about pocketing that one as a souvenir but then thought better of it.

"There are no more copies, you asshole!" she screamed.

"I wish I could just believe you," Harris said, selecting a toe on her right foot this time. "Problem is, I'm not a very trusting person."

CHAPTER 41

Allison checked her gun, reconfirming that it was loaded. She popped her trunk and pulled out a ballistic vest. The phrase bulletproof vest didn't quite work anymore since there were rounds specifically designed to pierce through the vests used by the FBI. She pulled it on and pulled the FBI windbreaker over it. A wave of déjà vu filled her with foreboding. Even though she rationalized that the feeling came from what happened with Sam Kraw, it didn't make her feel any less uneasy.

"We can't go out there," Mike said. "This is crazy."

She tried to look confident. "Given what this guy's done so far, do you have any doubt that he'll kill Natalie if we don't go?"

Mike turned away. "Still feel like we should be calling in backup. I guarantee that Garret wouldn't walk into something like this."

"No, he'd let the girl die," Allison said, pulling out a small leather bag before slamming the trunk door. The worst was that she knew Garret would be right in waiting. If she went in there alone she'd be breaking a dozen rules of engagement. If she dragged Mike along with her then it was going to be even worse. But saving Natalie was more important than her career, so she didn't even hesitate. "The guy asked for you too. I can't make you go––"

"––but if I don't, I'm a coward willing to let a girl die because I'm too scared."

"I was going to say I'd understand if you didn't, but I like your version better."

Allison opened her car door and looked over to Mike. "So?"

"Dammit," he said, opening his own door. "This better be an exclusive story."

"If we live through this, it's all yours," Allison said.

"That's comforting."

She threw the car into gear and raced down Harlow's deserted main drag. Everyone awake was over at the fire at the Smith-Shelly House and Allison and Mike were heading in the opposite direction.

The location given to them over the phone was only a fifteen-minute drive, but it might as well have been a helicopter drop into the middle of nowhere. A rusted-out sign on the road marked the entrance to Chaney's Quarry but the gravel road was overgrown with weeds that reached as high as the car's headlights. With the high beams on, Allison saw the faint outline of the path another car had recently taken through the weeds. This was the right place.

The car bounced along the road. They passed by a chain-link fence that looked to be mostly reclaimed by the forest growing around it and finally arrived at a hulking warehouse next to an enormous hole in the ground.

Allison parked the car some distance from the warehouse and turned off the engine.

"Now what?" Mike said.

Allison pulled out her phone and dialed. "Sheriff, this is Agent McNeil."

"Goddammit, where are you?" the sheriff shouted, loud enough that she had to hold the phone from her ear. "I have people looking for you. Thought you were fool enough to go back into the fire."

She could hear sirens in the background. It meant he was still at the fire and didn't know about his deputy yet.

"I'm sorry, but I need you to listen to me closely." She explained what was going on, where they were and what she needed the sheriff to do. To his credit, the only time he interrupted was when she told him about Deputy Cal back at the station.

"Wait. Say that again," was all he said. She heard him groan when she restated the bad news of his deputy's death, but that was it.

When she was done, the sheriff didn't say anything. All Allison could hear was the sounds of sirens and the commotion of a fire being fought. It occurred to her that the large man might very well have had a heart attack and was lying sprawled on the grass lawn.

"Sheriff Frank, did you hear what I said?" she said loudly.

"Yeah, I'm here, goddammit," he said. "Copy. Will have units en route to your location."

"Stay off the radios; anyone with a police scanner will pick that up. If someone breaks radio silence, this guy will kill Natalie."

"Copy that. We'll coordinate with cell phones." There was a long pause. "And you're gonna hold tight until we get there, right?"

"You bet," Allison lied. "Just hurry it up."

"Frank out."

"What was that all about?" Mike asked.

"By the time they get here, we'll either have this guy in custody or we'll be dead along with Natalie. If we showed up with a posse, he would have killed her and escaped. For some reason, this guy wants to talk to us. Especially you. Any idea why?"

Mike shook his head. "Not a clue. You know everything I do."

Allison reached for the leather bag she'd taken from the trunk. She pulled out a second Glock and held it out to him.

"You know how to use a gun?"

He took it, smoothly slid out the mag and checked that it was full before snapping it back into place.

"I hang out with a lot of law enforcement," Mike said. "I've spent a lot of time at gun ranges blowing off steam with the guys."

"It's different when it's a person," Allison said. The image of Sam Kraw's head disappearing in a cloud of red mist came to her. "Keep in mind we don't know how many people are in there."

"That's comforting," Mike said.

Allison climbed out of the car and Mike followed. They approached the big sliding doors that led to the loading bay of the warehouse. One of the doors was slid back on its rusted track to create an opening. Judging by where the weeds stopped growing, it looked like someone had opened the door recently.

"Let's split up," she said. "I'll go through here. You check out that door down there." She pointed to a door about twenty yards to the right.

Mike nodded and took the order without question. He jogged down to the door, staying close to the wall. While Allison waited for him to get into position, she leaned against the building, her heart knocking in her chest as the adrenaline pumped into her system. She was taking huge risks, propelled by the momentum of events. Her only operating philosophy had been to catch the killer, and now she added rescuing Natalie to that. But with even a few seconds pause, she felt needling self-doubt creep up on her.

Everything she was doing went against her training. The truth was that it was bordering on recklessness and she knew it. But she'd played out every scenario she could imagine if she played it by the book and they all ended with Natalie dead. Even though she'd just met the woman, she felt a disproportionate sense of responsibility to her and her murdered sister. Maybe it was because of the story of their abuse. Or that people their entire lives had abandoned them when they needed them most. She knew these women and she was willing to do anything necessary to save one and avenge the other.

Down the wall, Mike reached the door and stood ready, waiting for her signal to go in. A voice in her head whispered for her to call it off, to wait for Sheriff Frank to arrive with whatever law enforcement he'd mustered from surrounding towns. She knew they would have been called in for the fire; something like that was big news. There would be people from three or four towns away, so he was probably able to round up some decent firepower. But one look at the warehouse and the property and she knew it was impossible to block off all of the exits. Natalie would be dead and the killer or killers out of there before the first trooper rolled his car to a stop.

No, this was the only way to go. For whatever reason, the voice on the phone wanted to talk to both her and Mike. Obviously, there was something they had that he wanted. It was a bargaining chip, perhaps a small one and not enough to keep them from getting killed, but it was all they had.

She held up her hand toward Mike and counted down from three, then entered the warehouse.

CHAPTER 42

S he didn't like it.

The warehouse space seemed impossibly large, soaring upward three stories and with great lateral span that made it seem like an airplane hanger. Enough of the glass had been broken out of the upper levels of the structure that moonlight filtered in, painting everything in ghostly shades of grey. Metal walkways crisscrossed the area over her, following the path of guide tracks for old pulley systems that looked like they hadn't been put to use in decades. The floor of the warehouse, which appeared to have been some kind of assembly plant or a factory at one point, was littered with rusted shipping containers, old tires and piles of trash. A loud, irritated squeaking noise came from the biggest pile of debris near her and a dozen rats scurried away. She was just happy they were moving away from her because they were scared and not toward her because they were hungry.

She looked to her right and saw Mike briefly outlined in a shaft of moonlight before the door he used to enter closed behind him. Once it was shut, he disappeared into the shadows. She felt a pang of guilt for bringing him along. He was a civilian after all, not trained for this, nor paid to be here.

Of course, she was a behavioral analyst and not really trained for the field either. And she would be getting paid the same if she was taking her administrative leave on a beach somewhere. As she looked around her position, facing hundreds of spots where a sniper could easily pick her off, and with no plan of what she was going to do to rescue Natalie Bain even if she did find her, a beach suddenly sounded kind of inviting.

Bottom line, they had made the choice to be there and step into harm's way. There was only one way to go. She stepped forward into the dark, cavernous building, crouched low, gun drawn.

"Special Agent McNeil."

The voice boomed in the open space, smashing the silence. Allison flinched and threw herself against one of the shipping containers. The sound reverberated through the warehouse, making it impossible to peg where it came from.

"Thank you for coming on such short notice."

"Where's Natalie?" Allison called out.

"She's fine," came the voice. "Thanks to you. I was getting antsy."

"What do you want?"

"Is Mike Carrel here with you?" the voice asked, the fake gentility giving way to an edge of anger. "I told you to bring him."

"He's here," Allison said. "Bring Natalie out where we can see her and we'll talk to you."

"Not the way it works," the voice said. "I don't think you're taking this seriously enough. Look next to you."

Allison felt her throat constrict. She looked to the container on her left and saw nothing at first. Then, like magic, a red dot from a laser scope popped into existence two inches from her face, painting the metal surface. Allison held her breath as the dot moved over and took a position on her chest.

She fought to control her breathing and keep her wits about her. Logic told her that the shot would have already been taken without all the theatrics if that were the end game here. Still, being at the end of what she assumed was a high-powered rifle wielded by someone who had killed two people in the last twenty-four hours made it a little hard to relax. There was a chance that a sudden movement would throw the shooter off, but then what? In her exposed position and without knowing where he was, what chance did she have? What had just seemed like a really bad idea minutes before now seemed plain stupid.

"Why don't you tell Mr. Carrel what's going on and ask him to step out where I can see him?" the voice boomed.

"Bring out Natalie so we know she's OK," Allison yelled.

She didn't even register the movement of the red dot down her torso and coming to a stop on the outer thigh of her right leg.

The sound of the silenced bullet registered in her brain a split second before all of her nerve receptors were overloaded with an explosion of pain. The bullet ripped through her quad, blowing a chunk of it out the backside of her leg. The impact spun her around and she slammed to the floor. She screamed, a guttural call that was both pain and anger. She latched onto the anger only because giving in to the pain meant curling up into a ball and sobbing. If she did that, she knew she would die in a shitty warehouse in Harlow, West Virginia. That wasn't her plan.

"C'mon, Agent McNeil," said the voice. "It's not that bad. That was a clean shot. Right through the meat."

She dragged herself around the back of the container, pulled herself into the open end and sat against the interior wall, her chest heaving. She reached back and put a hand on the exit wound behind her leg and felt around. Besides the blood gushing around her fingers, there was a flap of skin and flesh hanging there. She put them back into the crater created by the bullet and pressed hard, groaning from the pain. She spotted an old piece of cloth farther back in the container, reached for it and dragged it to her. It was covered with oil stains and who knew what other kinds of chemicals, but it was better than bleeding out. She rolled it around her thigh a few times and cinched it tight.

"Mr. Carrel," said the voice, "if you're in here, I'd like for you to show yourself. Now."

Allison stilled her breathing, wondering how Mike would react. The shooter had just admitted he didn't know whether Mike was in the warehouse yet. That was an advantage. The play was to keep quiet and let the shooter keep talking to reveal his location. As long as he didn't also keep plugging her with bullets, it was the best chance they had.

"What do you want?" Mike asked, his voice seeming to come from higher up in the structure.

So much for their advantage.

"Ahh...there you are," said the voice.

Allison figured the shooter would be using his scope to search for Mike so she decided to make her move. She stood and found she could put more weight on her wounded leg than she anticipated. Gritting her teeth, she limped as fast as she could away from the container, heading toward a wreck of a delivery truck in the opposite direction of Mike's voice.

She braced for another blast and more pain, but it never came. She ducked behind the truck, breathing hard, tears streaming down her face from the effort. The run across the floor told her two things. First, that she could move better than she expected. And second, that Mike was the shooter's real target. She wondered why.

"Show yourself or I take another pound of flesh from the good agent," the voice said.

Allison thought about telling Mike it was a bluff, but it would give up her new position. She didn't have to.

"Come out so you can shoot me in the leg?" Mike said. "No thanks."

"That was just to get everyone's attention."

"You have it. Now what do you want?"

"That house where you started the fire. What did you find there?"

Allison froze, finally understanding the killer's motive for having them there.

"What are you talking about? I went there to get clothes for Natalie. Spotted the fire and helped get people out."

Allison crept out from the van and, hugging the outer wall, made her way around the edge of the warehouse. There was an old metal girder that lay on the floor, right where it had fallen from its old suspended position on the ceiling. This gave her a decent cover as she limped her way closer to the sound of the shooter's voice. She hoped Sheriff Frank would be an effective backstop in case she failed, but the thought also pressured her to move quickly because once the sheriff showed up, the game was over. Even if the sheriff was able to catch the killer, she doubted Natalie would still be alive. No, it was up to her.

"See, I have a tough time believing that," said the voice. "Here's what I think happened. You went to go look for young Natalie's computer, found it, then torched the place because you didn't have time to search for any other drives she might have copied it to. Am I right?"

The monologue gave Allison a good position on the man. A second floor balcony that overlooked the factory floor. She assumed the two dark rectangles in the wall beneath it were doors that went into management rooms in the back. That was where he must be keeping Natalie.

"Let's say we both have something the other wants," Mike said. "Now what?"

Allison stopped. Because of the sudden silence and not wanting to give away her position, and because she just caught what Mike had said. It had to be a bluff, but a dangerous one.

"Come out where I can see you and we'll talk about it," the voice said.

Allison crept forward.

"You might miscalculate and think I have the girl's laptop stashed somewhere that no one will find it if you kill me. That wouldn't help either of us," Mike said.

The killer fell silent.

Suddenly, there was a *zing* from the silenced rifle. Allison jerked her head in the general direction of Mike's voice, afraid she'd hear a thud as his body hit the floor. Instead she saw a spark where the bullet hit metal and heard it ricochet off into the darkness.

"That was just a warning shot," said the voice. "I could have already taken you out if I wanted. Just like I can take out Agent McNeil the second she crawls out from her little container."

Allison felt a twist of excitement in her chest. The shooter thought she was still in the container. She'd managed to get the advantage of surprise back on her side. If Mike could just keep him talking, she might be able to work behind the killer and get a shot on him. She crouched low and waited, knowing it was more important than ever not to make a sound. She had to time her moves to whenever the two of them were talking. As she waited, she moved her head from side-to-side, peering through the tangle of metal ahead of her from the fallen down trusses. There it was. A thin line of light outlining a door down a hallway that led off the main floor. Had to be Natalie.

"What do you want to do here?" Mike called out. "Obviously, we're not going to trust each other."

Allison moved toward the hallway. To get there she had to pass immediately under the balcony. It was a metal grid with small holes, not big enough for a bullet to pass through. She couldn't take a shot at him, but she'd also be protected if he spotted her.

She reminded herself that she still didn't know for sure if the voice was the only person she was up against. As far as she knew, there could be a dozen snipers positioned throughout the building. But given that no one had spotted her movement made her hopeful that the man on the balcony was working alone.

"Do you have the laptop?"

"Yes," Mike said. "It's somewhere safe. I've already told an associate of mine where to find it if something happens to me."

Allison felt her stomach drop as she heard the words. If he was still bluffing, he was a convincing liar. She found herself wondering if maybe he did have the laptop after all.

"Not sure if I believe that, but we'll go with it for now."

"You mean you can't afford to be wrong."

"I have the backup hard drive," the voice said. "But my employer hired me to get every copy."

My employer.

The words struck Allison like ice water. It meant that there was someone else pulling the strings and that it extended beyond the man on the platform. Clarence Mason was the first name that came to her mind. She hated that it did, but she couldn't help it. He'd had access to her location the entire way via the phone he'd given her. He'd tried to call her off the hunt. Now she wondered if that had been to give another operative a freer hand.

She shook the thought away. Intellectually she knew it was likely confirmation bias in overdrive. Her doubts about Mason had led her to stack up the evidence to support her theory, whether it was warranted or not. All that mattered now was that she knew there was someone else involved. Someone else she had to find and take down before Tracy was truly avenged.

"If you promised you'd get every copy, then you have a problem, don't you?" Mike said.

A flash of light danced across the upper windows of the old warehouse and the sounds of car engines wafted over the stale air. Allison saw the glow of a screen on the landing above her as the killer activated a phone. She couldn't see it, but she guessed it was a wireless camera set up outside.

"Now we all have a problem," the man said.

The rifle unloaded above Allison, rapid shots hammering into metal. She didn't need to look back to know that the container where the killer thought she was still hiding was taking a beating. The killer was about to make a run for it, so he no longer had a use for her as a bargaining chip with Mike. She realized that if she hadn't moved, she'd be dead.

Allison used the noise as cover to sprint down the hallway, putting as much weight on her injured leg as she could. She reached the door and flung it open. The bright light turned out to be two powerful camping lanterns. Allison squinted, her eyes adjusting from the darkness of the warehouse. It was a small office filled mostly with trash, graffiti on the walls, a single desk in the center of the room. Allison walked up to the desk, her chest heaving as dread filled her.

There, lined up in a neat row, were the bloody tips of four carefully painted toes.

Other than that, there was no sign of Natalie.

CHAPTER 43

Natalie contorted her body in the front passenger seat, doing everything possible to pry open the car door. But it was no use. Her arms were pinned behind her back. A thick rope tied her directly to the seat, the knot cinching tighter each time she struggled, digging into her ribs and making it hard to breathe. The zip ties binding her wrists and ankles cut into her skin until she bled. But even as she whimpered from the pain, she realized the slick blood pouring from the lacerations on her wrists might be her only hope.

The agony radiating up from her feet tried to send her off track, throbbing and bringing tears to her eyes. But she knew she couldn't stop. She'd fought the man the entire way from the building to the car. She'd fought him as he forced her into the front passenger seat and tied her up there. She'd fought him because she had no doubt in her mind that the man was going to kill her.

So the pain didn't mean anything.

In fact, she welcomed it.

It meant she was still alive.

She screamed in frustration as she yanked as hard as she could on her bindings, feeling a warm gush on her skin as blood spilled from the wound. But she didn't think of it as blood. It was just lubrication. And it was what she needed to get her the hell out of there.

She worked her wrist back-and-forth, trying to fold her fingers together to make them as small as possible.

There was some give around her right wrist, the zip tie sliding up higher than before. She felt a surge of hope and struggled harder against it.

It was agonizingly slow but, bit-by-bit, she worked it up her hand, sliding over the blood now pouring from her wrist. Up to the widest span of her hand between the knuckles of her index and little fingers.

Then it slipped over and her hands were free.

The second it happened, she heard an eruption of gunfire from the warehouse behind the car.

She pulled on the rope tied around her chest with her shaking hands. She wasn't free yet, but for the first time since the madness started, she allowed herself a glimmer of hope that she might survive.

CHAPTER 44

Allison spotted a door at the back of the room. There was blood on the floor. She checked behind her, expecting the killer to come barging through the door at any second, guns blazing. Instead, she heard feet banging on the ceiling above her and then a door slamming.

She imagined there must be a back staircase on the outside of the building. If she could time it right, then she might be able to get the drop on the killer as he ran.

She looked out the small window in the back door. After the bright light inside the room, it took a few seconds for her eyes to adjust to the moonlit night. It was better than the inside of the warehouse, but not by much thanks to a thin veil of clouds that diffused the light.

There was a car parked in the back. The massive hole of the rock quarry paralleled the back of the building and curved around the right side. But to the left were several dirt roads that disappeared into the thick brush around the property. She guessed Natalie was either in the car or already at the bottom of the quarry. She heard footsteps and craned her neck to see an old staircase above her. A shadow passed over her. The killer.

Allison turned the door handle, wincing with each squeak. Then, sensing the timing was right, she tugged hard to open it.

But it held firm.

Panic gripped her. She imagined for a second having to watch the killer climb into his car and simply drive away, with her stuck behind a door, unable to do anything about it.

She yanked harder on the door, all worry of making noise gone. It budged a little as the rusted hinges made a grating sound. She jerked on the handle, gaining an inch or two, enough to create a small crack to the outside. A quick search of the floor and she spotted a metal rod, a piece of an old shelving unit. She stuck it into the crack and pried the door back. Finally, the hinges gave way and the door swung open enough for her to get through.

She went out low, gun raised, just in case the door had made too much noise and tipped the killer off that she was coming. But a quick scan of her surroundings showed the man was nearly to the car, his back toward her. She took a knee, lifted her left hand to balance her right and trained her gun on him. From this position, with time to aim, even in the low light, Allison knew she was lethal.

All she had to do was pull the trigger and the night was over.

Tracy would be avenged.

Natalie, if she were still alive, could be saved.

Mike would escape uninjured.

She would acquire the hard drive of videos for Mason and get back to CID.

All it took was for her to pull the trigger and shoot a fleeing man in the back.

God, she wanted to. Every fiber of her being told her to take the shot. To end it right there. To be judge and jury and mete out the sentence she knew the judicial system would take forever to dispense. Vengeance, isn't that what she said she wanted more than anything? More than justice? And here it was, ready for her to take with a single shot.

Her finger added pressure to the trigger, but not quite enough. She was close, but not quite ready to go that far. Not yet. She knew that once she did, she'd lose something and never get it back.

"Freeze!" she yelled. "Stop right there!"

The shadow stopped, head cocked to one side.

Allison still wanted to end it. Part of her hoped the man spun around, gun in hand, shooting wildly in her direction.

But he didn't. Maybe he sensed that she wanted him to make a move. Wanted him to run after she'd told him to stop.

"Drop the weapon. Hands where I can see them," Allison barked. "Don't turn around before I tell you to."

She shuffled to her right and retook a knee, now lined up behind one of the metal supports for the staircase above her.

The man threw a rifle to his side and put his arms out.

"On your knees," Allison yelled.

The man didn't comply.

"I said on your knees."

She fired a shot at the ground to the man's side. The ground spit up dirt and gravel to tell the man how close the shot was.

"You don't know what you're dealing with here," the man said, slowly going to his knees. "You're in way over your head."

"Doesn't look like you're doing so well yourself," Allison said.

The man laughed. "You don't even know what's really going on here, do you?"

Allison felt her skin prickle. "Why don't you fill me in? Who hired you? Was it Mason?"

The man barked out a laugh. He looked over his shoulder and, even in the pale moonlight, Allison could see the scorn on his face.

"To think someone like you would be the one who finally—"

But he never finished the sentence.

A shadow ran from behind the car, wielding a piece of rebar, and took a homerun swing at the man's head.

Natalie.

Allison felt a pang of excitement that she was still alive, followed quickly by the dread that she was about to screw things up in a big way.

The man got his hands up at the last second and his forearms took most of the blow. Natalie reared back, grunting like an animal, and swung again and again.

Allison remembered the severed toes she'd seen. And the pain in the girl's eyes when she'd talked about her abuse as a child. All that pain and all that anger from being a victim was on display as she attacked her torturer.

But Allison knew it wasn't going to end well.

"Natalie! Move away from him! I have him covered!" Allison yelled.

But Natalie was lost to the world. She just swung harder as if she could break through the man's forearms to reach his head if she only mustered enough power.

In one of her backswings, the man swung his leg out and kicked her in the side of the knee. The rebar went flying and Natalie fell to the ground.

"Oh shit," Allison said, looking for a clean shot.

Natalie and the man rolled on the ground for a few agonizing seconds, Allison waiting for a moment of separation. It never came.

Instead, the man slowly stood up, Natalie positioned in front of him, a handgun jammed painfully under her jaw.

"OK, Agent McNeil," the man said. "Now it's time for you to put your gun down."

CHAPTER 45

Allison froze. She flashed back to the scene in the forest with Sam Kraw. While the situation seemed nearly identical, there was one major difference. Kraw was a twisted psychopath who liked to kill little kids. A coward that hid in shadows. The man in front of her now was a trained killer, or at least handled himself as one. The fact that he had the gun lodged under Natalie's jaw instead of at her temple meant that even if a hidden sniper were to take him out, the man's involuntary reflex would likely pull the trigger and result in Natalie's head being blown off.

"I'm right behind you," came a whispered voice from the doorway behind her. "He hasn't seen me yet."

Mike.

She resisted the temptation to turn around or even flick her head in the direction of his voice. She didn't want anything to tip off the killer that the advantage had changed once again.

"Try to draw him away from Natalie," Mike whispered. "Get me a clean shot."

"All right, let's take it easy," Allison called out to the man holding Natalie, but really talking to Mike. "Let's go slow, here. Take me instead of the girl, all right? I'm a more valuable hostage."

"Deal. Now come on out."

Allison didn't believe it for a second; the man knew he was running out of time. He'd seen the arrival of the police in front of the building. Sure, they were just locals, but locals carried guns too.

Allison stood, keeping her weapon trained on the man's head.

Natalie struggled in his arms and he snarled at her to make her be still.

"The place is surrounded," Allison said. "I've got federal, state and local on site. Choppers en route, will be here any minute. Let's just end this nice and easy."

The man shook his head. "Anyone ever tell you you're a terrible liar? Throw the gun."

Allison took a deep breath. If she didn't, she considered the man might decide to just shoot it out with her and then make his escape. With Natalie as a full-body shield, he would probably do all right. But he was looking for a higher percentage shot.

"Throw down your gun or I'll shoot her in the leg," the man said. "You know what that feels like."

Allison prayed that Mike was as good a shot as he said.

She tossed her gun and raised her hands.

"Now let her go," she said.

The man grinned. "Women. They can always be counted on to make the wrong decision."

He lowered the gun and shot Natalie in the leg. She screamed and fell to the ground. He turned his gun back to Allison and leveled it at her.

"She's coming with me," he said. "I promised her a slow ending because she wasn't very nice to me. I like to keep my promises when I can."

Allison braced for shots from Mike. They would come from right behind her. Any second.

Any second.

Silence.

Except for her heart pounding.

There was something wrong.

Mike was taking too long.

The man took aim.

Oh, Jesus.

She jumped to the right just as the man fired. Two bullets hit their mark. Allison twisted in midair from the force, smashing into the metal support beam next to her.

Her last image as she lay on the ground was of Mike walking out from the door. Gun raised. Aimed at the man. He was too late to save her, but there was still a chance for Natalie. Mike stepped past her without so much as a look.

Then everything went dark.

CHAPTER 46

Natalie looked up from the ground as the shots rang out, but she wished she hadn't. Allison's body twisted and jerked violently at the impact and then collapsed to the ground in a heap.

She tried to get up, but the pain in her leg sent the world spinning. The length of rebar was nearby, but what good was that going to do against a gun? Still, she dragged herself toward it. She wasn't about to just lie there and wait for the man to come finish her off or stuff her in the trunk of the car. After everything she'd endured in her life, she'd refused to run away when she'd gotten free from the car. And now she refused to die a victim.

Another gunshot behind her.

She flinched and tried to turn around to look for the source, but her body was rebelling against her. The world turned on its side and she found it hard to focus. A distant part of her mind, the part she'd learned to carve out for herself when she was being hurt, the same place she'd gone when her stepfather had forced himself on her over and over, stood by and watched with clinical interest. It wondered whether another bullet had just dug into her flesh. If so, she hadn't felt a thing, which was good as she didn't want to feel any more pain. But it also meant she was in worse shape than she thought. Pain was there to drive her forward. This drowsy feeling she had, this warmth creeping through her, that wasn't good.

Still, she let her eyes drift shut, the pull of the comfort there was just too welcoming.

"Let's talk about this," Harris said behind her.

Natalie's eyes shot open. Even in her weakened state she heard the fear in his voice. She liked that. Wished she were the one who'd put it there and she'd pay good money to see what had. It was the incentive she needed and, with what seemed like herculean effort, she rolled herself over.

It was the man who'd been with the FBI agent.

Gun in hand, he walked straight toward Harris, expressionless.

Harris, a bloodstain spreading from his shoulder and down his arm, stood with his hands to his side.

"This was never about you," Harris said, his voice sounding like he was under water. "Can't we work something out?"

"Where's the backup hard drive?" the FBI agent's friend asked.

"I have it. If you let me go, I'll just––"

The man put a bullet between Harris's eyes. Natalie watched in equal parts horror and fascination as the back of her tormentor's head blew out in a spray of tissue, bone and hair. The body teetered for a few long seconds as if it might continue to stand just out of long-standing habit, then it finally toppled to one side.

Natalie felt her body jerking and it took her a few seconds to realize she was sobbing. She had survived again. Beat up, in need of help, almost delirious from the loss of blood, but she was alive. Another man had tried to destroy her and failed. Even with all the pain, even as she fought to stay conscious, she felt a swelling pride in that.

A shadow passed over her. She looked up and saw it was the man who'd saved her.

She wanted to say thank you, and her lips might even have moved to form the words, but no sound came out.

"Shhh..." he said, sounding farther away than she knew he was. "You've lost a lot of blood. Hit an artery looks like." He looked over his shoulder. "They'll be here any minute. They might be able to save you."

He stood and walked away.

Might be able to save you.

Those words rolled over in her mind, tripping alarms as they went. Her body found one last store of adrenaline and her rising panic cleared her mind.

Might be able to save you.

She wasn't out of it yet. She was hurt worse than she thought and she needed help. With effort, she twisted to the side to look for the man. She assumed he was running for help, but he was bending down near Harris's body. When he stood up, she saw that he had Harris's gun in his hand.

"Get...help..." In her mind, she screamed the words, but they came out as a barely audible whisper. "Someone...help..."

The man walked back to her, scanning the warehouse as he did.

He stood over her, positioning himself so that she could see his face without having to move. She expected to see concern on his face, but there was none.

"Help," she whispered to him.

"I wish I could believe there were no more copies of that video," he said, shaking his head. "This is messier than I wanted it to be."

He raised Harris's gun.

"But I think the story will hold together, don't you?"

Natalie didn't understand what was going on. The man was supposed to be helping her. Why wasn't he trying to stop the bleeding? Why wasn't he getting help?

Then, somehow, even in her confused state, she pieced it together. It clicked. And once it did, all the energy drained from her. The defenses her mind had erected were torn down and all the pain came through in a torrent. She wailed, less from the pain, and more from the hopelessness.

The man seemed to understand her reaction. He nodded and gave her the gift of certainty.

"You're right," he said. "I'm the one." He raised the gun, holding it in his left hand.

She closed her eyes and tried to calm her mind. She refused to die in fear, cowering in front of any man. Instead, she forced herself to go to one of her favorite memories, the same memory that had been her escape during the years of abuse at her stepfather's hands. It was with Tracy at Smith Lake. They were just teenagers. Dreams and hopes intact, well before the world had torn them away. The two of them laid on the grassy shore, holding hands. She could almost feel the sun on her face even though she knew there were tears streaming down her cheeks in the real world.

In her memory, Tracy turned and smiled. "Everything's gonna be all right," she said. "Better than all right. Things are gonna be really great. You'll see." Natalie held on to Tracy's hand. Her last thought before the bullet ended her life was how happy she would be to see her beautiful sister again.

CHAPTER 47

Allison woke up pissed off.

Someone kept banging on the door to her room. A rhythmic pounding so loud that it felt like the room shook from it. She yelled for them to stop, but it did no good.

Bam. Bam. Bam. Bam. Bam.

She had half a mind to get up from her bed, open the door and catch the asshole making the noise in the act.

Only she didn't want to do that.

Because she knew who it was without getting up.

It was Sam Kraw, his evil grin filled with chiseled, yellow teeth. His eyes that looked right through her. He was standing outside her door with his head blown off, using a little girl's decapitated head to pound on the door. A wet, red stain growing with each beat as the little girl's face was smashed into a pulp.

She yelled again for him to stop. Screamed at him.

"Stop it, you mother fucker. Stop it or I'll kill you again."

But he didn't stop.

Bam. Bam. Bam. Bam. Bam.

280

Then Craig Gerty was next to her in the bed.

"You want me to stop him for you," he said. "I only need one thing in return."

He crawled on top of her, pinning her down. His hot breath and tongue on her face. Hands shoved between her legs.

She kicked and clawed, twisting away from him.

"Allison," came a different voice. "Calm down. You're OK."

Her eyes shot open. Craig Gerty was gone. Mike was there instead. Her neck was immobilized. She tried to lift her arms but couldn't. All she could move was her eyes. She saw an IV bag suspended to one side of her and a bag filled with blood to the other.

Bam. Bam. Bam. Bam. Bam.

That wasn't knocking on a door. It was the sound of helicopter blades.

Mike smiled and shouted over the noise.

"You're going to be fine," he said.

Allison remembered saying those same words to the man on the tactical team who died in her arms after Kraw's cabin exploded. The man whose face was half-gone, with shrapnel riddled through his body.

Hearing the words scared her.

Mike moved back to make room for a woman who attached a syringe to Allison's IV port. She wore medical gloves and a jacket that made her look official. More importantly, the woman had the look of steely competence given off by medical pros who knew what they were doing.

The woman noticed her staring up at her and smiled back.

"He's right, you're going to be OK," she said. "Can you move your toes for me?"

Allison did as she was asked. With her head in a brace she couldn't look down, but the woman seemed pleased.

"Good," she said. "Just hang tight. We're ten minutes out."

"N...na...n...nat..." Allison could have screamed from the frustration of not being able to get out the single word. The lights inside the helo were dimming. Or her eyes were drifting shut, she couldn't be sure which. Whatever she'd been given through her IV was doing its work but she fought against it, the need to know what had happened to Natalie burning in her chest. She struggled to remember what she'd seen before being shot but it was all a blur, like a dream scattering in the seconds after waking up.

She felt Mike take her hand and felt herself settle down. It was nice that he was there with her. If he was there, then he must have saved her. Must have saved Natalie.

She closed her eyes, allowing herself the comfort of his hand holding hers and the logic that if she was alive then Natalie must be as well. Slowly, the world drifted off, even the pounding on the door slowly faded into the distance and then finally disappeared altogether.

CHAPTER 48

Mike sat in Allison's hospital room draining his fourth cup of coffee, trying to decide what to do. Nothing had gone the way he'd planned. In fact, since the moment Tracy Bain had pulled the ski mask from his face in her Georgetown apartment, everything had pretty consistently gone to shit.

The life he'd spent the last decade so meticulously constructing had unraveled in just a matter of weeks. And now he was forced to just wait to see if the woman on the bed in front of him was going to wake up and finger him as the killer. There was no way he could tell what she'd seen, what she'd remember. All he could do was wait it out and be ready to take decisive action if things went the wrong way. It wouldn't be the first time he'd been in a tough spot.

What a ride his life had been. Even before his first kill, there had been years of thinking about it, preparing for the day. His interest had always been there; even as a teenager he was fascinated with serial killers and mass murderers. There were the greats: Dahmer, Gacy, Bundy. Then there were the young nut jobs like Klebold, Harris and Lanza. He'd considered that path for himself at one point. Going out in a blaze of heavy artillery, taking a record number of civilians with him before turning the gun on himself. But that ending seemed unsatisfying. As did the years of sitting in prison if he survived the inevitable capture, going through the endless appeals process as the state tried to put him to death.

No, early on he'd decided that the only way to scratch his particular itch was to do it smart and not give in to the desire to go on a spree. He wanted to do it like the guys he admired who got away with it for years. Only better because the only reason he knew about them was that in the end, they got caught.

On three different occasions while studying journalism and criminal justice at Colorado State, he followed young women to their cars at night, a knife and duct tape in his jacket pocket. But he always decided something wasn't quite right and he bailed out. There was a time when he thought he didn't have the nerve. That he was the guy who dreamed his whole life about skydiving, only to find once he was in the air that he was too scared to jump. To test himself, he adopted a small dog from a shelter a few towns over. It was a mutt, cute as could be, and ran up to him the second Mike walked into the play area with all the other dogs. The shelter worker insisted that people don't choose dogs, the dogs choose the humans, and that little Rex had obviously chosen him. Hours later, Mike drove Rex up into the mountains, the dog hanging out the car window, tongue out, his mouth somehow turned up into something Mike could have sworn was a smile. Mike stopped at a McDonald's to get his passenger a burger, which he scarfed down in only a couple of bites.

Finally, they took a random dirt road, an old logging trail, and drove fifteen minutes into the woods. Rex thought he'd gone to heaven, whimpering with excitement, ready to explore the great outdoors. Mike parked the car, let Rex out to pee, then stomped the dog to death with the heel of his boot. As he stood over the little carcass, he understood that he wasn't a sociopath; he did feel remorse over what he'd just done. But even greater than the sense of guilt was the incredible relief that he had it in him to take life, to scratch the itch that kept him up at night. He buried little Rex and, in a testament either to the power of canines or the horribleness of humans, the dog remained the only kill that Mike regretted.

Allison stirred in the bed and Mike stood, waiting for her eyes to open. That first look when she saw him would mean a lot, more than any words she might say. There was a chance she might have seen him kill Natalie; he couldn't be sure. And he needed to know. But he'd have to wait a little longer. Allison settled back down into the bed, her breathing smoothing out into a comfortable pattern. Mike sat back down, allowing his mind to wander back through his journey to the precarious spot in which he now found himself.

Right after college he'd sought out a job at the *Washington Herald*, writing about killers, learning about them, trying to understand them. It seemed to others like just the luck of the draw, a beat he pulled just like other guys at the paper might be assigned court cases or celebrity feuds. But there had been no accident. He threw himself into the work not only as a reporter, but as a student.

He quickly learned that his admiration was poorly placed. The real heroes were the guys who were still out there. The guys who didn't have the vanity to pick a *modus operandi* that ended up giving them publicity-friendly nicknames. The Boston Strangler. Son of Sam. The Zodiac Killer. They all blew it as far as Mike was concerned. Raising too high a profile that brought too much attention.

The truth is there are thousands of unexplained disappearances every year across America. Some of them are teenaged runaways, wives running from men who beat them, prostitutes getting away from their pimps, drug addicts wandering the landscape looking to score. These were the hunting grounds of men just like him. Quiet. Smart. Able to control the impulse to kill until it was just right. That was who Mike wanted to be like. Only better.

The first kill was messy and would have ended his career before it started if he'd done it in the States. Instead, he took a trip to Thailand by himself, enduring all the ribbing from his buddies about him taking a sex trip. He planned on doing that too, but in the end, he went to pop a different kind of cherry and prove to himself he had what it took.

The first one was a prostitute, so whacked on drugs that she didn't even seem surprised when he pulled out the machete purchased in the outdoor market earlier that day. Probably thought the Westerner wanted to play out a sick fantasy with her.

In a way, she was right.

Her expression changed once he clumsily plunged the blade into her stomach. She screamed louder than he thought possible, turned and ran from the room, the machete still lodged in her gut, flopping up and down as she ran. He didn't know what to do. The only other way out of the room was a high window. He pushed the bed that direction and was about to climb up on it when two men ran into the room and tackled him. The girl's screaming returned, coming closer to the room until she was pushed through, falling to the floor at his feet. Behind him, an angry man with a burn covering half of his face entered, brandishing the blood-soaked machete and shouting at him in Thai. Mike raised his arms to his face, thinking he was about to die, when he realized the man with the burned face had switched to English.

The trouble, it seemed, wasn't that Mike had tried to kill one of his girls, it was that he hadn't paid for the right to do so. A brief bargaining followed, a price set, then the man handed over the machete. The men left the room and the girl started to scream, understanding what was about to happen. And it did happen. Five different times on that trip, all bought and paid for from the man with the burned face. When he returned home, his buddies joked that he must have had a good time because he was like a different person. More confident. More assured. More comfortable in his own skin.

He couldn't have agreed more.

Allison stirred again. This time he saw her eyes moving behind closed lids, as if she were having a dream. He went to his darkest thought first, imagining that she was dreaming about the shooting at the warehouse, replaying the events, including seeing him blast Harris and Natalie. He cursed himself for not checking on her before the sheriff and all his local yokels had arrived. He could have just finished her off. If he had, he'd be home free. Now there was a chance, however slight, that she'd be able to finger him. Not that he would ever let it get that far. He'd spent a decade creating the perfect cover for himself and he wasn't about to let it get blown now.

It was no accident that he was regarded as one of the most respected crime reporters in the country. It was the result of incredible focus and intent. He knew that being around the same professionals tasked with taking him down was as dangerous as it was useful, but it gave him a thrill almost as strong as a kill. Almost. It was also a means to an end. By understanding the FBI's latest technology, by knowing how they thought about cases, it made sure he stayed ahead in the game. The real breakthrough had been befriending Garret Morrison, the ego-driven head of the FBI profilers who liked seeing his name in print nearly as much as catching a bad guy. Hell, he loved it more than catching bad guys. It'd been so easy to get himself in Garret's circle. A couple of puff pieces about how Garret was the mastermind behind the magic being done by the team he assembled and trained at CID. A couple of introductions to his friends at CNN so that any sensational murder ended with Garret's mug being beamed into homes around the world. Even a ghostwritten book on Garret's most interesting cases and how he was able to "read the minds of America's worst killers."

Mike kept Garret close over the next decade, easily pumping him for information under the guise of researching their next book together. The most important intel was the information withheld from the public on each case, small details about a killer's behavior or method meant to identify false tips and prevent copycat killers who replicated what they heard on TV. It was the perfect information for Mike. Once armed with all the details from Garret, Mike flew to another part of the country on the pretense of tracking down a story, and scratched his itch copying some other killer out there in the world who'd been too reckless and drawn the attention of the FBI. This way, if the body was discovered, the good folks at CID checked off their boxes and added one more body to the victim list on one of their ongoing investigations. It was perfect.

Or, it had been perfect until the day Garret told him all about Suzanne Greenville, the other call girl with the video cameras. Over too much whiskey, when Garret got to talking the most, he'd shared the details of the murder scene and how the cameras had been set up. Together, they tried to guess which DC politicos were stupid enough to go to some woman's house and pay for sex. Their conclusion: pretty much all of them. They mused about the power someone with those videos would have. The ultimate deck of cards to play with in a town where favors were never freely given.

Mike had left the bar already sold on recreating the set-up and getting his own insurance policy. He had no misconception that if he made a mistake big enough to be caught outright then no amount of influence would save him. But he didn't expect it would ever come to that. Still, it wasn't out of the realm of possibility that he might get connected to an investigation as a person of interest. If that were to happen, it would be important to have friends in high places. And if things got really bad and he needed a quick exit from the country, the higher the place the better.

Finding a call girl willing to play ball had been easy enough. A pretty young thing he'd bumped into at a gala on the arm of a much older man. She pitched him on hooking up later that night. He took her up on it, but instead of going to a room at the Four Seasons, he took her out for coffee and a long conversation. By the end of it, Catherine Fews, the only name she ever gave him, was on board with his plan. He set her up with some money to rent the place in Georgetown and installed the camera himself. She already had a clientele, but mostly with older men whose days of real power were behind them. They didn't do Mike any good. So, he started to subtly mention her name around town. Nothing obvious, just a word with the right people, a mention of an insane night he'd had with no strings attached. But then, because he was a creature of DC, he added that she wasn't taking on anyone new. The best way to feed a frenzy among powerful people was to tell them about something they can't have.

For nearly a year, it'd gone great. Some of DC's most powerful men, and a few women, had walked through the doors at the Georgetown address. And Mike's insurance policy had grown in value. When Mark Summerhays had fallen into the web, especially given the man's predilections, Mike couldn't believe his good fortune. But once the polls started to show him as a front-runner for the presidential nomination, Catherine got nervous. And he didn't like it when she was nervous.

He always knew how it had to end, but he felt sorry to close the doors on their enterprise just when it was getting good. He supposed it was because it was the first business he'd ever started and he felt a certain amount of pride in a job well done. Still, he had more videos than he needed, and he could envision a scenario where someone in Summerhays's inner circle tipped the Secret Service off to the existence of the Georgetown address. He wasn't about to risk Catherine sitting in front of a secret service interview. So, she had to go.

And that had been when the proverbial shit had started to hit the fan. Mike stood up from his chair in Allison's hospital room and tossed the paper coffee cup in the trash, shaking his head at the mistakes he'd made from that point forward. It would have been so simple to send Catherine on a trip somewhere for a well-earned vacation and then have her never show up. But his ego had gotten the better of him. Pulling off a kill right in DC, on video no less, was going to be a thrill like no other. And they never really pinned Suzanne Greenville on Arnie Milhouse, so he planned to give them a new lead in that old case.

The list of things he hadn't counted on happening since then was getting long.

The girl ripping off his ski mask. A second camera set up in the room. A professional hitman on the trail for the videos. Clarence Mason creating his own off-the-books investigation using his new hotshot agent, Allison McNeil.

For someone who prided himself on carefully controlling all variables, it was almost too much to bear.

I should just get the hell out of here, he thought, not for the first time. He could claim stress from the job, transfer his money overseas and just disappear. If things hit the fan over here, he'd read about it in some Internet café where he paid by the minute in some exotic currency.

Allison stirred, eyes fluttering open, trying to focus.

No, he would stick it out a little longer. All the loose ends might have been tied up just right after all. Natalie dead. Harris dead. The man's laptop and the external hard drive were his now. So was Natalie's laptop, which he'd recovered before setting fire to the Smith-Shelly House, destroying any backup copies Natalie might have made. The only missed opportunity was Allison. The local cops had burst through the back warehouse doors before he had a chance to confirm she was dead. The idiot Harris hit her twice in the chest, right in her vest.

She'd lost a lot of blood from the gunshot to her leg and taken a nasty knock to her head when she fell, but she was alive. With so many locals, there was nothing he could do about it. The question was whether she had seen him kill Natalie or not. The look in her eyes when she saw him would tell him everything.

He walked over to the edge of her bed and reached out for her hand. She opened her eyes and turned to him, blinking in recognition. She squeezed his hand weakly and smiled. It was the reaction he'd hoped for.

He returned the smile and forced his eyes to water just a bit. It might have been too much, but seemed to work. Allison noticed and squeezed his hand tighter.

As he thought through it all, he wondered if things weren't going to work out just fine after all. He had Harris's laptop and the backup disk. The girl's laptop was stashed away, ready for him to pick up. If the videos were tied up, then he would live through this. And maybe a romantic relationship with the FBI's rising star was exactly what he needed.

Maybe things were finally back on track.

He sat on the edge of the bed and softly gave Allison the sad news about Natalie Bain. When she cried, he held her in his arms and comforted her, told her that it was all over, that everything was going to be all right.

And, he realized, he actually believed it.

CHAPTER 49

The first call Allison made once her head cleared was to her dad. He picked up after only one ring and his voice sounded firm and strong.

"McNeil residence," he said. It was the way he'd answered the phone her whole life. Something about it got to her and she teared up.

"Dad, it's Allison."

"Hon, you all right?" he asked. "I've been worried about you."

She couldn't help the tears now. He was obviously having a good day, maybe one of the better ones he'd had for a while. She immediately felt a pang of guilt for not being with him.

"I'm fine, Dad," she said. "Just got caught up with work is all."

"Maria seems to think you're in the hospital."

Allison groaned. She'd texted Maria earlier to make sure things were all right. She wasn't supposed to mention anything to her dad. She didn't want to upset him.

"Yeah, nothing big though. Be home later tonight. We can hang out, all right?"

"I'd like that," he said. "Be like old times. I'll have your mom cook up a couple of pizzas."

Allison felt her heart sink and she heard an edge creep into her dad's voice. That anxiety that he knew something was wrong but couldn't quite put his finger on it.

"I haven't seen her though," he mumbled. "Must be picking Eddie up from school. Must be it," he said. "Getting forgetful, you know, baby?"

"I know, Dad," she whispered, not finding the energy or feeling the need to tell him that his dead wife wasn't picking their murdered son up from school. "I love you, Dad."

"Love you too, baby. Come home when you can. We'll hang out, like you said."

"Will do," Allison said, wiping tears from her cheek. "Can I talk to Maria please?"

A rustling sound and then Maria came on the phone. "He was having such a good day. I thought he should know. I'm sorry if I––"

The softness in the woman's voice took the edge off her being upset. "It's fine. Really." She took a deep breath. "I'm just sorry I'm not there."

"There'll be other good days," Maria said quietly.

But Allison knew they were already becoming infrequent and that there wouldn't be that many more before her dad slipped away altogether. She felt a sudden urge to get home. "I'm taking a plane home, so I'll be there tonight. Will you be there or someone else from the agency?"

"I'll be here," Maria said, an offended tone in her voice, as if Allison were purposefully reminding her of her place.

Allison picked up on it. It wasn't her intention at all. "Good. He likes when you're there. You're good for him. Really good for him."

There was a long pause on the line and Allison thought perhaps the woman hadn't heard her. She was about to ask if she was there when she replied.

"Thank you," she said quietly.

They said goodbye and hung up.

She took a minute to get her thoughts together and then called Clarence Mason.

"You've been busy," was how Mason answered the phone.

"I do what I can," she replied, matching his tone. She'd thought a lot about Mason and what his role had been in her little adventure. Part of her still suspected the killer was one of his guys. If so, there were deaths to answer for.

"I've spoken to the doctors up there," he said. "I was ready to send a team up, but they assured me you were all right."

Allison slid off her bed so that she was sitting on the edge. Her leg was wrapped, making her thigh twice its normal size. Her head throbbed from where she'd struck the steel support beam and there were two massive bruises on her chest from the impact of the bullets on the vest. All of it combined together to make her feel like one giant ball of pain. That was especially true once she'd made them stop the pain meds a few hours earlier. She wanted a clear head to think things through. She was starting to wonder if that had been such a great idea.

"You should try this some time," she said. "It feels great."

"I've been there more than I want to remember," Mason said, his voice drifting. "It's hard, but we recover and move on."

She realized he wasn't talking about her physical injuries anymore. She closed her eyes and saw Natalie's frightened face staring back at her, begging for help, and had to shake her head to get rid of the image. She wondered at a career like Mason's and how many ghosts like Natalie Bain he had circulating around him at night when his mind wandered into the past.

"We have people up there now going over the scene at the quarry. The locals have been mostly helpful. I hear the sheriff is a character."

"Do you have an ID yet?"

"Scott Harris," Mason said. "We know him. He's a fixer. International ties. Ostensibly consults on security issues, but several different parts of the community had active files on him. Let's just call it a hunch that Uncle Sam may have had need of Mr. Harris's talents on occasion."

"Did you send him up here?" Allison asked, deciding to go for the most direct approach. She wished she could see him to be able to read his body language, but she didn't want to wait. She had to know.

"No," Mason answered, not even pausing to acknowledge the accusation. "But I have a good idea who did."

"Who?" Allison asked, excited by the idea of a lead to whoever was responsible for setting Harris into motion. Still, she tempered her excitement knowing that if Mason was the one who sent Harris, the best way to defer suspicion was to cast it in a different direction. "I want to be part of the investigation."

There was a muffled sound and Allison heard Mason talking to someone in the background. She strained to listen but couldn't make out what was being said. When Mason came back on the line, he was distracted.

"We'll talk about it when you get back," he said. "I sent a plane. And Allison..."

"Yes?"

"No reporters tagging along this time. I have enough trouble with Garret when it comes to that."

Before she could open her mouth to explain the circumstances that led to Mike Carrel being with her, the line went dead.

She laid the phone on the bed and looked around the sparse hospital room. It felt far from home and, with her father's condition, even home felt like a fading idea. She felt so alone, isolated from her colleagues in BAU because of Garret's influence. She was on unsteady ground with Mason who she still didn't quite trust. She found herself thinking of Richard, amazed that it was only two days ago that she'd laid flowers at his grave. She'd given everything to her job, and what had it given her? Heartbreak after heartbreak. She was surprised to find herself wondering whether it was time for her to leave the Bureau. She could find another way to make a difference. One that didn't include all the petty politics and the rest of the bullshit.

Mike walked into the room holding two sodas and two hot dogs in paper wrappers. "I didn't know if you wanted anything," he said, lifting up the drinks and food. "These are for me, but if you want me to get you something..."

She grinned, feeling her melancholy and self-pity drain away. Maybe it was time to open herself back up again and see what might happen with this man who'd fallen into her life. At least he understood the horrors she lived with and the unique demands of her career. She returned Mike's smile as he took a seat on the bed next to her.

"Thanks," she said, reaching out for what he'd offered her. "I think I will try something."

CHAPTER 50

Allison stared out the car window as a young agent drove her and Mike back out to the quarry. At night, the place had seemed imposing, like a set piece in a horror movie with gaping black windows and curls of barbed wire. By day, the place looked like a dump. Piles of trash littered the property. There was an impressive collection of dead refrigerators, ruined tires and scrap metal.

Still, Allison had the chills as she passed through the doors into the main warehouse space, using crutches to take the pressure off her bandaged leg. The scene was lit with portable klieg lights and the crime scene technicians were busy scouring the area for bullet casings and other forensic evidence.

She'd been to enough crime scenes to know that while the crew would be thorough, there wasn't the energy present that would be there if they were looking for a way to catch a killer. For all intents and purposes, this was a closed case. The bad guy was in a body bag at the morgue and there was no reason to suspect that he hadn't been alone. Still, with the orders coming directly from Mason's office, she knew the resources wouldn't be pulled until the SAC, Special-Agent-In-Charge, felt he had done enough to make his boss happy. She wondered who was running the crime scene.

"Un-fuckin-believable," said a gruff voice behind her.

She turned and nearly said the same thing. Garret Morrison hobbled toward her on a pair of crutches.

"Garret," she said, making it sound like a dirty word. "I didn't know they were sending you."

"Someone has to clean up your mess," he said, clearly not happy to be there. "Mason asked me personally. What're you gonna say, right?" He turned to Mike and stuck out his hand. "You turn up in the damnedest places, Mike," he said. "Couldn't believe it when I saw your name on the prelim report."

Mike shook Garret's hand. "Just following a story. I figured once it got good, you'd be put on it."

"Damn right," Garret said, casting a look at Allison.

When Garret looked away, Mike gave her a shrug as if feeling guilty for stroking Garret's ego. Allison found it funny and had to bite her lip to keep from laughing.

"But don't know how the two of you managed to screw the pooch so hard, so fast," Garret said. "Local girl dead. Local guy gone missing next town over. Probably dead. Bad guy dead. Can't question a bunch of dead people, now can we?"

Allison glared at Garret. She always hated the way he talked about victims like they were a personal inconvenience to him. Even though she knew it was a coping mechanism to deal with all the horrific death around him on a daily basis, it didn't make it any less insulting.

"Tell me what you need from me," Allison said, wanting to get away from Garret as soon as possible. "Mason sent a plane for me and I don't want to keep it waiting."

Garret's face fell, not even bothering to hide his jealousy.

"You know the drill," he said. "I'll walk each of you through separately. We'll take it step-by-step, piece together how this went down. After that, I won't need you anymore."

"Sounds good," Allison said. "I'll want to talk to Sheriff Frank before I leave."

"Negative," Garret said.

"Excuse me?"

"My site. I'm SAC," Garret said. "I don't want you talking to the locals. They deal with me direct, got it?"

"Garret, you know what--"

Mike put a hand on her shoulder and she stopped.

"C'mon," Mike said. "Like you said, you don't want to keep the plane waiting. Get home to your dad," he prompted.

Allison nodded, stuffing her anger back inside.

"OK, let's get this over with."

"Good girl," Garret said. "Nice to see a man finally able to rein you in. This way. Start from when you walked into the warehouse."

Allison bit her tongue at the comment. She knew Garret was just trying to get a rise out of her and she wasn't about to give him the satisfaction. She followed him back to the main entrance to the warehouse, both of them hobbling like crippled penguins on their bum legs. Mike drifted off to hang out with a few of the other agents that were part of Garret's team. She noticed that he seemed to know everyone, calling the agents by their first names and falling into easy conversations as if he had just met some buddies at a neighborhood bar instead of a crime scene for a double homicide.

"So, you and Mike, huh?" Garret asked.

"What?" Allison said, realizing she'd been caught staring after Mike. She regained her footing and shot him a look. "Why? Jealous?" It was petty, but Garret had that effect on her. "Don't worry, he doesn't strike me as the monogamous type. I'm sure he'll still call you."

Garret just grunted his disapproval and pointed at the warehouse door.

"Walk me through it. Approximately what time did you enter the warehouse?"

Allison forced herself to concentrate and started the walk-through. She did her best to describe what happened, careful not to overstate what she saw or thought she saw at any given point. That was the classic issue with eyewitness reports. People in high-stress situations tend to blend what they feared they would see with what they actually saw. One eyewitness might see the suspect with a gun in their hand while another eyewitness with the same vantage point might see a knife. Both would pass a polygraph that they were one hundred percent certain of what they saw, so who was lying? Neither one. They saw what their brain interpreted.

Even armed with this knowledge, Allison fought to separate out what she actually saw versus what her mind told her she saw.

They followed her path across the warehouse floor. The pool of her dried blood where Harris shot her was taped off as part of the scene investigation. They both looked at it for a long second. She expected Garret to crack some wiseass remark, but he didn't. Instead, he marked the moment by nodding with a kind of grudging respect, then quickly moved on.

Together, they stood outside the container where she'd hid and talked about where she thought Harris was located during that time. They talked about the possibility of there being a second shooter. There was no evidence so far of one, but that was one of the reasons for the investigation. She did her best to recall where Harris had been while he was goading Mike to come out of hiding. She replayed in her head some of the things he'd said.

You went to go look for young Natalie's computer. Am I right?

Do you have the laptop?

That was the whole reason Harris had summoned them to the warehouse. He thought Mike had possession of the computer. She imagined the fire at the house again, saw Mike in the room beneath her, bent over as he ran through the fire. To her eye, it looked like he was just protecting himself from the blaze. But maybe she'd just seen what she wanted to see. If Mike did have the laptop, he likely would have covered it with his arms and run hunched over. And if he had the laptop, then––

"You still with me, McNeil?" Garret asked.

She refocused her attention. "Sure, a little foggy from the hospital is all."

"Need a break?"

On reflex, she thought of a comeback, thinking Garret was insinuating something about her strength or her grit. But there was none of that on his face. He didn't have a look of actual concern, but there was no judgment there either. Professional courtesy was the best description and even that blew her mind.

"Thanks, Garret," she said. "But I'm fine. Let's keep going."

They followed her path after leaving the container, under the balcony and into the back office where Natalie had been tortured. The tips of her toes were no longer lined up on the table. She knew they would have been photographed and then carefully placed into an evidence bag. Still, four circles of blood still dotted the table and made her stomach turn.

Allison left the room as quickly as she could and walked outside. The sun blazed and she squinted against the sudden glare. After her eyes adjusted, she saw the outline of two bodies on the ground.

"Which one was Natalie?" she asked.

Garret pointed to the one on the left. Allison walked up and bent down to the ground, awkwardly balancing with her crutches. She knew Garret was likely cataloging all the ways she was too soft to do the job, too emotionally invested, but she didn't care. She'd let Natalie down and the girl was dead because of it.

She heard Harris's voice again.

My employer hired me to get every copy.

My employer.

That was the phrase she'd been keyed on over the last couple of hours, especially since her conversation with Mason promising he had a lead on who'd hired Harris.

But now that she was on the scene and thinking it through, she remembered Harris had said something before that. Something important.

I have the backup hard drive.

My employer hired me to get every copy.

I have the backup hard drive.

She turned to Garret. "Where's the hard drive?"

Garret looked puzzled. "Are you talking about this mysterious laptop you and Mike say you were hunting down?"

"No, Harris was looking for the laptop. He thought Mike had it. But he said he already had the backup hard drive."

"We didn't find any hard drive," Garret said. "The team's doing a perimeter search now, but they've already gone over the immediate scene."

"No, he would have had it on him," she said. She pointed to the car. "He was leaving so he wouldn't have stashed it anywhere."

Garret looked annoyed. "I'll talk to the locals again, but they didn't say they found anything. But that Sheriff Frank was a real pain in the ass."

"Pretty big deal to hold back evidence like that, even for him," Allison said. "Sounds like a stretch."

"He was pretty pissed about jurisdiction. We had words," Garret said.

Allison nodded, imagining that it hadn't been a pretty sight between the two men. She didn't believe Frank would blatantly tamper with evidence like that, but something didn't add up. Harris had no upside from claiming to Mike and Allison that he had a backup hard drive, so why would he have bothered unless it was true? And then there was Harris's certainty that Mike had possession of the laptop. So certain that he'd risked giving away his position and called the FBI to come meet him. But why? Mike had assured her that he'd been bluffing that he had the laptop during his exchange with Harris. He seemed believable, maybe because she really wanted to trust him, but there was a nagging doubt eating away at her. Maybe he had recovered something in the fire. Maybe the nice-guy routine was just a cover for the reporter looking for the exclusive scoop.

Outside of Mike, there was something else bothering her. The bad guy was in a body bag in the local morgue, but she held no misconception that her job was done.

As far as she was concerned, this wasn't over until she found out who had hired Harris.

"How's the leg feeling?" Mike asked, coming up behind them.

Allison leaned on her crutches, noticing the pain a lot more once he mentioned something. She felt the OxyContin in her pocket and thought about taking one. But she wanted to keep her head clear so she resisted the urge.

"Not great actually," she said. "Feels like someone shot me."

"C'mon, Garret," Mike said, looking more concerned than amused at her attempt at humor. "Give her a break and wrap this up, huh? Girl's got a plane to catch."

Garret's face clouded over. Allison wasn't sure if it was because of Mike going to bat for her or because he knew that Mason had sent his private plane to pick her up and deliver her back to DC.

"Give me the play by play of the last part," he said. "Your statement is a little confusing here. You had a gun on Harris. He had the hostage. Then what?"

Allison's mind went back to the moments before she was shot. Natalie crying. Harris forcing the gun under the girl's chin.

"He had her. There was no way to disarm him. No doubt in my mind that he would kill her unless I put down my gun."

"And where were you?" Garret asked, looking at Mike.

"I thought you wanted to do this separately," Mike said.

"You're the one complaining about getting her out of here," he replied, an edge to his voice.

Mike looked at Allison, clearly uncomfortable. "I was in the doorway, watching the whole thing. I really thought that if she could get the killer in the open, then I could take the shot."

"So McNeil puts her gun down," Garret said. "Thinking you're going to stop him before he shoots."

"Yes," replied Allison, trying hard to keep her voice from shaking. It was less than twelve hours since Natalie had begged her for help. Since Harris had turned the gun on her and slammed two bullets into her chest. "I thought it was the only chance to save Natalie."

Garret sniffed the air derisively as if to say, *Well, that didn't work out so well, now did it?* If Mike hadn't been there, she had no doubt the son of a bitch would have said the words out loud.

"So when Allison threw her gun down, Harris shot Natalie in the leg, then came at Allison." Garret looked up from his notes. "So you had a shot on him? Before he fired at McNeil?"

Allison had already played the event out in her head a hundred times while lying in the hospital bed. She'd interviewed a hundred people after traumatic experiences and it was common for them to not remember anything in the minutes leading up to the event. Even people recovering from car crashes reported blank spots in their memory in the minutes before impact. It was as if the brain pressed the delete button on the incident for its own protection and scrubbed some of the extra data before just to be sure.

She remembered Natalie's face, she would always remember that. And she remembered Mike in the door behind her and the sense that there was a way out.

"I jumped to the right," Allison said, moving that direction. "That's the last I remember."

Mike stepped out from behind the pole and also went right. "I broke the same way so Allison was between me and Harris," Mike said. "I tried to maneuver to get a shot, but by the time I did, Harris started firing. First at Allison. Then one shot at Natalie."

"Two shots to the chest," Garret said. "You're just damn lucky he saved the head shot for the Bain girl."

Allison swallowed hard and felt a little dizzy. She had to lean more on her crutches. Of course she'd thought about that before, but standing in the spot where she'd come so close to dying affected her more than she imagined it would. Little sensory details of the night flooded back to her, disjointed, out of order. Harris holding Natalie hostage. The girl's dismembered toes lined up in a row. The bullets hitting her vest like a pair of flying sledgehammers.

But inside all of that, there was something else she couldn't put her finger on. Something in her gut that told her she was missing something important. She'd learned long ago to trust her instincts, but how could she trust them if they were giving her no more than a vague feeling?

She hung her head, suddenly finding it hard to breathe. Dark bands appeared around her peripheral vision and the white gravel she was standing on seemed to pulse with each beat of her heart.

"Are you all right?" Mike said, his voice echoing.

She cleared her head and discovered she was hanging from her crutches, facing the ground, breathing hard. Mike's hand was under her arm, propping her up. He took the small bag she carried over one shoulder.

She cleared her throat. "I'm fine. A little light-headed is all."

"What else do you need, Garret?" Mike asked.

Garret looked smug, as if he'd won something, but Allison didn't care. She just wanted to get out of there. She was thankful Mike was there. In the two men's relationship, Mike, although younger than Garret, had the role of the big brother. Garret was on his best behavior and even at that he was still a prick.

"C'mon, man, she's already walked you through everything," Mike said.

Garret closed his notebook and nodded to the sedan parked in the back gravel lot. "Martell will drive you to the airport," he said. "I'll want to talk to you again in DC."

"I'm going to walk her to the car," Mike said. "Be right back."

Garret looked even more annoyed. He pulled out two pieces of paper and laid them flat on his notebook. "Neither of you signed your statements."

"Can't we do that later?"

"It's a private plane," Garret said, sounding like a child. "It's not going anywhere."

Allison grabbed Garret's pen and signed hers and Mike did the same.

"I forgot you were a lefty, Mike," Garret said, angling the notebook the other direction so he could sign the statement more easily. "Probably why you're part of the liberal press."

Allison glanced down as Mike signed his statement. It hadn't struck her before that Mike was left-handed.

"The *Herald* is to the right of Fox News," Mike said. "The term liberal press doesn't get thrown at us much."

Garret folded the papers and put them back in his notebook. "Safe travels, McNeil. Try not to get anyone killed on the way home."

As they walked away, Mike whispered, "If I shoot myself in the leg, can I get out of here too?"

Allison smirked. "I don't think your boyfriend would like that. He's already jealous. Besides, you promised to drive my car back to DC."

They walked in silence for a few steps, Allison picking her way across the loose gravel, feeling a cold sweat spring up on her skin.

"I never apologized to you," Mike said abruptly.

"For what?"

"I...you know...you only put your gun down because you thought I had things covered," Mike said. "I almost got you killed."

"But you didn't. Here I am in all my damaged glory."

"I got Natalie killed," Mike said, the emotion heavy in his voice.

Allison stopped and made him look her in the eye. "Harris killed her. Not you. It was Harris."

Mike looked at her strangely, then nodded. "You're right. I have to keep reminding myself of that."

She turned and kept walking to the car. Mike slid his arm into hers but his touch that had felt like such a great comfort only minutes before, full of promise, full of potential, now felt strange and foreign. A cold shudder passed through her body and she wondered why.

CHAPTER 51

Mike watched the sedan pull out of the warehouse lot. So far, everything had gone even better than he could have hoped. There were no holes in the story. No gaps in the investigation that couldn't be explained. It helped having Garret there because even if something did come up, there was no way suspicion was going to fall on his good buddy Mike Carrel.

That had been a masterstroke and no accident. Mike had put that in motion with a phone call to him once Allison was safely in the hospital. While Garret had told Allison that Mason asked him to come up personally, the truth was that Garret had reached out to Mason and requested the assignment.

It'd been a whirlwind couple of days, at times nearly spiraling out of control, but he'd kept calm, been patient and it'd paid off. Now he could see a path out of the wilderness. Hell, it was more than a path, it was a smoothly paved road lined with gold. Not only did he have the laptop and the hard drive, not only were the only witnesses to the video dead, but he had a burgeoning relationship with the new star in CID. He imagined a protracted romance. He chuckled as he imagined what it would be like if he ended up married to her. A serial killer married to an FBI profiler responsible for hunting killers. It was almost too good.

The only thing he didn't like was the way she'd looked at him right before she left. There was a shift in her, so different from her reaction to him in the hospital when she'd cried in his arms like they were already lovers. He'd worried that something might be triggered when she visited the scene and he'd watched her carefully the entire time. But nothing stood out. Just the little bit at the end when she'd gotten weak and needed help to walk, and he'd felt her pull away instead of leaning into his body as he expected.

But was that really odd? The doctors hadn't even wanted to discharge her, let alone have her wander around a crime scene on her crutches. He decided it wasn't anything to worry about. If there was anything he knew, it was how to seduce a woman. Allison McNeil wasn't even going to be a challenge, he was sure of it.

He walked back to where Garret stood, reviewing his notes.

"Ready when you are," he said.

"McNeil, huh?" Garret asked, looking a little disgusted. "How long has that been going on?"

"Met her yesterday."

"No shit," Garret said. "And see what kind of trouble you got yourself into? I'd watch your step with that one."

"How'd that go for you?" Mike said, nodding at Garret's leg.

"Screw you," Garret said. "Come on, we need to fill out some paperwork. Let's walk through from the beginning."

Mike followed Garret back through the warehouse and out to the front door. They went through Mike's side of the story step-by-step, comparing it to his written statement, making clarifications and adjustments where needed. Afterward, they worked out together the sequence of how Harris shot Allison and then Natalie in the head, Mike claiming that the whole thing was a blur to him. It was a perfect case of confirmation bias. Garret knew with certainty that Harris had shot both Allison and Natalie, so every piece of evidence fit into that scenario. Mike almost had himself convinced that Harris had done the deed instead of him.

Shortly after Allison left, Mike excused himself to check his phone messages. Instead, he activated the Find My Phone app and waited as the map loaded. He only had a single bar out there so it loaded slowly, but when it finally did, it showed a blue dot traveling along the main highway. God, he loved technology. All he had to do was drop one of his phones into Allison's bag when he carried it around for her. It was a simple enough explanation when she found it there later, an oversight on his part, no more. But until then, he had real-time intel on her location.

While he finished up with Garret, he sneaked glances at the app, watching the blue dot stop at the local general aviation airport where Garret had told him Allison would be catching her plane. Then fifteen minutes later, the dot moved again, this time faster and not following any roads. She was on the plane and out of his hair. After a while, the dot disappeared as the plane ascended out of cell phone range.

"Do you need me here anymore?" he asked Garret finally.

"You're not going anywhere," Garret said.

Mike froze. Garret's voice had turned hard and serious. Something was wrong. Mike slowly turned, ready for anything. "Oh yeah? Why's that?"

Garret stared him down for a beat. "I think you know."

Mike resisted the temptation to look around for possible escape routes. He knew he had to remain calm until he knew how bad it was. He searched his mind for what mistake he'd made. Had he missed a surveillance camera on the old building? Did Allison actually see him finish off Harris and Natalie and the whole thing in the hospital and there at the factory had just been an elaborate set-up? Mike felt his heart pound. Garret's expression turned smug, as if the guy knew he had him dead to rights.

"I can't believe you thought you'd get away that easy," Garret said.

Mike squared his shoulders to him. If this was how it ended, he would go down fighting. He said nothing as he stared Garret down.

Garret matched him, eyes locked. Then, unbelievably, he burst out laughing. "Shit man, you should see your face. You look so damn serious. You're not getting out of here without hitting the bars with me tonight."

The enormous weight of thinking he'd been caught fell off his shoulders and he nearly gasped at the feeling. He disguised it with a laugh of his own to match Garret.

"Thank God," he said. "I thought you meant more paperwork. Drinking beers is something I can get behind."

Really, the last thing in the world he wanted to do was tie one on with Garret that night. But he needed to keep Garret close, especially since he felt threatened by his new relationship with Allison.

But Mike had a few loose ends to tie up first. And he needed to do those on his own.

"So hell yes, we're drinking tonight," Mike said. "If I ever needed a friend to talk to, it's now," he said, worried he might be laying it on a little thick.

But he needn't have worried. Nothing was too thick for Garret, who nodded knowingly. "I've been there, man. Pulling the trigger, even when it's a bad guy, it stays with you. It's good to get it all out."

Mike hated the idea of all the drunken hours of fake emotion he was going to be required to display that night. It sounded exhausting. But he knew it had to be done.

Just like recovering the laptop and hard drive had to be done as well.

"I'll call you in an hour or two to hook up," Mike said. "I just need to mop up a few things in town. Research, mostly."

"I thought you told McNeil you weren't going to file an article," Garret said, grinning like a fool, pleased to think he was back on the inside.

"I'm not. But I didn't say anything about a book. This has New York Times bestseller all over it," Mike said. "I imagine there's a role in it for you, coming in at the end to clean up the mess left by the young, inexperienced agent."

"Ohh, she's going to hate that," he said, obviously pleased.

"By that time I'll have gotten what I need from her and she'll be an ex-girlfriend, so it won't matter, right?"

As Garret laughed, Mike felt a wave of scorn for the man. He was so petty and predictable that getting on his good side was child's play. They parted ways with Garret still chuckling.

Mike walked back through the warehouse, looked around to make sure he was alone, then pulled aside a metal cover and reached into a small gap in the wall. He extracted the hard drive and thumb drive he'd found on Harris's body in the quick search he'd performed as the sheriff and his rag-tag posse closed in on his location. There had been a few nervous minutes when Mike thought the police might search him as a precaution. If they found the hard drive, and if it had on it what he thought it did, then it was game over. Luckily, with Sheriff Frank vouching for his identity and with Mike's Oscar-worthy performance of worry for Allison, they left him alone. In the confusion when the helicopter landed to transport Allison, he'd been able to slip away and stash the drive. Now, with it safely in his pocket, he breathed a little easier.

Mike climbed into Allison's car and checked his iPhone again. The Find My Phone app searched for a few seconds and then the map shifted over to Washington DC and pinged a blue dot at Reagan National Airport. Mike checked his watch, impressed with how fast Allison had made the journey. He guessed the director hadn't sent an old single-prop Cessna to pick her up. Must be nice.

As Mike pulled out of the gravel parking lot, the wheels crunching through the stone, he relaxed a little. Allison was out of the picture. Garret was in control of the crime scene and one hundred percent bought into his version of events. The only copies of the videos were in his possession and Harris was taking the blame for everything: Catherine Fews/Tracy Bain, burning down the Smith-Shelly House, Natalie Bain. All of it. Mike tried to forget the worry and fear he'd allowed into his life over the last week. Now, it just smelled of weakness, the exact opposite of how he was supposed to feel. He was a god, walking among normal men but also above them. A shadow. A nightmare. And it was time he goddamn remembered that.

He waved at the officers blocking the main entrance to the quarry and they let him through. There was media all over the place with small-market reporters doing their one-shots with the quarry sign behind them and satellite vans with their transmission poles reaching up into the sky. Having the local yokels be the first on the crime scene all but guaranteed nothing would remain a secret. But these were still locals and Mike didn't spot anyone he knew. That would come later. In the world of the twenty-four hour news cycle, the cable shows would have their anchors crawling through the underbrush trying to sneak a peek soon enough.

All the more reason to recover the laptop and get out of town as soon as possible.

If he hadn't felt so confident, he might have noticed he wasn't going about his errands alone. A single car, so far down the road that it was hard to even see it, pulled onto the road, kept its distance and followed him into Harlow.

CHAPTER 52

Mike parked the car half a block away from the charred remains of the Smith-Shelly House. There were uniformed men digging through the rubble, the fire inspection team he imagined, but he didn't worry about what they would find. His story checked out. Hell, he'd even dragged a few people out from the fire and got to play hero. Everyone accepted that Harris had set the fire so when they discovered evidence of arson, it would fit the story. The fire inspectors looked busy and he doubted they would be an issue as he recovered the laptop. Still, he watched for a couple of minutes to get an accurate headcount and see what they were up to. While he waited, he pulled out his phone and called Allison. She answered on the second ring.

"How was the flight?" he asked.

"Private jets are the only way to fly," she replied.

"Just become the director of the FBI and you can use it whenever you want," he said, getting out of the car, sliding his computer bag over his shoulder and walking toward the Smith-

Shelly House. He looked at the Find My Phone app and saw the blue dot still at the airport. It'd been there for a while, which was strange. He stopped walking. "What are you doing now? Going home?"

"No, Mason wanted to see me right away so I'm halfway to downtown," she said.

Mike frowned, staring at the blinking blue dot at the airport. She was lying to him. But why?

"Are you there?" Allison asked.

"Yeah, I'm here," Mike replied. He kept staring at the blue dot. If she was lying to him about where she was, then maybe she suspected something. "How's traffic?" he asked, trying to draw her out.

"Shitty. And get this," she said. "I left my bag on the plane, so I've got to figure out how to get that later. One of those days, right?"

Mike felt the tension release from his shoulders. Such a simple explanation. There was nothing odd going on. She'd just left behind her bag and the phone he'd stashed in it was all. A certain level of paranoia was healthy, but he felt himself dancing on the edge of what he considered an acceptable level. He needed to get a better grip on himself.

"One of those days," he agreed. "I'm staying up here one more night then driving back down." He paused for effect. "I can't wait to see you again."

There was an equally long pause on the line, then a soft reply. "Me either. Call me when you get into town."

They said goodbye and Mike felt the old confidence refill his veins. He was back in control. If anything, after a little more distance and time, he might look at this as his most impressive kill yet. To dance so close to discovery and still get away had been terrifying and exhilarating at the same time. It was the reason he'd killed Tracy Bain in front of a camera instead of in some empty field to begin with. But while it was exciting, it'd been too reckless. Discreetly killing Tracy, stashing her body and keeping the videos for a rainy day would have been the smart play. But he'd justified what he'd done with the idea that the murder scene would reopen a cold case and lead the police down a dead end. If he was being honest, all that was really just a pretext for him to live on the edge. And it was the exact kind of behavior he'd always hated in those who needed publicity to feel the rush.

His heroes, the killers who operated in the quiet dark alleys of cities, in the abandoned warehouses, in the truck stops crawling with runaways and prostitutes, the ones who went on and on without needing the fame, they would be ashamed at his grandstanding. As he walked past the burned-out husk of the house he'd torched the night before, he resolved to return to his roots and bask in the purity of his kills, not the thrill of evading capture.

The shed was a good fifty yards from the main house and tucked into the woods that backed the property. It was the perfect find when he'd searched for a place to stash the laptop after escaping the fire.

He imagined the investigators had given the place a quick once-over just to be thorough, but there was no reason to think the place held any clues, so he wasn't worried that it would have been turned upside down.

Still, walking up to the shed, he was relieved to see that it looked undisturbed.

He opened the door and stepped inside. There were windows on two walls so there was plenty of light, more than there had been when he'd hidden the laptop.

Mike moved a couple of ladders and wheeled the push lawnmower out from the back wall. He tipped it and reached underneath where, lodged under the mower blade, was Natalie Bain's laptop.

He pulled it out and wiped the dirt off its smooth metal casing. He slid it into his computer bag. Even if someone stopped him, he was just a reporter carrying his work laptop. With a quick look out the windows, he opened the shed door and stepped outside.

And came face-to-face with Special Agent Allison McNeil.

CHAPTER 53

Allison saw Mike's eyes flash to the gun in her shoulder holster. Wearing it without a jacket to cover it up was a conscious choice, as was the decision not to pull it on him. She trusted her intuition to get her this far and she wasn't going to stop now. The pit in her stomach that had been forming since she'd walked the crime site was like a living thing now, clawing at her insides as emotions fought for prominence. Anger. Betrayal. Even sadness. The only emotion apparent on Mike's face though was embarrassment.

Mike hung his head. "You caught me," he said. "I have no excuse."

"Natalie's laptop?" she asked, nodding at his bag.

He nodded. "Videos of a presidential front-runner with a call girl. And the video of her killer. Do you have any idea how big that story is?" he asked.

Allison watched his body language closely. Cataloging every look, every movement of his hands. "You interfered with a federal murder investigation," Allison said. "Do you have any idea how serious that is?"

Mike held his hands out wide and took a step toward her. "I'll give it to you that maybe I went too far––"

"Too far?"

"OK," Mike said, taking another step closer. "What I did was wrong. But what you were about to do was wrong too."

"What are you talking about?"

"Think about it," Mike said. "You were working this case off the books for the director of the FBI. What do you think would have happened to the videos if you gave them to Clarence Mason? You think he'd lock them up in an evidence drawer? No, he'd use them. Just like he's been using you."

Mike took another step.

"I hurt you," he said. "I can see that. I broke trust with you and I can't ever repair that." He touched the computer bag. "But this story is too big to get buried. And that's exactly what would have happened if I hadn't done my job."

"You went to Natalie's house, found her laptop and then set the fire to cover your tracks?" Allison's voice caught in her throat. "A woman died that night."

"The fire?" Mike asked. "I didn't have anything to do with that. Harris did that. You have to believe me. I went too far, I get that. But I'm no monster."

"What do you expect me to do now?"

"Just take a second," Mike said. Another step. "That's all I'm saying. Let's think this through. Not make any decisions right now."

"I don't know," Allison said, trying to appear indecisive when all she wanted to do was take a swing at him. It'd been a risk coming alone to confront him, but involving Garret would have just muddied the waters. She didn't need him falling over himself to take Mike's side. Or worse, if Mike was the killer, Garret would just end up tipping him off that she was suspicious because he'd never believe it without hard evidence. And that was the one thing she lacked. Besides, she'd been the one gullible enough to bring Mike along on this investigation. The responsibility to figure out what his real role had been was hers alone.

Mike smiled and took another step closer. "Let's just talk this through."

She nodded.

"That's good. I'll take that," he said. "We can sort this out."

Another step.

"Consider both sides."

Another step, so that he was right in front of her. His eyes flashed to her gun again. The moment of truth.

"Think through all the options," he said. "Including the option that you're just not nearly as smart as you think you are."

He dropped to a knee and punched her in her leg wound.

Hard.

The pain was like being shot all over again, white hot, so intense that the scream that came from her mouth felt like it might strip out her throat.

But her scream cut short when his hand clamped down over her mouth.

Her brain told her to fight back, but for that moment, the pain washed out everything else in the world. She gasped for air from behind his hand. Her eyes streamed with tears and the world pulsed around her.

There was pressure on her shoulder.

He was going for her gun.

She tried to throw an elbow into him but she was off-balance and missed. Unexpectedly, he let go of her and she spun from her momentum and fell to the ground in a heap.

When she looked up, the barrel of her own gun was pointed at her head. On the other side was a man she hardly recognized.

Wild. Crazed. Insane.

His eyes burning with contempt and hatred.

His face contorted like a mask twisting in on itself.

"It was you," Allison said, catching her breath. "The entire time. It was you."

Mike looked over her shoulder, checking for backup. Not seeing any, he grinned at her.

"You killed Tracy," Allison said.

"I like to think of her as Catherine Fews," he said. "It's how I knew her best."

Allison watched carefully as he paced in front of her, keeping the gun level. His initial surge of energy was giving way to agitation. She didn't have long and she needed to know everything before it ended.

"And Natalie. That wasn't Harris, was it? You killed her and then you killed him."

Mike stood over her, head cocked to one side.

"And you were going to sleep with me," he said, laughing. "Can you imagine? I mean, how screwed up is that?"

"You used me," she said. "Just like you've been using Garret all these years."

"Don't beat yourself up. That idiot gave me everything I needed to kill over a dozen people and not be caught," Mike said. "You just gave me Natalie."

Allison felt her throat constrict and her eyes sting. The words rang true. She had given him Natalie. She'd led him right to her.

"What am I going to do with you?" he asked. "Obviously, I have to kill you. But how?"

Allison didn't reply. Didn't want to give him the satisfaction.

"A bullet to the head might be fine. Here's the story. FBI agent, distraught after the death of someone she swore to protect, gets overburdened by the job, takes her own life at the site of the fire where a second person she tried to save had died the day before. Pretty compelling, don't you think?"

Allison stared back at him, defiant and unbending. She wondered if he'd noticed the bulge around her shin where her ankle holster was tied. With the gun pointed at her head, maybe he'd noticed it but didn't feel threatened.

"But before that, I need to know how you figured it out. What made you suspicious? Who else did you talk to about me?"

Allison remained silent.

Mike shook his head, feigning disappointment. Then his posture changed and he smiled. "You know what? I was just thinking earlier today just how much I enjoyed meeting your dad."

He was baiting her, but she couldn't help but react. "Turns out I was right about you from the beginning, Mike. You are an asshole."

He looked away as if considering something. "True, but your dad liked me. I think I'll pay him a visit." When he looked back at her, there was a wild, hungry look in his eye that made her skin crawl. "Trust me, I'll enjoy the visit more than he will. And it won't be short. I'll take my time. Go slow with him. Unless you tell me what you figured out and who else suspects anything."

Allison glanced over her shoulder through the trees. There was no one coming to her rescue. "It started with the fact that you had so much time right before Harris shot me, but you didn't stop him. You were right there, gun in hand. You had the means to save me, but you didn't pull the trigger."

"A civilian freezing in a life and death situation," Mike said, shaking his head. "Easy explanation. I can see that being disappointing but not enough to make you suspect me."

"Then I started to think about motive. What if you didn't shoot because you had actually wanted Harris to finish me off? As wild as that sounded, was there a reason you would do that?"

Mike held up the computer bag.

"Exactly," Allison said. "The videos. And Harris told us he had the hard drive already. And a backup on a laptop. Natalie was tied up in the car at one point, so he was obviously prepared to drive off. With him dead, there's no reasonable explanation why the crime scene guys didn't turn up the hard drive. That leaves opportunity. You were the last man standing. If Harris was telling the truth and the hard drive and laptop existed, then you had to have grabbed them for yourself before Sheriff Frank got there."

"*If* Harris was telling the truth," Mike said. "And there's no evidence he was. Did you tell all this to Garret?" He laughed. "No, I bet not. He would have thought you were crazy."

"Then there were little things," Allison continued. "When we did the enactment, you held out your right hand pretending it was the gun," Allison said. "Then when you signed your statement, you used your left hand. I thought back and you've been going out of your way to use your right hand. You knew from Maurice that I suspected the killer was left-handed."

"Again, hardly evidence."

Allison shrugged. "It was the small things that added up. So when I found your phone in my bag I suspected it was a tracking device. I'd recently had some experience with people tracking my movements through a phone, so it was the first thing I thought. But the second thing I thought was how great it was that you gave me the perfect opening to fake my own departure from the scene so that I could track your actions to see if my instinct was right. Honestly, I was hoping it wasn't."

Mike shook his head. "Sorry it didn't work out for you."

Allison laughed.

Soft at first, but then a little louder.

Mike squinted, confused.

"You know what?" Allison said. "I'm going to really enjoy studying you while you rot in prison. You're fascinating for none of the reasons you think you are."

Mike laughed, but he looked nervous. "You don't have anything on me. Even if you told all that to Garret, there's nothing there."

She reached into her pocket and he waved the gun at her. "Hey now."

She slowed down and pulled out a phone, pinching it with her thumb and forefinger. "Garret, are you there?" she said.

The color drained from Mike's face as he stared at the phone. There was a long pause. Too long. Allison felt her stomach roll over. What if Garret had hung up? Or if she'd turned the phone off by accident in her pocket? She stood with the phone held out in front of her, feeling increasingly foolish as the seconds ticked away. Mike began to smile.

"Guess it's just the two of us," Mike said.

Allison turned the phone toward her, dreading the idea of seeing a dead screen there. But just as she did, the answer she wanted finally came from the phone.

"I'm here," Garret said, sounding like someone had punched him in the gut. "On our way to your location."

Mike smacked her hand and the phone went flying into the bushes. If Garret tried to say anything else it was lost to them. When she turned back to Mike, his smile was gone.

"I don't know why you look so smug," he snarled.

"Because you're finished."

"You think I'm not prepared for this? I'll be gone before Garret gets here and they'll never find me." He aimed the gun at her head. "But they will find you."

Allison slowly kneeled down and pulled up her pant leg, showing him the gun there. "Remember you told me I wasn't nearly as smart as I thought I was?" She reached for the gun. "Well, it might not be saying much, but looks like I'm smarter than you."

Mike pulled the trigger.

Click

Click

Click

Allison didn't even blink. She knew the gun was empty. From the beginning, it'd been bait to see whether Mike was a reporter who'd overstepped his bounds, or a killer who needed to be taken down.

She pulled out her ankle gun and pointed it at him. "This is over."

"No!" Mike roared and lunged at her.

She shot twice. Once in his leg and the other in the shoulder.

He spun in the air and fell to the ground, grabbing at his wounds.

Allison watched him closely, his face twisted in agony. She didn't know whether it was more from the two bullets in his flesh or knowing that he'd been had.

He struggled to his feet, growling and drooling like a rabid dog. He came after her again.

She put another bullet in his other leg.

He dropped to the ground, howling in pain.

"Stay down," she yelled.

But he pulled himself up on his elbows, then dragged himself to his feet.

"You're going to have to kill me," he said, stumbling at her. "I'm not going to prison."

She dodged easily and kicked him off balance. He fell to the ground hard, screaming in pain. And he appeared ready to stay there.

Allison walked closer, careful to keep her distance in case he lunged again. "Remember I told you I wanted revenge more than justice?" she said. "Seeing you rot in prison like a caged animal...that's the best revenge I can think of."

"They're all still dead," he said. "Doesn't...ch—ch—change...anything."

"Maybe," Allison said. "Neither does this." She stepped on the gunshot wound in his shoulder and he screamed in pain. "But damn if it doesn't make me feel better."

She heard voices coming through the forest. It would be the fire inspection guys first, then Garret and his team would come next. There would be a lot of questions to answer over the next few weeks. Uncomfortable ones about how a serial killer had essentially infiltrated the FBI's Behavioral Analysis Unit, including Allison's own involvement in bringing him to Harlow. But there was one question she didn't want answered publicly.

Minutes later, as Mike was read his rights in front of a flustered Garret Morrison and carted off on a stretcher under armed guard, there was no sign of the laptop or back-up drives that had caused so much pain to so many people.

That was something Allison intended to take care of personally outside of official channels.

CHAPTER 54

Libby stood up when Summerhays walked into the room. He had a fleeting mental image of serious men and women standing up in the Cabinet room, or of generals and admirals rising in the situation room in deference to the Commander-In-Chief. Libby realized that Summerhays probably spent his entire life feeling that people ought to stand up for him whenever he arrived, only now he could envision it with the sound of "Hail to the Chief" filling the air.

Bile rose in the back of Libby's throat and he had to grab the back of the upholstered chair to steady himself. His palms were slick and he felt the trickle of sweat down his rib cage.

"Libby, my man," Summerhays bellowed, generating jealous looks from the staff accompanying him. It was the way on successful campaigns. Once victory seemed inevitable, talent flocked in and vied for the candidate's attention. It was a zero-sum game and the stakes were no less than having the ear of the man clearly on track to become the next leader of the free world.

"We need to talk," Libby said softly.

"Sure, sure," Summerhays said, turning to an aide handing him a stack of papers.

Libby cleared his throat. "I mean now."

"In a minute."

"No, *now*."

The words came out louder than he meant them to, so loud that they seemed to nearly echo in the large hotel suite. Libby felt his heart pound in his chest. The flurry of activity by the entourage slowed noticeably, going from frenzied action to just enough to appear busy while waiting for the train wreck about to happen.

Summerhays hardly looked up from the paper he was reading. After a couple of beats where Libby considered that perhaps the man actually hadn't heard him, Summerhays quietly said, "Can you all give us the room please?"

Libby marveled at the way people stumbled over themselves to be the first out of the room. Twenty-thousand-dollar-per-week consultants nudging interns out of the way to squeeze through the bottleneck at the main door. No one wanted to be the one Summerhays looked at and wondered why his direct order hadn't been followed faster.

The last staffer left the room and closed the door with a bang.

The second it shut, Summerhays threw down the paper in his hands. "What the hell was that?" he asked. "You can't talk to me like that. Not anymore."

"It's Harris," Libby said. "I told you not to use him."

Summerhays looked pale. "The video. It is...is it going to..."

Libby shook his head. "No, it's not that."

Summerhays exhaled heavily. "Thank God. Jesus, don't do that to me."

"This isn't about some goddamn sex tape," Libby said. "Harris left a trail of bodies behind him. I told him he wasn't to hurt anyone. Under any conditions."

"Then good thing he was working for me instead of you, isn't it?" Summerhays said. "Christ, Libby, don't go losing your edge on me. Not now."

"My edge?" Libby said. "He killed people."

"Do you know how many people do that for a President? The military does it every day."

"Oh my God, you've lost it," Libby said. "You knew this was going to happen, didn't you?"

Summerhays shrugged. "I knew Harris wouldn't leave any loose ends. If that meant a few nobodies had to die, then so be it. Sacrifices have to be made. For the greater good."

"You knew I'd call Harris," Libby said. "You even suggested it later, even though you already had him working on this. You were directing him personally, but you still got me involved. Why would you…" He watched Summerhays cross the room to a liquor service and pour a drink for himself. The smug bastard didn't even offer him one. "Now I see. If they trace Harris back somehow, it's to me, not you."

"Like I said, sacrifices have to be made," Summerhays said. "The important thing is Harris neutralized a threat. That's all that's important."

"Who are you?" Libby asked.

"I'm the next President of the United States," Summerhays said, raising a glass toward Libby. "Thanks to you."

"I need some air," Libby said, crossing the room toward the door.

Summerhays grabbed his arm as he passed.

"We're in this together, Libby. To the end." He squeezed painfully. "Don't you ever forget that."

Libby nodded. He opened the door and the swell of the campaign washed over him. Staffers pushed past, filling the void he'd left in the room behind him, all lining up to do the bidding of the great Mark Summerhays. He took one glance back and saw Summerhays take a seat on the couch, glass in hand, calmly holding court over the madness.

Libby pushed his way through the throng of people in the hallway, past the Secret Service guards afforded Summerhays due to his front-runner status and into the elevator. He went down to the third floor and got off. This seemed like a wasteland compared to the hustle and bustle of the top floor but he thought the silence was appropriate. It was a funeral after all.

He knocked on room 312 and his father opened the door. Libby had been to the room earlier, it was where they had set him up with the wire, the same wire that had just exonerated him and ended a man's presidential run.

They shared a moment, just the two of them, father and son.

Mason reached out his hand and Libby took it, shaking it slowly.

"I'm proud of you," he said.

"Yeah? Well, I'm not so proud of myself," Libby said.

"The team is going to make the arrest now. I don't think you want to be here for it."

"No," Libby said. "I'm all right. I own part of this. I'm going to see it through."

Mason nodded and opened the door for him to come into the room. Libby walked through and immediately heard the playback of his voice on the speakers. He looked at a monitor and saw video from the tiny camera they'd installed in his suit collar. It wasn't lined up perfectly on Summerhays but it was close enough.

A young woman he didn't know stood watching the monitor, leaning heavily on crutches, one of her legs wrapped in a heavy brace. When she turned to look at him, he was struck that someone so beautiful could look so angry.

Mason waved her over.

"Special Agent McNeil, this is Libby Ashworth. My son."

The agent extended her hand and he shook it.

"Turns out a video was the man's undoing after all," she said.

"So the other videos were never found," Libby said.

Mason looked to his junior agent, a mysterious smirk on his face. "I think Allison is the only one who knows the answer to that question," he said.

Allison shook her head. "We found a video of the killer, Mike Carrel, but that was the only one ever recovered." She looked at Mason. "It's probably better that way, don't you think?"

Mason smiled. "Probably."

"Excuse me," Allison said. "The Attorney General is about to make the arrest. I'd like to be there for it."

"Of course," Mason said. "You deserve it."

"Thank you," she said, handing Mason an envelope. "This is for you."

Mason took the envelope and opened it as Libby watched her leave. "What's her story?" he asked.

"She's young," Mason said, grinning as he read the letter. "But she has real promise in the Bureau."

Libby indicated the paper Mason held in his hands. "What did she give you?"

"Her resignation letter," Mason said.

"Really," Libby said. "I guess you were wrong about her future with the Bureau."

"I'm often wrong, but rarely about people." Mason put a hand on Libby's shoulder. "Sometimes it just takes them a while to come around."

CHAPTER 55

"You all right, love?" Jordi asked, turning his wide girth in the driver's seat to look at her. The fact that he'd ventured out into the real world at all was a testament to his concern for her.

"Sure," she replied. "Just a little tired is all."

"You sure about this? Quitting and all?"

Allison looked at her dad's house and nodded. She'd been home to check on her dad since coming back from West Virginia but only for an hour at a time when she could. Mike Carrel's capture and then the circus around Summerhays had taken all of her endurance. Matching wits with Clarence Mason on a good day was hard enough but the relentless, if cordial, questioning by him about what really happened in Harlow sapped her of all her strength.

In the end, she had no doubt that Mason knew she had the videos. It was too convenient that she had recovered the video of Catherine Fews/Tracy Bain's murder and nothing else. The first responders on the night Allison was shot were questioned again and still nothing. Finally, Mason had asked her the only question worth asking.

"If you had the videos, would you give them to me?"

Her answer was quick and unequivocal. "No."

He'd already assumed the answer, so snapped back with the second question, an old interrogation tactic. A quick response is often the most truthful response.

"Why not?" he'd asked.

"There are a lot of people who still remember Tracy Bain as the high school student athlete with a future in front of her. They deserve to keep that memory."

Mason had kept quiet. Waiting.

Finally, Allison added, "And I don't trust you with them."

Mason had laughed at that. An unexpected response.

"God, you do have brass balls, don't you?" he'd said before turning serious. "Let me explain my intentions and see if I can earn your trust."

The two of them had sat down and had a frank conversation about Mason's feelings about Mark Summerhays, what Mason suspected about the man but couldn't prove. How his goal wasn't to blackmail congressmen into appropriating funds for the FBI, but to prevent his beloved country from electing a criminal to its highest office.

Together, they hatched the plan to achieve his goal without the videos. They would send in Libby with a wire. Allison had thought Mason too confident that his son would not have crossed the line and ordered Harris to kill if necessary, but she was willing to play along. In her mind, once they started talking about it they would incriminate one another and the chips would fall where they would. As long as she got to watch the person who set Harris in motion do a perp walk, she was happy. The fact that it had worked and Mason had seen his son vindicated was just icing.

"Do you want me to walk you in?" Jordi asked.

"I look that bad?"

"Worse."

She punched him in the arm. He smiled, but then looked at her seriously.

"Get some distance. Take a break," he said. It was his real voice, without the fake accent he usually adopted. "You've been around so much death, maybe you should try life for a while?"

She leaned over and gave the big man a kiss on the cheek. "Thanks, Jordi. I think you're right."

"While you're at it," Jordi said, his accent back in full force, "call that cop you told me about, go out on a date and get a good shag. It always works for me."

Allison felt herself redden. Neil Briggs, the officer who'd flirted with her at the hospital crime scene had left her a message, making it clear it was a social call. She'd made the mistake of telling Jordi about it. She laughed as she climbed out of the car. She knew better than to answer. Jordi always grabbed the last word so it was best to just let him have it early.

She waved as he pulled away then went down the driveway to her house, both her body and soul hobbled by the events over the past year. Tortured by Arnie Milhouse. Burying Richard. Holding the dying men during the botched raid on Sam Kraw. The woman from the fire dying on the ground next to her. Natalie pleading for her life. It was too much. More than she ever wanted to bear. Too much sadness and too much pain for a lifetime, let alone a single year. She wanted no more to do with it and her letter to Mason had made that clear.

She walked into her house and heard the TV on in the back room.

"I'm home, Dad," she called out.

No response.

"Dad?"

She walked down the hall, the sound of the TV getting louder. She fought a rising sense of panic that something was wrong. That her father was dead, either by natural causes or from some part of her career dealing with the darkness in the world finding its way into her house. She quickened her step.

"Dad?"

She turned the corner and took in the sight.

Her dad and Maria were on the couch, the TV playing an old black and white movie, John Wayne in Stagecoach if she wasn't mistaken. Her dad sat upright while Maria was fast asleep, her head on his lap. He waved at Allison, put his finger to his lips and pointed to Maria. Carefully, he lifted himself off the couch and replaced his lap with a cushion. He pointed to the kitchen and tiptoed that direction. Allison followed.

"Looks like she's a big John Wayne fan," she said with a laugh.

"She likes those mushy love stories," he said. "I pretend to like them but as soon as she falls asleep, I switch the channel."

"You know, she works for you. If you want to change the channel, you can just do it."

"She quit the agency last week," her dad said. "She's just...you know...here now. I hope that's OK."

His speech was so clear and his thoughts so quick, that for a second she allowed herself the idea that he'd been miraculously cured. But she chastised herself. There were good days and bad, she knew this, and the trick was to take things as they were and enjoy the good as it came.

She threw her arms around his neck, gave him a hug and kissed both of his cheeks.

"What's all this for?" he said.

"For being a scoundrel," she said.

He grinned and gave her a wink. "You know what we should do?"

"What?"

"Make some hot chocolate, go out in the backyard and see who can name the constellations. Remember we used to do that?"

Allison blinked back tears. "Yeah, I remember. It's really cold out there. Are you sure--"

"Come on," he said. "I'll see if Eddie wants to join us. He's probably sleeping. Teenage boys. They're always...always...teenage boys are always..."

Allison stepped into his arms and laid her head on his chest. She wrapped her arms around him in a tight embrace as his voice faded away.

"It's OK, Dad," she said. "I'm right here."

She felt him take a long, shuddering breath, then he held her out at arm's length.

"Just two hot chocolates," he said. "Me and you. Just like old times."

"Just like old times," she agreed.

She made the drinks, found a warm blanket for them to share and then they went outside and cuddled up under the stars. Her dad told the old stories, clear as if he were reading them off a sheet. They laughed together at the punch lines to funny stories they'd both heard a hundred times. Cried as they recalled their sweetest memories as well as their saddest.

But as the sky lightened in the east, her dad's memory faded, retreating back into the darkness so impatient to claim his mind forever. Rather than cling to it or chase it, Allison just laid her head on his shoulder and they stopped talking. As the sun rose and chased the shadows from the world, she held on to her dad and took comfort from the strength in the arms wrapped around her.

Finally, they went back inside. Maria had moved from the couch to the master bedroom and her dad padded along the hallway in that direction. Allison kissed him goodnight, went to her bedroom and collapsed onto the bed, not bothering to get undressed or get under the covers.

But before she could drift off, she heard her door open. It was her dad, a glass of water balanced carefully in his hands. He gently placed it on her bedside table, then patted her head the way he had when she was a little girl.

"It's going to be all right, hon," he whispered. "You'll see."

He left the room, closing her door gently behind him.

Allison reached out and touched the glass with the tips of her fingers. She smiled, surprised to find that she agreed with him. With a cleansing breath, Allison settled into her bed, cleared her mind and fell into a deep, restful sleep, better than any she'd had in years.

Author's Note

T hank you for reading this book. Without you, the reader, I'd be scribbling away for only my own pleasure. I'd be awake before dawn, mainlining caffeine while my five kids and wife slept upstairs, telling these stories only to myself.

Don't get me wrong, I'd still do it. I love the process so much that I'd still do it if I had to pay for the privilege. There's something about clawing my way through a story, excavating characters and building a world where surprising things happen that really cranks my motor. I don't think I could stop if I tried.

But having you share the journey with me is gravy. And damn if it isn't good tasting gravy.

We're all busy. Modern life demands our attention in ways unfathomable even a decade ago. Jobs that follow us home. Twenty-four-hour news channels. Kids on three or four sports teams at a time. Holidays. Family. Keeping up with our friends' fake perfect lives on Facebook. It can seem overwhelming. At least to me it does.

Finding the bandwidth to invest hours, days even, into reading a novel, is nothing short of a miracle. But, for me, there's nothing better than the immersive experience of reading a good story well told. When you choose to read KILLER PURSUIT or any of my books, you give me your trust that I will deliver that experience to you. I hope that I have done so to your satisfaction with this novel. I hope that I delivered the goods and that we're square. If I fell short, please know I took the attempt seriously and did my level best. And if you enjoyed it, then I'm one happy guy. Like I said, gravy.

If KILLER PURSUIT was a good ride for you, please drop me a line and let me know. Even better, drop a quick review on Amazon or your favorite online site. Best of all, tell your friends as word of mouth is the way most people choose their next book to read.

I appreciate your support and your trust. I hope I prove to be deserving of them both.

Best,

Jeff Gunhus

About The Author

Jeff Gunhus is the author of the Amazon bestselling supernatural thrillers, *Night Chill* and *Night Terror* and the thriller *Killer Within*. He also writes the middle grade/YA series, *The Templar Chronicles*. The first book of the series, *Jack Templar Monster Hunter*, was written in an effort to get his reluctant reader eleven-year-old son excited about reading. It worked and a new series was born. His book *Reaching Your Reluctant Reader* has helped hundreds of parents create avid readers. As a father of five, he and his wife Nicole spend most of their time chasing kids and taking advantage of living in the great state of Maryland. In rare moments of quiet, he can be found in the back of the City Dock Cafe in Annapolis working on his next novel. If you see him there, sit down and have a cup of coffee with him. You just might end up in his next book.

www.JeffGunhus.com

www.facebook.com/jeffgunhusauthor
www.twitter.com/jeffgunhus